DARK SAHALE

By

Sam Ferguson

DARK SAHALE

Text Copyright 2017 Sam Ferguson
Artwork Copyright 2017 Dragon Scale Publishing

ISBN 10: 1-943183-25-2
ISBN 13: 978-1-943183-25-8

Front cover art by Bob Kehl

Books by Dragon Scale Publishing

Table of Contents

Chapter 1

Lady Arkyn pulled the forest green hood back around her pointed ears and looked around. It was night, but the darkness didn't hamper her vision as it would a human's. She surveyed the back alley leading up to the manor house and then stole across to the back door. A large dog's carcass was lying in the grass some fifteen yards away from her. Its head was cruelly twisted around its body and the long tongue was hanging limply out the snout.

Whoever had been here before her had been driven by pure rage to do such a thing. More than that, they were strong. She slipped into the back door, careful not to disturb the broken glass along the floor from the slim window nearby that had been smashed to gain access to the back of the house. In the rear parlor were two more bodies. One male, the other female. The butler had had his throat ripped out. The woman had been hit with something large and heavy alongside her head. Their crumpled corpses were stacked atop each other, suggesting a very quick-moving assailant.

Arkyn silently walked through the parlor and into the kitchen. Nothing was disturbed in that room. An onion sat upon a cutting board with the knife carefully placed next to it. A pot of water was on the stove, but the fire below had not been started yet. Two fresh pieces of wood were placed inside, with a bit of kindling and paper in place to make the ignition easier.

She passed over the marble floor and pressed the swinging door open. She walked through a velvet carpeted hallway and into the dining room. She closed her eyes and shook her head as she sighed in disgust. Four guests and another servant were dead in that room. She moved past them and out into another hallway. She walked around a large staircase and to another parlor room. She stepped down three marble stairs and surveyed the room. Two additional guests were there. One of them was still upright in a high-backed chair with a tea cup held in his right hand. The tea had spilled during the moment of attack, staining the man's brown pants and the arm of the chair. His brown eyes were open, forever frozen in a stare of terror.

Arkyn moved forward and gently closed the man's eyes. Then she looked to the woman who was lying face down on the floor. She couldn't see the wound from this angle, but the large pool of blood surrounding her body told her all she needed to know.

She turned around and went across the entry foyer and into the drawing room. There were three slain guards there, each wearing platemail. One was missing his head, another had been run through with a large spear. The third was missing his left arm and his helmet was quashed in at the top, with streaks of blood that had dried to the outside of the visor.

"Very strong indeed," she commented wryly as she studied the wounds. It would have taken superhuman strength to run a spear through the armor the second guard had on, not to mention how powerful a strike would have to be in order to nearly flatten a steel helmet.

In the back of the drawing room, a bookcase had been hurriedly pulled aside. Books lay strewn about the floor around it, attesting to the frantic escape attempt. She went into the hidden passageway. Stone surrounded her on all sides, and the dank odor of mold and earth flowed into her nostrils. She had to turn sideways to avoid bumping her shoulders on the walls. Such a narrow hallway would have made a rushed escape nearly impossible, as she was an elf, built slender and lean. A man with wider shoulders would have struggled a fair amount more than she to get through the twisting hall.

She followed it down a spiraling path until she came to a large entryway. A mess of tangled and broken iron bars greeted her. She inspected them carefully, using her elf-vision to see in the darkness. She realized that what she was looking at, had at one time been a portcullis. Whoever had tried to escape had managed to make it this far and then seal the way behind themselves. She turned around and ran a hand over the stone walls. She felt scratches and gouges in the rock. The pursuer had been big, but strong enough to force himself through the narrow passage and then barrel through the portcullis as if it was nothing more than thin planks of pine.

Lady Arkyn stepped into the large chamber and looked around. An underwater stream babbled softly in the distance, and another tunnel led out, likely to the sea.

She doubted that the intended victim had ever gotten close to that final stretch of tunnel however, for the boat was still lashed to a pair of metal stakes.

Lady Arkyn turned to her left and scanned the thick darkness. She saw the body prone on the floor, near a large chest.

"Here, Lady Arkyn," a voice called in the darkness.

Lady Arkyn nodded and walked toward the murder victim. "You could have lit a torch, Njar," she said.

Wood smacked onto the stone floor and an orb of light appeared over the image of a large, black-furred satyr. "I left the light off, in case the first person to find me was not you," he said. "I am not exactly welcome in these parts."

3

Lady Arkyn laughed. "After the last war we had, I would assume that all of the old blood would be gone by now."

Njar bleated and shook his head. "Humans are a stubborn lot. They are slow to forgive, and even slower to change their minds if they have decided that someone else is responsible for their plights."

"Not all," Arkyn said.

Njar smiled and met her eyes with great golden orbs. "True, not all humans are such."

Lady Arkyn moved to the body and knelt beside it. "I am unfamiliar with this man," she said. "I know this manor had been empty for many years, as has much of Winter's Beak, but I am not aware of who ever owned this manor."

"His name is Willow."

"Like the tree?" Arkyn asked.

Njar nodded.

"Strange name for a human to take."

Njar shrugged. "He is not human," Njar said. "Not entirely, that is."

Arkyn cocked her head to the side. "What do you mean?"

Njar sighed. "I have known Willow for many decades. He used to reside not far from Viverandon, though Winter's Beak has always been his ancestral home. He was born and raised in the forests, and so his parents named him for the tree under which they shared their first kiss."

"But what is he?" Arkyn asked.

Njar looked past her. "Where is Erik?" he asked. "I thought you two were traveling together."

Arkyn frowned slightly and nodded slowly. "We did, for three years after the great battle with Tu'luh. Then, we parted ways."

"Tu'luh," Njar said as he spat upon the ground. "That is one creature I hope rots away in the hell fires of

4

Hammenfein. Many lost their lives because of that dragon's stupidity. Never let it be said that humans are the only stubborn, blind race upon the face of Terramyr."

Lady Arkyn nodded her agreement. Tu'luh had been the cause of not one, but two great wars. First in Hamath Valley, some five hundred years prior, and more recently all along the southern parts of the Middle Kingdom. It had taken not only Erik, but many great and legendary heroes to defeat the Red Dragon. Fortunately, all of that was behind them now.

"Where is Erik now?" Njar pressed. "He will be most interested in this."

Arkyn shrugged. "He is somewhere south of the orcish lands, but don't worry, I can send a Night Hawk after I know more about what we are dealing with here."

Njar nodded. "As I said, Willow is no human. He is a sahale."

Lady Arkyn gasped. "Sahale? Are you sure?" She pulled off a long, forest-green glove from her right hand and then reached out and touched the dead man's neck.

"Of course I'm sure," Njar snipped. Njar turned Willow's head and bent the right ear down to reveal a small, crescent-shaped birthmark. "The sign of the sahale," he said flatly.

"Then, why didn't he change into his dragon form?" Lady Arkyn asked. "He could have easily defeated an intruder if he had." The sahale were a race of half-humans who could shift into dragon forms at will once they had reached their age of maturity, usually around seventeen years. The fact that Willow had remained in his human form suggested there was something more at play here.

"I'm not entirely sure," Njar said. He held out a fur-backed hand and slowly made a circle above the corpse. "But, I believe he was prevented from changing. I think the murderer used some sort of spell that blocked the dragon blood from performing its magic."

"Can such a thing be possible?" Lady Arkyn asked.

Njar shrugged and leaned heavily upon his staff. "It's the only conclusion I can come to. Tell me, did you recognize any of the guests?"

Lady Arkyn rose to her feet and folded her arms, still staring at the body lying on the floor in front of her. "No," she said flatly. "If they are of the noble class, they are not people I am familiar with."

"Much has changed since Nagar's Blight chased the dragons from the Middle Kingdom some five hundred years ago," Njar said. "Now that the curse is lifted and Tu'luh has been slain, things are shifting once more, and all of it for the better, I'm afraid."

Lady Arkyn nodded. She knew that many of the inhabitants of the Middle Kingdom were less than eager to have dragons return to the land. The fact that the progenitor of all dragons on Terramyr, Hiasyntar'Kulai, had only remained in the Middle Kingdom for a short while before flying back to the east didn't help things either. Both races had respected his position, and now the loss of that buffer was keenly felt. No one knew exactly why he left, but it created a vacuum of power as other, lesser dragons came to the land and did not have the great Ancient One to look to. Most of the time the dragons kept to themselves, but there had been skirmishes. Some started by humans, of course, but a few incidents were likely the fault of adolescent dragons who were still unaccustomed to coexisting with humankind.

"Five hundred years is a long time," Lady Arkyn said. "Even to dragons. Time away can change them as well as those of us who remained within the Middle Kingdom."

Njar nodded. "Yes, the Middle Kingdom will struggle to find its balance once more. However, I fear that this incident will only lead to a deeper divide between the species. I mentioned the people upstairs, but what I didn't say was that they were all sahale as well, even the guards and the servants."

6

Lady Arkyn felt the blood drain from her face. *All of them?* She had no idea so many sahale existed. "Who would go to such trouble to murder thirteen sahale?"

Njar shook his head. "That is why we need Erik. I need the two of you to hunt down the killer and stop him. This travesty cannot go unanswered. If the younger dragons ever learned that so many of their kin had been brutally murdered, they would likely seek revenge. One or two attacks on villages by dragons, and the delicate peace we are trying to nurture will be ripped apart." Njar sighed. "There is something more," Njar added. "Look at the eyes."

Lady Arkyn bent back down to Willow's corpse and inspected the man's eyes. "No," she gasped quietly. "This can't be."

Njar stepped closer. "I noticed it when I walked in. My kind are more sensitive to the shifting of magic and the traces of energy left behind by it. I had hoped that perhaps it was part of whatever spell had prevented the victims from changing into their dragon forms and defending themselves, but as I inspected the manor, I realized I was horribly wrong."

"A shadowfiend was here," Lady Arkyn said. Now that she was studying the eyes more carefully, she could see the tell-tale sign of dull, gray pupils and faded irises. "Whoever it was had not only murdered the sahale, but had drained them of their power."

"As you know," Njar said grimly. "A shadowfiend absorbs the powers of his victims, making himself stronger with each kill. Often times they will prey upon wizards to gain magical advantage, but now we have something else. As the dragons return, they offer new powers to shadowfiends that have not previously been available to them in abundance."

"A shadowfiend is hunting down dragon-kin and taking their powers," Arkyn whispered. "Such a foe would be nearly unstoppable."

"And that is why I summoned you and Erik. You are the strongest pair I know of. You have to stop the killer before he grows too strong, and, you have to do it quietly so that neither dragons nor humans learn of the danger that has come to the Middle Kingdom."

"Not a simple task," Lady Arkyn said.

"A profound understatement," Njar replied.

"What of Master Lepkin and Lady Dimwater? Surely they can help."

"If you know where to find them, then I will call upon them as well. As you know, Kyra Dimwater and I are very close, but she has shrouded herself from me. I cannot scry her location, and I have no idea where to even start looking. More importantly than that, searching for her would spend time that we likely don't have. There are not many sahale left in Terramyr. I knew most of these. They had gone far away from the Middle Kingdom. There are a few families yet, but I imagine they will be traveling here soon. Terramyr as a whole has never been kind to the sahale folk. They have been feared and hunted by almost every race. Their only true home has ever been here, in the Middle Kingdom."

"We have to stop the murderer before the others arrive," Arkyn agreed with a nod. "Do you have any clues where to look?"

Njar shrugged. "This one is powerful. I cannot see the event that took place here, not even with the Pools of Fate. Nor can I track the shadowfiend from this point. I have, however, uncovered other clues that lead me to believe there is a shadowfiend by the name of Alkantar hiding in Pracheloor Cave, which is a large network of tunnels within a set of three mountains along the northern shores of the Middle Kingdom about three hundred miles east of Far Point. If I were you, I would start there."

"You aren't coming with us?" Arkyn asked.

Njar shook his head. "No," he said. "I will try to contact other sahale from my tower in Viverandon. With any luck, I can convince them to stay away from the Middle Kingdom for a while. However, even if not, there are matters there that demand my attention."

There was a hint of fear in the satyr's voice told Lady Arkyn that something very serious had happened in the satyr's home as well. "Tell me what's wrong," she said.

Njar shook his head. "Viverandon is my concern. Yours is the Middle Kingdom. I have helped you as much as I can. I must return now to my people. You must hurry, the city guards will be back in the morning."

"I can help you," Lady Arkyn said.

"Not with this," Njar replied. "Now go, and be sure not to be seen." Njar stamped his staff on the ground and a great slit of gold light tore through the air a few feet away. He waved his left hand and the slit widened, tearing through the fabric of space. Through the rift, Arkyn could see a lush and beautiful forest city. A great tree stood at one end. She had always longed to see Viverandon in person, but had never been able to get more than glimpses through Njar's portals through the years. "Lady Arkyn?" Njar said.

The elf looked to her friend and waited for him to speak.

"Do be careful, my gut tells me that the forces at play here are more dangerous than anything you or Erik have ever faced before."

"More dangerous than Tu'luh?" Arkyn asked.

Njar nodded solemnly. "I believe so." He then turned and walked through the portal.

The rift closed with a crackling sparkle of blue and green light, and then Njar was gone.

Lady Arkyn looked down to Willow's body. "What could be more dangerous than Tu'luh?" she asked herself.

Chapter 2

Erik tossed and turned on his bed. Beads of sweat accumulated on his forehead and matted the hair against his pillow. His limbs moved in erratic jerks and swings, twisting the blanket over his body as he murmured and groaned in his sleep. He was having another nightmare. In his mind, he saw a large fireball fall from the sky and explode into the walls of a large city. Flames shot out around the impact site and smoke billowed upward, thick and black. A man upon a great horse emerged from the flames, carrying a sword as long as most spears, and wider than an ax blade. With one swing, the remainder of the walls crashed down around the city. The hulking man rode his horse into the city, issuing fire from his mouth and clearing whole buildings with his sword as the weapon seemed to grow to impractical proportions with each additional swing. Men and women shrieked and ran in terror, but none escaped the wrath of the horseman.

Erik stood on the cobblestone streets, facing the strange creature and determined not to let him destroy the rest of the city. He pulled his weapon and moved forward to fight. He blocked the first swing of the horseman's sword, but the impact against his blade drove him to the side and crushed him against a stone wall.

The horseman looked at Erik with fiery, white eyes and opened his mouth. Fire, hotter than anything a dragon could produce, erupted from the horseman's mouth and shot outward toward Erik, but it didn't come quickly, it moved slowly through the air, as if the horseman delighted in watching Erik squirm. Erik tried to push the humongous sword away, but the weapon held firm, pinning him to the wall. The young warrior couldn't move, and he couldn't escape.

Just as the fires came close enough that the heat burned the oil from his forehead and dried his skin, something grabbed his arm.

"Erik," a voice called.

Erik turned and saw Tu'luh the Red, the immense dragon that had caused so much pain and destruction in Terramyr. Somehow he was here, grabbing hold of Erik and pulling him away from the horseman's fire attack. As soon as Erik was free, he lashed out at Tu'luh.

"Get off of me!" Erik shouted as he pushed with all of his might.

Suddenly the fires of the nightmare were gone, and a young monk crashed into a dresser along the wall a few feet away from Erik's bed. Erik panted crazily, his adrenaline surging and his anger boiling. It took him several seconds to realize what he had done. By that time, the young monk was already picking himself up off the floor and brushing his robes off.

"My fault," the monk said. "Shermin told me not to try and wake you from your night terrors by touching you."

Erik nodded and scowled angrily. "You should have used the water," Erik said hotly. Since his arrival, Erik had warned the others of his nightmares, and instructed them to use a cup of water to splash his face rather than try to wake him with physical contact. It was dangerous, as he couldn't always control his body's reactions.

"I'm sorry," the monk said. "I forgot the water, and given the way you were fretting about, I didn't want to waste time getting the water from downstairs and risk letting you fall out of the bed."

"Better that I fall onto the floor than you get hurt," Erik said, the anger in his voice softening a bit as he came more fully to his senses. "Are you all right?"

The monk nodded. "I am fine. A bit of a bruised ego, perhaps, but a monk should not have an ego in any case, so I suppose it is for the best."

Erik smiled and wiped his forehead. "What is your name?" Erik asked.

"I am Nolan," the monk said. "I usually work the lower gardens," he added. "But as Shermin was busy with other affairs tonight, I volunteered to be your watcher." Judging by Nolan's tall, lanky build, Erik guessed the monk to be about seventeen. He had a head full of black curls and a pair of thick glasses resting on the bridge of his pointy nose. A patchwork of freckles dotted the young monk's cheeks as well, completing the awkward teenager's appearance.

Erik nodded. "Nolan, my sincere apologies. Thank you for waking me, but next time, perhaps get the water first."

Nolan smiled. "Of course," he said with a slight bow of his head. "Is there anything you require before going back to sleep?"

Erik shook his head. "I won't be going back to sleep, but I don't need anything either. Thank you."

Nolan wrung his hands and knit his brow as if trying to formulate something in his mind. "Can I ask you something?"

Erik nodded. "If you like."

"Brother Shermin told us that you had agreed to fight the demon that plagues us every few months, so I understand why you have stayed with us."

Erik nodded. "Yes, the spell that holds the demon in his plane is deteriorating. When Shermin discovered that I am a sahale, he asked if I would stay on and wait for the next time the spell weakened enough for the demon to come."

Nolan nodded eagerly. "And, I am certain you will defeat it too. But, what I don't know is why you came here in the first place. Had news of the demon spread to your lands, or had you come for some other reason?"

"After I left..." Erik caught himself before telling the young man that he had lived with a tribe of orcs. "Several months ago, I was in one of the villages down in the valley below. I was looking for a place to try and find a way to calm my nightmares. I overheard one of your brother monks while buying supplies. The shopkeep was ribbing him about giving up the life of a soldier to become a hermit in the mountains."

"That would be Brother Lucas, he was a great knight before coming here," Nolan cut in.

"Yes, well, after hearing Brother Lucas talk about finding peace here, I thought I might give it a go. I came here shortly thereafter. Finding your extensive library was a nice surprise as well," Erik said with a smile.

Nolan looked over to the desk nearby and stared at the pile of books. "What are you studying, exactly?" he asked.

"Well, I had hoped to find information on sahale, but absent that I have found a few things of interest. Most of them deal with the Four Horsemen."

Nolan's eyes went wide. "That's one of my favorite subjects too!" Nolan reached into a leather pouch at his side and brought up a leather bound journal. "Look, I have made sketches of what I think they look like." Erik was about to refuse, but Nolan shoved the book into his hands.

Erik opened the book and flipped past the first couple of pages until he came to the first sketch. "You have talent," Erik commented as he studied the image. There on the page was a masterfully rendered sketch of a large human warrior riding atop a six-legged horse. An oversized sword hung from the horseman's waist, and a great scythe was in his left hand.

Erik flipped the page and found another two horsemen sketched out in charcoal.

"I draw what I think they will look like, of course," Nolan said with a sheepish grin. "I don't know what they actually look like, but…"

Erik smiled. He flipped past the last horseman and then saw a large dragon's head. In neat handwriting below the image was written the name "Tu'luh the Red" in ink. "You drew this as well?"

Nolan nodded. "Well, the rest of the book contains other important figures that I have read about." Nolan tried to stand up and reach out for the book, but Erik was intrigued now. After Tu'luh there was a rendering of Nagar the Black, the elf sorcerer that had worked with Tu'luh to create a terrible and dark magic. As he continued, he saw other images, some he recognized, and others presumably taken from historical figures in the closer regions surrounding the monastery that he had not heard of. There was an orc chief as well. Then, near the middle of the thick book was a drawing with a face he would have recognized anywhere.

"This is Master Lepkin?" Erik said as he looked up to Nolan.

The young monk was wringing his hands nervously. "Yes, well, it's a work in progress. I'll take it back…"

Erik held out a hand to stop Nolan. "Hold on, this is good. So you have the book separated into categories then. Villains in the front, and heroes in the back, am I right?"

"Yes, but—"

Erik pulled back away from Nolan's reaching hand and continued flipping through the pages. "I'm almost done," he promised. The next page had a drawing of Lady Dimwater. It wasn't entirely accurate, but the quality of the illustration was brilliant. He continued through the book until he came to a page that had a sketch of him. Erik stopped and stared at the image. It took him by surprise to see himself in the book.

"Sorry," Nolan offered in a quiet voice. "It's just, I never met a hero in real life before…"

Erik looked at the image. His likeness had been captured well, almost too well. It was obvious that Nolan had been watching him during his stay at the monastery. The drawing showed Erik in a dashing pose with sword drawn and sparkling as he held it up high. The caption underneath read, "Erik Lokton, The Champion of Truth."

"I'm not sure that I am a hero," Erik said as he closed the book and gave it back to Nolan. "Certainly Master Lepkin and Lady Dimwater belong in the book, but I am not sure I do."

"But I have heard of what you have done," Nolan said. "Shermin has told us. You are possibly the greatest hero to live. You have defeated dragons and wizards and…"

Erik held up a hand. "Nolan, it's getting late," he said in an attempt to change the subject. The truth was, Erik wasn't sure he was a hero at all. Along with the nightmares that plagued his sleep, he had enough doubts about who he really was during the day to make it nearly impossible to accept the title of hero. Besides that, nothing he had done in the war against Tu'luh had been on his own anyway. There had always been others to help him through most of the toughest parts. "Master Lepkin has given a lifetime of service," Erik put in. "If I should spend the rest of my life trying to live up to his legacy, I should be lucky to become half the man he is."

Nolan took the book back and then went for the door. "May I ask, just one more question?"

Erik sighed impatiently. "As long as it's a quick one."

"You said you came here to learn more about sahale, but you are one. What more would you need to know that you can't figure out for yourself?"

Erik thought for a moment. He had sahale blood running through his veins all right, but since beginning his travels, he was discovering much that he had not expected.

15

There was a darker side to having such powers, or perhaps he had a darker side to him thanks to his specific blood line. He wasn't sure. That was what he wished to figure out. He looked up to Nolan and shrugged. "I guess, just as a boy needs a father to learn what it is to become a man, a sahale needs a mentor to show him how to navigate the balance of being both man, and dragon."

Nolan nodded and reached for the handle on the door. "And here I thought we monks were supposed to have all the wisdom and answers," he said. "I'll retire downstairs again and let you sleep. Should you need me again, I will bring water the first time." Nolan smiled and went for the door, taking with him the candle he had brought with him, and leaving Erik alone in the darkened room.

Erik watched the door for a few moments and then straightened out his blanket and lay back down, staring up at the ceiling. Instead of giving in to sleep, however, Erik spent the rest of the night staring at the ceiling, plagued by concerns about his own inadequacies, and suspicions that his biological heritage was more dangerous than anyone understood.

He left early the following morning, taking to his usual meditation spot. Since he had arrived at this monastery, Shermin, the apparent leader of the monks, had insisted he meditate daily. It was supposed to help Erik clear his mind and connect with the deeper parts of his soul so he could find inner peace. Sometimes it worked, others it didn't, but after a night like the one Erik had just experienced, he was more than eager to give it a shot.

As he looked down now, he could see that the bluff where the monastery sat was some three miles away. He could just make out the dot that was the monastery for the Monks of the Southern Light, a religious order similar to the priests in Valtuu Temple. They were not blind, as those in Valtuu Temple, but they did revere dragons and sought after wisdom and knowledge, despite the fact that their knowledge of

16

dragons was far lesser than even the most basic neophyte of Valtuu Temple. They worshipped the Old Gods, Icadion first and foremost. They were more than simple historians though, as they sought to spread their religion to the regions around them, and had an active missionary service. Many of the nearby towns owed their active traditions of worshipping Icadion to the Monks of the Southern Light.

Erik was not particularly religious himself, but the monks were kind and welcoming to him. What he liked best was their silent courage. It was Shermin, a short, bald monk in his forties, who had first figured out Erik's true nature. When he announced it to the others, they had all gathered around him as if they were meeting someone they had been waiting for a very long time. Although each of them would later try to get more information out of Erik about his nature, as Nolan had the previous night, none of them seemed to shrink away from him in fear. It was refreshing to be around people with minds open enough to accept all kinds of people without judgment.

He spent the entire day sitting upon the snow-covered mountain peak, staring out at the valley below. Winter had come early to the southern lands, but it was not gray and dreary as winter could sometimes be. The snow was crisp and pure, draping the land in a carpet of brilliant, sparkling crystals. The dusted trees and the wintry slopes on the mountain looked like something he would imagine for a snow elf realm, if there were such things. His sword was lying next to him as he silently watched an eagle soar through the air, scavenging for whatever it could find.

There was a mighty river that was born from a spring in the mountains just a ways off to the east. The raptor would likely find food there if it couldn't find a southern snow hare first.

He thought about joining the eagle in flight.

He loved flying.

The sensation of total and complete freedom was unlike anything he had ever felt. Throughout his journey he had been careful to shift forms only when he was sure others weren't watching. A flying dragon was sure to draw any nearby orcs. How those people loved their battles, and dragons were among their favorite foes. The humans of the south were not like those back home in the Middle Kingdom either. They were frail and skittish. Even looking upon him with just his armor and weapons in his human form was enough to set off alarms in most villages near here.

In addition to not wanting to startle the locals, Erik took special care to avoid his dragon form in settled areas because whenever he was in his dragon form, a strange desire would creep up on him from the deepest recesses of his soul. He couldn't be sure why, but when he saw the masses fleeing or running, there was a small part of him that almost wanted to give them the battle they so feared. Whether it was a product of the dragon blood running through his veins, or perhaps a darker taint painted upon his soul, he couldn't be sure.

There was a beast somewhere inside him that he couldn't explain.

As he sat upon the mountain, looking down and trying to calm his inner self, he thought about the conversation he had had with Nolan after the nightmare. He was thankful that the young monk hadn't pressed for more information about Erik's sahale side. Erik was not fond of discussing that part of his lineage. It was more than a little disconcerting to the young warrior that his father was Dremathor, a shadowfiend with latent sahale blood, and his grandfather was Allun Rha, the grand wizard who had created the only magic powerful enough to ensure victory at the Battle of Hamath Valley. Allun Rha was a hero to most people in the Middle Kingdom, but Erik had gotten an intimate look at the repercussions of the magic created by his grandfather. While Tu'luh the Red and Nagar created a curse that would use the inherent evil within a creature to turn them into mindless drones, Allun Rha had only been able to overcome Tu'luh by using a similar approach. The Illumination, the book containing Allun Rha's spell, essentially created his own slave army to combat Tu'luh the Red by reaching into a creature and manipulating their desires for good until they, like Tu'luh's slaves, obeyed Allun Rha completely. The idea that anyone related to Erik could so callously melt the minds of so many, and create soul-bound drones to fight for him was mind boggling. Erik had spent the years of that war fighting to help others, and even now felt guilty just for having used the remainder of Allun Rha's army to fight in the final battle. Trying to imagine actually being the one to enslave people in such a way... well that made Erik sick to his stomach.

Mostly.

There was also another part of him, a part that he was trying to quash in his meditations and his never-ending wanderings that saw the logic to the method. Those who had been enslaved and used to create Allun Rha's Golden Army would have died and succumbed to Nagar's Blight. Perhaps their sacrifice was necessary. Expending a few hundred to save thousands almost appeared as an intelligent strategy to the young warrior. Morality was not an easy question in the face of such overwhelming odds. Erik knew this, but it was the fact that a part of him, no matter how small that part was, actually liked the strategy that caused him to question himself.

Perhaps Allun Rha had been more tainted than even he realized. When visiting the old wizard in his tower, Erik had noticed certain... quirks. It was obvious that everything involved in the events leading up to the Battle of Hamath Valley had left a blight on Allun Rha's character. Perhaps it went deeper than that though. After all, Erik's biological father was known to the world as Dremathor, a ruthless, conniving shadowfiend who had been as brutal as any other Erik had ever heard of. Perhaps there was a genetic predisposition for evil in his heritage. Or, maybe it was something in the dragon blood that, when mixed with the blood of a human, created something strange and dark.

Erik shook his head. Once, he had thought he knew exactly who he was. He was the young hero that had fought to save the Middle Kingdom. He was The Champion of Truth. He was the defender of the weak, in the same knightly tradition as Master Lepkin. But now, he was not so sure. It wasn't just the strange tendencies or the impulses to lash out either. There were the nightmares, and the increasing sense of insecurity they brought with them.

This was why he had felt that he and Minrielle Arkyn had needed to travel separately for a while. Nolan had only gotten the brunt of Erik's fevered dreams once, but Lady Arkyn… Erik shook his head. Even now the thought of rearing against her whenever she tried to wake him from his nightmares caused him pain and great shame. Though the two had grown quite close in the three years they had traveled together after leaving the boundaries of the Middle Kingdom, it was better this way. Once, he had given her a promise ring, intending to marry her once they returned to the Middle Kingdom and could have a ceremony surrounded by their friends, but he had to find a way to tame himself first.

Lady Arkyn had not been easily persuaded to leave him on his own. But, as time went along and his nightmares seemed to worsen, becoming more frequent and often eliciting dangerous reactions from Erik, even she had to admit that time apart might be beneficial for Erik to help calm his inner self. She had mentioned finding a particular grove of trees in one of the southern forests. It was supposed to be an old elven holy site that would help with such things. The last time they had spoken, Erik promised to find that grove and set things right, and reaffirmed his wish to marry her if she would have him back afterward.

She had told him to be quick, so their time apart would be short.

He was working on that as quickly as he could, but he never found the grove of trees. An orc settlement had overrun the site, and Erik was forced to try and find an alternative method to subdue his inner demons. Their time apart was already far more than he would have ever expected. It had been four years almost to the day that he and Lady Arkyn had parted ways.

Since then, in addition to his introspection and meditations, he sought for peace by helping those he could, offering whatever services others might need that he could provide. Most villages in this region were quick to turn him away, too afraid of strangers to even let him in and take a chance. Had they only realized that he was sahale, and thus able to turn into a dragon at will, they likely would have all died of fright on the spot.

He did find some areas where he was more than a little useful, but those quests had been bloody, and did little for his inner demons. He had fought against a horde of Tarthuns that had come down from the Eastern Wilds in search of new, undefended territories to sack. Once, he had even found himself taken in by a tribe of orcs for several months while he united with them to fight a common enemy. That experience had opened his eyes significantly. To see and learn about those he had fought so hard against at Ten Forts only a few years prior had been enlightening to say the least. It also led him to a new method of caging his demons. For, as he now understood the orcs to be of no less value than humans, he discovered that he was able to extend mercy to other foes he encountered. He learned that by simply keeping this merciful approach to any battle, he was better able to keep his own lust for battle quieted, and chain those inner, darker tendencies more successfully than his biological father and grandfather seemed capable of.

21

Erik tried to shake the doubts from his mind. It was nearly supper time, but the day's meditations had not gone as well as he had hoped. Instead of clearing his thoughts, he found himself bombarded by everything that he felt was wrong with himself. Still, never one to give up easily, he took a deep breath of cold air and closed his eyes as a gust of wind picked up and blew a drift of snow into his face. He cleared his mind and focused only on the scent of the clean air, and the coolness it brought with it. He remained there for nearly another hour before he finally managed to shirk the doubts and fears that had kept him awake the night before.

A bell chimed in the distance. It was faint, but Erik knew that it signaled supper was ready.

Erik stood up, grabbing his sword on the way, and then stretched. He wasn't wearing his armor, just a tunic and a pair of pants. He removed his pants and shirt and wrapped them around the sword. He tied the bundle together with the straps on the scabbard, and then he hurled the sword out over the edge of the drop off.

With a mighty yell and a wide smile, Erik leapt off after the twirling weapon. He closed his eyes as the light enveloped him when he called upon his dragon blood. His bones stretched and strengthened. His muscles, tight and already firm and larger than most men, grew and thickened. From his back sprouted a pair of magnificent wings. The leathery skin stretched from the bones and caught the air. His tail shot out behind him and gave him perfect balance as he let out a thunderous roar and blew a ball of fire out into the open air.

No longer was he in his human form. Erik had once again taken to wing.

He angled downward and soared with amazing speed.

Erik caught the falling sword with ease and sailed toward the bluff where the monastery stood. With expert precision he tilted his wings up at the last moment, catching the air and flying upward, narrowly avoiding slamming into the top of the bluff. He hovered over the bluff just ten feet off the ground, and then he dropped his sword and returned to his human form, completing the transformation just before falling to the ground.

He pulled his pants on first. Then he slipped the tunic over his head and arms.

"You are getting faster," Shermin said with a humble nod.

Erik smiled at the monk. "Practice makes perfect," he said.

Shermin held up a finger and arched a brow. "*Perfect* practice makes perfect," Shermin said.

Erik smiled wider. It sounded like something Master Lepkin would have said during one of Erik's many sparring lessons.

As the two walked into the towering monastery, Erik wondered how Master Lepkin was faring. He knew that Lepkin and Dimwater had had a child, but he had not seen them since Fort Drake, and that was many years ago. Erik had still been in his teens then. He was now twenty-three. Lepkin's son would be five or six now, if Erik remembered his birthday correctly. He cast a wistful glance to the north, and then disappeared behind the impossibly heavy oak door.

He could smell mutton stew even before he arrived in the dining hall.

Seven places were set, one for each of the six monks who permanently resided in the monastery, and one for him. The other monks that worked the lower grounds with Nolan, ate on their own until they were invited to the table once it was perceived by others that their wisdom and knowledge was sufficient.

Erik sat at the head of the table, as Shermin had insisted since discovering that Erik was sahale.

Once they were all seated, Shermin led the group in prayer. Each of the monks bowed their heads and folded their hands in front of them. Erik did likewise.

"All-Father, we thank thee for the life thou hast bestowed upon us. We thank thee for the knowledge that thou hast provided for us. We thank thee for the wisdom that thou hast planted within us. Guide us as we seek the higher truths. Teach us as we seek to understand. Protect us as we seek thy will. Amen."

"Amen," all of the other monks said in unison. Erik remained politely silent. To him, Icadion and the other Old Gods still seemed quite distant. History told him that the Old Gods had abandoned Terramyr centuries before, and that Demi-gods now ruled in their places. He wasn't about to stomp on the religion of those he was staying with, but he wasn't too keen on joining them either.

They all dug in with their spoons, eager to taste the meal that Derian, the best cook among them, had created for their lunch. Derian was relatively new to the monastery, and hailed from a village two hundred miles to the east. He had come seeking knowledge from the monastery, and had wound up staying on. Fortunately for all of the monks, Derian had been an aspiring chef working at a small inn before his arrival. To hear Shermin talk about it, the monk would explain that Derian's arrival had changed the way they ate in much the same way that spring brings flowers and trees into bloom.

Apparently, none of the other monks could make anything to speak of.

Derian was especially pleased today, as he should have been. Erik had eaten mutton stew on many occasions prior to this. It was a dish that was extremely easy to turn into swill with tough meat. Derian, on the other hand, had created a savory masterpiece with delicious, tender chunks of meat set in a garlic broth among carrots, celery, and onion. It was by far the best mutton dish he had ever tasted. Despite their vows to give up greed and gluttony, the large pot that could have easily fed thirty people was entirely consumed by the seven of them, another testament to Derian's skills.

After supper, Erik retired to his chamber, which had previously been an office for transcribing manuscripts, and stared out the window. It had started to snow again, and the dark gray clouds did not look as though they would be emptied any time soon. The young man went to his bed and pulled a leather bound journal out from underneath. He opened it to write inside, but found himself sitting and staring at it blankly for several minutes. The monks had encouraged him to record his travels, and use the journal not only as an accounting of each day's activities, but as a supplement to his daily meditations. Shermin promised it would endow him with additional wisdom and insight, and help him take note of his progress as he wrestled with the less desirable traits within himself. So far, despite having been at the monastery for several months, Erik had four pages.

Everything he had done in his life prior to arriving at the monastery had taken three pages worth of space. That included his impression of the orphanage he lived in as a small child, the time he spent with Trenton and Raisa Lokton, his loving and departed adoptive parents, as well as recounting the war against Tu'luh and his travels since leaving the Middle Kingdom.

There were more details he could write, he knew, but the exercise made him uncomfortable. He doubted anyone would ever believe half of the things he had claimed to have done, and he himself needed no reminders. How could he ever forget what he had been through? Janik's betrayal. The blood feud with House Cedreau that claimed the lives of Lord Cedreau, his youngest son, and Erik's father. The battles he had won, with Master Lepkin and Lady Dimwater at his side every step of the way. Al and Jaleal too. Master Orres' self-sacrifice, and the joining of forces with legends like Peren,

Gorin, and Lady Arkyn. No. He didn't need to write it all down in a book. The images, sounds, and smells were with him every day now. It was all a part of him. Even if the human part of him could forget, he was not entirely human. He was, after all, sahale. He had met face to face with Hiasyntar'Kulai, the Father of the Ancients and progenitor of all dragon kin upon the face of Terramyr. More than that, he had ridden the great dragon through the clouds. He had studied in the palace of the Immortal Mystic. He had seen and done things that even most dragons could not claim to have done.

And all of that was accomplished before he had even reached the age of maturity according to the customs of the Middle Kingdom.

Perhaps that was why there was only one page written after the account of those other things. What did he have to write about now that could ever compare with what he had already done?

He blinked at the blank page and sighed. "I'll try again tomorrow," he said as he slipped the book back under the bed. Erik moved to the desk and pulled a large, brown leather book out of a drawer.

It was an archaic text, with many phrasings that were nigh impossible to decipher. Still, the prize of knowledge that it dangled before Erik was too great not to strive for. The book was written about the Four Horsemen, compiled by a strange group of hermit wizards known only as the Cult of Zammin. Shermin was certain that the Cult of Zammin knew how to call the Four Horsemen down to Terramyr, which made Erik wonder whether they might also know a way to defeat them.

As was evident from just the previous night, Erik could never rid his mind of the vision which the treacherous Red Dragon had conveyed to his mind so long ago in the secret chamber below Valtuu Temple. After all these years, Erik could still see the images as clearly as the day Tu'luh had shown them to him, and not just during the night either. If

Erik closed his eyes and focused even to a small degree, his mind would see the terrible images in full detail. There was nothing he could do to escape them.

It was a horrible, nightmarish peek at the future.

At the time Tu'luh had shown him the vision, Erik had been told that it was meaningless, a simple illusion created by Tu'luh to scare him into joining forces with that crazed and deluded dragon. Erik had believed that to be the case, until the vision started coming to him in the night.

The first time it happened, Erik and Lady Arkyn were traveling through the southern reaches of the orcish lands. They had been together for about two years by that point. Erik thought it was a simple nightmare, but then each night the vision would return. After two weeks, the vision progressed beyond what Tu'luh had ever shown him.

The visions became nightly occurrences, but each night with subtle changes. Sometimes he fought with the horseman, as he had before Nolan woke him. Other times he would watch helpless as the horseman destroyed city after city. Then, there were the nightmares wherein Erik would actually join with the horseman, and help bring death and destruction to the very homeland he had fought so hard to protect. Lady Arkyn had tried to help calm him at night, but more often than not had ended up getting a response similar to Nolan. Though she swore she was never harmed, and could never be afraid of him, Erik knew that he had to find his answers alone. His time at the Monastery of the Southern Light hadn't yet helped him with his nightmares, but at least he had uncovered some things about the horsemen.

If his attempts at translating some of the texts were accurate, the Cult of Zammin knew of another person that worked with the horsemen, a guardian of sorts, or perhaps a judger of worlds, Erik couldn't be sure based upon the texts he had read so far. What he did know, was that the man carried a long, silver spear, and was often dressed in green, hooded robes, beneath which was a jerkin made of dragon skin and a black tunic. It was the tunic that was important, for it was said by the Cult of Zammin that the tunic would bear a particular symbol upon the collar. Erik had spent hours memorizing that symbol.

If he ever met the guardian, he wanted to know it right away, for he had some questions to ask of that man.

He studied the tome until long after the sun had dropped behind the western horizon. Shermin, accustomed to Erik's long hours of study, brought a small snack of bread and fruits meal up to him and set it on the desk next to Erik. Erik thanked Shermin with a smiling nod, but hardly touched the food. He was too busy reading. One day he would have to thank Al, the king of the dwarves in Roegudok Hall, for instilling the love of reading in him. Even Master Lepkin had never succeeded in igniting a passion for reading in Erik the way that Al had. As a young teenager, Erik would have given up after half an hour, but now he was so focused that he feasted upon the words, picking them apart and doing his best to drain them of the precious knowledge contained in their riddles and ancient idioms and metaphors.

Only when his eyes grew heavy enough to close on their own did he finally decide to end his studies for the night. He closed the book, careful to place a small ribbon of red silk inside to hold his place. He then put the book back in the drawer and stood up. He glanced out the window after blowing out the candle. The clouds had gone now, revealing hundreds of thousands of stars in the night sky. They twinkled brilliantly above him while the moon bathed the snowy mountains in her light. Erik leaned out and took a breath of crisp night air and then turned to his bed.

Chapter 3

Erik was quickly able to fall asleep. His mind was focused on the studying he had done that day, and so runes and symbols danced in his head as he drifted off into a deep sleep.

That was when he heard the strange call.

It wasn't quite a squawk, nor was it a screech. It was something between the two, only barely audible. He turned back to the window and peered outside. In the distant darkness, he could just make out the glittering trail of purple and gold sparkles. A second call came, louder this time.

"A Night Hawk," he said softly.

A flurry of thoughts ran through his weary mind. He knew only a handful of people who could use Night Hawks. Lady Dimwater was one, and Master Lepkin was another. Perhaps King Mathias was dead. He was, after all, well beyond the age of most men. If the king had died, Lepkin might send for Erik to have him help with the transition of power. Erik knew only all too well how many nobles had squabbled over the throne just a few years prior. Or, maybe Lepkin needed him for something else. Erik wasn't sure what else Lepkin would want though. Even if some creature were foolish enough to attack Master Lepkin and Lady Dimwater, the two former masters from Kuldiga Academy were more than capable of defending themselves. He wondered whether Al might send for him; he did miss his dwarf friend. Or possibly Jaleal, the diminutive gnome warrior that had shared in Erik's quests, had sent the messenger. A knot formed in Erik's stomach as the magical bird drew closer. None of those possibilities struck him as the reason for the Night Hawk's call.

When Lady Arkyn had finally been persuaded to let him travel alone, she had promised to send a Night Hawk if she should need to contact him. The knot in his stomach grew and began to pull at him as if to drag him through the floor. Night hawks were not usually the bearers of uplifting news.

He stood waiting, which was all he could do. There was no real point in guessing what might need his attention. He would know soon enough. The great, magical bird sped through the skies like a shooting star, leaving a trail of illuminated dust in its wake. It was nearly as large as Erik's dragon form was, but it was much faster than any physical being. It crossed the vast openness between them in less than a minute, and then shrank down to the size of a large owl and lighted upon the stone window sill.

"Well then, what have you got to tell me?" Erik asked.

The bird dipped its glowing head toward Erik. Erik reached out and put a hand upon the bird. A series of images flashed through his mind. He saw the dead bodies. He saw the claw marks in the secret hallway. He saw Njar and Minrielle standing over another body. Next he saw a small city from a bird's-eye-view and the words *Winter's Beak* came into his mind. The feeling of urgency from Minrielle was overwhelming. Erik digested the distress call and then backed away from the bird.

He had never known so many other sahale existed. To find out about them in this way flipped his stomach and he nearly retched on the floor.

The message ended and the bird chirped once, raising its head to look at Erik with beady black eyes.

Erik nodded. "Tell her I'm coming," he said. "I'll be there as quickly as I can."

After Erik sent the Night Hawk back with his response, he turned and went for the door. He stretched out his hand and pulled the portal open only to find Shermin approaching, holding a small bucket of water.

"I felt a disturbance, is everything all right?" Shermin asked.

Erik nodded. It was uncanny how Shermin was so tuned in to his surroundings when he was on duty as his watcher for the night. "I have received some disturbing news from my homeland, I will need to leave as soon as possible."

Shermin's face grew long and the monk sighed. "The demon will not come for another two months. If you do not stay to fight him, then he will continue to demand sacrifices." Shermin's eyes welled with tears. "If we refuse his sacrifice, then he will destroy our monastery, and he will ravage our library. All of the knowledge we have accumulated will be lost forever."

"I understand," Erik said.

"When there is a champion willing to fight, then the demon is appeased when he defeats them. But, if no champion comes to our aid, then the demon's mercy can only be purchased by sacrifice. The last two times he has come, no one has been willing to fight. We were able to buy our way out by sacrificing two bulls and three goats, but he warned us last time that he would need a human, or else he would come for the monastery."

Erik nodded. "I am not leaving before facing the demon," he said resolutely.

Shermin sighed in relief and stepped forward to fall upon Erik's shoulders with his hands. "Oh, thank you, Master Lokton, thank you!"

Master Lokton. He was still not used to the title. "Call me Erik," he told Shermin for the thousandth time.

Shermin nodded and patted Erik's shoulders. "Of course, of course," the monk said. Erik knew that the man had no real intention of speaking with him so informally. "Thank you, again, for staying. If the demon were to ever get his hands on what he seeks, then it would mean destruction for many people in these parts."

"So you have said," Erik replied evenly. Shermin had told Erik of a magical spell used to banish the demon long before. While it did allow for the demon to return to this plane once every seven months, it did keep the monster trapped in an alternate plane the rest of the time. It also protected the monastery from direct assault, but the magic was growing weaker now. As the years had passed, the protections it afforded were decaying, allowing the demon to come ever closer as it grew stronger. If the demon ever got its hands on the book, then the spell would be broken entirely, and it would be allowed to reenter this world, free to wreak havoc as it pleased. "I will not be staying long," Erik said.

Shermin squinted at him, confused. "But, you just said you would face the demon?"

Erik nodded. "There is another way to fight him."

Shermin shook his head. "No, to speak his name would break the banishing spell."

"Only if I failed to slay him," Erik said.

"No, I cannot allow such a reckless decision," Shermin said with his hands up in the air. "No. It mustn't be done!"

"If you give me his name, I can summon him forth. Then, I will kill him. You do believe that I am the one spoken of in your prophecy, do you not?"

"It isn't a matter of belief," Shermin argued.

"Yes it is," Erik said. "Everything is a matter of faith. In times of trial, we must step into the darkness, full of courage, and void of doubt and fear." Erik smiled as Shermin sighed.

"You have learned much since coming here," Shermin said. "You must understand, that if you summon him, and he overpowers you, then he will be free in this plane. We have guarded his name since his banishment. We have gone to great lengths to ensure that no one outside of these hallowed walls could ever whisper his name."

"I have slain dragons and demons before," Erik said. "I will not let you down."

"Pride goeth before the fall," Shermin replied, quoting one of the monastery's famous proverbs.

Erik nodded. "It isn't pride to know your own strength," he said. "To know thy enemy is wise, but to know thyself is true power," Erik said, quoting another proverb used in the monastery.

Shermin nodded solemnly. "I will have to confer with the others. The decision to give you the name must be unanimous. If even one monk refuses, then you cannot have the name."

"I understand," Erik said. "Shall I go with you?"

Shermin shook his head. "No, I will go. Please, rest for tonight. In the morning, you shall have your answer."

Erik nodded and returned to his room.

As he laid down to sleep, he heard a fluttering of wings at the window. He looked up and saw a large, black raven. His heart skipped a beat. He had not seen a raven at his window for many years. The first time had been as a young teenage boy. The raven had come and tapped at the window to warn him of an impending attack. Since that night, he had hated ravens. Over the last several years, he had even gone out of his way to kill ravens he found along his travels. Killing the messengers of death was his way of trying to hold the evil at bay and maybe, just maybe, preventing a raven from ever lighting upon his window sill again.

Apparently, despite his best efforts, it hadn't been as effective as he had hoped.

"Don't you dare tap on my widow," Erik snarled as he sat up quickly and threw his hands out to scare the bird.

The raven *caw-cawed* at him and then tilted its head. It was not about to fly away. It hopped twice to the side of the window and then tapped on the stone. *Tap-tap-tap-tap-tap-tap.* Pause. *Tap-tap-tap-tap-tap-tap.*

"NO!" Erik shouted as he charged the raven. The bird launched away into the night.

It was never a good omen to see the raven at the window, but so close on the heels of the Night Hawk, surely the two had to be connected. Erik closed his eyes and tried to remember the meaning of different sets of taps. He knew the pause in the middle was a break before repeating the message. The first time he had seen the raven at his home in Lokton Manor, there had been sets of three taps.

Three taps meant that death came for you, but could be averted.

The memory of the first real battle he had ever experienced came flooding back into his mind. Blacktongues had ravaged his home. They were merciless in their marauding. He had been their target, but they had not cared about other lives either. That had been the first time he had killed a man. He had died defending old Louis and his wife from a savage Blacktongue. Even now, after experiencing many other battles, it was the first one that still clung to the back of his mind like a shadow, ever following him.

He shook his head and forced his mind to think about the raven.

Four taps meant that the recipient of the raven's message would die that night.

Five taps mean that someone in the household would die.

What was six taps? He paced back and forth for a moment, exhaustion from his hours of study stalling his efforts to remember the meaning. He closed his eyes and tapped his forehead six times, recreating the raven's message.

"Six taps… six taps," Erik whispered to himself.

A knock came at the door.

"Enter," Erik said.

"I was busy with the others, and then I heard you shouting," Shermin said. "Are you all right, Master Lokton?"

Erik shook his head. "A raven came to the window."

Shermin put two fingers to the sides of his mouth and spat on the floor. "Ravens at the window are an ill omen," he said decisively.

"Do you recall what six taps means?"

"A set of six, are you sure?" Shermin asked.

Erik nodded. "Positive."

Shermin shook his head and his shoulders drooped. "I am sorry, Master Lokton, but it means that one of your friends will be killed tonight."

*****

Braun woke from a dream and set his feet on the cold, marble floor of Lokton Manor. The large man went to his window and peered outside. The two guards on patrol were just passing by as he watched. A quiet, silvery mist was creeping over the fields beyond the stone half-wall. The moon was full and bright, bathing the entire area in soft light.

The large man turned and slipped his boots on. As House Lokton's Man-at-arms, he was never one to be caught unawares, so he always slept in trousers and a tunic that covered him well enough to handle anything that would arise on short notice in the night. He grabbed his sword belt and latched it around his waist, and then he exited his room. He looked down the hallway and sighed as he saw the doors to

Trenton and Raisa's room closed. A golden chain sealed the double doors so that no one could enter. Braun had rebuilt the manor exactly as it had been before, right down to the last stone. He had hoped that Lady Lokton would once again be able to find her place there.

Her sorrow had been so great after the death of her husband that nothing he did ever brightened her mood. Hiasyntar'Kulai, the Father of the Ancients, had come mid-way through completion of the rebuilding process. He had taken Lady Lokton with him. The dragon reunited Lady and Lord Lokton on the other side of the rainbow bridge, granting them both a joyous life in Volganor, the Heaven City.

Out of respect, when the manor was completed, Braun had sealed their rebuilt bedchamber. No one would ever be allowed inside, unless Erik Lokton returned and took up his place as the head of House Lokton.

Braun sighed as he thought of Erik. It had been several years since he had seen his young charge. Braun would have gone out into the wilderness to find Erik and join him, except that Lady Lokton had given Braun strict orders to stay with the manor and protect the people that worked and lived on Lokton lands. He turned and walked down the hall.

He stopped suddenly, the hairs on his neck standing on end. He turned and scanned the shadows. There was nothing there but paintings and statues that had been recommissioned after the house had been completed. Still, he couldn't shake the feeling he was being watched.

*****

Lady Arkyn woke in the early morning hours. The sky outside the cave she slept in was still dark. Clouds covered the moon's face as a chill wind wafted into the tunnel. She rubbed her arms and grabbed her bow. She couldn't see anything in the cave, but the years of experience told her she was in danger.

Lady Arkyn tip-toed to the cave's mouth, and that's when she saw them.

Skulking, dark forms crawling through the underbrush and up the forested hill toward her cave.

They weren't guards, she knew that much. City guards would not crawl upon all fours like animals.

She set an arrow to her bowstring and smoothly pulled back. She scanned the forms stalking toward her. She could now see the daggers and curved short swords they held in their hands. Their intentions were clear.

Lady Arkyn fired the first shot.

A woman shrieked as the arrow bit into the back of her neck. She jerked and convulsed, and then went still.

The other forms stood erect and began sprinting as they shouted their war cry.

The elven archer counted forty of them charging in fast. She was good, but even she wasn't fast enough to stop all of them before they would reach her. She quick-fired three more shots. Three more attackers fell to the ground. Two male, one female.

An arrow zipped by her head and slapped off the stone wall behind her.

That was her cue to turn.

She ran back into the cave, her legs gracefully propelling her forward over the stones on the ground. She stopped twenty yards inside, turned back and fired two more shots. Both arrows struck the same attacker. He fell with a sick *thump* as others charged in behind him.

In the darkness she had a slight advantage. Her pursuers were human, and their eyes could not find her in the blackness of the cave, but she could easily see them with her elf sight. More than that, the pursuers' silhouettes were easily visible against the night sky that was framed by the mouth of the cave. Sitting in the dark where she was, even if she had been human she would have seen them well enough to aim her shots. She knelt and fired arrows until her quiver was empty. Eighteen arrows streaked through the tunnel and piled bodies at the mouth of the cave. That made for a total of twenty-three slain. As she had been traveling light, she had no spare quiver to fall back on. The angry, snarling attackers were swarming the mouth of the cave now, obviously realizing that she had no more firepower to send their way.

She was about to turn on her heels and scurry along, when she heard a strange language being chanted at the entrance. It was familiar, somehow. A dark and ancient tongue that brought evil with it. Goosebumps formed along her skin.

A green glow descended upon the fallen like a mist, and then those who had been slain began to stir and rise once more. They pulled the arrows from their bodies and broke the shafts before discarding the pieces along the cave floor.

Lady Arkyn cursed under her breath. "Erik, where are you?"

*****

Braun stepped out into the night and sniffed the air. His muscles were tensing, ready for a fight. He couldn't see anything around the manor, but he could *feel* it. Something was there, in the darkness. Blood was going to be spilled.

He fingered the handle of his sword and tugged at it just enough to ensure it would slide smoothly from its sheath. His eyes studied the mist-covered fields and then scanned back toward the barns and stable buildings. The horses were quiet. There was no sign of movement.

The large warrior quietly made his way down the front stairs of the manor and then walked along the perimeter of the building, scanning the bushes and shrubs near the walls for concealed assailants. A less experienced guard might have laughed it off as overactive nerves, or perhaps a simple case of the jitters brought on by being woken from a dream suddenly, but not Braun. There was something unmistakably evil nearby. He hadn't found it yet, but whatever it was, he was not about to allow Lokton Manor to be attacked again.

"Where are you?" Braun whispered into the night. "Come out and face me."

The two guards on patrol rounded the western corner of the house and nearly jumped out of their boots when they saw Braun. They snapped to attention real quick, but remained silent in response to him putting a finger to his lips.

"Have you seen anything unusual?" he asked as he approached.

They shook their heads.

"A quiet night," Arnis said.

"Not a thing out of place," Remi added.

"I want you to go inside," Braun ordered. "Remi, you head to the alarm bell. Arnis, you close the front doors, lock them, and alert the others."

The two of them were fairly new to the estate, but they knew better than to question their commander. They nodded quietly and then hustled their way to the entrance of the manor. Braun watched them to make sure the doors were shut as he asked, and then he made his way for the mist-covered field. He wasn't able to say why exactly, but he felt drawn to the field.

He nimbly leapt over the stone half-wall and trekked out into the mist. The swirling vapor hugged at his waist, obscuring his view of the grass below. His gut told him that there was an unspeakable evil, so he drew his sword. If he could just find whatever it was that was disturbing him, he could yell back to the manor. Remi would hear him and sound the alarm. He was sure of it.

He walked far beyond the distance his voice would carry and still found nothing. The pit in his gut grew larger and thicker, threatening to drag him down to the ground, but he ignored it. He was the protector of House Lokton. If there was danger, as he was sure there was, he was not about to turn and run from it now. He walked out past the large graveyard that had been put in after the large battle that had destroyed the manor. The gravestones stood still and silent, their shadows mingling with the mist as he walked by.

Seeing the stones gave him an idea of where to look.

His heart thumped heavily in his chest as he recalled the warlock, Gondok'hr. The fiend was powerful as he was cunning, and had masqueraded as Senator Bracken in order to shore up his power and launch his assault upon the realm. The body of the warlock had not been buried in the cemetery. The marked graves were only for the honorable heroes that had fallen fighting against the evil Gondok'hr stood for.

Gondok'hr had been burned in a pit, and then covered with layers of stone and dirt. Four palo santo trees had been planted in the soil above the grave as well, in an attempt to cleanse the area of the evil ashes that now polluted the ground.

Braun went into the woods, stepping lightly and cautiously. He was incredibly silent, especially for a large man. He neither broke any twigs under foot, nor rustled the undergrowth as he went into the woods. He slithered through the forest like a ghost. He came upon the place of Gondok'hr's burial and then knelt behind a sizeable boulder as he peered around. A dark figure was hunched over the pit, mumbling something that Braun couldn't quite understand. Black mist writhed upon the cursed ground, appearing almost like oil.

The figure stopped and stood erect. He turned, but Braun couldn't see the figure's face in the darkness. The figure pointed to one of the palo santo trees and an orange spark leapt from his finger and struck the tree. The wood shattered outward and the tree was no more.

Braun ducked back around the boulder, his eyes blinded by the brilliant explosion. He took in a steadying breath and let his eyes readjust. Then, he leapt out from behind the boulder and charged the intruder.

"This ends now!" Braun shouted.

The dark figure snapped his fingers and a wave of air slammed into Braun, picking him up and throwing him back ten feet to slam into the base of a large tree.

"I am sorry to see you, Braun," the figure said as he took two steps toward the large warrior. "I had not intended to hurt anyone in House Lokton."

Braun screwed his face up and grunted as he struggled to his feet. The voice was somewhat familiar, but he couldn't quite place it. "Who are you? Show yourself!"

The figure laughed. "I am sorry, I truly am," the figure said. He snapped his fingers again.

The black mist began to coalesce into several large forms. Black figures groaned and stood in the darkness. Only then did Braun realize that it was not a mist at all. They were spirits, or specters, brought into existence by the intruder's evil powers.

"Be gone!" Braun demanded as he lifted his sword into the ready position. "I cannot allow you to disturb this area."

"Oh, but Braun, I have come for Gondok'hr's ashes."

Another man may have asked why, but not Braun. He was not a man of words, but of action. He charged down once more. The first dark form lunged at him. With a flash of his sword, Braun cut off the creature's arm. The humanoid hissed and staggered backward.

The intruder then turned his back to Braun. "My servants will deal with you. I have other matters to attend to." A green light extended out from the intruder's hand and permeated the ground until the whole area began to glow. The remaining palo santo trees withered on the spot, shriveling and shrinking against the weight of the evil being wrought upon them.

"Rise, Gondok'hr, rise!" the intruder said.

"NO!" Braun shouted. A rush of anger flooded his body and caused his strength to surge. He cut down the dark servants as he waded deeper into the throng and toward the intruder. At first it appeared as though the battle would be an easy task, but then those who were cut down began to rise again, coated in the same green light as the ground. Even the arm Braun had severed came back to life and tried to reached out and grab Braun's ankle. Braun managed to stab the dismembered arm and fling it away.

He struck out wildly, cutting two more of the things down, but the rest of them kept coming.

Something cold shattered through his chainmail and pierced his left shoulder. Braun's left arm went limp and heavy. He turned and kicked at his assailant, striking a wight in the chest. Another one snarled and came in from the right. Braun turned just in time to cut off another attacker's arm at the elbow. He stabbed straight into the creature's chest. The monster fell back.

"Don't make this harder than it has to be, Braun," the cloaked stranger said from somewhere behind the throng of foul creatures.

Braun put his weight into a full vertical chop that connected with the top of the fiend's skull and continued down to split the wight in two. He then lunged forward and hacked off another wight's head. He moved for a third, but before he could reach it, another came in from behind and tore at his right arm. Chainmail links snapped like dry twigs as sparks mixed with a spray of blood. Braun's sword arm fell, tingling for only a moment before the heavy numbness took over.

He grunted and launched a backward kick that knocked the attacking wight away. Braun was no fool, he knew he couldn't win, but he was not about to make it easy on his enemies either. With his arms dangling at his side he spun and jumped between savage kicks. He caught the nearest wight in the groin, and then followed up with a left-footed round-house

42

to the face that knocked the wight to the ground, cracking its skull on a stone. Another wight rushed in. Braun stopped it with a massive stomp to the creature's chest. Ribs caved and snapped under the force as the wight's limbs jerked forward before the whole body flew backward to knock into three more of the creatures.

It seemed every shadow in the area gave birth to more of the sinister beings. Wights surrounded him now, and he was drowning in a sea of gnashing teeth and dagger-like claws. He fought valiantly, but in the end he was caught by a severed hand that had crawled toward his ankle. The fingers ripped through his pants at the ankle. A terrible, shooting pain blasted through Braun's right leg up to his hip. His limb felt as though it were stone. He could no longer move it. He stumbled and fell.

The darkness closed in as his body grew cold and heavy.

As his mind gave in to death, the large warrior wished that he had been able to do more to protect House Lokton.

*****

Lady Arkyn sprinted through the dark cavern. She had scouted it well before deciding to use it for refuge, and knew that near the end was a smaller shaft that would allow her to escape upward. Better than that, there were two vents that spewed a vile mixture of natural oil and an odorless gas. She would lead the attackers there, and then she would hit them with something that was sure to break the reanimation spells.

The stumbling steps were gaining speed as the lumbering creatures followed her through the cave. The woman was still chanting and making clicking noises. Lights flared into life in the cave, momentarily blinding the elf while also aiding the attackers. She knew she would have to move much faster if she were to have any hope of reaching the shaft

She sprinted nimbly through the tunnel, avoiding the occasional rock hurled haphazardly after her. After three minutes of hard running, she came to the end of the cave. Two waist-high mounds rose up from the cave floor. Black goo bubbled and spurted out the tops as green and yellow vapors hissed and rose into the air to coalesce along the stone ceiling. She turned sideways and stepped between the two mounds, careful not to let any of the black liquid touch her. She pulled her dagger and stared upward through the shaft. She could just make out the open night sky above the twenty-foot long chute. Lady Arkyn took in a breath and then ran up the back wall, leaping at the last moment for the chute, with her arms stretched upward. She stabbed her dagger into the compact dirt on one side and threw her left hand against the other side, grabbing onto a thick root. Her shoulders burned as she pressed into the sides and slowly pulled herself up. The thirteen seconds that passed before she could pull herself up enough to wedge her knees and back against opposite sides of the chute felt like an eternity. When she had found this escape route, she had been so confident it would provide a quick exit, but reality was proving that she had overestimated her abilities.

It took great effort to shimmy up the chute, managing only a couple of feet in the first minute. The shaft broke to the right a bit, which proved difficult to navigate as even her narrow shoulders barely managed to squeeze through the opening. Luckily, however, that very bend in the chute provided her with an excellent foothold so she could stand and rest her hands and shoulders before continuing to propel herself upward. The next third of the tunnel went fairly quickly.

She could hear the angry shuffling of feet below. They were close.

Lady Arkyn moved faster. She would need her hands free in order to use her tinder kit and drop the spark down to the gasses in the cave. She was five feet below the surface when a dark form came into view. She froze, hoping it wouldn't be able to see her in the darkness of the shaft. How had they known of the shaft?

"Get me a torch," the man said from above.

Lady Arkyn cursed her luck. She didn't have long now before being discovered, and there was nowhere to go. She looked down and saw several forms walking below her. One of them bumped into one of the bubbling mounds and recoiled with a shriek when some of the hot liquid hit his arm.

Lady Arkyn closed her eyes and leaned back into the tunnel with her spine as she pressed into the opposite side with her feet. It was now or never.

She took out her tinder kit and also a rag and bit of wood. The elf could only hope that the vapors had not come up into the shaft. If they had, then she might only be igniting herself, but there was little choice anyway. There were too many below to fight, and the ones above would have the advantage. Her only course of action now was to try and take as many of them with her as possible.

She whispered a silent prayer and then used the tinder kit to light the rag and bit of wood. Once she had a flame, she heard excited shouting from above.

"There, there!" a man said.

Arkyn moved her left leg and angled the burning mass of cloth and wood so she could drop it.

One of the reanimated creatures looked up and grunted at her.

"Catch this," she said as she let go. She watched the flames flicker in protest as the mass of fire rushed downward. Her breath caught in her throat when it hit the side of the tunnel and bounced, sending sparks outward, but the flame lived on until it fell directly into one of the two bubbling mounds.

Whoosh-whomp! BOOM!

Fire and stone erupted violently. A rush of heat assaulted Lady Arkyn. She tried to shield herself from it,

45

closing her eyes and covering her face with her hands. The stinging blaze went up her pant legs and licked at her body as it passed upward for a moment, and then it stopped. From below her there was a sick, wet thumping sound. She looked down and saw the top half of a man's body stuck in the bottom of the shaft. Somehow, the explosion had thrown him upward, sealing off the chute from below and sparing her life.

Never one to waste a good turn of luck, Lady Arkyn scampered upward as quickly as she could. When she reached the top, two men were rolling to their hands and feet two yards away, while another was putting out flames on the front of his tunic by slapping himself and running around wildly while screaming hysterically.

Lady Arkyn left the screamer alone and went for the two that had obviously been able to dodge the flames that had shot upward through the chute. She came down hard with her dagger, slicing the first in the back of the neck. He cried out and fell forward. The second man turned to see what was wrong and took Arkyn's dagger through his left eye. The elf used the heel of her boot to unstick her blade and then went back to the first man. She dropped down, flipping her dagger upside-down as she moved, and drove it through the base of his neck.

She then stood and looked for the panicked man. The flames were larger now, engulfing his torso as his tunic burned.

Lady Arkyn calmly walked toward him, placing herself in his path as he turned and ran back her way, still slapping the flames and oblivious to her. She lashed out with a quick kick to the man's jaw. Bone cracked as his skull jerked backward. His screams became garbled mumbles and he fell onto his back. The flames flared outward and then died down a bit as the tunic was nearly consumed.

"Stop, drop, and roll, my friend," she said as she came down hard, plunging her knife into the man's heart. She pulled her dagger back and then kicked the body down the steep hill, watching it roll as the last of the flames died out.

Lady Arkyn sheathed her weapon, and then turned to escape into the night.

Chapter 4

Erik found the other senior monks in a large chamber. There were no decorations on the gray and brown stone walls. The monks here believed that in order to debate problems and come to true wisdom, there should be no distractions. The floor was cracked and worn smooth with age. It had been repaired in some places, but never had it been replaced with marble or expensive tiles. There weren't even chairs in the deliberation chamber. They believed that no problem was so difficult that it couldn't be solved while standing.

Shermin saw him enter the room and offered an empathetic smile.

Erik replied with a nod, but he couldn't try to return the smile. The raven was still fresh on his mind. Logically, he knew that he had been too far away to reach any of his friends during the night. Even in his dragon form, it would take days to cross even as far as Ten Forts. It was what he didn't know that was eating at him. He had no way of knowing which of his friends had been in peril, and that was destroying his peace. His first guess had been Lady Arkyn, as she had sent the Night Hawk to him, but there was no way for him to know for sure at this point.

In any case, he had to try to force that to the back of his mind now. He was needed desperately in the north, but he would not be able to leave until he had fulfilled his promise to the monks.

"We have decided to give you the name," Shermin said without pretense. "Each of us shall give you a letter. When you have all of the letters for the name, you will have to figure out the order in which they are to be placed."

"You mean you don't know?" Erik asked.

Shermin shook his head. "The letters are purposefully mixed as an added safety measure, but I suspect you can figure it out easily enough." Shermin approached him and placed a hand on his shoulder. He leaned in close to Erik's ear. "My letter is A."

Shermin then left the room.

The next monk approached. "F," he said quietly.

The third came next. "D," he whispered.

The remaining monks each gave him the last letters, R, Y, N, G, respectively.

Erik exited the chamber and quickly made his way outside only to find Shermin standing in the grass a few yards outside the monastery.

"My family has served here for generations," he said softly as he turned to regard Erik. "Since even before the demon came to plague us. The first born male of each generation has dedicated himself without exception, but I shall be the last," he said.

Erik cocked his head to the side. "Why is that?" he asked.

"My father and mother perished many years ago during an orc raid, my three brothers along with them." Shermin's eyes grew moist. "I am the last of my family. It would be a shame if the demon were to outlast my line."

Erik nodded. "You will see the demon fall today," he promised.

49

Shermin smiled and tossed his head back as he took in a great breath and let the sunshine hit his face. "May Icadion grant you victory," Shermin said. "And, I am sorry about your friend," he added. "I know what it is to lose someone close."

Erik nodded, understanding now that Shermin had lost nearly everyone he held close. "Thank you," he said. In truth, Shermin's words did little to comfort Erik, but the young man was no stranger to loss either. Many of his friends, some closer than others, had died in years past. His adoptive father as well. Death wasn't something he was used to, but it was something he could push down into the recesses of his soul in order to accomplish the work at hand. For now, he was Erik, The Champion of Truth, the slayer of demons. There would be time for mourning later.

He marched out across the long yard until he reached the edge of the plateau. He knelt down and closed his eyes as he rehearsed a spell Lady Dimwater had given him the last time they saw each other. He had long ago committed it to memory, but wanted to run through it once before the fight. A knot formed in his stomach as he rose to his feet and drew his mighty sword.

"Always nervous," he said to himself. It seemed no matter how many battles he won, there was always a bout of jitters and fear before another. He called the letters to mind. He viewed them floating before him, imagining how to arrange them. As he did so, he called upon his power to see the truth.

Letters fell into place.

The demon's name was Fangryd.

Erik glanced over to the monastery where Shermin was standing and watching. None of the other monks had come outside. Shermin had his hands clasped together and his mouth was moving, likely in prayer. Erik looked down at his sword. It was not the same weapon that Master Lepkin had given to him, but it had many of the same properties. In fact, it had the same hilt. Though the original weapon had been destroyed, this new one had been forged using Telarian steel, the only metal known to withstand a dragon's flame and remain cool to the touch. The orcs that Erik had lived with had some amount of the material, and had helped him re-forge a new sword in the pattern of the old one. They were the one people who could understand the significance of such a gesture, a reaching back to the past to create something remarkable. The endeavor had turned out better than even Erik had hoped. Not only did the weapon look like the old sword, but the dragon's flame enchantment had been lying dormant inside the hilt all those years. Once a blade had been laid into the hilt anew, the enchantment had taken hold, allowing Erik to summon fire onto the sword as he had with the original weapon.

He traced the fingers of his left hand over the flat of the blade and took in a deep breath to steady his nerves once more.

"Let's get this over with," Erik said.

"Fangryd, I summon thee by name!" Erik shouted into the air.

Nothing happened.

"FANGRYD!" Erik shouted again. "I command Fangryd to appear!" The early morning sky grew dark. A warm wind from the north carried black and green clouds over the plateau. A pair of tornado funnels formed, whirling in the air above Erik. Dust and debris whipped around him as the twin tornados danced around each other, slowly and methodically extending their tails downward until they landed upon the ground.

"Who dares to summon me?" a voice thundered from within a cloud of blackness born of the tornados.

Erik stood firm. "Fangryd, I order you to come out and show yourself."

"Hmm, I can feel the darkness in you, but you are not what I expected," the voice said.

Erik paused for just a moment. What did the demon mean that it could sense the darkness within him?

A guttural laugh emanated from the darkness. "Yes, yes, I can see it now. You are fighting against the darkness inside of you. Then why have you summoned me? You have no power to control me, boy."

"I have not summoned you in order to control you," Erik shouted.

"Then, I shall feast upon your bones, and I shall relish in the freedom you have so foolishly granted me."

Erik let his feelings flow through him and into his sword. White flames danced upon the black, Telarian steel as he readied himself. "Come out, demon," Erik said.

A long, thick leg with massive, rock-like growths along the front extended outward from the darkness. A long, deadly claw stabbed into the ground, shaking the entire plateau. The leg then flexed as a second came forward. A red glow grew from within the black cloud until it finally broke through, revealing an ever-burning face much like a bat's. Long fangs extended below the creature's jaw, dripping with acidic venom that hissed and ate through the dirt wherever it landed. Two more legs followed the head and body. Overall, it was like staring at a large spider. The head and face were in the front, with a bulbous, flaming body behind it. Six legs protruded outward from the body, with two shorter limbs jutting out from under the head.

"You do not know the powers you have stirred," Fangryd laughed. "I have devoured wizards and sorcerers in the blink of an eye. I have slain warriors by the hundreds. I am older than the stone upon which you stand, a demon from another plane, and another time."

Erik smirked. "I know what you are," Erik said.

"Oh, then you have either come to kill me, or you have released me in the hopes that I will in turn grant you some of my power," Fangryd surmised. "You are doomed in either case. No human can defeat me, and I do not share my power. Had you fully given yourself to developing the darkness lurking in the depths of your soul, then perhaps you could have commanded me, but you are foolishly trying to suppress it."

"I have come for neither of those purposes," Erik said.

The demon's wicked smiled widened. "Then do tell me what it is you think you are doing, for you are nothing but a bug to be squashed under my claw."

"The monks here claim you have slain many people, and by your own words, you have killed many more. I have come to offer you a chance at redemption." Erik kept the ideal of mercy at the forefront of his mind, pushing away any doubts the demon was trying to stir within him about his own character.

"Redemption?" the demon scoffed. "Is that why you fight against yourself? Is that why you have abandoned your true destiny?"

Erik could only barely hold back his growing anger and contempt for the beast. "I am the master of my own fate," he shouted. "I shall say it again, I am here to offer you a chance to redeem yourself and make amends for what you have done."

"I have seen the gods," the demon said. "I have even slain a few of the gods of my home world. I need no redemption."

Erik continued, focusing solely on his mission, as he saw it, to offer mercy to all those who could truly make use of it. As he tried to see the demon for what it might be, instead of what it was, he became empowered by the surge of strength welling up inside of him. "It will not be an easy road," he said. "You will have to spend many years making restitution, but I am offering redemption."

Fangryd laughed, and acidic venom dripped onto the ground, smoking as it ate through the stone. "The mighty do not seek forgiveness," Fangryd said evenly. "Even if I did, why should you care?"

Erik smiled confidently. "I was taught that every life is precious." He thought not only of the orc tribe he had grown fond of, but of the lesson Master Lepkin had taught him very early on in their training. Every creature has a family, a friend, a higher purpose, and the monster is often as deserving of the knight's rescue as any damsel in distress may be.

"Even a demon's?" Fangryd asked. He brought his face closer and sniffed, nostrils flaring wide.

"The tenet must apply to every creature, or it can apply to none," Erik said. "So, make your choice, shall you work toward redemption and forsake your evil ways, or shall you choose death?"

Fangryd laughed and pushed up to his full height, towering over Erik by twenty feet. "Foolish human. What threat could you possibly pose to me?"

"Then you refuse to change?" Erik clarified.

"I refuse," Fangryd said.

Erik recited the spell he had practiced. A bolt of lightning tore through the sky and a mighty howl split the air, but there was no thunder. Fangryd turned, raising one of its spiked legs as Silverfang, Dimwater's mighty wolf companion from another plane, came charging in toward the demon.

"This is what you have?" Fangryd laughed. "A dog and a fire-sword? I have devoured legions. No human shall stand before me!"

Erik stabbed his sword into the ground and called upon his inner power to shift into his dragon form. The transformation was fully completed by the time the laughing demon turned back to face Erik. The young warrior smiled, drawing his scaly lips back to reveal his own fangs. Mighty claws dug at the earth and stone beneath him. "You err, Fangryd, for *I* am no human, and now you shall pay for your crimes."

Fangryd's eyes darted up and down Erik's dragon form, as if trying to comprehend it all.

54

Silverfang closed in and leapt up at the demon's underbelly. The magical animal's bite was not enough to penetrate the thick shell underneath, but it did distract Fangryd one more time. The large demon scuttled to the right and tried to stab at the wolf. Silverfang effortlessly dodged each claw as it slammed down into the dirt.

Erik lunged forward, showering the demon in a great wave of fire. With his forelegs, Erik grabbed Fangryd's front two legs and snapped them at the knee joints as easily as one might break a crab leg at the dinner table. Fire and black smoke billowed out from the open wounds. Fangryd reared back and prepared to spit his deadly acid, but Erik was ready for that.

As the vile, acrid stuff streamed toward him, he held up the severed legs and blocked the deadly venom. He then leapt up over Fangryd, smashing down upon the top of the demon's head with his own acid-coated legs. The thick, rock-like shell on the legs was enough to withstand the acid, but the top of Fangryd's skull was another matter entirely. The skin melted away, revealing white bone. Erik continued to pummel Fangryd, driving the demon down to its belly.

Fangryd lashed out with its two legs on its left side. Erik blocked the first by catching it with his right rear leg. The second demon leg was batted away by the thrashing of Erik's tail. Fangryd tried to regroup as Erik pressed the fight, but Silverfang came in fast and hard, snarling and positioning itself just a few feet away from the demon's fiery face.

The distraction worked once more. Fangryd flinched away from the wolf, likely expecting the animal to lunge at its eyes. It brought its shorter arms out defensively, and that's when Erik came down hard with the severed legs. There was a wet cracking of bone, followed by a shower of sparks as the skull split open. Green ooze poured out and Fangryd began to twitch.

Erik dropped the severed legs before the acid could reach him, and then he pressed upon the thorax with his left

55

foreleg, pinning Fangryd to the ground. With his right foreleg, he reached out and drove his talons through Fangryd's middle leg's trochanter, the joint between the thorax and the leg. The limb snapped off with a fiery *pop!* Erik then grabbed the lower end of the leg as Fangryd tried to squirm free. Erik used the claw as a dagger, and drove hard into the skull fracture, stabbing deep into the demon's brain.

Fangryd went limp.

The flames and sparks shooting forth from his open wounds died down. The fire protecting Fangryd's face dissipated, and more green ooze leaked out from the demon. Erik dismissed Silverfang, and then took three steps back from the demon before pouring out an inferno so hot that it incinerated the carcass.

Erik then took his human form once more and started for the monastery. The fight had not been overly exhaustive, but the amount of fire he had needed to produce to destroy the body had left him drained. He staggered toward Shermin, who was rushing to help him. They went up into his bed chamber, leaving his sword in the dirt near the battlefield. Erik slept for the rest of the day, rising only after the sun had set and the moon was high in the sky.

He threw his covers off only to find that he had not clothed after his transformation. He hurriedly put on his clothes and then stretched. The sound of music and laughter came in through the window. Erik stepped to the window and saw the monks outside, along with perhaps forty villagers. A large bonfire was burning in the place where the demon had fallen. People were eating, dancing, and laughing. He smiled. He packed the rest of his belongings, which were few, into a sturdy back pack and then went down the stairs. Had he been able to, Erik would have slipped away without saying good bye, but Shermin caught sight of him and rushed over to call everyone else's attention to their hero.

"Behold, the warrior who has slain the demon!" Shermin shouted as he lifted Erik's hand into the air.

The others cheered and clapped. Many of the villagers approached him, grabbing his free hand and shaking it, patting him on the back, or trying to hug him through the throng of people. An old lady kissed him on the cheek and thanked him. He nodded and tried to move away from them as quickly as possible without appearing rude. Fighting demons was not quite as hard as accepting praise. By the time he was able to pull away, his cheeks were thoroughly flushed and he was avoiding eye contact so as to dissuade others from continuing to thank him for what he had done.

Shermin sensed Erik's uneasiness, and with the help of the other monks, redirected the villagers to their dancing and their food. Erik circled around the large fire and pulled his sword out of the dirt. He sheathed the weapon and then stared out over the valley. He couldn't see much of it, as the fire hampered his ability to see into the darkness of night beyond the plateau, but he could sense a definite shift. The evil that had lorded over this area was now vanquished.

"Where will you go?" Shermin asked quietly as he came up beside Erik.

"I am needed in the north," Erik said.

Shermin extended a hand. "Accept the thanks of an old monk?"

Erik took Shermin's hand in his and gave it a hearty shake. "It is I who owe you thanks," he said. "The books I have been able to read, and the new knowledge I have been able to learn, have helped greatly."

"Did you pack the book written by the Cult of Zammin?" Shermin asked, glancing at Erik's backpack.

The young warrior patted his backpack. "I did," he said.

Shermin smiled and looked out into the night. "I assumed you would," Shermin said.

"If I can decipher it, I will have a copy sent back."

Shermin shrugged. "There must be some sort of cypher somewhere. If you can send a copy back, we would appreciate it, but even if not, if all you ask for slaying the demon is a book, then you can have it without any further obligation. As I have said before, however, it is my firm belief that if the Four Horsemen come to Terramyr, there will be nothing you or any of us can do to stop them."

Erik didn't respond. He let the words roll around in his head. He had learned a lot about the Four Horsemen since he first heard about them several years before, but nothing indicated they were stoppable. In fact, nothing he read or learned even hinted that the gods could stop them. By all accounts, if the horsemen came, then it was far too late to save the world. The only way to keep them at bay was to try and maintain order and balance.

That was no simple task.

"May the road rise to meet your feet, and the sun always shine upon your path," Shermin said.

Erik smiled and then made his way toward the stairs carved into the hillside and started down. Though the monks were more than accepting of Erik's ability to change into a dragon, there was no reason to scare the villagers who had only just gotten out from Fangryd's shadow. He descended half way down before he was certain that he was far enough away so as not to be seen. He walked to the edge of the stairs and peeked over the rails. Had the sun been shining, he would have seen the ground some thousand feet below where he stood, but as it was a very dark night, the drop off appeared to fall away into nothingness.

He used his belt to wrap his belongings together and stuffed his pants, shirt, and boots into the backpack. Once everything was secure, he tossed the bundle over the rails and then leapt out after them. The transformation happened a couple of seconds slower than it had when battling the demon, but it was quick enough to allow him to catch the falling equipment nonetheless. He stretched his wings and soared out into the darkness.

In his dragon form, he could see much better, easily discerning homes and campsites as he soared away from the monastery. He flew out to the forest and then ascended upward to take advantage of the many lingering clouds in the night sky. As the cool air rushed over his body, he couldn't help but wonder if Lady Arkyn was all right. He beat his wings faster. Tonight, he was going to see just how far, and how fast, he could fly without taking a break.

Chapter 5

Njar stroked the fur atop his head, smoothing it back repeatedly as he stared at the pattern of tea leaves in his cup. He saw three symbols. Change. Trouble. Death. The old satyr reached for his book on tasseomancy, hoping that perhaps there was something he was missing, or possibly that the symbols had alternate meanings. He flipped through the pages, looking up each symbol in the order they appeared in the cup starting with the symbol nearest to the cup handle, and then working his way around the cup in a clock-wise fashion. From what he understood, the events were going to happen very soon.

The satyr chief stood up. As he rose, he bumped the table with his knee. The teacup shook and sloshed the little bit of remaining liquid around in the cup. Njar looked down out of habit and noticed that the three symbols had remained unchanged, but a fourth had appeared. Betrayal.

"No," Njar said to himself. "Surely, that cannot be a correct reading. I only bumped the table, I did not perform the entire ritual."

He turned and left his home, but the symbol of betrayal was burned into the back of his mind, nagging and pulling at him and worming doubts and suspicions into his very soul.

There was only one place to go.

The Pools of Fate.

He would try to understand the tea leaf reading by calling upon the Pools of Fate to show him the future. He made his way quickly, holding his staff in his right hand and stamping the ground with it with each step he took. It was mid-afternoon, so most of the other satyrs were indoors, likely enjoying a short nap or perhaps eating a light snack. Satyrs were fond of their afternoon meals.

Njar arrived at the Pools of Fate and looked out across the waters. The surface was still and calm. He held out a hand and called upon the energy of Terramyr. A vibrant green flowed up to meet his hand. He absorbed the energy and then converted it to create the spell he would need to peer into the future. His staff began to glow. He touched it to the water and stirred the end of the staff around in a circle three times while chanting the spell.

In response, the water began to glow a bright blue. The hue lightened until the water appeared almost as if it were a liquid crystal. For a few moments, Njar could see into the depths of the pool and straight down to the bottom.

A chill ran up his spine as he looked upon a pair of shackles embedded in the lake bed. He shook his head to fight off the unpleasant memories of a time when he had been imprisoned there by a dark, evil creature, and continued with his spell. The energy flowed out from the staff and into the water. Bubbles boiled into the water from the end of the staff, and then a great mist rose up before him. He pulled the staff from the water and stamped it on the ground twice. The mists thickened.

From years of experience, Njar knew that the mist would soon take shape, and show him glimpses of what he was seeking. He waited as the gray mists swirled around in the air above the pool. His skin tightened as the atmosphere around him grew cold. He heard the sound of footsteps coming from behind him, so he turned to see who would dare intrude upon him at this time, but no one was there.

The mist flowed out and around him.

He floated up off the ground.

The satyr bleated and tried to stamp the ground with his staff, but instead he found himself tilting forward.

"No," Njar said to no one in particular. "Time to put an end to this!" He spoke the words to end the spell, but nothing happened. The mists pulled him out over the waters. His heart began to beat faster and he had trouble breathing. All at once the memories of being trapped at the bottom of the Pools of Fate flooded into his mind and he began to panic. He clawed at the swirling vapors around him, but could not wrench himself free. He tried to call out, but found that he was hyperventilating, and could not actually speak with words. A black tendril rose up from the pool and Njar froze in terror.

Not again. I can't do this again!

The tendril seized Njar's staff and yanked it from the satyr. It then disappeared down below.

The gray mists turned dark, blotting out the sun.

"NO!" Njar cried as he finally found his breath. "I control the Pools of Fate! I am in control. They listen to me!"

A voice laughed in the mist.

Njar stopped fighting and tried to turn himself toward the sound of laughter. "Who's there? Who dares attack me here?"

"Don't you know?" the voice called out. "Can't you recognize me?"

Njar peered into the black mists, but saw nothing. The voice did sound familiar, but it was warped somehow, distorted by the Pools of Fate. "Show yourself!" Njar demanded. "Face me honorably!"

"What would you know of honor?" the voice asked. "Njar the Trickster. Njar the Meddler."

These were titles Njar had never heard before.

"Njar, the Backstabber," the voice continued.

Njar tensed. That one he *had* heard. He had not earned it, but a group of humans from the Middle Kingdom had saddled him with it long ago, after an unfortunate event that led to the deaths of many humans.

Had someone come at last to seek their revenge?

No.

No human could have found Viverandon. The home of the satyrs was well hidden, constantly moving, and guarded by powerful magic. This intruder had to be something else. Something... more.

"Show yourself," Njar repeated. "I will not tolerate this much longer."

"You have no choice, old friend," the voice said.

The mists parted and Njar saw a man walking toward him, hovering over the water of the pools below. He was a large man with dark, nearly black skin. His eyes were brown and fixed intently on Njar. He wore red silk robes and a pair of green velvet shoes that had long, up-curled toes. In his hand, he carried a brown staff. Njar recognized the shadowfiend at once. It was Dremathor.

"This can't be, you're dead," Njar said.

"Death can be overcome," Dremathor replied evenly. An evil grin parted his lips as he folded his thick arms. "I have come for revenge," Dremathor stated dryly. "You owe me, you back-stabbing goat."

Njar bristled. It was one thing to be called a trickster or a meddler, but it was quite another to be called a goat. For satyrs, calling them a goat was one of the most denigrating things a person could say.

"What have I done to offend you, Dremathor?" Njar asked hotly. "We came to an understanding. You agreed to the plan!"

Dremathor shook his head. "You know, death has a way of changing a person's mind. Seeing the things I saw, feeling the things I felt."

"How did you return to the plane of the living?" Njar asked.

"How I did it is not important. It is what I intend to do now that should concern you." Dremathor's voice was as ice, stabbing into Njar's heart. "I am coming for what I am owed, and I am going to repay you for everything you did to me, goat."

Dremathor stepped toward Njar and pulled a spear of sick, wicked blackness out of the mists.

Njar tried to raise his hands and perform a counter spell, but his limbs were frozen at his sides. He glanced at his arms only to see strange, dark creatures writhing in the mist. There were several of them swirling in the waters below, but two had managed to approach undetected and grab Njar's arms.

"Wights," Njar grunted as their paralyzing magic flowed through his body.

"Yes, well, I made a few new friends too," Dremathor said. "I suppose I forgot to mention that part." He stepped forward and stabbed the spear through Njar's chest. The satyr felt his skin rip open as the tip of the weapon bit into him. It forced its way between two ribs and then bit into Njar's heart. A sharp coldness shot out from Njar's chest. He tried to scream, but no sound came out of his mouth.

The spear was ripped free and then Dremathor laughed again.

"Nonac is next," Dremathor said.

Njar's eyes shot wide. If Dremathor could get to Nonac, the sacred tree that guarded Viverandon, then none of the others would be safe from his wrath. Njar tried to will himself into action, but the strength left his body, and drained from his mind. He slipped into the waters below as the mists disappeared and Dremathor vanished.

The satyr chief's body floated toward the bank of the Pools of Fate. For a while, he lay upon the dirt barely breathing as his legs bobbed up and down with the water. Then, as the feeling started to return to his arms and legs, he opened his eyes. He was confused. Hadn't he just been stabbed? He weakly struggled to push himself up onto his side so he could examine his chest. He was wet, but otherwise unharmed. There was no hole in his chest. Encouraged by this discovery, he forced himself to sit up and inspect his arms. There was no damage there either, as there should have been if he had been attacked by wights.

It must have been a vision.

Yes, that was it. The Pools of Fate had shown him what was to come. A future encounter with Dremathor. But how could that be? Dremathor was dead. There was no way to conquer death and come back into the world of the living, especially in Dremathor's case. The shadowfiend had voluntarily allowed his powers and strength to be absorbed by another. As far as Njar knew, Dremathor would have no powers left. How could he have escaped to the plane of the living?

Had Dremathor tricked him all along?

Njar patted his wet, but otherwise intact chest and shook the loose water from his body. He was a target, now. He would have to watch his back. The symbols in the tea cup were becoming clearer. He looked up into the sky, now void of clouds and bright as the moment he had stepped out of his home. The satyr then realized that his staff was gone.

He performed the spell that summoned it, but nothing happened. He snorted angrily and recited the spell aloud. Still, nothing happened. A third time he tried to summon his staff, and then he heard a faint laugh carried upon the soft breeze.

He looked out to the Pools of Fate and saw a soft, golden glow coming from below the waters.

The liquid cleared enough for him to see that his staff was now chained to the lake bed, in exactly the same place he had been imprisoned. His heart nearly stopped in his chest. The encounter was not wholly metaphysical in nature. Something *had* assaulted him, and it had seized his staff. Njar felt a deeply-rooted fear gnaw at his soul.

Dremathor had said that Nonac was next.

The great tree, the barrier to Viverandon, was in danger.

Abandoning his staff, he turned and ran from the Pools of Fate. He could hear the laughter growing louder behind him, but he didn't stop. He had to make sure the tree was safe. Whatever it took, Njar had to protect Nonac.

He ran through the village and across the fields until he came to the edge of a lush, dense forest. A mighty oak tree stood tall and proud. The massive sentinel reached out to Njar with its energy. They did not communicate in ways that most people understood. There was no exchange of words or sharing of thoughts. Rather, it was an ebb and flow of essence and life energy that the two utilized. Nonac sensed the turmoil within Njar, but assured the satyr chief that all was well.

Njar sighed in relief, happy that for now they were still safe. He knew that should Nonac ever fall, then Viverandon would be unable to move itself. Worse than that, the doorway into the magical realm would be thrown open wide for anyone to enter. Since most humans despised their kind, Njar couldn't allow that to happen.

He walked up to the tree and placed his hand on the thick, rough bark. "I am glad you are well, my friend," Njar said. "I can remember sitting in your shade as a youngling, and I would that you should be standing still when my youngling's youngling's youngling come to seek refuge beneath you, old friend."

The energy flowed back and forth, communicating the message Njar wished to send.

The tree responded with warm, clean essence.

Then there was pain.

Njar cried out as his right hand merged with the tree. His skin fused to the bark, and a great channel was opened between them. Something dark and evil stirred within Njar's bosom. It felt as though a sharp-spined hedgehog were walking backward through his body, striking and stabbing at everything in its way. The ball of twisted magic burrowed its way through Njar's arm as the satyr chief screamed in pain and struggled to pull himself free of Nonac. A great pressure built in Njar's hand, and then there was a sensation of sharp pain followed immediately by a sensation of release and emptiness.

Nonac quivered, and Njar was released.

The great tree sent out angry energy and shook Njar to his core.

"What?" Njar asked. "No, I haven't betrayed you!" he shouted. Nonac quivered and the earth around the massive sentinel shook with it. A thick root emerged from the ground, slowly pulling up bits of turf and popping as smaller offshoots broke free of the main root. The tree's anger flowed into Njar again. "But I haven't betrayed you!" Njar protested. "I only…"

He looked down at his chest and smoothed away some of his fur. There, he saw a line of scar tissue over his heart. He had never been wounded there before. Somehow, the spear that had gone through him was real. A dark spell had assaulted him, and infected him with something terrible. Njar looked up at the quaking tree. His mouth fell open and he gasped as one of Nonac's leaves turned gray and fell from the branches above.

Nonac was in trouble.

A great gust of wind came at him from behind, bringing with it the laughter he had heard earlier.

"You tricked me," Njar said aloud. "You infected me with something, knowing I would rush to protect Nonac, and thereby used me to slay my greatest and oldest friend."

Dremathor laughed again, and then the wind disappeared.

Nonac shuddered violently. The lifted root swung through the air and batted Njar several yards toward the grassy field. He tumbled to a stop, coughing and gasping for air. The blow Nonac had given him hurt greatly, but not nearly so badly as the knowledge that he had been used as the instrument of Nonac's death. The bruise on his body would heal, but not the scar across his heart.

"I am sorry, my friend," Njar said as Nonac withdrew its energy from him. "I didn't know. I promise."

Another leaf fell to the ground.

"Dremathor, I will find you, and I will kill you," Njar swore as he struggled to his feet. "I shall not let this evil stand!"

*****

Erik had shifted into his human form four miles outside of Winter's Beak. Although he was anxious to answer Lady Arkyn 's summons, he was apprehensive about being spotted flying over the several smaller villages that lined the road leading out of Winter's Beak. As it was, the few farmers that did see him coming were quick to get out of his way, glancing nervously at the large sword he carried and shewing their children indoors. He had once seen townsfolk react to Master Lepkin in a similar way. Back then, he had never thought he would be headed down a path that would have others treating him that way.

He hurried along to the city. Rows of tall trees closed in at the edge of each farming village, pressing the sides of the road until the next grouping of grain fields or ranging area forced the forest to open up again. It would have been a pleasant walk, if not for the Night Hawk's message constantly playing in his mind. He increased his pace, jogging in the long stretches between villages and slowing to a quick walk when he came upon people. By doing so, he was able to cross the entire distance to Winter's Beak in less than forty minutes.

When he arrived at Winter's Beak, he could feel that something was not right. The salty sea air carried with it the cold fingers of death. There was no smoke or sign of battle that he could see, but he could feel its lingering effects. He slowed as he walked into town through the main road. Tall row-houses loomed over him on the right, while shorter, square homes and shops stood on the left. There was a decent number of people moving about outside, oblivious to the aura of gloom that hung over the town. As the buildings on the left gave way to a thoroughfare, Erik saw down the sloping hill and out to the docks. Only a couple of ships were in the waters, but that was not unusual for Winter's Beak. While it had once been a thriving port, it was now little more than a rest stop for weary seamen who lost their way in the many storms of the northern seas. Even from where he stood Erik could tell that two of the warehouses were no longer in use. Their boarded windows and sagging roofs plainly told of the town's fate.

Still, for all of its hardship, Winter's Beak was home to several lesser noble families. Some of them were new nobles, having earned titles in the war against Tu'luh, while others were more established, wealthy families that despite the overall downturn in the area, still had enough gold to live on for generations to come.

Erik had often wondered why families like that didn't offer more to the communities they resided within. Having spent his early childhood as an orphan, and then somehow becoming the adopted son of a nobleman himself, Erik could see that there was clearly enough to go around for all. While he didn't condone the theft of money or forced redistribution of their wealth, from his father's example he had learned that very rich men could offer much to their communities, and be all the better for it.

He himself was now a landed lord, but he didn't hoard his inherited wealth. He used it to employ people who worked the lands, provided for their protection, and had over the last few years, used large sums to invest in various development projects throughout the kingdom. He made a mental note to send a letter to Braun and ask him to identify some project worth funding in Winter's Beak, and then he continued walking through the town.

He went another four blocks before he heard a whisper coming from an alley on his right. He moved toward it, recognizing Minrielle Arkyn's call. As he left the view of the main street, she stepped out of the shadows and removed her hood. Her delicate, yet strong features were as beautiful, if not more so, than the day she had left nearly four years before. Her ears were pointed and regal, her eyes the color of jade, twinkling as she offered him a warm smile. He felt his heart flutter when she spoke.

"Hello, stranger," she said.

"Hello," he replied. He had missed her even more than he had anticipated. "I got your message." He wanted to go in for a hug, but under the circumstances, he figured that might be a bit out of place. He had a job to do. They could embrace later, assuming she still felt the same way as he did after all this time.

Lady Arkyn's smile disappeared. "I'm sorry we couldn't meet under happier circumstances," she said.

Erik recalled seeing the bodies through the Night Hawk's message. "Do we know who did this?" he asked.

Lady Arkyn shook her head. "The city guards are involved now. They have searched the manor and boarded it up."

"Do they know that the others were sahale?" Erik asked.

70

"No. The people of Winter's Beak have no experience with such things, and there are no outward signs of their true nature, except for the birthmarks, which aren't likely to cause any major alarm. Each of the bodies found were in their human form. Njar did give me a lead to investigate." Lady Arkyn glanced over her shoulder. That was when Erik realized she didn't have her bow with her.

"Where is your bow?"

Lady Arkyn shrugged. "I was attacked several nights ago. It was lost in the battle. Listen, we need to hurry. There is a shadowfiend that Njar believes may either be responsible, or at least know where else to look for clues."

"A shadowfiend?" Erik asked. Those were dark creatures. Every shadowfiend had been human once, born without magical powers, but driven by their insatiable lust for magical power they made pacts with demons to acquire magic. Worse than that, they could feed upon their victims and absorb their power. "If a shadowfiend killed these sahale, then he would be very powerful after absorbing their strength," Erik whispered.

Lady Arkyn nodded. "That is why we have to hurry. For now, we have the element of surprise on our side, and we have you," she said with a gesture toward Erik. "You are the most powerful sahale. There is no one else I would rather track this murderer with. Njar said he is in Pracheloor Cave, nestled in a set of three mountains some three hundred miles east of Far Point."

Erik felt a knot tighten in his stomach.

It wasn't often he wanted to shy away from a fight. He had willingly thrown himself at Tu'luh the Red on multiple occasions, as a fourteen year old he had once stabbed Tukai the warlock with a fork, and he had slain the warlock Gondok'hr at Lokton Manor, but this was different. If Erik could defeat demons while in his dragon form, then what could a shadowfiend with the power of several sahale running through his veins accomplish?

Lady Arkyn must have noticed his hesitation, for she stepped forward and wrapped him in a warm embrace. "It's good to see you," she said again, although her voice was not as happy as it had been when she had first greeted him. "I am glad to see you are all right."

Erik smiled and hugged her back. The momentary nervousness left him and he resolved himself to finding the culprit responsible and bringing him to justice. Shadowfiend or not, Erik was the Champion of Truth, and he had more than a few tricks of his own. "I am glad to see you are well too," Erik said.

He paused then and thought of the raven. Now that he knew Lady Arkyn was alive and well, who among his friends had the raven marked for death that night at Erik's window?

Chapter 6

Erik and Lady Arkyn traveled the two hundred and thirty miles north to Far Point in two days, camping and resting during the day and flying by night as Erik was easily able to carry Lady Arkyn on his back while in dragon form. Only after they had flown sufficiently far from Winter's Beak did she tell Erik about the strange necromancer that had attacked her.

When they arrived in Far Point, they were greeted at the gates by a pair of shabbily dressed men wearing leather hauberks and carrying spears. They were not professional soldiers, but Far Point was known for having a sizable number of volunteers working the city guard since the end of the recent war, as they had supplied most of their professional guards to bolster the army at Ten Forts and Fort Drake.

"State your business," one of the men said as he scratched the side of his face.

"We are traveling through," Erik said. "Just need to purchase some supplies."

"Your name?" the other guard said as he leaned on his spear and smiled at Lady Arkyn.

"I am Lady Arkyn." She turned and gestured to Erik. "And this is Lord Erik Lokton."

The guard stood up straight as a pole and quickly moved to salute Erik. "Sir! It is an honor to have you here."

Erik looked to Minrielle, but she only shrugged.

The other guard took a step forward and examined Erik from head to toe. "This is Gerald Kigsel. You saved his life once, at Fort Drake."

Erik turned to Gerald. "You fought at Fort Drake?" he asked.

Gerald nodded. "Yes, sir, I did. I'm sorry I didn't recognize you. My left eye went blind after the battle, and my right eye doesn't see as well as it used to."

"You can relax," Erik said as he moved close enough for Gerald to see him return the salute. "I am just a man, same as you," Erik said.

"But you're not," Gerald said. "I saw what you did in that battle. Everyone there saw it."

Erik sighed. "Well, I'm sorry for the loss of your eye, but I am glad you survived."

"If you are looking for a place to stay, my family would be honored to treat you to a nice meal and a bed. My wife is the best cook in these parts. It may not be fancy food, but it will fill you up and leave you happy."

"He's got that right," the other guard said. "I'm over there four nights a week myself. Good food." He patted his burgeoning belly and smiled. "Real good food."

Erik shook his head. "I'm afraid we cannot stay. We are here only to purchase a bow and a few other supplies before moving on."

"I have a bow," Gerald said. "Only, I can't use it very well now, on account of my eyes. I'd be happy to give it to you."

"That's not necessary," Erik started.

"No," Lady Arkyn cut in. "I would like to see the bow. It would be an honor."

"Cover my shift, Bender," Gerald said.

74

Bender nodded. "Just make sure I get some of the leftovers from tonight's supper."

Gerald clapped Bender on the back and then hurriedly escorted the others through the open gates.

"Gerald?" Lady Arkyn began. "If you can't see very well, then why are you posted at the gates?"

Gerald laughed. "Far Point is short on man power," he said. "Our previous governor sent all able bodied men to the war. Some to Ten Forts, others to Fort Drake. I may not be the ideal guard, but I can fight if needed, and Bender still has sharp eyes." The man shook his head as a big smile overtook his face. "The last time I saw you, Lord Lokton, you were flying through the air and blazing your way into glory. What happened to you after that?"

"I've been busy traveling," Erik replied. "And please, call me Erik. I'm not keen on titles."

Gerald nodded and led them through a series of meandering streets. As they walked, Erik realized that nine out of every ten people he saw were either women or children. There were hardly any men to be seen.

"The war must have hit Far Point hard," Erik commented.

Gerald nodded silently. He then pointed to a narrower road and led them to a short house made of brick. He opened the door and ushered them inside while calling out to his wife. "Naomi, we have company."

Erik stepped through the doorway to see a nice, simple home. A hearth and oven were placed on the far left wall. A small, round table that seated four was pushed up against the front wall to allow for more walking space when not in use. Behind the kitchen area was a large blanket that separated it from what Erik guessed was a bedroom. To their right was a set of apple and bread crates. Several simple pieces of furniture appeared to have been fashioned from the materials of similar crates, including small tables, stools, and chairs.

Gerald saw Erik looking at the furniture and smiled proudly. "In my spare time, I make furniture out of old crates. They may not have the craftsmanship you're used to, but they're solid and sturdy. Go on, try out a chair." Gerald gestured emphatically to a chair.

Erik obliged the man, removing his sword as he slowly sat back into the chair. The wood groaned slightly, but nothing moved or gave in to Erik's weight. "It's good work," he said.

"I even made a set of bunk beds for my sons," Gerald said excitedly. "I can show you—"

"Gerald, dear, I'm sure they're hungry. We can show them your work later," a sweet voice said as a woman stepped out from behind the blanket hanging from the ceiling. "You two look famished, I have cheese and bread for now, and I can cook up some stew if you are okay to wait for a while."

"Thank you for the offer, but we don't mean to impose," Erik said.

"Nonsense," Gerald replied with a smile. "If not for you, I would not have come home to my family at all."

The woman stopped and looked at Erik. "He is a bit larger than you described, but otherwise he is exactly the way you said," she noted. "I have something for you." She turned and disappeared back behind the curtain only to come out a moment later with a bundle in her arms. "This belonged to my brother. He died in Axestone. We don't have any sons to give it to." She set the bundle on the table and then pulled the table out for them to be seated. "Please, take a look, won't you?"

Erik glanced to Minrielle and then moved to the table and removed some of the cloth to see what was wrapped inside. Lady Arkyn gasped when the scimitar was fully uncovered. Erik gently picked it up and tested the weight. He pulled the blade from the sheath and admired the shine. It had been polished recently, and the edge was as perfect as the day it had been forged. "It is exquisite," Erik said. "I can't accept such a gift, better it stay in the family."

"No," Gerald said quickly. "It isn't polite to refuse a gift. Please, do us the honor of accepting it. Perhaps it will save your life, as you saved mine at Fort Drake."

"My husband was one of the archers there," the woman told Lady Arkyn. "He has recounted the battle several times. I am sure I could never repay you for sending him back home to me."

"I was only doing my duty," Erik said, feeling more than a little embarrassed by the attention.

"So the bow you mentioned, that would be your bow then?" Lady Arkyn asked Gerald.

Gerald nodded. "It's a fine weapon. Passed down in my family for generations. The family legend is it was made by elves."

"Gerald!" his wife scolded.

Gerald's cheeks flushed as he realized what he had said. "Sorry, I didn't mean anything by it."

"It's all right," Lady Arkyn said. "I take it as a compliment. Besides, show me the bow and I can tell you whether the family legend is true."

Gerald's bright smile returned to his face and he wagged a finger in the air as he turned and disappeared behind the curtain. "Just one moment!" he said. There was some shuffling about behind the curtain, and the sound of wood scraping along the floor. Squeaky hinges opened up, and then Gerald bounded back to the main room. "Here it is," he said proudly.

Lady Arkyn took the bow in her hand and inspected it carefully. She ran her fingers along the bowstring and then up and down the limbs of the bow itself.

"Well?" Gerald asked impatiently.

Lady Arkyn smiled. "It is indeed an elven bow," she said with a nod. "Fine craftsmanship, and sturdy too."

77

"I knew it!" Gerald said as he clapped his hands together. "My fourth great-grandfather got that bow as a gift from the elves!"

Lady Arkyn nodded. "I have some coin here," she said.

"Oh no, you can't pay me for it," Gerald said.

Lady Arkyn shook her head and continued to produce her coin purse. "An elven gift is not something we can take back. Once an item like this has been given away, the only way an elf may receive it back is to pay for it. Such is our way."

Erik watched her carefully, but he didn't say anything. Even without his power of discernment, he knew Minrielle well enough to know that she was lying. The bow was well made, but it was not the work of elves.

Lady Arkyn set the coin down on the table and pushed it toward Gerald. "In my culture, this is the only way I could accept this from you."

Gerald scratched the back of his neck and looked to his wife. "Well, that hardly seems fair. I mean, I owe you my life. I shouldn't be getting money from you. It feels dishonest."

"Don't think on it for another second," Lady Arkyn said. "If I can't pay you for the bow, then I can't take it, and seeing as I don't have bow, you would leave me in a tight predicament if you don't allow me to pay you for it."

Gerald bit his lip and then grunted. "All right, but only if you make sure to stop back this way sometime in the future. Perhaps I can repay you with a favor of some sort. My daughters have taken up the family business of piloting small ships through the narrows and straits in the waters around here. Maybe they could give you a tour sometime. I used to enjoy going out onto the water when my vision was working fully."

"Deal," Erik said, eager to get this part of the visit over with. The four of them passed the time eating stew, drinking cider, and swapping tales. Erik tried to get Gerald to do most of the talking, but the man was more than a little insistent that

Erik should talk of his exploits. By the time the meal was through, they had become good friends. Erik even allowed Gerald to give him a thankful hug upon departing.

"Remember, the offer for a tour of the narrows is an open one, it never expires!" Gerald called after them as they exited the house.

Lady Arkyn and Erik waved good-bye and then proceeded to leave Far Point. Once they were out of sight, Lady Arkyn took the scimitar for herself, since Erik already had a magical sword. She also slung the bow over her shoulder and situated the quiver.

"Nice folk," she commented as they left the eastern gates.

"Why'd you lie to Gerald?" Erik asked. "About the bow being made by elves?"

Minrielle smiled and shrugged. "Not every lie is a bad one. Who am I to crush a family legend?"

Erik nodded absently. "I suppose," he replied.

"They're good people," Lady Arkyn insisted. "From the looks of it, they could use some cheering up. She lost her brother in the war against Tu'luh, and he lost most of his sight. From the way she acted when she gave you the scimitar, I suspect their family suffered heavy losses all around, otherwise the scimitar should have passed to her brother's sons."

Erik nodded. "Likely if he had any sons, they died as well," Erik said.

"Besides, I could see how uncomfortable the gift made you. So, I figured I could make everyone a bit happier. They have had their legend verified by a real elf, and you have not had the embarrassment of receiving a gift without giving something in return."

"Am I really so transparent?" Erik asked.

"You may be the Champion of Truth, but you aren't the only one who can read people," Lady Arkyn said with a wink.

Chapter 7

Erik and Lady Arkyn moved to the edge of the forest and looked out across the valley to the set of three mountains. Unlike normal ranges where the mountains rolled along a line, these three jutted up like spears stabbing at the clouds. None of the peaks touched each other. Instead, they formed a kind of loose triangular valley between them.

"If the shadowfiend Njar spoke of is the murderer, he will likely know we are here," Lady Arkyn said.

Erik nodded. "If Njar knew of this shadowfiend, why didn't he warn us of him long ago?"

Lady Arkyn sighed. "Perhaps Njar had planned to work with him," she supposed.

"Work with him?" Erik echoed.

Lady Arkyn shrugged. "You know Njar, he likes to take in pet projects. He never fails to see the possibility of rescuing a lost soul."

Erik knew that all too well. During Erik and Lady Arkyn's first few months of traveling together, she had told him several stories about Njar's exploits. For Erik, learning that his own father was in fact a shadowfiend was more than a little bit unnerving. As a child in the orphanage he had often wished he could understand his origins, but after Lady Arkyn had revealed everything that Dremathor had done before Njar was finally able to successfully turn the man from his evil ways, he wanted nothing more than to forget all of it. *Sometimes, ignorance truly is bliss,* Erik thought to himself.

She told him of several other instances when Njar had reached out to help save other lost souls. Njar's intentions were always pure, of course, but the outcome was not always favorable. Still, Erik had to give the satyr credit, for he did far more good than harm.

In addition to helping to rehabilitate shadowfiends, or wayward wizards, Njar also had a soft spot for helping younger people in distress. For example, he had learned that Dimwater and Njar were quite close friends, and shared a long history together, starting when Lady Dimwater was in her first year at Kuldiga Academy. Without his help, she may have grown up to be a very different person, considering the violence and adversities she had to go through, beginning with her mother's murder at the hands of a shade.

Looking back on those first couple of months with Lady Arkyn, Erik realized now that he had learned more about his friends from Lady Arkyn than he had ever understood in all the time traveling with them while on their mission to destroy Tu'luh the Red and Nagar's Blight.

Erik looked out toward the three spires jabbing at the clouds above. He wondered if Lady Arkyn might be right. Had Njar tried to work with the shadowfiend here and failed, or had he not yet gotten around to approaching this particular individual? As he looked at the cave, wondering whether the shadowfiend inside was responsible for the murder of thirteen sahale, he was forced to whisper a silent thanks to Njar for his work with Eldrik Cedreau.

Eldrik, who now went by the name of Aparen, was on quite the dark path not so long ago. After House Lokton and House Cedreau had clashed in a war that resulted in the deaths of Lord Cedreau and Eldrik's younger brother, Timon, Eldrik had taken up company with a coven of witches. Eventually he had slain Lord Lokton and had even become a shadowfiend himself. There was no telling what kind of havoc Eldrik would have wreaked upon the Middle Kingdom had Njar not intervened.

Likely, the person hiding within Pracheloor Cave was someone who was like Eldrik, except that this time Njar apparently had failed to rescue him before he turned to the darker arts. Erik, on the other hand, was determined not to give in to the temptation of his own power. As a human, he was stronger than most and better with a sword than any except Master Lepkin only. As a dragon, well, Erik was unrivaled in the Middle Kingdom.

He never spoke about it, but there was always a seed of lust that threatened to sprout in the back of his mind. Ideas that flashed through his head in an instant, urging him to take the throne for himself, or if not the throne, then to carve out a holding of his own by tooth and claw. Even when he thought of the holdings of House Lokton, which now were rightfully his to rule with his parents both deceased, there was still a hunger for more.

This is why he had given the demon at the monastery the option of seeking mercy.

The idea of offering mercy, of trying to find the value in each life, kept Erik humble. It forced him to think through any actions he might take. By understanding the consequences of his dealings with everyone around him, he was better equipped to quench those lusting thoughts for power before they could take root in his mind. He had once given in to emotion. He had let himself fight without caring for another. As a result, the blood feud between House Lokton and House Cedreau had boiled into a bloody and costly war.

Though he knew now that his father, Trenton Lokton, would always have been the target of the evil senator's plans, he knew in his heart that if he had not lost control on that sunny day back in the courtyard of Kuldiga Academy, Lord Cedreau and Timon would still be alive. More than that, Eldrik would never have turned to the witches for power, and would not have become a shadowfiend in the first place.

That was Erik's burden to carry. He had caused those wounds, and now he had an obligation to make sure he would not misstep so grievously ever again. That was why the shadowfiend in Pracheloor Cave was going to be offered mercy as well. Erik would not take upon himself the titles of judge and executioner. He was here to stop bloodshed. If he could do it without killing another, then so much the better.

"How do you want to go in?" Lady Arkyn asked, ripping Erik from his thoughts.

"Do we know much else about him?" Erik asked. "Does he keep servants or guards? Does the cave have any additional openings other than the entrance?"

Lady Arkyn shrugged. "I know only what I have told you. The shadowfiend who lives here is named Alkantar. He is not one to be trifled with, but Njar didn't seem convinced that he was the murderer."

"Only that he was the closest and best lead," Erik finished with a nod. Lady Arkyn nodded in agreement. "Well, there is a way to get him out," Erik said. "One summer, our stables were infested with snakes. They were harmless, but the horses wouldn't sleep in their stalls, and some of the men around the house reported bites that were painful and swollen for two or three days at a time."

"Mountain racers," Lady Arkyn said with a knowing sigh. "I have dealt with them on occasion."

"My father taught me how to use controlled burns of the hay to smoke them out. We had to be careful not to burn the stables, of course, but it worked."

"It would be hard to burn an entire system of caves," Lady Arkyn said.

Erik pointed to the tops of the mountains. "Perhaps instead of fire, we can use water."

"You want to melt the snow pack?" Lady Arkyn asked as she looked up to where Erik was pointing.

"It's one way, but if there is a significant chance that Alkantar is innocent, we might not want to put him on the defensive."

"So then, we could sneak into the cave," Lady Arkyn said.

Erik shrugged. "Or, we could just march to the entrance and announce ourselves." He looked at her and winked. "You could stay behind, hidden somewhere with your bow. I could go to the entrance. If Alkantar is after sahale power, then he should be greatly interested in me."

"If he comes out as a dragon, there will be little I can do with my arrows," Lady Arkyn said.

Erik thought for a moment. Tactically, he liked the idea of trying to flood the caves best, but if he was to offer mercy, then he couldn't very well assault someone who might be innocent. Then again, a shadowfiend by its very nature was anything *but* innocent. They were unnatural, cursed creatures that were all responsible for murder in some degree. Magic in the Middle Kingdom was passed from parent to child much in the same way as skin color or physical stature. However, without exception, shadowfiends had all used dark rituals to steal their magical power from someone else, killing the victim in the process. From that point, they fed on other creatures to increase their power. They were somewhat like vampires, except that shadowfiends were very much alive, and much easier to kill, provided you could get close enough to them. Knowing this, Erik felt a bit better about assaulting the mountain, but he still had to temper the predator instinct that was beginning to rear itself from within. That, dark, shadowy part of his soul liked the idea of flooding the caves the best. It wasn't just the tactical advantage, it was the total victory over any foes that might be in the caves that was tempting him.

He suppressed the thoughts by returning his focus to mercy. He had to keep mercy at the forefront of his mind. By offering it, even to a suspected murderer, he would hopefully be able to keep the beast within himself at bay.

"We surprise Alkantar, and then we question him," Erik said at last.

"I could move to that thicket of ferns next to those boulders," Lady Arkyn said as she pointed to a place two thirds the way across to the cave opening. "I should have a good enough vantage point from which to attack, so long as it isn't a dragon."

Erik nodded. "I will change into my dragon form now. Best to confront Alkantar face to face."

He removed his sword belt and prepared for the transformation. He set his clothes near a tree and then closed his eyes and called up his power.

Nothing happened.

He opened his eyes and looked around. The hairs on the back of his neck began to rise as a chill ran down his spine. He hurried and tried to change once more, but again nothing happened. Something was blocking his power.

"It's a trap!" Erik called out.

He barely had time to pull his pants on before something lunged out of the bushes, deadly claws stretched out toward him. Lady Arkyn put down the beast with a single arrow that burrowed deep into the thing's left eye.

Erik summoned Silverfang. A flash of lightning struck down without thunder. The massive wolf appeared before a pair of animated skeletons that were advancing on Erik and Lady Arkyn. Silverfang wasted no time in ripping their bones apart, snapping limbs and cracking vertebrae before discarding the enemies into a pile of chewed and splintered bones.

Erik drew his sword and Lady Arkyn turned to face the opposite direction. They scanned the trees while Silverfang sniffed at the air.

"He knows we're here," Lady Arkyn said.

"Then let's not keep him waiting," Erik replied. Seeing that the area was clear around them, he quickly put his clothes back on and the three of them ran out from the trees and into the valley. The ground rumbled beneath their feet. Dark forms started to rise from the grasses around them. They sprang up like vapors from a geyser spewing blackness into the air. Then they took form, with arms and legs becoming the first discernable appendages.

"Wights!" Lady Arkyn shouted. "Don't let them touch you with their claws or you will be paralyzed."

Silverfang rushed in, danced around two of the creatures and then lunged at a third from behind. The wolf savagely tore at the creature's neck. It hissed and wailed as it fell to the ground.

Lady Arkyn went to work with her bow, firing an arrow into the skull of two nearby wights. They each fell to the ground only to rise up a moment later and yank the arrows free.

"We're in trouble," Lady Arkyn said.

Erik unleashed his power as he had before, summoning the white, searing flames to his blade. "Let's see how they fare against this."

He spun in fast and hard, catching the nearest wight in the chest. The monster's flesh popped and sizzled against the heat as it fell backward to the ground. The wight did not get up. Erik glanced up to the monster that Silverfang had killed. Its head was hanging limp by a thread of connective tissue and black skin, but it also was not rising.

"Cut off the heads, and you kill them."

Lady Arkyn drew a long scimitar and went to work. She ducked under a powerful swipe of nasty, green claws, and then came up to lop off the wight's head with a single swing. The head and body fell to the ground, never to move again. She then spun around, narrowly avoiding the reaching grasp of another wight. She countered hard and fast, severing the wight's arm at the elbow. The creature recoiled and hissed in pain, but the severed arm kept crawling toward her leg.

Erik stepped in with his fiery sword. He went for the injured wight, chopping the monster in half at the torso.

Lady Arkyn stabbed through the grotesque arm, pinning it to the ground until the rest of the body died. Four more wights fell by Erik's blade, and then the valley went quiet. Silverfang ran a wide perimeter, scouting for any additional enemies. Lady Arkyn put an arrow to her bowstring after sheathing her scimitar and the pair walked toward the entrance. When they were still about twenty yards away from the cave's opening, a man appeared there, dressed in furs and leather.

"Are you Alkantar?" Erik asked, his sword still ablaze.

The man folded his arms and looked past them to the field. "I see you have met my doormen," he said grimly. "It has been a long time since someone has dared come to my home, looking for trouble."

"I have come to ask you about Winter's Beak," Erik said bluntly.

"Bah," Alkantar said with a dismissive wave. "A bleak and dreary town. Hardly worth talking about, let alone assaulting me over."

"So you deny murdering anyone there?" Lady Arkyn pressed.

Alkantar arched a white brow and stepped out into the light. He blinked his black eyes a few times against the brightness of the sun, and then he raised his left hand and snapped his fingers.

Erik heard a sharp whimper and turned his head to see Silverfang plucked from the ground and hovering in the air, legs clawing at an invisible force that held it captive.

"I deny nothing," Alkantar said. "I have killed many in my life time."

Erik called upon his power to see beyond the words Alkantar spoke. He had trained hard at Valtuu Temple to use his magical gift to discern truth from error. Not only could he tell if someone was lying, he could also see when they omitted the truth. "I didn't come for games, Alkantar," Erik said. "Did you murder thirteen sahale in Winter's Beak in the last few days?"

Alkantar shook his head. "No."

Erik nodded and extinguished the flames on his sword. "Do you know of a satyr named Njar?"

Alkantar nodded his head. "I do. Is it he that sent you?"

Erik gestured to Silverfang. "If you didn't murder the sahale in Winter's Beak, then we are no threat to you. Release Silverfang."

"Oh, I think not," Alkantar said. "You have destroyed many of my servants, and they are not easy to create."

Erik didn't wait to see what Alkantar intended to do. He used the spell Lady Dimwater had taught him to send Silverfang back to his own plane. In an instant, the wolf disappeared.

Alkantar stiffened and emitted a low growl. "I see you are not without a few tricks of your own."

"Njar sent us to talk with you. He thought that you might know who attacked the sahale in Winter's Beak," Erik said. "Will you speak with us?"

"Njar…" Alkantar shook his head slowly. "How is the old goat these days? It has been many decades since I have heard from him."

"Winter's Beak," Erik pressed.

"What is in it for me?" Alkantar asked.

"Mercy," Erik said.

"Mercy?" Alkantar repeated. "I have no need of mercy from a young whelp such as yourself. Perhaps you didn't realize, but my magic is superior to yours. Who do you think enchanted this area so that you could not change into your dragon form?"

Erik bristled. "I am the Champion of Truth. I have vanquished—"

"Yes, yes, I understand. You are very important and strong," Alkantar interrupted. "I, on the other hand, am stronger. Shall I demonstrate?"

A blast of air slammed into Erik so hard that he flew back ten yards and then landed hard on his back. An instant later, Lady Arkyn was floating in the air and grabbing at her throat, her legs kicking beneath her.

"Stop, this isn't what I wanted," Erik shouted.

"Oh?" Alkantar asked skeptically. "The trees in the forest are my ears. I heard your plans to flood my caves!" The shadowfiend then motioned to the valley. "You were eager enough to cut down my servants as well."

Erik rose up to his feet. "The flood was just to get you to come out so we could control the situation. Your wights attacked us."

"You control nothing!" Alkantar said. "Don't you understand that I can see the darkness within your soul? I can see how the bloodlust grows in your heart. You wanted to fight, no, you wanted to destroy me!" He turned and stretched his left hand out toward Lady Arkyn. "Now you will pay for your trespasses!"

Erik's form vanished.

So did Lady Arkyn's.

Alkantar looked around, confused. "Where are you?" he shouted.

Erik's sword slipped around Alkantar's neck from behind just as Lady Arkyn appeared a few feet off to the side, her bow drawn and aimed at the shadowfiend's chest. Even Silverfang was back.

"I tried to warn you," Erik whispered as he tightened his grip on Alkantar and slid his blade across the shadowfiend's neck just enough to make sure Alkantar understood that he was caught. "I am the Champion of Truth," Erik continued. "Not only can I see through deception, but I have become fairly adept at creating diversions myself."

"Ah, clever boy," Alkantar commented. "You used illusions to trick my senses. Impressive, but when you let met loose, I will kill you, make no mistake."

"Answer my questions, and we need not fight."

"Very well," Alkantar said, sounding more than a little deflated at being outsmarted. "What is it you wish to know?"

Lady Arkyn moved in quickly and tied Alkantar's wrists and ankles. They sat him down on a rock at the mouth of the cave. Silverfang moved in close, snarling in Alkantar's ear while Erik moved to stand in front of the shadowfiend.

"You say you didn't murder the sahale in Winter's Beak, then who did?"

"Ah, so because I am a shadowfiend, I must certainly know every other shadowfiend, and their business, is that it?"

"Njar said you would know," Lady Arkyn said flatly.

Alkantar nodded. "I know who it was, but you are foolish to try and stop him. He is one that has defied fate. His strength is more than you can imagine. If you go up against him, you will fail."

"Who is it?" Erik pressed.

"I have a question for you," Alkantar said suddenly. "Do you know why he hunts the sahale?"

Erik paused and glanced to Lady Arkyn.

"Oh, this is delicious," Alkantar laughed. "You have no idea, do you? Njar hasn't told you yet, has he?"

"Told us what?" Lady Arkyn asked.

"That it is not the shadowfiend you should be worrying about," Alkantar said. "You should be scared of the dark sahale."

"The dark sahale?" Erik echoed. "What are you talking about?"

Alkantar scoffed and shook his head. "You think shadowfiends are dangerous? Wait until you see the dark sahale. He is going to be the undoing of this world. His power will swell, and his attacks will leave countless dead."

"You lie," Erik said.

"You know better than that," Alkantar said sourly. "You are the Champion of Truth, and you know that I am not lying."

Lady Arkyn turned to Erik. "Is he telling the truth?" she asked.

Erik nodded. "At the very least he believes he is telling the truth," Erik replied.

"If you do not believe me, then let me show you," Alkantar said. "I can show you the threat that is lurking in the darkness."

"I don't trust him," Lady Arkyn said. "It's a trick."

Alkantar shrugged and looked off to the valley. "For all I know, you are the dark sahale, boy," he said before turning his head back to Erik. "Tell me, how many have you killed? Why should you be the judge of me when you have taken more lives than I?"

"I do not take lives for pleasure or gain," Erik said quickly.

"Ah, but does a wolf not feed upon the deer?" Alkantar said. "I am no longer a man, I am more. I must, from time to time, feed myself. Are you and I so different?"

"I've heard enough," Lady Arkyn said. "He doesn't know anything useful."

She drew her bowstring back as far as she could and aimed at the shadowfiend's head. His black eyes glowered at her.

"Oh, but I do," he said. "For I know how the other one stopped the sahale in Winter's Beak from transforming into their dragon forms. I can show you where that spell came from, for I learned it from the same place as he did."

Erik held out his hand. "Wait," he told her. "We need to know more about this." He stepped in closer and hoisted the shadowfiend up to his feet. "I will not untie you until after you have told us all you know."

"As I said, I can show you. Come, down into my chamber."

"No, Erik, it's a trick," Lady Arkyn said.

Erik shook his head. "I sense no deception. He is not lying about the spell. He knows something, and what he shows us may help us find answers."

"She stays here," Alkantar said. "You can bring your wolf, but your archer stays here."

"I go where he goes," Lady Arkyn said flatly.

Erik shook his head once more. "No, stay here. It will be all right. I won't be long."

Lady Arkyn shot Erik a look that was more than contemptuous, but he held firm. He loosened the cords around Alkantar's ankles just enough so the shadowfiend could walk, and then he followed him deeper into the tunnel.

Yellow candles floating in the air gave them light as they descended into the bowels of Pracheloor Cave. The air grew musty and dank. The ground became soft and damp. Silverfang hung a few paces behind them the whole way, head low and muscles tense, ready to pounce at the earliest hint of danger. Alkantar remained silent as he led the way. Erik constantly called upon his power of discernment. He searched not only for harmful intentions from Alkantar, but also checked the surroundings for hidden traps or hiding enemies.

Only when they came to a large chamber with a rectangular desk did he allow himself to relax.

Alkantar sat at the desk and spoke the words that summoned a large book shelf. There were tomes in many different languages. Erik recognized orcish, dwarvish, elvish, and others. As he scanned the titles, he saw one that looked very familiar.

He reached out and pulled the book out to inspect the runes on its spine.

"That was written by elders in the Cult of Zammin," Alkantar said.

Erik nodded his head. "I have seen another book of theirs," he replied.

"They are the ones who taught me the spell," Alkantar said. "When I was younger, I was a neophyte in their order, many, many decades ago."

"You know what this book says?" Erik asked.

Alkantar nodded. "It is written in a language devised by the Cult of Zammin. All of their earlier members were instructed in the language."

"Then teach me," Erik said.

Alkantar shook his head. "There is no spoken language," he said. "It is a system of runes. Some of them are representations of letters, but others are pictographs. It would take you a long time to learn it."

Erik assumed that he could use his other book, which was partially translated, to help him understand this one, but he would need some sort of cypher to speed things along. "Can you write down a cypher?"

Alkantar shook his head. "No, if you want to learn how to read that book, then you must go to the Cult of Zammin, who reside far to the north, across the sea and beyond the northern orcish tribes at the base of the mountains that surround our lands and cut us off from the rest of Terramyr.

"The Impassable Spine," Erik said with a nod.

"Many have tried to cross the treacherous peaks, but only dragons and mighty wizards have ever succeeded." Alkantar shifted his weight and cleared his throat. "That book is not what I promised to discuss with you." Alkantar motioned with his chin toward a large, red leather book. "Pull that one, and you shall see that which you seek."

Erik set the book from the Cult of Zammin down on the desk and reached for the red book. He pulled it out and searched for a title. "What is this book?" Erik asked.

"It is the book of forgotten prophecies," Alkantar said. "It was written by the Order of the All-seeing Eye."

Erik nearly threw the book onto the ground. The Order of the All-seeing Eye was a most troublesome group of warlocks. They had sought to help Tu'luh the Red curse all of the Middle Kingdom with Nagar's Blight, a powerful spell that contaminated and could control the hearts of dragons. If perfected, that same spell would be powerful enough to work upon all living creatures in the Middle Kingdom, turning everyone into mindless drones and slaves.

"That order is destroyed," Erik said sourly.

"Yes, so I have heard," Alkantar said. "Tukai died after trying to capture you, and the others died shortly thereafter, mostly by your hand, if I am not mistaken."

Erik nodded. "Why should I believe anything in this book?" Erik asked as he turned and thumped it down on the desk in front of Alkantar.

Alkantar laughed and sneered evilly. "Tukai's prophecy came true, did it not?" he asked. "Was Trenton Lokton killed by the hand of his own son?"

Erik felt a rage boil up within him that he wasn't sure he could control. "Be careful what you say next," Erik warned.

"I have no love for those warlocks," Alkantar said. "However, their prophecies are valuable. They offer quite a bit of insight into the future. Not one of them has failed to come to fruition."

"The warlocks twisted their prophecies, and used them to gain power and influence," Erik replied.

"Oh, and the pious priests at Valtuu Temple never abused their power?"

Erik stood stoic and quiet.

"You know I tell the truth," Alkantar said. "Think of the first Prelate you met at Valtuu Temple. Did he or did he not, try to coerce you into taking the Exalted Test of Arophim early? If I am not mistaken, he sent his own warriors out to capture you after you had fled the temple."

That much was true, but even then Erik understood the prelate's motivations. "The Prelate was in a desperate situation, as were we all," Erik replied. "I bear no ill will toward the man."

"Intriguing," Alkantar said. "Now, open that book and go to the end. The last three pages will describe the dark sahale."

"I will not read the trickery of warlocks," Erik fumed.

"But you have the gift and power of discernment!" Alkantar shouted. "Surely, this task is not beyond your powers, is it?"

"I am not chasing a sahale, I am looking for a shadowfiend who murdered a dozen sahale in Winter's Beak."

"But perhaps you are on the wrong side," Alkantar said. "What if the shadowfiend is working to protect the Middle Kingdom from the dark sahale? What if by saving the sahale, you doom the rest of us to oblivion?"

"No, I can't believe that."

"The bond between humans and dragons never lasts," Alkantar said. "It always breaks down. Even now the two species are unable to rediscover the harmony that used to exist between them. It won't take much to ignite the fires of hatred, and once that happens, war will ravage this land."

Erik shook his head. "No," he said.

"You see nightmares," Alkantar cut in. "You see the Four Horsemen. You know what they are capable of. You seek a way to stop their coming, but fail to see the obvious path set before you." Alkantar spoke a spell and the cords binding his wrists and legs melted away. Erik pulled his sword, but then his body was frozen in place, as if held by invisible chains. "Don't make this harder than it has to be," Alkantar said. "You may be the Champion of Truth, but you have let yourself come into a spider's den."

Erik struggled against the invisible chains, but to no avail.

"Don't you know that a shadowfiend is most powerful in his lair?" Alkantar asked. He stretched his arms out to the side and then his human form began to warp and shift. Thickly corded muscles flowed into his arms. Spikes jutted out from his shoulders as fangs grew from his jaws. The black eyes grew in size as the shape of Alkantar's face became much more animal than human.

"I am Alkantar, the Trapper. I am surprised that Njar never warned you. You see, he once made the error of assuming that I was peaceful because I didn't leave the comfort of my cave. What he didn't realize, was that I have more than enough quarry willing to come into my home. Daring adventurers, eager apprentices, unlucky wanderers. If my wights don't get them first, then I pull them into my home, much like a spider lying in wait."

"What of the dark sahale?" Erik asked with great difficulty.

"Oh, that was all true, but since you are more concerned with the other shadowfiend, why should I let you escape? You would only get in his way, and his work mustn't be stopped. Besides, for all I know, you could be the dark sahale. You have killed countless in your wars, and you have already defied the fates once. Who is to say you wouldn't turn to a darker path if pressed against something you couldn't ever understand?"

Alkantar raised his right hand and brought Silverfang over to the desk. He laid the animal down on its side. Silverfang tried to fight against the spell, but this time there was nothing it, nor Erik, could do.

"I think I shall devour the wolf first," Alkantar said as he licked his blueish lips. "I can feel a great power coming from him. What plane does he come from, do you know?"

Erik remained silent, still trying to push against the invisible force that held him in place.

"No matter, I shall consume its essence, and then I shall take yours. It will be good to taste the power of a sahale." Alkantar smiled and moved in slowly toward Silverfang's neck. The wolf snarled, but went rigid as the spell pulled at it and held it down.

Alkantar moved in, jaws opening wide so his fangs could bite into Silverfang's thick neck. He came in closer, obviously relishing each passing second. Then, right as he moved to bite, Silverfang snapped his head up and bit into Alkantar's neck. There was a sick, wet tearing sound as the wolf pulled at the monster's throat.

The spell holding Erik in place faded away at once and he jumped into action, leaping over the desk and drawing his sword. The white flames erupted around the blade just as the cold, Telarian steel bore down on Alkantar's skull. The bone cracked in two and the black eyes went dull.

"Didn't you know?" Erik began. "Silverfang is immune to paralysis spells, he is a master of them himself. He was only feigning capture." Erik booted the shadowfiend to the ground. Silverfang continued his work until there was a loud *cr-snap!* Alkantar's head rolled awkwardly until his nose came to rest behind his left shoulder, throat torn out and neck broken.

Erik knelt beside Silverfang and petted the animal on the back of the head. "Well done," he said. "If Alkantar was the spider, then you were the assassin bug."

Silverfang licked his snout and then turned to face the tunnel they had come in from. His hackles were up and he started to growl in a low, menacing rumble.

"Right, time to go!" Erik said. With Alkantar now dead, he was free to transform himself. In the blink of an eye, his body ripped through his clothes as scaly limbs replaced his human ones. The tunnel needed widening, but with his dragon strength he had no problems burrowing his way upward. Silverfang ran ahead of him. They could both hear Lady Arkyn battling something outside the cave.

As Erik had suspected, leaving Lady Arkyn outside was playing into another trap that Alkantar had arranged. He and Silverfang burst through the cave opening to find a team of wights running after her. She had managed to slay a few, but six more were chasing her through the valley. Fortunately, she was quick on her feet and deadly with her sword. A wight's head fell to the ground just as Erik took to wing.

He opened his mouth and gathered his fire in his chest as Silverfang let out a long howl, the signal for Lady Arkyn to turn and run out of the way. No sooner had she put thirty feet between herself and the wights than Erik unleashed a cone of fire that engulfed the monsters entirely, reducing them to smoking ash.

When the battle was over, Erik dropped down near Lady Arkyn and transformed back into his human form. The she-elf turned and pulled a spare pair of under garments from a satchel she wore at her side and handed it to Erik.

"Next time, I get to play prisoner and you can deal with the wights," Lady Arkyn said.

Erik smiled and dressed himself. "Alkantar would never have gone for that. We had to let him believe he had the upper hand."

Lady Arkyn shrugged and eyed Erik from head to toe. "It appears we need to find you some new clothes."

Chapter 8

Erik finished scouring Alkantar's lair for clothes and then burned the corpse and collected the ashes into a vial as protocol demanded. The ashes of every slain shadowfiend were supposed to be sent in to King Matthias. The first time Erik had seen this done was at Spiekery, when Lady Dimwater defeated Balt'ezar the Brown, a wicked and vile shadowfiend masquerading as a priest requiring human sacrifice. After she had killed the monster, she had burned the body and collected the ashes.

Now, Erik was doing the same thing, and not for the first time either. Alkantar marked the tenth shadowfiend that had fallen at Erik's hands. He had also fought three demons, including the one at the monastery, and several other things that most dared not face even within the confines of their own nightmares.

He closed the vial and tucked it into a satchel, provided courtesy of the dead Alkantar. He then left the tunnel, never to return to this forsaken cave again. He had thought about collapsing Pracheloor Cave, but decided that in the interest of time, his strength would be better put to use traveling.

With all of the necessary tasks completed, Erik looked around the lair for anything else that could prove useful. He started with the books, smiling to himself as he realized Tatev, the librarian from Valtuu Temple, would have done the same thing. The types of books before him were a veritable treasure trove of foreign cultures and peoples. He saw books written in Common Tongue, Tarthun runes, Elvish, Dwarvish, and even Orcish. He had only seen the one book written by the Cult of Zammin, which was now being perused by Lady Arkyn, but he did find another book that proved of interest.

"Minnie," Erik called out, using his nickname for her. "I found something that says it is written by Kyra Dimwater. Could this be accurate?"

Lady Arkyn moved over to him, tucking the large tome she was studying up under her left armpit. "What is the title?" she asked.

"A Treatise on Dragons, Their Strengths and Weaknesses, with Excerpt from The Chronicles of Kendualdern," Erik replied. He flipped through the first few pages and found a short introductory note in the inside. "This book uses my own first-hand account of interactions with dragons, as well as factual accounts of dragons who lived upon Kendualdern, my favorite of course being Gorliad, the dragon prince."

"Erik, you have stumbled upon Lady Dimwater's lost manuscript!" Lady Arkyn said. "She spent years writing this."

"How did it end up here?" Erik asked as he looked around. "Certainly she wouldn't give such a book to Alkantar."

Lady Arkyn shook her head. "No, it was lost at some point during her travels. It's a long story, but she and I were beset upon by a band of Blacktongues once, and we lost many things that we had been traveling with. This book was one of the things we lost."

Erik nodded and tucked the book into his satchel. "Then we shall return this to her the next time we see her."

"Are you sure about the direction we should be heading?" Lady Arkyn asked as she rummaged through the book written by the Cult of Zammin.

Erik nodded. "I have done some research on them privately, before coming here. Everything I learned would seem to corroborate Alkantar's notes."

"But why would he leave notes?" Lady Arkyn asked. "I mean, why would he have a paper in the back of this book with directions to find the cult, let alone a hand-drawn map?"

Erik shrugged. "He said that he knew who was behind the murders. Perhaps he is more involved than that. Maybe he was responsible for training the murderer. After all, he had a spell that kept me from transforming into my dragon form. Perhaps they both had the same master."

"And that master is somewhere in the cult?" Lady Arkyn asked as she closed the book.

"I think so. Either way, the Cult of Zammin seems to be our only clue at this point. It is the only thing linking Alkantar with the murderer. We'll take the books and Alkantar's map with us."

"So then, should we fly?"

Erik shook his head. "No. I don't want to draw undue attention to ourselves, and more importantly, I don't want to be ambushed by someone else who can prevent me from changing. If they can stop the spell from being used, then who is to say they can't also reverse it? If they should do such a thing while we were in mid-flight, all the armor in the world wouldn't save us from crashing to our deaths."

"So this is something we have to fight on two legs then," Lady Arkyn commented with a nod. She smiled then and gave Erik a wink. "That's all right, you're cuter in your human form anyway." Erik smiled at the compliment. He thought of telling her then how much he had missed her, but the moment passed before he could find the words. Lady

Arkyn turned and gathered a few additional supplies and turned to leave the cave.

"We'll go back to Far Point," Erik called out after her. "It's time to take Gerald up on his offer to give us a tour of the seas in the north."

They retraced their path back to Far Point. Other than a light snow storm, they met no obstacles. However, when they reached Far Point, things seemed quite different from just a few days before. Well-armed guards stood before the gates. A trail of smoke rose up from behind the walls, stretching high into the sky.

"What happened here?" Lady Arkyn whispered.

Erik shrugged. Then, the wind shifted and carried with it the scent of sulfur. He knew in an instant what had caused the fire. "A dragon fight," Erik said.

"What?" Lady Arkyn asked. "Impossible."

Alkantar's warnings of a dark sahale came back into Erik's mind.

The guards took one look at Erik and then ran back to the gatehouse. He couldn't hear what they were saying, but their shouting was anything but happy.

The gates creaked and groaned as they were opened from within the city.

Erik stopped in his tracks. He would have recognized the warriors for what they were by their spiked and ridged Telarian armor. Each of them carried spears, swords, and hand axes, ready for battle. Four dragon-slayers emerged from Far Point, accompanied by a taller man in dark robes.

"I don't like the looks of this," Lady Arkyn said. "What are they doing up here?"

The other guards disappeared through the open gate only to emerge a few seconds later, pushing a large cart, upon which stood a massive wind-lance, a weapon not unlike a scorpion launcher. What differed, was the target each weapon was designed for. While the ballistae, and scorpion launchers were created to slay human foes, the wind-lance was invented and perfected for one purpose; killing dragons.

"I am Erik Lokton, son of Trenton Lokton," Erik called out as the four dragon-slayers continued to advance on him.

"We know who you are," one of the men called out.

"Then surely you understand that I am no threat to Far Point, or to any other city in the Middle Kingdom, Erik replied sternly. "What is the meaning of this display?"

Three of the dragon-slayers stopped and readied their spears.

"Erik, I don't recognize any of them," Lady Arkyn said.

The fourth dragon-slayer removed his helmet and tucked it under his left arm. The strong Telarian steel was well oiled, and seemed to move effortlessly as the warrior approached them. He strode up to Erik within arm's reach and then stopped.

"The day after you left Far Point, the city was attacked," the man said.

Erik nodded. "I can see the smoke. If you are asking for my assistance in tracking the assailant, you are making a piss-poor impression."

The warrior scoffed. "I am not here to impress you. I am here to do my job."

"And what is that?" Lady Arkyn asked.

"To keep out dragons, and… other trouble makers."

"Do you know who Erik Lokton is?" Lady Arkyn asked incredulously.

"I know *what* you are," the man said. "You are part dragon, and therefore you are not coming in." Lady Arkyn started to object, but the dragon-slayer spoke over her. "Challenge me and you will find three more as determined as I am to keep you out of Far Point. If you get past them, you will have to face the wind-lance, operated by a crack team that owes its loyalty to us." He then turned to Erik. "And before you think to take your dragon form, I should warn you that Master Dilbin is fully capable of preventing you from transforming."

Erik perked up at this. Was Master Dilbin a member of the Cult of Zammin? Or had he been at some point in the past? "Where is Dilbin from?" Erik asked. "I haven't heard of him before."

"He hails from the north," the warrior said. Erik shot Lady Arkyn a curious glance. She returned the gesture with an understanding nod. "I must also warn you that we have been alerted to the savage murders of many people in Winter's Beak. I find it most curious that both towns have seen destruction, and both have had you as guests in the recent past."

Erik slowly drew his sword and set the point on the ground. "I think you forget your station," he said. The white flames flowed out onto the blade. "I am an agent of the king. As such, I have authority to go where I please, when I please. I am on official business, and you are impeding *my* investigation."

"We do not recognize your authority," the dragon-slayer said.

Erik shook his head in disbelief. "Where are you from? I knew Tillamon, and I have trained with Master Lepkin, and I even met many dragon-slayers, but I have never seen one act the way you are now."

"Tillamon was an old fool!" the warrior spat. "Lepkin is a traitor. He is a dragon himself. And you are just like him. We are the true dragon-slayers, we are the Sons of the Blade, and we will not rest until the Middle Kingdom is safe again."

Erik turned and looked at Lady Arkyn.

The elf stepped forward and leaned in. Her green eyes were like daggers, and her fingers tensed, hovering just over the handle of her scimitar. "Are you saying you would defy King Mathias' agent?"

"I am saying all of Far Point will," the rogue dragon-slayer replied evenly. "Mathias sent most of the men folk from Far Point to die. The governor's own sons are dead now as a result of a war that benefitted none but the dragons."

"That isn't true!" Lady Arkyn said.

"Yes it is," the warrior said. "Otherwise we would not be cowering in our own homes while dragons darken the skies above us. We would not be yielding our country to outsiders. We would fight them off, and repel this invasion."

"But it isn't an invasion," Lady Arkyn argued. "This is the way the Middle Kingdom always used to be, with men and dragons working together for the good of mankind."

"Does *that* look like something good?" the warrior shouted as he pointed to the wafting smoke.

Erik, sensing the tension rising to a tipping point, put his hand on Lady Arkyn's shoulder. "Come, we should go."

"Yes," the warrior agreed angrily. "You should."

"Know this," Erik said quietly. "I am not responsible for the destruction here, nor the deaths in Winter's Beak, but I will find the one responsible, and when I do, no mercy shall be given."

"If you speak the truth, then perhaps there may be a place for you among the ranks of true patriots," the warrior said. "But if you throw in with the dragons, we will offer you no quarter."

Erik pulled on Lady Arkyn's shoulder. The two turned to walk back toward the forest when the rogue dragon-slayer called out after them.

"Also, you might like to know that your friend Gerald is in the dungeon, along with his wife and daughters. If you are responsible for this, and they knew about it, they will all swing on the gallows."

Lady Arkyn's hand grasped the handle of her scimitar and she started to pull upward, but Erik seized her wrist and held it in place.

"Don't," Erik said harshly. "He is baiting us."

"How does he know about Gerald?"

"Someone undoubtedly told him about our dinner with the family. Come," Erik said as he pulled her along. "We don't want a fight here."

"Yes we do," Lady Arkyn said.

"We'll come back during the night," Erik replied. "We won't leave them in the prison, but we can't risk an open confrontation here. That will only strengthen their position."

"As agents of the king we have the authority to put them down," Lady Arkyn replied.

"Just because we can do something, doesn't mean we should."

Lady Arkyn sighed and Erik could feel her hand relax. He let go of her and the two walked back to the forest.

"Sorry," Lady Arkyn said after a few moments of silence. "It's just…"

"I understand," Erik said when her words trailed off. "I feel the same way."

They camped a mile away from Far Point, careful to stay deeper in the woods and away from the road. They chose not to light a fire, instead opting to forego dinner and make do with the bits of dried bread they had remaining. From their position, they could see to a narrow spot on the road, and took turns watching and waiting. Just before dusk, a patrol of well armored guards marched along the road, apparently ensuring that Erik and Lady Arkyn had truly gone.

"Shall we attack?" Lady Arkyn asked.

Erik shook his head. "Let them return unharmed. I don't want there to be any unnecessary bloodshed. We'll wait until it's dark, and then we'll go back into Far Point."

"So along the coast then?" Lady Arkyn asked.

"That would be the easiest way in probably," Erik said.

"I should go without you," Lady Arkyn commented.

Erik shot her a confused look.

"If their wizard is trained to work against dragons, then I would bet he can sense when dragons are close."

"Like Alkantar," Erik commented with a sour frown. "It makes sense, but I'd rather go with you."

"Don't worry about me, I've been doing this kind of work for years."

Erik started to say something, but he knew she was right. He reached out and took her hand in both of his and squeezed gently. "Just, don't get caught."

*****

Lady Arkyn crept along the shoreline shortly after midnight. With her elf eyes, she could easily see in the darkness. As she and Erik had suspected, there were fewer guards along the coastal shores of Far Point. The docks jutted out into the misty waters, with only a few large vessels anchored there. Each of the larger ships had their own guards. Even from the shore, Lady Arkyn could see them walking the decks. She continued her scan of the area. Several smaller schooners and the like were moored, but they appeared empty. There were a few buildings, warehouses and the like, which she could use to conceal her movements. As luck would have it, there was no northern wall.

So long as she avoided any guards, she would be able to slip in.

She moved quietly through a dilapidated warehouse with a caving roof, ducking down behind an old crate when a pair of guards walked by. After they passed, she moved stealthily to the nearest house. It was a small building, but the large rose bushes helped conceal her movement. She worked her way up an alleyway ascending a hill and then crept along the back of a series of row houses until she came to the jail.

There were four guards in front of the building. Two standing at the door and sharing a smoke, two more seated and playing a game of cards across a makeshift table formed by two small crates stacked atop each other. There was a light shining through the window in the front, with another two guards visible inside. She ducked back behind the row houses and worked her way through the shadows until she managed to circle around to the back of the jail. She frowned when she saw no rear door. There was a window on the second floor, but there were also three guards at the back of the building.

She was going to have to get creative.

Lady Arkyn crouched low in the shadows, considering her options, when a large man came around the side of the jail house. With her keen sense of vision, she easily recognized him as the rogue dragon-slayer from before. He was still dressed in full armor, and using his spear as one might utilize a walking staff. He approached the guards at the back of the jail. All three were quick to snap to attention and salute him.

"Any sign of them?" the dragon-slayer asked.

"Nothing, sir, quiet as a graveyard back here."

The dragon-slayer cursed and shook his head. "They'll come for Gerald, I know they will, and we will have to be ready. When they try to come looking for him, we'll make sure the people of Far Point know who they can trust."

"Yes sir," the others said in unison.

"Stay alert," the large warrior said before turning and going back around to the front of the jail.

There was something about the way the dragon-slayer spoke that caused Lady Arkyn to doubt her current plan. If they were laying a trap, and expecting them, then the smart thing to do would be to keep Gerald and his family somewhere else, while filling the inside of the prison with enough guards to ambush her and Erik.

She quickly abandoned her position and retreated back through Far Point. Her first destination was Gerald's house. She snuck by the two sets of patrol guards walking the streets and made it to the house without difficulty. When she arrived, she found a single guard posted outside the front door. There was a light coming from the window, but from her vantage point across the street in a narrow alleyway, she couldn't see into the house.

She checked the roofs surrounding her for other guards, and then darted across the street and into an alleyway that would allow her access to the back of Gerald's home. She had to turn sideways and slide between two brick buildings, but she eventually made it into their rear garden, which was a small pad of dirt with raised planter beds in wooden frames for growing vegetables. Another guard was pacing back and forth through the small area. Lady Arkyn pulled her scimitar and waited for the guard to turn back toward the house. She came out hard and fast, cracking the man on the back of the skull with her scimitar's handle. She guided his unconscious body to the ground and then moved to the door. She found that it was locked, but the nearby window wasn't. She pulled the window open and slipped into the house. She could see two young women sleeping in a single bed, likely Gerald's daughters. A few feet away was another bed with Gerald and his wife. Lady Arkyn smiled upon seeing they were still safe. She then saw a shadow dance upon the drawn curtain that separated the bedroom from the kitchen area.

Lady Arkyn crept silently to the curtain and peered around. A lone guard sat nursing a rather large bottle of wine without the aid of a glass. His eyelids were droopy and he was quietly humming a tune to himself while bobbing his head up and down. It would be easy enough to silence him. Lady Arkyn snuck up behind him and wrapped her left arm around the man's exposed neck while using her right arm to pull back on her left wrist. Her taught muscles easily closed off the blood and air supply to the guard's head. He was asleep within seconds.

She then turned and went back for Gerald and the others. She woke them as quickly and quietly as she could, and then led them out the back door. Leaving the city proved to be just as easy as getting in. The family followed her through the shadowy alleys and streets until they neared the docks.

Gerald pointed out their ship. It was a slim schooner designed to be operated by a crew of three. The only problem was there were four guards on board. Lady Arkyn suggested stealing another ship, but Gerald assured her that all of the other vessels capable of sailing through the Breaks, a grouping of islands to the North West, would require crews of at least six. Gerald's wife was not skilled in sailing, neither were Lady Arkyn or Erik.

It seemed Lady Arkyn would need to use her bow after all.

She instructed the family to wait in one of the abandoned warehouses while she took care of the guards. She stole her way toward the docks, careful to watch for the patrolling guards making their rounds along the streets. She found a hidden position on the interior of a collapsed warehouse wall some forty yards away from the docks. The shadows and rubble would conceal her position well enough so long as the foot patrol walking the road between her and the docks didn't catch her first. Not only would she have to take down all four of the guards quickly enough to avoid an alarm, she would have to time the assault for when the patrols had their backs to the docks.

She waited impatiently, counting the minutes off in her head as she studied the patrols. The four guards on the schooner would be easy enough. Two walked in rounds atop the deck, while one stood near the port side, studying the warehouses with his inferior night vision. The fourth was leaned back in a chair, arms folded across his chest, appearing to be fast asleep.

Once the patrol on the road walked far off into the shadows, Lady Arkyn went to work.

She took in a breath and waited for the two guards on the boat to turn their backs to her. Then her first arrow was set loose. The guard standing port-side caught the missile with his forehead, and began to fall backward. Before his body hit the deck, two more arrows bit into the pair of guards circling the deck, one in the neck, the other in the back of the head. As the bodies hit the ground, the fourth guard startled awake and lifted his head only to be rewarded by a perfectly aimed arrow that tore through his skull and toppled him onto his side.

Lady Arkyn then sprinted for the spot where she had left Gerald's family. The five of them dashed across the road and toward the schooner. They didn't have much time, Arkyn knew, so she posted Gerald in the spot where the first guard had been standing, quickly throwing the guard's hauberk over to the startled man.

"Here, take his spear," Lady Arkyn said. She then told Gerald's wife to go below deck while the two daughters donned armor and began pretending to patrol the deck. Lady Arkyn placed her bow at her side and slipped into the fourth guard's hauberk just in time to sit in the chair as the guards patrolling the road stopped and began to turn around to retrace their route.

The daughters walked slowly enough that they untied the moorings a bit more with each pass around the deck. If they were lucky, the guards on the road wouldn't notice anything strange. Just to be sure, Lady Arkyn kept her eyes on the patrol. If possible, she would avoid killing any more guards, but she was more than ready for the alternative.

The patrol passed along the road and off into the distance the other way.

The daughters fully untied the last mooring and then Gerald took over, whispering and signaling with his hands. Lady Arkyn stood and surveyed the docks all around, not wanting to be caught by surprise in case there were other guards nearby.

The schooner lurched into motion as the skilled crew took her away from the dock.

There was no turning back now.

Just as the schooner put the docks behind it, the patrol on the road came running down the docks. One was readying a bow and the other was grabbing at something dangling around his neck. Lady Arkyn sighed and launched an arrow before the whistle ever touched the guard's lips. He fell to his knees and then slumped forward as the second guard fired his arrow at them. Lady Arkyn glanced at the arrow for only a moment before realizing it would never reach them. The guard had not judged the distance correctly. She fired a second arrow and dropped the bowman. He staggered backward and then splashed into the water.

Gerald and his daughters expertly piloted the craft out from the bay and into the open seas before anyone else noticed their escape. They sailed due east to pick up Erik, who was waiting for them along the coast.

Chapter 9

An elderly man sat at a meager, well-worn desk, pouring over a list of names and places. His shaky hand traced the words on the pages.

A woman sat on the rickety bed a few feet to his left. She cleared her throat expectantly.

"Just a moment," he said as he studied the passage. "The tomes of prophecy are hard to read."

"The book before you is no tome of prophecy," the woman replied. "It is a genealogical record."

"It is written in a similar fashion," the old man said. "I should know, I was once the prelate of Valtuu Temple. I can recognize the writings of the ancient mystics when I see them."

"Odd choice of words," the woman mocked. "With eyes as dull as yours, I doubt you *see* much of anything anymore."

The old man nodded silently, taking the berating. His eyes were dull in the ways of normal vision. His natural-born sense of sight had been offered long ago as a sacrifice when he joined Valtuu Temple. However, he was not entirely blind. He had the gift of true sight, an ability that allowed him to see auras and magical energies. It was a skill that was highly prized by certain people, especially while searching for forbidden knowledge.

The ancient mystics had entrusted the priests of Valtuu Temple with their prophecies, and secrets, but they took great pains to ensure that only the priests would be able to unravel the codes. To any normal person, a book would have several written passages, many of which would contradict each other, but to a priest with true sight, the hidden knowledge was plainly laid out before them, written with a kind of magic that never faded with age. Of course, even then there were tricks used by the mystics to keep the more dangerous pieces of information away from wayward priests, but the ex-prelate knew those tricks very well. The only two people who might have had as much skill as he did, were Marlin and Tatev. The first had succeeded him as prelate after he was banished by Master Lepkin several years before. The second was Valtuu Temple's librarian. Both were now dead.

"You certain that you need to know all of these names?" the ex-prelate asked.

"Are you certain you wish to be breathing tomorrow?" the woman replied.

The old man smiled. Given the fact that he could see auras, he had identified this particular woman as a very real threat. Her magical abilities were greatly advanced, far superior to his own. While he was mainly schooled in the arts of healing and deciphering mystical tomes, this woman had a dangerous power surging through her that rivaled anything the old man had encountered before, save for Lady Dimwater. Her voice was soft and pretty, but her demeanor was harsh and strong. He knew better than to tangle directly with her.

In the end, he didn't disagree with what she wanted, he just liked to poke the bear a bit, as it were.

"I have identified a few more families, but these lines are not originally from the Middle Kingdom. They are recorded as residing much further away."

116

"Where exactly?" the woman inquired.

The old man shrugged. "Take your pick," he said. "You can find sahale on nearly every continent. Of course, you and your master have already slain the most renowned family lines closest to the Middle Kingdom. The others, I would imagine, are less powerful, and should prove easier marks than the ones we summoned to Winter's Beak."

"Are there no others here, close to us?"

The old man sighed and glanced back down to the page. "There are two more," he said. "One is written in this book, and the other I know of personally, though I know not exactly where he is."

"Tell me," the woman said.

The ex-prelate nodded. "The first resides in the north, in a place called Hermit's Hole. He is a strong one, so your master will need to take care."

"My master will have no trouble dispatching the beast," the woman spat.

"Oh, no doubt, no doubt," the old man said.

"And the other?"

The old man frowned and turned to face the woman. "The other is Erik Lokton." A strange swirl of colors flowed through the woman's aura, a mix of anger, confusion, and what appeared to be admiration. It was a confusing reaction to the old man. "You know him?" he asked.

"Who doesn't?" the woman asked cryptically.

The ex-prelate nodded, as if that answer satisfied him, but he could see that the woman was hiding something. Still, he decided best not to poke the bear again… this time. "He should be easy enough to find, if your master wants to tangle with him as well, but I should warn you. If the sahale in Hermit's Hole is a threat, then consider Erik much more so. He defeated Tu'luh the Red, among many others. He shall not be an easy target to slay."

"You are needed for the names and locations of strong sahale individuals," the woman cut in. "You are not required, nor asked, to be an advisor on strategy."

The old man bowed his head in deference. "As you say, m'lady." The woman got up to leave and made for the door. "If I could ask a favor," the ex-prelate said. The woman stopped and turned to listen over her shoulder. "If your master does decide to go after Erik Lokton, then I want to be present for his assassination."

"Out of the question," the woman said.

"Then bring me back a souvenir perhaps? A finger, or an eye?"

The woman exited and closed the door behind her.

The ex-prelate laughed softly to himself and turned back to the book on his desk. Of all the things he thought he would do in his older years, tracking down sahale and helping a madman kill them had never crossed his mind. Whether it was due to his current status as a fallen priest, ousted by the order that had required so much of him for most of his life, or an innate cruelty that had always been a part of him, he couldn't be sure, but he was discovering that he rather liked playing for the side that chased and slew dragons.

*****

Njar rummaged through the endless bottles and vials on the shelf. Eye of newt, frog's tears, crocodile saliva, jars of various herbs for poultices, even the dried tail of an ox wrapped in borglin vines atop a bed of volcanic salts. No matter how desperately he wished for it, he could find nothing to aid the ailing Nonac. The massive tree that had guarded the satyrs for ages was now in need of protection and help, and Njar was not prepared.

The satyr snarled and grabbed the side of the wooden shelves and overturned them, shattering jars along his floor and spilling their contents. He walked toward the stone wall off to the side of the room and waved his hand. A doorway appeared, granting him access to an inner library hidden within the center of his home. As he stepped through the portal, gold and blue flames burst into existence. There were seven book cases here, each situated at the point of a seven-pointed star drawn in gold inlay along the black marble floor.

This was the inner sanctum of the satyr chief, the accumulation of centuries of knowledge and wisdom. He moved to stand in the center of the room, firmly planting his feet down in the middle of the star. The doorway to the house closed, sealing off all contact to the outside world. Njar stamped his right foot three times. The stomps echoed in the chamber and a rush of wind came from above, circling the satyr. He stamped his left foot three times, and the floor seemed to vanish, revealing a vast, empty void beneath him. The bookcases still stood on the points of the golden star, suspended in the magical chamber. Njar clapped his hands, and the walls receded into the void. The torches that had hung on them now hovered in the air, still and constant like stars. The circling wind rushed faster and faster, tugging and pulling at Njar's fur. Then it shot upward and the ceiling vanished, revealing a sky full of stars and wondrous colors.

The chamber's transformation was complete. Now, he would be able to confer with those that had come before, and hopefully with Terramyr herself.

"Ancestors, I call out to you now. Wake Mother Terramyr, and guide me to understand her wisdom." He continued on with the chant until the first of the torches along the wall flickered and nearly died out.

A silver outline, almost like that of a thick mist, appeared near the torch.

"Njar, what troubles you?" the form asked in a voice that was at once both thunderous, and soft.

"Nonac has been poisoned, and we have been attacked," Njar said with a bowed head. "I have failed in my duties, and now I do not see the way out."

"You have not failed," the form said, remaining where it stood. "This was always meant to be."

Njar shook his head. "No, we are in peril. A powerful shadowfiend threatens to destroy us all. If Nonac falls, then so shall Viverandon."

A second torch flickered, and a second form of mist grew in the void. "Njar, this day has been coming for a long time. Now it is up to you to face it with dignity, honor, and courage."

"What day do you speak of?" Njar asked. "I know of no prophecy that speaks of this. Nonac is to stand for all time."

A third form appeared, and Njar held his silence. He had never seen more than two spirits at any one time in the sacred council chamber. He had heard that in times of great importance more spirits could come, each one representing a point on the star, which in turn symbolized Terramyr's chronological epochs. To see three meant that this was indeed a serious event, and not just because of the danger it posed.

As Njar stood there, more forms appeared in the darkness, each coming to stand near the star. He spun around, counting six of the satyr spirits and then found himself barely able to breathe. Were the spirits angry with him? Did they blame him for Nonac's disease?

"I will do what I can to make this right," Njar said. "I swear I will find a way to heal Nonac, and I will put a stop to the magical assaults on Viverandon."

None of the spirits spoke. They stared at him with silvery, unblinking eyes. All of the torches flickered and died, leaving Njar in total darkness. Several seconds passed, and then the fires burst back into flame. The fires grew and began to arch over the center of the star above Njar's head. As the blue and gold flames mingled, a seventh form began to take shape. Its limbs were not made of mist, as the other spirits were, but of living flame. The fiery satyr descended from the air and gently touched down a few feet away from Njar. This one, Njar knew, for only one satyr chief danced with the power of fire, and that was Rameun, the third chief of Viverandon. Njar fell to his knees and bowed his head in reverence.

"Njar Somoricliar, the Son of Thunder, lift your head," Rameun said.

Njar raised his eyes, but was hesitant to look upon the powerful spirit of Rameun.

"Look upon me," Rameun demanded. "Set your eyes upon mine so there can be no misunderstanding."

Njar reluctantly looked to Rameun. "I am sorry," Njar said in a trembling whisper.

"You have been betrayed," Rameun replied evenly. "This was always to be so. We have seen it coming since the beginning."

"Then why have I not seen it?" Njar said. "Why should I allow my house to be destroyed? My home, my people, everything that I love?"

Rameun stepped forward, his form burning with a bright orange flame and eyes of gold. "For millennia, we satyrs have protected the balance. We have sought to keep the evil from overtaking the light in Terramyr. That is the purpose we were created for."

"Then why allow me to fail?" Njar cried out.

Rameun stepped toward him and knelt down before Njar. "Because, the Son of Thunder would have seen a way to prevent this tragedy, if allowed to foresee his destiny in the Pools of Fate."

The first form of mist came closer and added, "Sometimes we must travail through the pain to attain our true purpose. There is nothing like the fire of tribulation that will help burn away the impurities that weigh us down."

Njar shook his head, failing to understand. "What could be so important that it is worth losing Nonac?" Anger swelled within him like he had never felt before. Anger, pain, and resentment. If these satyrs knew what was coming, they should have warned him. The Pools of Fate should have shown him. What was the wisdom in letting everything come under such an attack? "How can I keep balance like this?" Njar pleaded. "Tell me! All my life, I have sought to do the right thing. I have helped others temper their desires and lusts, I have pruned the dead growth on the trees of men's spirits and thus allowed them to blossom into fruitful beings that have protected Terramyr, so why this? Why is this my reward?"

Rameun reached out and put his flaming hand on Njar's shoulder. To Njar's surprise, the fire did not hurt. "Because no longer are we to seek balance," Rameun said. "Terramyr senses a great danger. The events of late have pushed her into a corner, and her very existence is threatened once again, not only by the rebellious, fallen gods, but from forces beyond the stars that have begun to take notice of her. The only way to protect the Mother now, is to do away with balance, and to conquer our foes."

Njar's mouth hung open. "Do away with balance?" he said incredulously. "But balance…"

"Balance was the tenet of the past, now we must show our strength. A new age is dawning, and those who would threaten Terramyr must be destroyed."

Rameun placed his other hand on Njar's forehead and the two were whisked away to another plane.

Hot air stifled Njar's breathing and stung his nose and lungs. A heavy pressure bore down on him from above as thick clouds, bursting with lightning and hail rolled in. He looked around to get his bearings, and saw several forms moving in and out of the shadows dancing on the edge of a burning city.

Winter's Beak was ablaze. Dragon's flew in the sky, and dragon-slayers fought from the ground. Women and children were shrieking and running for their lives, carrying only what they could hold in sheets and blankets that had been turned into hasty sacks. Walking in their midst, firing magical missiles at the sky, were men in hoods, led by a singular beast, a shadowfiend with spikes and great fire erupting from his mouth.

"What evil is this?" Njar asked as he coughed against the blistering air.

"This is the near future," Rameun said. "Nonac will die, and Viverandon will be exposed. How you handle that fact will decide whether the brutality you see here becomes reality, or dies as one of hundreds of possible futures that is not triggered."

"How do I stop this?" Njar asked as a large, silver dragon swooped down and bathed several buildings in a wave of fire. Screams of dying people were drowned out by the thunderous response of the shadowfiend and his minions as they fired lightning and other spells into the air. The dragon was ripped in twain, and his sizzling body fell to the ground, crushing three houses under its weight.

"If you save Viverandon, then this future will come to pass, and the number of the dead will be vastly more than if you had let Viverandon fall."

"Let it fall?" Njar echoed. "You want me to abandon my people?" Njar shook his head. "I cannot do that!"

"Then Terramyr will die, bathed in the blood of her children."

Njar looked back to the ghastly scene before him. The rage boiled hot in his chest. He watched as the shadowfiend commanded an army of men against the dragons. The two forces were evenly matched, balanced even. Njar took in a breath of the stifling air, allowing it to scorch his insides without flinching. Once, he had seen a young girl reach into the past during a vision at the Pools of Fate. She had reached into the past and touched the events. The change had been slight, but it had been real.

The satyr chief did not question whether he could do the same now. He simply let his rage propel him forward. Without his staff, he strode toward the city and approached a group of four dragon-slayers. They each wore their tell-tale Telarian steel armor, which was designed to withstand the heat of a dragon's flame.

They saw him coming and motioned for him to help.

"The dragons! Help us defend ourselves!" one of the men shouted.

Njar shook his head. "No." In his mind's eye he saw the dying Nonac raising its root to attack him once more, and the feeling of total betrayal that had plagued him ever since now boiled into a rage the likes of which he had never experienced.

"Help us!" a wizard called out from the side as he aimed up at a dragon with a spell.

"No," Njar replied as he kept walking closer.

"That is right, fair satyr, help us wipe these creatures from the land!" a red and black dragon roared as it flew overhead.

"No," Njar replied. He was not there to help any of them. It had not made sense before, but now Njar felt the meaning of what Rameun had said. The time for balance was past. Now it was time for strength. Njar dashed forward and slammed into the wizard, the top of his horned-head breaking the wizard's ribs and denting the man's chest inward.

Three of the four dragon-slayers came to the wizard's aid, but Njar roared at them and summoned a mighty snake of coiled lightning. The silver and blue cords shot out from his hands and blasted into the first, and then held him in an electrifying embrace while reaching out for the second, and then the third. Telarian steel was impervious to fire, but metal

124

was a great conductor. The men shook and jerked until their legs gave out and they fell to the ground.

A mighty roar sounded above as the red and black dragon soared toward what little remained of Winter's Beak. Njar looked up and summoned the powers of Terramyr herself. A green energy shot up in columns, stretching from the ground to the sky. The dragon crashed into them, breaking his left wing and cracking his neck. The beast fell to the ground, where Njar cast a spell to bind the creature with thick vines that covered every inch of the dragon and then began to squeeze until it stopped wriggling.

A blast of blue fire streaked in toward Njar then as the shadowfiend turned his attention to the satyr. Njar dodged the flame only to see a trio of dragons sailing toward him. The fourth and final dragon-slayer was also preparing to strike, a long spear in one hand and an axe in the other.

"Surrender now," the dragon-slayer shouted. "You cannot hope to defeat us all!"

Njar smiled. "No."

The vision ended in a flurry of fire and lightning. Njar moved through his enemies like a tidal wave crushing sand castles on the beach. When he finished, a smoldering heap of bodies lay at his feet. He turned to regard Rameun, who was standing where he had been at the beginning of the vision. The fiery satyr smiled and bowed his head to Njar. The other six ghosts from the sacred council chamber appeared and knelt on the ground, three to Rameun's left, and three more to his right.

"The Son of Thunder has awakened," Rameun said. Rameun then knelt on the ground as well, and the vision went dark.

*****

Erik and Lady Arkyn stood at the front of the schooner. The fog was thick in The Breaks, making for slow, treacherous travel with a lot of sudden, sharp turns to avoid rock outcroppings. Gerald and his daughters proved more than capable though, steering them through safely enough. Erik found himself more than a little uncomfortable however. Whether it was the limited field of vision, or the worry that they were being followed, he couldn't be sure.

Gerald's wife assumed the position of cook, working in the kitchen below deck to provide meals for everyone on board. On the menu today was shark, since they had come upon a lone shark that had bumped into the vessel and tested the hull with its teeth. Lady Arkyn had quickly put it down, and they all had worked to pull the thing aboard the ship. Gerald had cleaned it, tossing the innards to the sea and then happily let his wife take over preparing it from there. With any luck, the shark meat would last them the entire voyage, which was only expected to take a few days.

Half of the reason they had come through The Breaks was to harvest kelp for adding to the various dishes Gerald's wife would prepare. Erik had never tasted kelp before, but it had proved a better experience than he had expected. It was thick, but not tough. Firm in the center and soft on the edges, it was like nothing he had ever had before. He liked it best in soup, especially with the shark meat, but it wasn't bad dried and wrapped around seared bits of meat either. Had life not worked out for him the way it had, Erik thought he might have made a good seaman. The food was good, the air was different and fresh to him, and the rocking of the ship was a lot more fun than he had expected. It was nothing compared to flying, of course, but it was fun nonetheless.

A break in the fog flashed before them just enough for Lady Arkyn to spot a large column of rock jutting out of the water.

"Rock on the starboard bow!" she cried.

The schooner tilted and swung left as Gerald's daughters worked the rigging and he expertly used the wheel to pass by the column. Erik smiled at Minrielle. She gave him a wink and then walked away, heading for the kitchen below deck. Erik let his eyes linger on her for a moment. His smile widened considerably, and then he turned back to lean on the railing of the ship. He had worried that seeing her again might be awkward after being apart for so long. He was more than a little happy to find out that he was mistaken. It was as if the years had been nothing at all. He surmised that was likely in part due to the fact that she was an elf. She would live for a long time, hundreds of years, in fact. In light of that, what was one or two spent apart?

Perhaps after this business was finished and the murderer was caught, he might take a page out of Master Lepkin's book, and settle down for a while. With any luck, Minrielle might join him.

For now, he contented himself with reading from Lady Dimwater's book. It was a thick tome with well over a thousand pages. Since it was organized by topic, Erik had a hard time deciding where to start. Ultimately, he decided to begin with the summary of 'Ascension' which was about Gorliad, the dragon prince Dimwater had mentioned by name in her introduction page. As the schooner rocked back and forth, he lost himself in Dimwater's recounting of the story, and was for once able to clear his mind of all the doubts and fears that plagued him so long as he put himself into the world of Gorliad.

Chapter 10

Njar found himself lying on the floor in his inner sanctum. The torches burned weakly upon the walls, but the doorway to his home was still closed. He pushed up to his feet and rubbed a hand over his face. *What just happened?*

He spun around, looking for Rameun or the other satyr spirits, but he saw none. He was alone. He hurriedly waved his hand and opened the doorway out of the inner sanctum. He rushed out, hopped over the mess of broken glass and spilled ingredients, and made his way outside. His stomach formed a knot and his throat started to dry as he thought about the implications of his vision. Had the attack already hit Viverandon? Had his actions in the vision sped up Nonac's degeneration?

He ripped his door open to find that not only was Viverandon unharmed, but the other satyrs were outside, playing and working. He saw younglings kicking a ball around a large tree and chasing each other. Older satyrs worked in their gardens or drew water from the stream nearby. Birds sang in the trees, and the sky was clear.

He trekked out toward Nonac, hoping that somehow the tree had regained its strength. If all of the others were going about their business as usual, then surely Nonac must have fended off the magical attack that Dremathor had sent.

Njar made his way to the tree and was utterly devastated to see that a sickly gray color was creeping into a large number of leaves. Nonac was not healing. He ran toward the pair of satyrs set to guard the tree.

"Good morrow, Njar," one of them said as he turned and offered a slight nod.

Njar returned the greeting. "Why have you not sent for me?" Njar asked, pointing up to the gray leaves. "Nonac is sick, can't you see?"

The two guards glanced at each other and then up to the massive tree.

"I see nothing wrong," the first guard replied.

"Nor I," said the second.

"Come, look at the leaves," Njar said.

The two looked up and shrugged.

"There, look!" Njar exclaimed as a pair of leaves fell from Nonac's branches. "The falling leaves, don't you see them?"

The two guards shook their heads and looked to Njar. "Are you feeling well?" one of them asked.

"Of course," Njar said impatiently. He walked up to the tree with the intent of inspecting its condition more closely, but a large root ripped itself from the ground. *Thwack!* Njar went tumbling backward across the ground.

"Njar, are you all right?" the guards asked in unison.

A wind blew in from the north, carrying that same, sadistic laughter. "They cannot see it, old friend. Their eyes are not open to the truth."

Njar jumped up, the rage boiling in his chest. "Show yourself!" he shouted. The two guards stopped short of reaching out to him and looked at each other, perplexed. Njar realized how silly he must have looked, and shook his head as he brushed himself off. "Nonac is ill," he said simply. "Keep your eyes open and your wits clear."

The two guards nodded silently.

Njar then turned and walked back toward his home. There was nothing more he could do here. Nonac refused to let him close, and no one else could see the approaching danger. If he kept acting the way he did, they would declare him mad and exile him. He couldn't let that happen. He needed to stay in Viverandon. Dremathor was coming soon, and Njar had to prepare.

Rameun's words came back to him as he walked. Njar stopped and glanced back at Nonac. Could he let Viverandon fall to save the world? Would he be able to turn his back on all that he loved?

The wind came in again, soft and subtle, carrying Dremathor's sinister laugh with it. It mocked him, enjoying his slow fall from grace. Njar shook his head. He would not be able to let Viverandon fall. No matter what it meant to the world, he could not stand by and let Nonac die and leave his home defenseless. Rameun had said it was time to show strength.

Njar took in a breath and spoke to the mocking winds swirling around him. "Go on and laugh now, old friend, for I am not going to wait here for you. It is time for the shadowfiend to know what it is to be hunted."

"Oh?" Dremathor's voice replied as the wind continued to blow. "What does an old goat like you have that can ever harm me?"

Njar clenched his fist. "Just you wait," Njar said. "I let you come in with a firebrand and set my home alight. That is not a mistake I shall leave hanging."

"The wise satyr will forsake his precious principles of balance and turn to the ways of the warrior?" Dremathor's voice laughed in the wind. "Oh, I think not."

"Think what you will, you drooling cur, for it does not change the path I am on now." Njar reached out and gathered a green mist from the field, summoning Terramyr's essence. With it, he reached out and grabbed the wind, holding it in place. As he did so, a translucent face appeared in the wind. It was that of Dremathor. Njar twisted the green energy around the shadowfiend's ethereal neck and squeezed. "I am Njar Somoricliar, the Son of Thunder, and I am coming for you, Dremathor, and anyone else who stands in my way."

Dremathor's eyes went wide. Njar squeezed until the apparition exploded in the energy's grasp and melted away on the wind. This time, there was no sound of laughter. Njar smiled and headed for his home. He had not set his hands on his father's sword for quite some time, but now seemed like the correct moment to take it up once more.

*****

Erik and Lady Arkyn waited as Gerald's daughters dropped anchor and the schooner came to a halt.

They were only fifty yards away from the shore of a beautiful island of sandy beaches and sweeping grasses. Some distance beyond the beach was a thick forest of tall pines. There was no visible road, but Lady Arkyn knew where they were headed.

"You sure we can't change your mind?" Gerald asked as he came up to Erik.

"No, the road from here will take us into more danger," Erik replied. "You should head south. If you can, make your way to Lokton Manor. Ask for Braun, he'll take care of you."

"I wish I could go with you," Gerald said as he wiped a tear from his dull eye. "The salt in the wind," he explained.

Erik smiled and allowed Gerald the cover story, but he could see that he was very sad to see him and Lady Arkyn

131

depart. "Stay safe, my friend," Erik said as he extended his hand.

"And you," Gerald said as he shook Erik's hand.

"Don't forget, I have some dried shark meat and seaweed wraps in this pouch," Gerald's wife said as she hurried up from below deck. "You ever need any more good food, you know where to find me," she added.

The daughters were silent, but they waved and smiled appreciatively as Lady Arkyn and Erik got into the small dingy and began rowing to shore.

Gerald watched him from the deck until they landed on the beach, and then he gave the order to raise the anchor and unfurl the sails. Erik smiled as the ship turned and headed back for the fog. "Good people," he commented. "The world could use more like them."

Lady Arkyn agreed with a nod. "A few hundred men like Gerald could change the world," she said. "All it takes is a good, solid family with a wise mother and good father, and most of the world's problems would sort themselves out. There's always a rotten egg here or there of course, but on the whole I have found a good, strong family can make a world of difference."

Erik nodded. "It did for me," he said. He didn't even want to think where he would be without his adoptive parents. They had taken him in, taught him, and guided him. He had been greatly blessed by the gods, he knew. Of course, it helped that he counted Master Lepkin, Lady Dimwater, and Al among his family as well. He may have started without a family, but now he had become more fortunate than most, and he knew it.

They pulled the dinghy up onto the shore and flipped it upside down in the grass. They then began to walk along the grasses when a strange sound filled the air. Erik and Lady Arkyn turned to see the fog burn away from the surface of the water. A large ship was closing in on Gerald's schooner. There was a great amount of shouting coming from both ships, but there was one voice that rang out clearly over the seas.

Gerald called for help. "Erik! Erik! Help us!"

Erik ran toward the shoreline and leapt up into the air, summoning his power to transform himself into his dragon form. Instead of changing, his bones felt cold and his limbs grew heavy. It was as if an unseen chain of thick, heavy links was coiling around him. He crashed into the water with a splash.

Lady Arkyn was there in an instant, pulling him up.

"To the dinghy!" Erik shouted.

Lady Arkyn grabbed him and held him back. "It's no use!" she shouted.

"ERIK!" Gerald's voice cut the air like a knife.

Erik turned in time to see a volley of arrows darken the air between the two ships. The missiles landed all over the schooner. Gerald's daughters fell to the deck, but Gerald held fast to the wheel, working as best he could to steer away from the much larger ship. Time seemed to slow then. Erik tried to summon his power once more, but again he was prevented from using it. He could only watch helplessly as the attacking ship closed in. The massive ship bobbed up out of the waves just enough for Erik to catch a glimpse of the long, sharp ram extending out the front before it bored into the hull of the schooner. Gerald was thrown to the deck. He struggled back to his feet only to be rewarded with a second volley of arrows that concentrated on him.

Erik turned away as Gerald's arrow-filled body fell down for the last time. The schooner cracked and broke apart. The last sound Erik heard before the larger ship crashed through the shattered schooner was Gerald's wife screaming for her husband and daughters. The large ship then ran her over in the water, and she was not to be heard from again.

"Come, we have to go," Lady Arkyn said. "There is nothing we can do."

133

Erik tore away from her and walked out into the water. He called upon his power again, fighting against the magic that bound him to his human form. Tears streamed down his cheeks as pain racked his body and the pressure around him squeezed tighter and tighter.

"Erik, we have to go, now!" Lady Arkyn shouted. "They are coming this way. We can't fight off that many archers. We have to run."

Erik heard the words, but he wasn't paying them any heed. He was the Champion of Truth, he could break through the curse if he focused hard enough. He knew it. He struggled against the magic for another two minutes as the large ship came toward them.

A single archer leaned back, aiming his bow up at the sky. He let loose. The missile arced through the air and landed thirty yards short of where Erik stood.

"Erik," Lady Arkyn said loudly. "We don't have much time. They'll be in range soon, and then they will all fire at us. We have to go!"

"I can do this!" Erik shouted. "I have to!" He called upon the dark corners of his soul where he kept his most painful memories. He called them up now, hoping the extra surge of anger they would cause within him would help him break through the bonds of the spell holding him in his human form. He saw Marlin die once again. He saw Salarion fighting as a slave for Tu'luh the Red. He relived watching Tatev's murder at the hands of Tarthuns. He saw his father in chains upon the senate floor. Then he saw Janik in the woods near his home just before he had revealed his true nature and turned on Erik.

Erik shouted as his body started to transform. The bones elongated and broke, the muscles stretched and ripped, and then the spell gripped him tighter and snapped him back into his human form. He cried out in agony as his heart thumped within his chest and he struggled for breath. There was nothing he could do.

This realization came just as the first archer's next arrow landed one foot to Erik's left.

All of the archers pulled back on their bows.

"Run!" Erik said as he turned and grabbed Lady Arkyn's arm. They darted for the dinghy and dove under it just as a barrage of arrows thudded into the ground following them up to the small boat. Several missiles came close to the dinghy as well. "Let's move!" Erik said as he put his back to the middle seat in the dinghy and gripped the forward seat. He stood up straight, using the small boat as a large shell to protect them as they ran for the forest.

Arrows thunked into the wooden hull and bit into the dirt around them, but nothing was strong enough to get through to them. They kept running for the trees as quickly as they could as arrows kept following them.

"If we can make it to Gontin, I know the captain of the guard there," Lady Arkyn said. "He'll lock the town down and stop these men from getting to us."

Erik nodded and continued to concentrate on his job holding the boat between them and the arrows.

Another volley thudded into the wooden boat. This time one of the arrows broke through so that the head grazed Erik's right forearm, but he didn't let the surprise slow him down. They continued to sprint until they reached the edge of the forest, and then he dropped the dinghy and they ran for their lives.

The bushes scraped at their legs as they darted in and around the trees. The arrows stopped following them now, limited by the range as the ship likely ran up against the shallower waters. Erik's chest was filled with fury that propelled his feet forward faster than he had ever run before. As they drove deeper into the forest, he felt something else, as if bands were unloosed from around his body. Erik stopped, holding his hand out to steady himself against a tree as he heaved for breath.

"What's wrong?" Lady Arkyn shouted as she came around. "We can't stop now, we have to move on!"

Erik looked at her and offered a single nod. "Go on, then, go to Gontin. There is something I must do."

"No, Erik, you can't. There are too many of them. You can't go back!"

Erik felt the power rise in his body. He now knew that there was indeed a range to the wizard's spell.

"You can't go back!" Lady Arkyn shouted again. "What are you going to do? You'll never get close enough to them in your dragon form."

Erik smiled. "Lepkin always told me that the brain was my best weapon." He knocked his knuckles against a tree. "I only have to circle high enough above the ship to remain out of the wizard's reach. How far would you say we have run? A half a mile?"

Lady Arkyn shook her head. "More like a quarter, maybe a tad more."

"Then that shall be easy. "Step back please. I don't want to hurt you." Erik took off his clothes and tossed her his sword. "Go on in to Gontin, if you wish, I will catch up with you."

"No, if you are going back to fight, then I will hold the position here," she insisted.

Erik nodded. "There isn't much time." He let his power surge through him and he changed into his dragon form. He let out a mighty roar and then ripped four large oak trees from the ground as easily as a man might pull weeds. He leapt into the air, climbing higher and higher with each beat of his wings.

Gerald's murder would not go unanswered.

He flew high into the air, until he had passed well beyond a quarter mile, and then he turned for the ship. He flew hard and fast, covering the distance he had run in mere seconds. He could see the several rowboats heading to shore with their landing parties; archers and swordsmen armed and ready to do battle. They pointed at him and shouted as he tore through the air above, but there was nothing they could do. Their puny arrows were nothing to him in his dragon form. The wizard was on deck aboard the main ship. He saw Erik too, and was busily waving his hands, no doubt trying to force Erik back into his human form. Unfortunately for the wizard, Erik had judged the effective distance very well.

He flew over the ship and then raised two of the trees in front of him. He used his dragon fire, tempering it slightly so as to light the trees rather than consume them, and then he dropped them over the ship. He circled above, watching the flaming bombs fall toward the vessel. For good measure, Erik brought the other two trees up and lit them as well. He put a great amount of strength into throwing the last two, hoping that the wizard below wouldn't be able to stop all of them. The crew rushed about, pulling the anchor up as quickly as they could, but they were too slow for the burning trees. The wizard managed to knock one of the trees aside, but the other three struck their target. Two crashed through the main deck, while one crushed the main mast and lit the sails and rigging.

Archers in the rowboat were hopelessly aiming their bows up and firing at Erik, but the missiles stopped well short of him and turned back to fall toward the sea. Erik turned and flew back toward the forest. He ripped four more large trees without slowing down for an instant and then circled around once more. He lit the four trees and zeroed in on his target. The ship itself was already going down, but he had to ensure the wizard was killed. Only then would he be able to engage the other warriors more effectively.

Erik sent four fiery trees down at the wizard, who was stumbling and struggling to keep his balance on the ship as its rear end rose up out of the water and slowly sank downward.

The poor fool never had a chance. The first tree struck the wizard and crashed through the upper deck, pushing the wizard's broken body along with it. Flames roared out as the ship was pulverized.

Erik let out a mighty roar and swooped down. The archers in the nearest rowboat fired their arrows, but Erik swallowed them in a wave of fire that consumed the arrows and then pressed forward to obliterate the rowboat. He moved on to the next, and then the next. He then moved to the fourth and final rowboat when a familiar form stood and held his arms out to the side.

"My armor is made of Telarian steel!" the rogue dragon-slayer shouted. "It is impervious to your flames!"

Erik sneered. "Then let us see how you can swim in it!" He spewed out his fire as the rogue dragon-slayer raised up his shield to block himself from the fire. The boat around him turned to ash and he fell into the waters below. He and the other dragon-slayers splashed about for a bit, and then the weight of their armor dragged them below the surface and down into the murky, dark depths.

The mighty sahale then ascended toward the clouds and circled around the site of the wreckage several times. Satisfied only once he had made sure there were no survivors, he returned to the forest and changed back into his human form. He found Lady Arkyn waiting for him at the edge of the trees, holding out his clothes and staring out to the smoke that had risen above the sea.

"That was quite a sight," she commented.

Erik nodded and dressed. "I only wish I could have gotten to the dogs before they had caught Gerald and his family."

Lady Arkyn smiled. "At least we may be comforted in knowing that Nagé will come for their souls, and escort them to the halls of the honored dead in Volganor. They shall have peace."

Erik looked at her, and then glanced to the water. "That is the injustice of this world," he said bitterly. "A good man should not have to die in order to find peace."

Chapter 11

The moon was high in the night sky by the time Lady Arkyn and Erik arrived at the gates of Gontin. The walls were about forty feet tall, obscuring any view of the inner city they might have had. There were two men walking the ramparts above, and three guards at the gate below.

"A bit late for a pair to be traveling in these parts," one of the guards said as he set down a pipe and picked up a book. A second grabbed a torch and followed the first as they came out to meet Erik and Lady Arkyn. "If you are planning on coming inside, I will need your names and your mark."

"Is Captain Deringer around?" Lady Arkyn asked.

The guard stopped and looked at Lady Arkyn. He smiled, curling his thick mustache upward. "Lady Arkyn, it has been a long time. You don't look a day older than you did ten years ago."

"That is the blessing of an elf," Lady Arkyn said. "How have you been Farnsworth?"

"I've been well. The Mrs. is as ornery as ever, but Sally and her husband had their second child last summer, so she has other things to fuss about now, which keeps her from nagging me so much."

"Congratulations!" Lady Arkyn said.

"Personal or official?" Farnsworth asked.

"This visit is one we want to keep a bit tighter," Lady Arkyn replied.

Farnsworth nodded and offered a wink. He turned and handed the book to the other guard. "Tell the others at the gate that we have no visitors. We'll be omitting this from the logs."

"As you say, Lieutenant," the other guard said with a slight bow of his head and shuffled off back toward the gates.

"Who's this then?" Farnsworth said, indicating Erik.

"Erik Lokton, at your service," Erik said with a slight bow of his head.

"Lokton eh?" Farnsworth repeated with a nod. "I knew your father, Trenton."

Erik stiffened and cocked a brow. "You did?"

Farnsworth nodded. "A right fine fellow, your father. I never attended Kuldiga Academy, but your father did a summer of field work out here. He stayed with my neighbor's family actually. I found him to be honorable, if not a bit mischievous." Farnsworth gave a smile that indicated to Erik that perhaps the old guard had joined in on Trenton's mischievous behavior. "I was saddened to learn of his passing, my condolences." Farnsworth offered his hand. Erik took it and the two shook quickly before Farnsworth escorted them to a small door near where he had been sitting that led into a small office on the outside of the gatehouse. "If you wish to see Captain Deringer, I can summon him here for you," Farnsworth offered.

"I would appreciate it," Lady Arkyn said.

Farnsworth nodded and gestured to a kettle on a stove. "There might be some tea left, could probably use a little fire under it to warm it up again, but you're welcome to what I have."

"Thank you," Erik said. He then turned and called out for Farnsworth to wait a moment. "Would you also happen to have the capability to deliver a small package for me?" he asked.

"I can arrange for that, what did you have in mind?"

Erik fished out Lady Dimwater's book about dragons that he had found in Pracheloor Cave. "I would like you to have this book sent to Lokton Manor, but whoever takes it must be very careful with it. I do not want it damaged in any way, or lost."

"I shall make the arrangements personally in the morning. Consider it taken care of." Farnsworth took the book and then turned to leave, closing the door behind himself. From inside the waiting room, they could hear the man door being opened in the larger gate for Farnsworth to pass into Gontin.

"I thought you would read that some more on the next leg of our journey," Lady Arkyn commented.

Erik shrugged. "After what happened with our first ship, I think it might be better to have it waiting in my library at home. I don't want to risk it sinking to the bottom of the sea and being lost forever."

Lady Arkyn nodded. "This used to be a larger fortress," Lady Arkyn said. "Before the seas were claimed for the Middle Kingdom this was an outpost that was self-governing. It gets its name from the first ruling family. They were formidable seamen, back before they were tamed."

"Tamed?" Erik asked.

Lady Arkyn grinned. "This was a fortress for pirates and plunderers," she said. "They launched all sorts of raids up and down the coasts. For years they were untouchable."

"So how did the Middle Kingdom annex them?" Erik asked.

Lady Arkyn slapped Erik's shoulder. "A pair of sahale princes convinced them that it was more profitable to join the Middle Kingdom and create an official navy of sorts."

Erik laughed at that. "I suppose even the best of pirates are no match for dragons," he said.

"Dragons have shaped much of the Middle Kingdom," she replied. "From the very beginning, when the Ancients helped form Roegudok Hall and the dwarves that live there, we have ever been under their watchful eyes and powerful wings."

Erik moved toward the tea and poured himself a bit of the tepid liquid. He took a slow sip to test the flavor. Mint tea, his favorite. He drank the first cup quickly, and then poured a second to savor. He offered some to Lady Arkyn, but she declined. They sat at the table in silence, Arkyn watching the door and Erik sipping his tea.

The last time he had had mint tea this flavorful was back in Lady Dimwater's tower at Kuldiga Academy. He smiled thinking about it now, but he had become friends with her only after breaking into her study. It seemed such a childish thing to him now, but at the time he was sure he would uncover some great mysteries about the renowned Lady Dimwater. In a way, he guessed he had. That had been his first encounter with Silverfang, and the first time he had experienced the mighty wolf's paralyzing magic that could not only hold a man motionless, but instill in them a fear that melted their willpower. Except for Erik, that is. Even as a young teenager, Erik had possessed a greater amount of will and fortitude than most. He had been able to break through the spell and take a swing at Silverfang. Of course, had he known then what he knew now about Silverfang's fighting abilities, he would never have dared to make such a bold move. He smiled wider, thinking about the wolf who was now bequeathed to him by Lady Dimwater and had been a most wonderful companion since. Erik couldn't help but think that perhaps it was his courage the first time they met that had endeared him to Silverfang so, for the wolf was always eager to answer his calls now.

Of course, there had been more to that night. Lady Dimwater had caught him, and instead of expelling him from the academy, she made him serve with her on assignments. Not long after that night, she had taken him on a mission to Spiekery, and vanquished a shadowfiend there. It was Erik's first taste of magical battles. It had all seemed so marvelous at the time as he watched Dimwater battle a monster that had preyed upon a village for years. Now, he was just as capable of carrying out such missions himself. Alkantar served as a reminder of that point, showing just how far Erik had come in such a short amount of time.

Erik sighed and shook his head as if to clear his mind of everything.

"Something wrong?" Lady Arkyn asked.

Erik looked at her and offered a half-smile. "Something Alkantar said about the Dark Sahale," he replied. "Just, it sounded similar to something else I heard recently, that's all."

"What?" Lady Arkyn pressed.

"There was a demon in the mountains far to the south. He was plaguing the people in that area, and they had called upon me to help them defeat it." Erik took in a breath as he recalled the abominable creature that he had summoned forth from its banishment. "The demon said that it too could sense the darkness within me, that I had been destined to be a great master of..." his words trailed off and he shook his head. "Just, Alkantar said he sensed the darkness within me too."

"Horse-apples," Lady Arkyn said flatly. "You are going to let a couple of monsters sow seeds of doubt into your mind? You know everything you have accomplished, everything you have fought for. Everyone has a bit of evil inside of them, that's what makes us mortal. It is the fight to overcome our base desires and gross temptations that make us great."

Erik shook his head. "No, there is more to it," he said. "I have had a nagging feeling that agrees with them.

144

Sometimes, when I fight, I enjoy it. I never used to, but now, I sometimes find myself too willing to fight and destroy."

Lady Arkyn raised her left hand and tugged at the fingertips of her forest green glove. "Erik, I have known since the first time I saw you what kind of man you are, and what you could become. It is what drew me to you. Even while you were trapped in Lepkin's body, I could see who you really were," she said.

"Minnie," Erik whispered. "There are thoughts and feelings flooding my mind and soul that I am afraid I cannot control. What if I am not that same person you met several years ago?"

"There is something I want to show you." Lady Arkyn pulled the glove off and revealed a simple band of gold around her left ring finger. "Do you remember the night you gave this to me?"

Erik's frowning face lit up into a bright smile. "You still wear it?" Despite the depressing thoughts that he was concentrating on at the moment, the sight of the ring on her finger lifted his spirits considerably.

"Why shouldn't I?" Lady Arkyn asked.

"I just thought, after four years…"

Lady Arkyn shook her head. "Four years is nothing to an elf, and less than that to a sahale I should suspect. You asked me to marry you, and do you remember what I said?"

The door opened, abruptly ending the conversation. Erik sighed inaudibly at the interruption. Minrielle smiled at him and put her glove back on.

A tall, well-built man strode into the room quickly and made a straight line for Lady Arkyn. She barely had time to stand before the man pulled her into an embrace. Erik watched silently as Lady Arkyn's cheeks flushed just a bit.

"It's good to see you, Minrielle" the man said.

Lady Arkyn pushed back and pointed with her hand to Erik. "Captain Deringer, let me introduce Lord Erik Lokton, the Champion of Truth," she said formally.

Captain Deringer let his eyes linger on Lady Arkyn for a few moments before turning to bow toward Erik. "Lord Lokton, a pleasure to meet you in person. I was called up to serve in Fort Drake, but the war was over before I arrived."

Erik set his tea down and rose to shake hands with Captain Deringer. "A pleasure," he said.

Captain Deringer then turned back to Lady Arkyn. "What has it been, ten years?" he asked.

Lady Arkyn nodded and moved back into her chair.

Captain Deringer grabbed a chair and slid it next to hers. "I know you're here on official business, but before we get into that, I have to ask you, why didn't you return, Minrielle?"

Lady Arkyn glanced to Erik with her green eyes and fumbled for words while tapping her left index finger on the table. Finally she reached up and smoothed her hair back and changed the subject. "I hear Farnsworth has a new grandchild," she said. "Do you have any family news to share?"

Deringer shook his head. "You should know the answer to that, Min-min," he said.

Erik was not the jealous kind, after all, he had been away from Lady Arkyn for four years himself, but he had never heard about this Captain Deringer, and there was obviously a story here. But, given the conversation that Deringer had walked in on, Erik was more than a little curious about the history between Deringer and Lady Arkyn. Still, he would rather hear it from Lady Arkyn herself, and not learn about it from Deringer, so he cut in before the captain could go any further. "We require a vessel to sail north," he said.

"Yes, the sooner the better," Lady Arkyn put in as she turned her body ever so slightly away from Deringer.

Deringer's smile faded and he looked to Erik. "Ah, I see." For such an abrupt rebuttal to his advances, he took it well, shifting directly into business mode without so much as a confused expression or a flashing frown. "Am I permitted to know the nature of the mission, or is it best simply to arrange for the best vessel at my disposal?"

"We are keeping things quiet for now," Erik said. "We need something fast that can get us up into the northern territory."

Captain Deringer nodded. "Rafe is the best I have," he said.

"Rafe would do well," Lady Arkyn replied. "He's not just a good sailor, he can keep his mouth closed when needed. I have used his services before on official business," she said.

"When do you need to leave?" Deringer asked.

"We'll rest for the night, and then be off before first light."

Deringer leaned back in his chair and folded his arms. "The fishing vessels will leave about an hour before dawn. It should be easy enough to slip out ahead of them. One moment, I'll have Farnsworth go and instruct Rafe."

Lady Arkyn nodded. Deringer went to the door, leaned out, and spoke softly to Farnsworth. The guard nodded and walked toward the gate. Deringer closed the door once more and came back to the table.

"Is there anything else you require?" Deringer asked.

Lady Arkyn nodded and glanced nervously to Erik. "There is, but it's a bit complicated."

Deringer smirked. "It always is, with you," he said.

"There are rogue dragon-slayers about causing trouble. They have taken over Far Point and instituted their own kind of martial law. Furthermore, they chased down the vessel that brought us to the southern end of this island and attacked it, sinking the vessel and killing a family onboard."

147

Deringer's smile faded and he leaned forward on the table. "If you need protection, the entire city guard is at your disposal." He then looked to Erik. "I have heard of your reputation, but I have also heard of late that there are wizards who can stop people like you from transforming into your dragon form."

Erik stiffened at these words. Just how much did this Captain Deringer know?

"No, Erik handled the ship that pursued us," Lady Arkyn put in quickly.

Deringer's eyebrows shot up and then he smiled and offered Erik a nod. "Well then, your reputation is obviously well-deserved."

"How did you know of the wizards?" Erik asked, ignoring the compliment.

Deringer's smile darkened and he took in a sober breath. He turned to Lady Arkyn and hesitated before he spoke, as if trying to find the right phrase. "I am not so blind to see that you have moved on, while I have not." His words hung on the air for a moment. Erik watched carefully as Lady Arkyn glanced down to the table, unwilling to meet Deringer's gaze. "What I need to know now, is whether I am still among friends?"

Lady Arkyn nodded. "Whatever you have to say, it will remain between the three of us," she assured him.

"Very well," he said. "Then you should know that about a month ago, a stranger came to Gontin. She had long, black hair, beautiful blue eyes, and was very attractive. She was attended by two servants, something we don't see much of out here in Gontin. She stayed only for one day, and while she was here, she visited with Lord Oswald, do you know him?"

Lady Arkyn shook her head.

"Lord Oswald is an old resident of Gontin. He mostly kept to himself, but he was a good citizen. He was wealthy, but not miserly, and the town loved him for it. Anyway, it is not unusual for him to receive visitors at times. Businessmen, inventors, and even scholars have all come to him over the years, seeking capitol with which to fuel their dreams and visions, but this woman was different. I don't know exactly what she wanted from him, for he wouldn't tell me, but after she left, Lord Oswald packed up and left town."

"What does this have to do with wizards?" Erik asked.

Deringer held up a finger. "Gontin has a secret," he said. Deringer glanced to the door and then leaned forward. "Do you know much of our history?" Deringer asked Erik.

"I gave him the overview," Lady Arkyn replied.

Deringer nodded. "Well then, you know that two sahale came and changed this town from one of pirates and murderers into something respectable, yes?"

Erik nodded.

"Did you know that one of the sahale remained here?"

Erik looked to Lady Arkyn, who had put a hand to her mouth.

"I thought they both left," Arkyn said.

Deringer shook his head. "One left, after Nagar's Blight came to the Middle Kingdom, but the other stayed. In his human form, he was unaffected by the curse. He remained as a kind of...agent for lack of a better term. In any case, I tried to send him after the woman to see who she really was. He was careful, but they must have seen him. The two servants turned out to be wizards. They attacked him along the coast when he caught up with them. In order to defend himself, he tried to shift into his dragon form, but somehow their magic stopped him. He suffered great wounds during the ensuing fight. He only barely made it back to Gontin, but by then Lord Oswald had left and the woman was too far for me to chase."

"Can I talk with him?" Erik asked. "It would be a great help to our current mission."

Deringer shook his head. "I would that you could, but he died of his wounds not three days afterward. He wasn't able to discover who the woman was, and her name and mark have disappeared from our logs. The guards that had been on duty the night she arrived all died in their sleep the same night Lord Oswald left. I am sorry, there is nothing more I can tell you."

"So there are at least two wizards who can perform this magic," Lady Arkyn said.

"Likely more than that," Erik posited. "Alkantar could do it. The wizard in Far Point could do it."

"Yes, but the wizard is dead, and so is Alkantar."

"So you have run into this problem more than once," Deringer said.

Erik nodded. "Twice at least, plus the problem in Winter's Beak."

"What happened in Winter's Beak?" Deringer asked.

"I'm sorry, but we shouldn't talk about that," Lady Arkyn said.

"No, but the note Lord Oswald left for his steward indicated that he was on his way to Winter's Beak. Some sort of…gathering, I think it was. No one has heard from him since. Has something happened there?"

Lady Arkyn and Erik looked at each other.

"Was Lord Oswald a sahale?" Lady Arkyn asked.

Captain Deringer shook his head. "No, of that I am certain. My family has known his for generations. They have lived in Gontin since the beginning. They are rich and powerful, but they have no magical ability to speak of."

"Are you certain?" Erik pressed. "This is important."

Captain Deringer nodded. "Lord Oswald was born after my father. My grandfather told me stories of some of the family's eccentricities and behaviors. I am certain they are a family of men, nothing more."

"Then why would he be summoned to Winter's Beak?" Lady Arkyn asked Erik.

Erik shook his head and sighed. "Without being able to ask him, I doubt we will ever be able to answer that."

150

"Captain Deringer," Lady Arkyn started as she tapped her fingernail on the table. "Send dispatch to Winter's Beak. A terrible atrocity has occurred there, and it sounds as though Lord Oswald may be involved somehow. You should inquire of their city guard whether they know of Lord Oswald's whereabouts."

"That's it?" Deringer asked. "You aren't going to give me anymore to go on than that?"

Erik reached into himself and called upon his power. As the Champion of Truth, he could discern not only whether an individual was lying, but what their true intentions were. "Captain Deringer, if it were discovered that Lord Oswald were part of the crimes committed in Winter's Beak, what would you do?"

Captain Deringer straightened in his seat. "Then I would help bring him to justice in whatever way I could."

Erik listened to the words, but he relied more upon his power to feel the captain's answer. He could sense no guile in the man, and therefore decided to allow him into their circle of trust. "Captain Deringer, what I am about to tell you does not go beyond you. Not even Farnsworth may know of it."

Deringer narrowed his eyes and kept his silence, obviously thinking on the proposition for a moment before responding with a single nod. "I am at your service," he said.

"Several sahale were lured to Winter's Beak recently," Erik said. "They were all murdered. They were found in their human forms, obviously prevented from using their dragon forms to defend themselves."

"Could they have been poisoned?" Deringer asked.

Erik shook his head. "There were signs of definite struggle." The Champion of Truth took in a breath and measured his words carefully. "We believe a shadowfiend to be the offender."

"A shadowfiend?" Deringer asked. "I thought they were all slain?" He looked to Lady Arkyn. "Is not your group's first priority to seek out and destroy shadowfiends and necromancers?"

Lady Arkyn nodded. "We do our best, but a few have managed to remain hidden. Erik and I slew one not more than a few days ago in Pracheloor Cave. We suspect there are others."

"I see," Deringer said. "I will send the dispatch to Winter's Beak. However, if I discover something you should know, how will I get the information to you?"

"Have you ever heard of the Nighthawk?" Lady Arkyn asked.

Deringer nodded. "I have never been able to perform the spell, even with the instructions."

Lady Arkyn screwed up her face and frowned. "But, the summoning does not require magical power to perform. All you have to do is read the words as they are on the page."

Deringer put his hands up in the air. "It's never worked for me. I tried it several times, attempting to find you."

Arkyn blushed and then bit her lower lip.

"It won't be necessary," Erik cut in quickly. "If Lord Oswald is involved, then you should move forward and handle it."

"And if he has thrown in with a shadowfiend?" Deringer asked. "I have a few good men, but we are not known for our magical prowess in Gontin. What good would swords do against such a creature?"

A flash of golden light erupted in the room.

Erik stood and drew his sword, Lady Arkyn leapt out of her chair and turned with her bow at the ready, and Captain Deringer pulled his own sword, watching Erik and Arkyn for the signal to strike.

"Forgive the intrusion," a voice called through the light as the line expanded into a portal to another place. "It is I, Njar Somoricliar."

Lady Arkyn relaxed and put her bow down. Erik and Deringer put their weapons away as well.

A large satyr with black fur stepped through the opening. Two lines of red paint streaked downward from his left eye, and a strange design was painted in red upon his right cheek. At his hip was a belt carrying a wickedly curved scimitar. A bow was slung over his left shoulder, and a quiver of arrows poked out over his right. He wore a chest guard of ringed leather, and a special helmet that allowed for his horns to go through two large openings sat upon his head.

"Njar?" Lady Arkyn said as she eyed him.

"Forgive me, it took a long time to locate you both. The Pools of Fate have been tainted, and Nonac is dying."

Lady Arkyn gasped and clapped a hand to her mouth.

Erik knew little of Viverandon, the home of the satyrs in the Middle Kingdom, but he knew enough about Nonac to realize the gravity of the situation. "What can we do to help?" he asked.

Njar shook his head. "I will watch over my people, but I came to warn you. I was attacked in Viverandon, and I now believe I know who is responsible for the attack in Winter's Beak."

"Who was it?" Lady Arkyn asked.

Njar turned to her with sad, golden eyes and said, "Dremathor."

Lady Arkyn stared at Njar with an open mouth.

"Are you sure?" Erik said.

Njar nodded. "I am sorry Erik, but it is true. He came to me at the Pools of Fate. He attacked me there, stole my staff and tainted the Pools. Then, he lashed out at Nonac, the guardian of my homeland."

Erik closed his eyes and shook his head. "This can't be," he said.

"I'm sorry, but I feel a bit out of the know," Deringer said.

153

Njar turned to Arkyn with his face and pointed at Captain Deringer with his hand. "Can he be trusted?" Arkyn nodded. "Very well then." Njar turned to address Captain Deringer. "Dremathor is a shadowfiend, and more to the point, he is Erik Lokton's true father."

Captain Deringer whistled through his teeth. "A sahale and a shadowfiend by blood?" he commented.

Erik shook his head. "Dremathor is *not* my *true father*. As for his biological contributions to my existence, a shadowfiend is not a creature made by birth. I am not infected by such filth."

Deringer patted the air and shook his head, instantly realizing his misstep. "I'm sorry, forget I mentioned it."

"Dremathor is dead," Lady Arkyn said.

Njar nodded. "He willingly gave himself," he said. "His life essence was allowed to be consumed by another, in the hopes of aiding a younger, troubled soul. At the time, I thought Dremathor's actions pure, but now it appears as though he had ulterior motives all along that I failed to see."

"I'm sorry," Deringer started, "I don't follow. What do you mean he allowed his essence to be consumed?"

"A young shadowfiend had lost his way in this world. He was being manipulated by a coven of witches. They used his thirst for revenge to twist him and control him. They promised him great power, but did not fully inform him of the repercussions of his actions. The boy's name is Eldrik Cedreau."

"Eldrik is the one who murdered my father," Erik said.

"Dremathor?" Deringer asked, obviously struggling to keep up.

Erik shook his head. "No, I do not claim Dremathor as my father. He is a disgrace, and was not the man who cared for me. I speak of my true father, Trenton Lokton."

Deringer nodded. "So Eldrik murdered Lord Lokton. Then how did he come upon Dremathor?"

Njar sighed. "That was my doing. I have ever been a meddler. I have often sought out wayward souls and worked to bring them back into balance with the natural order. Many years ago, I worked with Dremathor. Eventually it appeared as though I had gotten through to the human part that remained deep within the shadowfiend. He ceased preying upon others, and began to live a reclusive life, taking an oath to set things right at some point if the opportunity ever presented itself that would allow him to atone for his sins in some degree. That opportunity eventually came, when Eldrik, already turned to a shadowfiend by the cunning witches, wandered into Dremathor's lands. Dremathor sent the boy to me, and made the boy swear to work with me.

"I worked hard with Eldrik, who had taken to calling himself Aparen by that time. It was not an easy feat, but eventually I managed to show him the error of his ways. He made a grand recovery, and even proved to tip the balance in the war against Tu'luh the Red."

Erik nodded. "Eldrik helped me defeat Tu'luh at Fort Drake."

"You worked with a shadowfiend?" Deringer asked. "But, I have never heard of that before. Why is it not widely known?"

Erik scoffed. "Those who write the history of our kingdom deemed it unseemly to give a shadowfiend credit for saving the realm. Those who survived the battle, which were few, were led to believe that Eldrik was a magical illusion used to distract Tu'luh while I alone engaged the dragon in battle. The truth, is that without Eldrik, we might have very well lost that fight."

"Yes," Njar said. "Men are often apt to omit the true method of victory if it would tarnish their own glory and perceived honor."

155

"Where is Eldrik now?" Deringer asked.

"Far to the west," Njar replied quickly. "He sought a life of peace after the war, and has established a small community where people of all kinds can find rest. Were we not in such a hurry to find Dremathor and stop him now, I would call upon him for help, but he is too far away to summon."

Deringer nodded. "Very well, so how did Dremathor give his life essence to Eldrik?"

Njar nodded solemnly. "As part of Eldrik's final rehabilitation, there was a last ritual and test. Dremathor offered his power to Eldrik. I assisted with the transfer. Eldrik had turned from evil by then, and was dedicated to helping Erik fight against Tu'luh the Red. At the time, I thought Dremathor was offering himself for the good of the cause, and to help atone for the wrongs he was guilty of by giving his power to Eldrik. It appears I overlooked something, however, for Dremathor has found a way to cheat death, and he has returned as strong as ever."

There was a silence in the room then for many moments. Erik looked to Njar, and then to Lady Arkyn. The satyr would not meet his gaze, and Lady Arkyn could only shrug helplessly.

"You know," Deringer said. "It is said that the greatest trick the devil ever performed was to convince the world that he did not exist. Perhaps there is something to that in this case."

"Yes," Njar replied sourly. "It would appear so. Thank you for the golden wisdom of men." The tone in his voice was enough to convince Deringer to sit down and keep his mouth shut.

"What will you do?" Arkyn said, pointing to Njar's sword.

"I have had a change of heart," he said. "Once, I sought balance, but now I seek justice."

"Are the two not the same?" Lady Arkyn replied.

"No," Erik answered for Njar. "They are not. Balance requires mercy. True justice does not understand the concept of mercy."

Njar nodded. "I am going after Dremathor, and I am going to stop him."

"Where is he?" Erik asked.

Njar replied, "I located him in the south, at his old tower. I will go there, and hunt him."

Erik grunted. "Should we go with you?" he said. The idea was a stark departure from their plans to travel northward to find the Cult of Zammin at the base of the Impassable Spine mountain range, but Erik was starting to connect a common thread. "If my sahale blood comes from Dremathor, but Dremathor himself could never change into dragon form as his gift was latent, then could it be possible that he is the one who murdered the thirteen sahale in Winter's Beak? Perhaps he is trying to awaken the gift in himself by taking it from others."

"It is possible," Njar said. "However, I did not sense that kind of power within him. Though my gift is not as advanced as yours with regard to discerning a person's full powers, I am fairly talented in my own right, and I would like to think that I would know if he had consumed sahale essence."

"We could aid in defeating him in either case," Erik offered.

"And what of Alkantar?" Njar asked.

"We slew Alkantar," Erik reported. "While in Pracheloor Cave, we have discovered clues that will lead us north to find the Cult of Zammin."

"You believe they are involved?" Njar asked.

Erik nodded. "I don't know how deeply, but it would appear that the magic used to keep sahale from shifting into their dragon forms originates with the Cult of Zammin. But, if Dremathor is the Dark Sahale…"

"The Dark Sahale did you say?" Njar echoed as he reached up and tugged gently on his goatee. "Where did you hear that expression?"

"From Alkantar," Erik replied.

Njar sighed heavily and shook his head. "I have heard whispers of such a thing, while using the Pools of Fate over the years. I..." Njar turned and looked at Lady Arkyn. "I thought I had taken sufficient steps to avoid that particular fate."

"What do you mean?" Erik asked.

The satyr turned back to face Erik. "When I choose to work with individuals who are, let's say, on unrighteous paths, I prioritize those that have been shown by the Pools of Fate to have far-reaching effects throughout the world. The Dark Sahale was something I worked very hard to avoid." Njar tugged harder at his goatee, pulling all of the coarse hair taught and dragging his chin downward a bit. "No... if such a thing were still a danger, I should have known through the Pools of Fate. I..."

"What can you tell us?" Erik asked.

Njar shook his head. "No, not yet. Let's focus on the tasks at hand. I will continue with finding Dremathor and putting an end to his treachery. It would make sense that Dremathor would have a larger network in order to pull off the kinds of attacks he has. The Cult of Zammin is a secretive bunch, and they are excellent at shielding themselves from observation. Even the Pools of Fate have never been able to pierce their veils and shadows. Though, from what I have learned of them over the years, I am surprised to hear that you believe them to be involved. I have seen them as similar to satyrs, seeking balance rather than power and dominion."

"Times change," Erik said. "Perhaps they have strayed from what they used to be."

Njar sighed. "Well, then this is where we part ways for now. You should go northward. Find out what you can about this magic that can bind sahale to their human form, and whether they have any connection with Dremathor."

"I do have a personal interest in them as well," Erik said with a nod. "So long as you are certain you can handle Dremathor on your own. It appears they may have knowledge about the Four Horsemen that exceeds anything else I have access to."

"The Four Horsemen…" Njar repeated as he grimaced in disgust. "That is a subject that has haunted me all my life."

"You cannot go alone," Lady Arkyn said.

Njar shook his head. "I am not alone. While most of the others in Viverandon did not believe me, I do have a few loyal warriors following me to slay Dremathor. I promise you, when the day is over, Dremathor will not stand victorious. Go north, discover the secrets that cult is hiding, and rid the world of that terrible spell they have. If it continues to spread, who knows what other kinds of magic can be created that would hurt not only the sahale, but perhaps other dragon kin as well. We must not allow a wedge of division to come between men and dragons. The Middle Kingdom cannot stand if it fights itself."

"May the Gods favor you," Erik said out of habit after living with the Monks of the Southern Light for so long.

Njar smiled. "I do not lean upon the Old Gods, young friend. I draw power from Mother Terramyr herself, and believe me, she is as wroth as I. Dremathor shall fall."

With that, Njar stepped back through the portal and the opening vanished, leaving the three alone in the room once more.

"Why wouldn't the other satyrs trust Njar?" Erik asked Lady Arkyn. "I sensed no deception in his words. What was it they couldn't see?"

Lady Arkyn shrugged. "We'll have to ask him the next time we see him. In the meantime, once we finish our business in the north, we will need to return and see if there is anything we can do for Nonac. If the old sentinel is sick, then the satyrs are in far more danger than Njar is willing to admit."

"I see now why you two keep secrets," Captain Deringer said with a thoughtful nod as he stared blankly at the table. "I will work on finding Lord Oswald, and I will consider myself lucky that my task is not as complicated as yours."

"If you want an added twist, then just think on the fact that Dremathor is, in fact, the son of Allun Rha."

Captain Deringer frowned and pointed at Lady Arkyn. "You mean, *the* Allun Rha?" Lady Arkyn nodded, smiling slyly. "The one who defeated Tu'luh the Red at Hamath Valley over five hundred years ago?"

"The same," Lady Arkyn replied.

"So that makes you…" Captain Deringer turned to point at Erik. "You're the grandson of Allun Rha?"

Erik nodded. "As you said, we have complicated lives."

Deringer rolled his eyes and pushed back from the table. "Allow me to lead you to Rafe. I think I have had enough talking for one night."

Chapter 12

Njar and his seven warriors stepped through a golden portal and out onto a tall hill overlooking a lush forest. The air was cool and soft, blowing gently from east to west.

"Where do we find the shadowfiend?" one of the satyr warriors asked.

Njar smiled and shook his head. "First, we must find his tower. It is hidden with a spell, as it was in the past when he was alive." Njar pointed out across a marshy valley.

"I see nothing," the satyr replied.

"Precisely," Njar replied. The satyr chief knew that if Dremathor were still counted among the dead, then the tower would have been plainly visible, for Dremathor's magic that hid it would have ended.

"Does he know we are here?" another satyr asked.

"If he does, then he is staying his hand," Njar said. He hoped that the wards and charms he had cast would be enough to conceal their arrival, but he had no way of knowing for sure. He scanned the ground below the hill, looking for any sign of movement. He knew that Dremathor had been a powerful shadowfiend in life, capable of commanding hosts of skeletons and other creatures. Of course, if Njar's experience at the Pools of Fate was any indication, then Dremathor now controlled beings even more deadly. "When the sun sets there will be a few moments when the light of dusk will help me identify where he is. All invisibility spells have reflections, you just have to know where and how to look when the sun is in the right position."

"And then we attack?" the satyr warrior asked.

Njar nodded. "And then we attack, with full force."

The other satyrs paced back and forth, whispering words to spells and practicing their sword strikes. Njar could sense their nervousness, but he did nothing to quiet them. Better to let them be nervous for a while, as fear could be a powerful motivator, if harnessed appropriately.

They waited while the sun began its descent in the west. Orange and pink hues lit up the clouds as if by fire. The puddles of water below reflected the beauty, but Njar did not allow his focus to be turned from his task. He scanned for the slightest anomaly. As the colors of the sky began to turn to red and purple hues, Njar saw the telltale wavy lines rising from the valley below. It was subtle, like a mirage one might find while traveling, but unmistakable to the experienced satyr.

He raised his right hand and uttered the words of a revealing spell. A massive, silver bolt of lightning streaked down from the clouds and dashed itself into the mirage with a great clap of thunder. Immediately following the thunder was a high-pitched shattering sound, as though a great window had been blasted apart with a metal rod. The waves disappeared from the land to reveal a simple, round tower of black stone.

"Not exactly what I expected," one of the warriors stated.

"Do not be fooled by the simplicity of its design. This tower has been the death of thousands," Njar said. He then turned and smiled at the warriors beside him. "However, I should note that not one individual from those thousands were satyr. I have been here before, and I know the way. Stay with me, and we will win the day!"

The satyrs raised their weapons and their fear melted from their faces, replaced with determined gazes that emanated with power and courage.

"Come on, we don't have much time before he will be able to repair his spell." Njar rushed down the hill, with the warriors close behind him.

Once they reached the valley floor, they began running much faster. The grass *whooshed* around them with each step as the knee-length blades swiped their furry legs. They leapt over a brook to land in marshy grass and lilies, but they were nimble animals capable of traversing many different types of terrain without slowing down or losing their footing. The mud and muck sucked in with each step, trailing grime and pungent black goo behind their hooves. The acrid smell of death and decay assaulted Njar's nostrils, but he ignored it, as did the others.

Ahead and to the right, an arm bone reached up from a puddle of murky water. Bones continued to snap and pop into place as a skeleton rose from the liquid. Njar whispered a spell and a blast of lightning struck down from the sky and obliterated the skeleton, sending bits of flaming bone all around the puddle.

Two more creatures rose up, but Njar had chosen his companions well. Magic fire consumed the skeletons in an instant, and the group did not so much as slow their pace as they continued through the pitiful defenses guarding the outer part of the marshy valley.

Another skeleton rose from the ground several yards off and prepared to hurl a javelin, but Njar sent a blast of blue fire at the creature, exploding its skull and knocking the rest of the bones to the ground.

"On the left!" one of the warriors shouted.

Njar turned to see a massive snake making its way toward them with unearthly speed. Each of the satyrs managed to dodge the gargantuan serpent's attack, but Njar had to dive head first into a thick puddle of black water and sticky mud. The grit and grime rubbed into Njar's fur, but he didn't have time to clean himself. He could hear the snake turning around and heading back in for another attack. The thing was at least thirty feet long, and nearly as thick as a tree trunk. Njar quickly pushed himself up to his feet. The ooze clung to his skin, creating a string of slime between his fingers and face as he wiped the muck away from his eyes. The snake was hurtling toward him, but the other satyrs launched into action. They blasted it with spells and hacked at it with scimitars and halberds.

The snake died as quickly as it had appeared.

The ground trembled then as something squirmed beneath the surface. Njar stared at the ripples in the black water for a moment, trying to understand what was happening. Before he could react, a second snake burst out from under the ground, shooting through a black puddle and taking one of the warriors down with its massive fangs. Only the dead satyr's lower legs stuck out from the snake's mouth as it continued to emerge from the hole in the ground.

A second satyr rushed in, but the snake turned its plate-sized, yellow eye on the satyr and the warrior was turned to stone.

"Basilisk!" one of the other warriors shouted.

Njar quickly averted his eyes from the massive monster. All of the satyrs turned and fled, knowing that to look into the basilisk's eyes meant a quick and unavoidable death. Njar sprinted for all he was worth, heading still for the tower. As he did so, he called out instructions to the others. "Summon dartwings!"

He wove the spell in the air with his fingers, but he didn't dare stop to see his creations. Small, cat-sized creatures with small, leathery wings appeared with each utterance. Their blind, white eyes would render the basilisk's main power useless. The dartwings each shrieked terribly as they sensed the basilisk's presence. Njar could hear the beating wings tear at the air as the dartwings launched their assault.

He had never before fought a basilisk, but he knew enough about dartwings to understand that the two creatures were mortal enemies. The satyrs summoning a horde of dartwings was somewhat analogous to desert tribes in the south using a mongoose to slay a cobra. The dartwings would tempt and taunt the powerful basilisk, all the while remaining unharmed by the basilisk's eyes, and when the moment was right, they would strike and kill the monster before devouring its carcass.

A mighty hiss erupted behind Njar, and several dartwings shrieked and screamed. He had to fight his urge to turn and look, knowing that even a passing glance of that deadly basilisk's eye would mean his demise, but it was difficult. He had always wanted to see a battle between the two creatures.

Fortunately, the basilisk was entirely consumed with fighting the dartwings, and Njar was soon rejoined by the other five surviving warriors.

"We have to hurry," Njar said as he pointed to the tower. The wavy, mirage-like lines were rising from the ground again, obscuring his view of the tower. Njar called upon the lightning once more, but a strange shield around the tower flashed into view, stopping the lightning in the air several feet above the tower with a horrendous thunder-clap that almost ruptured Njar's eardrums.

More skeletons rose from the murk and muck, but the satyrs dispatched them with relative ease. Off in the distance behind them, the screams of the basilisk became more frenzied and pained.

A gray cloud gathered around the top of the tower, sucking the wind toward it and making a loud, humming sound as it gathered strength.

"Watch out!" Njar shouted as he noticed the magical assault forming above them. He strengthened his wards around the group just as a hail of fire and ice rained down upon them. The blocks of ice shattered against an invisible shield and the fire spread out across it, hissing and smoking in desperation as the satyr's magic kept them safe.

A large group of skeletons, clad in rusty armor and holding broken, but still deadly, swords and axes, rose up between Njar and the tower. The undead creatures clanged their weapons on old, decaying shields and opened their clicking jaws in a silent yell of defiance. Had any of the monsters actually had voices, Njar was certain they would have sounded quite menacing, but as it was, their futile attempt at a rally cry served only to embolden Njar and his warriors.

"Nothing stands in our way!" Njar shouted.

All of the warriors began weaving their hands in the air as best they could without sheathing their scimitars. Lightning, fire, and other spells flew toward the throngs of skeletons before them. Bones and armor shattered upon impact. Smoke rose from the ash piles and sparks exploded from broken bits of metal and charred bone.

The skeletons ran forward. There must have been two hundred of them, but the spells cut into large numbers with each strike. The satyrs ran forward, undeterred. The skeletons were reduced by two thirds before the two groups clashed at the base of the tower.

Njar spun and took the head off of three skeletons before leaping up into the air and pummeling a fourth with his solid hooves. The skeleton's armor bent inward, and then the ribs cracked and shattered. Njar came down with his sword, splitting the skeleton's skull in half, and then he sent another round of lightning through the enemy force. Blue and green fires erupted through the enemy as the other satyrs worked not only their scimitars, but their magic as well. Within seconds, the skeletons were defeated.

The satyrs erupted with a cheer, but Njar held a hand up to quiet them.

The skeletons had been a buffer, a diversion to buy Dremathor more time.

Several dark figures were wriggling up from the ground at the base of the tower. A few more were oozing out of the stone wall itself, forming into shape only after slithering between the cracks in the mortar.

"Wights," Njar said.

"Terramyr help us," one of the warriors exclaimed.

Njar sheathed his scimitar and held his hands out, palms down toward the ground.

"Protective circle!" one of the warriors called. As Njar knew they would, the others formed a defensive buffer between him and the forming wights. They would buy him whatever time they could, so that he could perform his spell.

"Mother Terramyr, giver of life and progenitor of souls, hear my words," Njar spoke as he used his power to reach down into the ground. As his energy moved down into the earth, another force rebuffed him, pushing him away. As he had expected, the very ground around the tower was cursed. "Mother Terramyr, giver of life and progenitor of souls, hear my words!" Njar repeated louder. "I call upon you..." Njar's words stopped as he realized that the words of this spell were not why he was attempting to summon the world's energy. The original spell called upon Terramyr, and her energies, to help restore balance, but that is no longer what he was after. Njar sought justice. Njar sought an end to all evil. There was no more place in his heart for merely struggling for a harmonious balance.

Evil was not a natural force, like death, which could be balanced against an equally natural force such as life. Evil was not the counterpart to good, but the absence of good. One could never strive for balance between something and nothing. There was only the massive void, threatening to swallow everything in its darkness. Evil had to be destroyed, pushed out of Terramyr, and replaced with good.

"Mother Terramyr, I call upon your strength to enact justice!" Njar shouted. He pushed his powers deeper into the earth, reaching down into the ground and fighting through the forces struggling against him. He had to connect with the power that lay deep below the surface, and bring it up to aid him. In Viverandon, such a feat was easy, routine even. He could use the power to restore dying flowers, or heal the sick in his home. Here, however, Dremathor's blight had scarred the land, and made it dead. The very ground refused to yield to its master.

The wights attacked. Their screaming and wailing was matched by the sounds of scimitars slicing through sinew and shattering bones. Magic exploded around him, but Njar did not so much as open his eyes. He trusted in his warriors and focused all of his energy on reaching the heart of Terramyr.

"Grant me the power to bring justice!" Njar shouted over and over again.

Something brushed against his back and he heard the dying grunt of one of his warriors, but still Njar drilled deeper with his magic, searching for Terramyr's response. The other warriors shouted spells and commands to each other. The wights continued to scream and hiss.

"You cannot win," a voice said as a cold, deathly wind floated across Njar's face. "This is my home, the seat of my power. You couldn't even stop me at the Pools of Fate."

Njar ignored the taunt and focused harder on his magic. He pushed everything he had deep into the ground. Columns of green energy flowed from his hands and pulsed downward into the murky ground.

He smiled when he heard the shrieking dartwings enter the fray.

"They're attacking the wights, keep up the pressure!" one of the warriors shouted. The sound of claws tearing at flesh joined in the cacophony of battle. Njar called out to Terramyr once more, begging her for power. With his eyes closed, he did not see that she was already responding. At his feet, around the two columns of light, blue and yellow flowers were beginning to spring forth and bloom as Njar drove the curse out of the ground.

Something sharp scratched Njar's leg and he felt his right calf go numb. He cried out and almost fell, but shifted his weight to his left leg just in time.

"Terramyr, Mother of all Living, HEAR ME!"

Something took hold of Njar's energy. It seized it, and then squeezed hard. His body jerked forward, nearly toppling to the ground as he struggled to maintain his spell. Then there was a feeling of great swelling. The ground beneath his hooves rose upward and trembled. The wights screamed as the satyr warriors shouted rallying cries and pressed the attack. The dartwings were silent now, likely slain by the savage wights. Njar's focus remained on his spell. He had to reach Terramyr's power. It was the only thing he knew capable of clearing the wights and granting him access to Dremathor.

A mighty, deep rumble churned the ground and then there was a massive explosion. It was not a physical explosion, for the ground did not erupt or break apart, but there was a great ball of green energy that expanded outward from Njar's position as quickly as a burst of lightning and as hot as a rush of magma. The wights shrieked and then were obliterated. The tower cracked and crumbled, and the very sky flashed white as if lit by the brilliance of three suns, chasing away the incoming darkness of night.

Flowers and vines grew up from the ground, snaking over Njar's hooves and out from him in a wide radius until the entire valley was cleared of the murky marshes and healed with lush, beautiful land.

Njar, breathing heavily, fell to his knees. A vine with white flowers grew from the ground and covered the scratch on his leg. Instantly, the feeling came back to his leg and his strength returned to him. To his horror, all of the satyr warriors, save one, had been slain by the wights. Their broken bodies were covered with vines similar to the one that healed his leg, and then pulled into the ground.

"They shall be remembered," Njar said. He looked to Rajeh, the one remaining warrior, and saw the satyr's wounds. He had been paralyzed. His left leg was broken in two places, and there were bite marks on his chest and shoulder. Blood streaked down his furry face, but the satyr only smiled.

"I am honored to have been a part of this," he whispered.

Njar looked to the tower and felt a surge of power rush through him. "Your part is not yet done," Njar promised.

A nest of vines slithered out, growing over Rajeh's body. His wounds healed and he gasped as his lungs took in a great breath. The vines stood him up, and he found himself whole and ready to fight.

"What shall two satyrs do to me?" a voice cried out over the now lush and flower-filled valley. "You have broken my tower, but *I* still live!"

Njar rose to his feet and stared as the rubble of black stones was pushed away from the pile and Dremathor stood, apparently unhurt.

"I had hoped I was incorrect," Njar said as he surveyed Dremathor. "I had hoped that my visions at the Pools of Fate were wrong, and that you had remained dead, with your honor intact." Now, seeing Dremathor in person, Njar knew for certain who it was. He had the same dark skin, the brown, hate-filled eyes that Njar had seen the first time they had met in person, and he was very much alive. He even wore his customary red silk robes and a pair of green velvet shoes that had long, up curled toes that peeked out from under the robes.

"You should not have doubted," Dremathor replied. "I have returned, and I am not to be done away with so easily. Now, one of us must die."

Njar nodded. "Justice shall be served this day," he said. "Then I shall restore Nonac, and your efforts shall be for naught."

Dremathor laughed wickedly. "Nonac! The old tree is dead already."

"No, it fights your disease."

Dremathor shook his head. "Silly satyr, always so sure of yourself and your visions that you fail to suspect that someone else might have the upper hand. There was a traitor in your midst, and while you have come here to assault my home, I let you deal with my servants while I finished my assault on yours. Viverandon has fallen, and I have feasted upon the souls of your kin."

Njar trembled with rage. "No! I was just there! Nonac lives, and you lie!"

Dremathor sneered. "Silly goat. You once helped me die to ease my pain." The shadowfiend held his hands out wide. "Let me return the favor."

"NO!" Rajeh shouted and rushed forward. The satyr slashed through Dremathor and the robes fell to the ground, empty.

Dremathor's laughter echoed over the valley. "Your friend is right, enough talk." Dark clouds rolled in from every direction, dispelling the light Njar had brought.

"We need more help," Njar muttered. As if in answer to his plea, four areas on the ground began to glow a bright, vibrant green. From the dirt rose a sprout in each area. The four sprouts grew fast and strong, thickening and multiplying as they reached twelve feet in height. Then they branched out and formed arms and legs. Atop their wooden heads, a pair of

171

satyr horns grew out, and the faces of those who had fallen to the wights grew from the wood and smiled at Njar.

"We are here, Njar Somoricliar. Mother Terramyr has heard you."

Njar turned as shouting erupted from far off behind him. Two more tree-like creatures emerged from the ground, one pulling a basilisk fang from his shoulder, and the other shaking off flakes of gray stone.

"You have an army, Njar, allow me the same courtesy," Dremathor's voice called. The clouds thickened and black lightning struck the ground in several places around the ruined tower. The black stone from the rubble was pulled out toward the black lightning, and formed into strange creatures of stone, bound together by magic.

Njar pulled his sword once more and turned to the large warrior-trees around him. Rajeh signaled for the creatures to follow him. The ground trembled as they ran toward the stone golems. Everything crashed together in a battle unlike anything Njar had ever witnessed before. Stone golems would break off a tree-warrior's arm only to have the tree regrow and come back stronger. The tree-warriors shot out strong vines, strangling and holding the golems in place while the stone creatures ripped through the vegetation. It appeared they were at a stalemate, with Rajeh hopelessly hacking at the rock with his scimitar and dodging their savage blows.

The satyr chief looked to the sky and uttered the words of another spell. A green beacon of light erupted from the ground beneath him to pierce the great clouds. Dremathor was there, hiding in the vapors above the ground.

"Come down and fight me fair, you coward," Njar shouted.

Dremathor shook his head. He pulled his hands back and gathered balls of silver and black lightning, allowing their strength to build before discharging them toward Njar. The satyr called upon Terramyr's power, pulling a wall of earth up between him and the magical assault. Dirt and turf exploded around him, but the lightning did not make it through. Njar then summoned large plants under himself. A great, sturdy leaf unfurled beneath his hooves as the stalk shot upward. With his left hand, he held onto a branching vine for stability, while his sword was ready in his right hand. The stalk shot upward at an alarming speed, reaching up over the wall of earth and careening for Dremathor before the shadowfiend realized what was happening.

Dremathor shouted angrily and spun in a fury of smoke and mist. When he emerged a second later, he had great, bat-like wings, four arms, and two harpy-like legs replete with talons. He opened his fang-filled mouth and issued forth a bout of fire, but the stalk grew a shield of leaves and thick, green stems that blocked the flames.

The growing plant slammed into Dremathor and drove him upward. Dremathor clawed savagely at the vegetation, but the vines grew back twice as fast as he could cut through them, ensnaring his arms and wrapping around his waist and neck. Njar was lifted out as the leaf he stood upon dropped him upon a stretching vine that snaked out and around the entangled Dremathor.

"It ends here," Njar shouted as the vine shot toward Dremathor. The shadowfiend only barely managed to turn his head to see Njar before the satyr chief plunged his scimitar deep into Dremathor's back. The tough hide gave way and allowed the blade to slice through the softer tissues underneath until it slipped through the back of the ribcage and through Dremathor's heart, and finally out the front of the creature's chest. Dremathor howled in pain as fire erupted from his wound. Njar put his left hand onto the handle of his weapon and used all of his strength to twist the blade inside Dremathor. He felt the ribs struggle at first, and then pop as they broke under the pressure. Dremathor shrieked in an unearthly manner before his body began to spasm.

Njar ripped his bloody blade free of the shadowfiend and watched as the giant stalk he rode upon shot vines into Dremathor's open chest. They threaded themselves out the back and then wrapped around and plunged down the anguished Dremathor's open mouth. Within seconds, he was entirely consumed by a mess of vines. Then, as if that weren't enough, Njar lifted his hand to add his magic. Each of the hundreds of vines sprouted sharp, knife-long thorns, cutting Dremathor's screams short.

The shadowfiend was dead.

The remaining clouds dissipated and the stone golems below crumbled to dust.

The giant stalk gently returned Njar to the ground, and then sprang back upright, growing yellow, blue, and purple flowers along its trunk and many vines.

Rajeh approached with a smile on his face. "It is over," he said.

All six of the tree-warriors were with him, smiling with their wooden faces and bowing to Njar.

"There is one thing left before we can return home," Njar said. He turned and sheathed his scimitar as he looked out at the expanse of the cleansed valley. He reached into a small pouch at his belt and pulled a single seed, that of an aspen tree. He bent down to the ground and planted it. Rajeh knelt beside Njar and the two held their hands over the seed, uttering the words of a prayer so sacred and ancient that it has no written words. When they were done, the first aspen grew out of the ground and reached for the sky. When it attained its full height, it stretched out with branches and unfurled magnificent leaves of gold and green.

"This will be the first of many," Njar said. "The aspens will ensure this valley remains clean."

Rajeh nodded and placed a reverent hand on the new tree.

174

"We must stay," one of the tree-warriors said sadly. "Our purpose is fulfilled."

Njar looked to them with tears in his eyes. "I am sorry to have lost you all. You have performed with honor, and helped our people more than I can ever explain."

"We will not disappear," a second tree-warrior said. "We shall remain here, in this valley. Should you have need of us again, return to this tree and whisper your prayers to Mother Terramyr. Then we shall come."

Njar watched, astounded as the tree-warriors walked to the new aspen tree. They each placed their wooden hands on the tree's trunk, and then vanished.

"Mother Terramyr has created a new race," Rajeh said.

Guardian spirits of the world," Njar said with breathless awe. "We have been favored today." He then thought of Nonac, and his mind recalled the words which Dremathor had spoken. "Come, we should return home." He walked away from the tree, Rajeh close behind, and opened a portal to Viverandon. He was overjoyed to see through the portal that everything was intact. The sun was shining brightly, for even though it was night in the valley were Dremathor's tower had been, night and day behaved differently in Viverandon than in other places on Terramyr. The sun could be called upon at almost any time, according to the will of those living within Viverandon. Njar smiled as he saw satyr younglings playing in the fields.

"All is well," Njar said. "All is well."

They stepped through the portal, happy to return home victorious, and anxious to find a remedy for Nonac.

Chapter 13

By all accounts, Erik found Rafe to be a relatively ordinary man. He had long, black hair pulled into a single braid at the back of his head, spoke with an interesting northern accent, and no more looked like a daring adventurer than he did a simple fisherman. Yet, his skill with their ship was more than obvious. Rafe by himself could do what Gerald and his daughters did as a team, and he was faster at it. The ship was a little smaller than Gerald's, about sixteen feet long with a single center mast, but it looked no less complicated to pilot than Gerald's to Erik's untrained eye. Rafe worked the rigging and the wheel without requesting help at all the first day. Erik couldn't be sure how far they had traveled, but it seemed they were going much faster than Gerald's ship. The prow of the ship almost bounced off the incoming waves as Rafe carried them across the water.

Lady Arkyn sat on a bench overlooking the starboard side of the ship, seemingly lost in thoughts. Given the lull in activity, Erik thought it appropriate to see what answers he could get about Captain Deringer. He went below deck and grabbed some bread and dried meats, along with a water skin, and then went to her.

She noticed him coming and offered a smile, but Erik could tell by the way her eyes seemed to remain fixed on a distant point that she was deep in thought.

"So, Captain Deringer seems to be a good man," Erik said, hoping he was breaching the subject lightly enough.

"Subtlety is not your strong suit," Lady Arkyn replied with a laugh. "If you want to know about him, just ask directly."

He offered the waterskin, which she took and drank from. "You two have history," Erik stated. "I was curious, that's all."

"It was a long time ago, in human terms at least."

Erik took a bite of bread, chewed and swallowed, and then said, "Didn't seem to be long enough for him."

Lady Arkyn took a bit of dried meat and held it in her hand. "It wasn't a long relationship. It was not even an entire summer. I was never as committed to it as he was. Sometimes men have a hard time letting go."

"Or maybe that's just your effect on us poor, helpless souls," Erik teased as he took a drink.

"Ah, so now you think I have some sort of charm spells at my disposal?"

Erik smirked and closed the waterskin. "You charmed Deringer pretty well, me too I suppose."

Minrielle fidgeted with her left glove. "So in the last couple of years, you haven't changed your mind?" Lady Arkyn asked.

Erik shook his head. "No, why do you ask?"

Lady Arkyn shrugged. "I don't know. I guess because you asked me to give you some space. I wasn't sure if that had more behind it than you let on. Four years of 'space' could be enough for a man to change his mind."

Erik went quiet and looked out to the water. Wanting to be alone had indeed had many reasons behind it, but none of them had to do with her, exactly, at least not in the way she was making it sound. He had only wanted to keep her safe, and to keep her from seeing a part of him that he didn't like, and wasn't sure how to control or come to terms with. He tried to think of how to explain it as she watched him stare at the open sea.

"Did it?" Lady Arkyn pressed.

Erik shook his head. "Not in the way you think," he said. "It was a lot of things, but mostly it was just me trying to understand who, or what, I was, and am. Like I mentioned back in Gontin."

"Because of the war against Tu'luh?" she asked. "Many warriors have nightmares after such experiences. And, if you are talking about what Alkantar and the other demon said, then you already know my feelings on that. You are a man of good character. All of us struggle, but you will come out on top in the end."

Erik nodded. "Not only that, but that is a large part of it. I am still worried about the Four Horsemen. I have this nagging feeling that they are going to come, and that there is nothing I can do to prevent that."

"That will be long after our times have ended," Lady Arkyn said.

Erik shook his head. "But that's just it," he started. "I am sahale, that means dragon blood flows through my veins. In very much the same way that you would outlive any man you chose to be your partner, I will live long after you have…" he couldn't bring himself to say it.

"Is that perhaps part of why you asked me to leave? You're afraid of my death?"

"No," Erik said with an exasperated sigh. "I'm not explaining it right. You and I have talked about life many times. I know that you, despite having a longer life span than humans, have learned to take joy in the moment, and not worry so much about the future. I am trying to do that as well. With you, I think I could be happy for as long as we're together, but it is the fact that I will live for hundreds, maybe thousands of years beyond that which bothers me. You may not be here when the Four Horsemen come, but I very well may be. I have seen so much suffering already, I don't want to watch the end of the world."

"You mean, you don't want to be helpless to stop it," Lady Arkyn said.

Erik nodded. "More than that," he said. "Sometimes, in my dreams, I actually help them destroy our homeland."

"Preposterous," Minrielle said quickly. "Those are just nightmares, nothing more than your own fears being processed by your mind while you sleep. You should not give them so much power over you."

"I am trying to work out the problem as best I can," Erik said. "But I have only been able to find a couple of clues here and there. So far, everything I see points to the fact that they are unbeatable. Even the gods shy away from their power. No one understands them, and no one can stop them."

"So we take joy in the moment," Minrielle said. "We do what we can to right the injustices of this world while we live, but we understand and accept that the end might come any day. Maybe today, maybe next week, or maybe a thousand years from now. The appointed time of its coming doesn't matter nearly so much as how we live our lives in the meantime." Erik smiled. He always felt better after talking to her. She smiled at him and took his hand. "You have people who love you back at Lokton Manor. Perhaps after this you should return home and see the good you have brought about there."

Erik nodded. "That sounds good."

"So," Lady Arkyn started with a coy smile. "Do you have anyone in your past I should be aware of? After all, you were alone for four years."

179

Erik laughed and nodded playfully. "There was this one orc princess, actually. She had great teeth and a wonderful set of muscular legs."

"Oh!" Minrielle broke off a piece of bread and tossed it at Erik.

He responded by shrugging and taking another drink. "Her name was Griselda," he added after he finished drinking.

"I'm sorry I asked," Minrielle replied. "Don't let me keep you from your green-skinned lover. Please, by all means, return to her arms once this is over. Just watch out for those tusks when you move in for a kiss." Minrielle shook her head and looked out at the sea.

"No, I think I will go home, as you suggest," Erik said.

"Oh, well, then take her there. I am sure Braun will be pleased to serve an orc mistress."

Erik laughed again. "Actually, I was hoping you would join me," he said. Erik reached out and took her left hand in his.

Before Lady Arkyn could respond, Rafe cut in with a warning shout.

"We are coming up on Natchy Moors. You two should get below deck."

Erik gathered the food while Lady Arkyn sighed.

"I have always tried to avoid the Natchy Moors," she said. "If we weren't in such a hurry, I would have had us sail two days out to the west just to avoid them."

"What are they?" Erik asked. "You didn't mention them when we spoke with Captain Deringer or Rafe."

"There is not a good explanation for them," she replied. "To some, they are considered to be the manifestation of Hammenfein within the mortal realm. To others, they are considered cursed."

"Neither sound like good choices," Erik said as he looked off to the north. He could just make out a thick curtain of fog rising up from the waters near the far horizon.

"Come, we will need to do as Rafe says. Don't worry, he has gone through them once. He'll get us safely to the other side."

Erik and Lady Arkyn quickly went below deck.

*****

Njar struggled to open his eyes. A terrible, high-pitched ringing assaulted his ears and his head was pounding. As he took in a breath, the air burned his lungs. His fur was matted to his skin with a thick coating of sweat, and blood trickled from his nose and lip.

What happened? Njar wondered. The last thing he remembered was stepping through the portal and… He rubbed his sore eyes and forced them open. The air was boiling hot against the soft tissue of his eyes. He recoiled and covered his face as he closed them against the pain. The burning in his nostrils and lungs grew worse as he continued to take in breaths. He began coughing and choking. His mouth was dry and all of his joints hurt. He couldn't think clearly with the ringing in his ear growing louder. He tried to move his legs, and only then realized that he was lying on his side. He felt the ground with his hands and opened his eyes just narrowly enough to see the ground while avoiding the intense heat.

The earth below him was dry and covered with scorch marks. Ash swirled along the ground, driven by the currents caused by the high temperatures in the air. An ember landed on the back of Njar's right hand. He stared at it blankly at first, and then shook it off when it melted some of his black fur.

Where am I? He got onto his hands and knees and then pushed up to a kneeling position. The difference in temperature he experienced on his head and neck compared with the lower parts of his body was astounding. If it was hard to breathe before, it was nearly impossible now. He lowered his head toward the ground, fighting against the fit of coughs that beset him. After he regained control of his breath, he stayed low to the ground and looked around, forcing himself to open his eyes enough to see his surroundings.

There was a ditch of some sort a few meters ahead of him. It looked familiar, but he couldn't quite place it. He crawled toward it, curious about its familiarity. As he peered down from the side, he saw a sliver of water at the bottom of the ditch. This had been a stream of some sort.

He looked up along the length of the ditch and saw a pair of cement footings. They were both cracked and broken, but he knew they had once held a bridge. He looked to the other side of the ditch and saw another two footings, although in worse shape than the closer pair.

Everything looked so familiar. He was sure he knew the place. He turned around, but saw only a vast, open stretch of dry land. There were no plants or buildings of any kind. There were wisps of smoke rising from the ground and smaller piles of ash lining the dirt in various places, but nothing recognizable.

Njar tried to summon a protective shell around himself, but his magic failed him.

"Too tired," Njar told himself absently. He slowly rose to a standing position, giving himself several seconds with each couple of inches he moved upward so he could try to adjust to the intense heat of the air. When he finally was upright, he held a hand before his eyes and spun around in place. The land was so foreign to him. Smoke and vapors rose up from the ground, riding the great thermal energy upward to the gray sky. There were no animals or structures that he could see, but yet he felt as though he should understand where he was.

He walked away from the ditch for several meters, searching for any clue of what had gone wrong. The last thing he remembered was the portal. He had been on his way home. Rajeh had been with him.

"Rajeh!" Njar called out.

No answer.

The satyr chief put his hands to his mouth and shouted at the top of his lungs. "Rajeh!" Still no answer. He walked down a gently sloping hill until he came to a large depression in the ground. The earth here was black, as if burned by a dragon.

But what dragon would do such a thing?

Was he in the wastes near Demaverung? If so, how had he gotten there?

Njar's heart caught in his chest as he thought about a particularly gruesome option. Perhaps he had stumbled into Hammenfein. Perhaps Mother Terramyr had not approved of his quest for justice after all, and he had been sent to face the hell fires of the Old Gods. There was no way for him to know. He walked toward the large depression in the ground and carefully descended into it. The further down he went, the cooler the air became. He was more than a little happy to have escaped the terribly hot air above, and was able to fully breathe easily once he reached the bottom of the fifty foot deep hole in the ground. He looked around and marveled at the size of the depression. It spanned several hundred feet before him, and at least half that to either side of him.

He decided to cross the depression, choosing to use the cooler air to help regain his second wind before climbing out the other side and continuing his trek out of wherever he had mistakenly teleported himself to. He walked along, marveling that there was no ash in the bottom of the depression. To be sure, bits of ash and dead embers were beginning to float down into it now, but there were no piles or lines of ash as there had been on the higher ground.

Perhaps this depression had been a lake.

That would make sense with a stream nearby.

Njar walked along the bottom of the depression, his hooves sinking in the dry dirt beneath and kicking up a bit of dust. Then, as he reached the center of the dry lake bed, his hoof struck something hard. Njar frowned and glanced around himself. He couldn't see any structures nearby, but the thing under him felt as solid as metal. He bent down and cleared the dirt away with his hands. As he moved the pale, brown dirt to the sides, he started to see something cylindrical emerge. He hurriedly brushed it off and revealed a golden rod.

The fog left his mind and he now knew exactly where he was. This was no golden rod. It was his staff. The same staff that Dremathor had taken and hidden at the bottom of the Pools of Fate. Njar grasped the staff and yanked it free of the dry lake bed, his mouth agape and his eyes filling with tears. If this was his staff, then he was standing in the Pools of Fate. The vast wasteland above was Viverandon.

"NO!" Njar shouted as he sprinted back the way he had come. He clambered out of the dry lake bed, ignoring the heat and allowing it to sear his lungs as he ran back toward his devastated home. As he pictured Viverandon in his mind, he realized that the piles of ashes coincided with where houses had once been.

"NO!" Njar cried as he fell to his knees. "This has to be some sort of trick! This is an illusion, that is all."

"There is no illusion," a sly, wicked voice called from behind him.

Njar wheeled around, staff ready for battle. There stood a man, his face hidden by a large hood. "Dremathor! How could you still be alive?"

"Misdirection is one of the first strategies of battle," the voice cackled. A pair of bony, white hands reached up to pull the hood back.

Njar narrowed his golden eyes on the man before him and attempted to use his staff to summon a great blast of lightning. No sooner had the spell materialized, than it backfired and struck Njar full in the chest, launching him several yards backward to thump onto the scorched ground.

"Did you honestly think Dremathor worked alone to achieve this?" the man said as he floated toward Njar. "No, my meddling friend, I say he did not!"

"I know you," Njar said. "Your true name is Gondok'hr."

Gondok'hr laughed and nodded. "Quite right, Njar Somoricliar, quite right."

Njar struggled to get up, but found his body lacked the strength.

"Let me show you something," Gondok'hr said.

A rush of air whisked by as Njar was flung away from his spot. A mere two seconds later, he landed on the ground next to a large tree. Njar saw the gray, dead bark on the massive tree and knew at once that Nonac had fallen.

"I wanted to thank you for letting us into your home," Gondok'hr said. "It would not have been possible without your help."

"Why?" Njar asked breathlessly.

"Why?" Gondok'hr repeated with a wicked grin. "Because you are in the way."

"I did not betray Nonac!" Njar shouted. "You infected me. I had no knowledge of my condition."

Gondok'hr shrugged. "It makes no difference. You were a useful pawn in any case." The warlock held his arms out wide and smiled. "Njar Somoricliar, the last satyr chief! How quickly do the mighty fall!"

Njar pressed himself upward, using his willpower as much, if not more than his physical strength. "Dremathor is dead!" he shouted as his right hand reached down and pulled his scimitar. "And I shall reunite you with him."

"Valiant, but I think not," Gondok'hr said. He raised a hand and gathered a dark ball of energy in front of him.

Njar struggled to step forward, but then a voice entered into his mind.

Hold still.

The satyr froze, confused by the command. Who was left alive that could speak with him by mind? None of the satyrs could communicate like that except for him, and he could only speak in that way with one other entity.

Forgive me, I could not see.

A mighty root emerged from the ground, flexible and moist from hiding so deeply in the earth. Gondok'hr wailed in frustration and launched his spell, but the root was faster. It shot out and whacked Njar across the chest. A blinding light erupted around him, and Njar realized that Nonac had used its power one last time, except instead of transporting all of Viverandon to a new location, it was only sending Njar. The satyr chief whispered his thanks just as the ball of dark energy slammed into the root, shattering Nonac's last limb, and finally slaying the great giant.

Njar landed hard on the ground at his destination, but managed to stay conscious just enough to look around. He found himself in a lush bed of ferns and tall, soft grasses. Flowers nearby attracted a few large bees, and birds sang overhead. Wherever he was, he was safe, for now. His eyes closed as he swore he would exact justice on Gondok'hr. Fatigue overtook him and he lost consciousness.

*****

Erik and Lady Arkyn remained below deck as strange wailing sounds came from beyond the door. Something scratched along the hull of the ship and then snarled loudly.

"Shouldn't I go up and help?" Erik asked.

"No," Lady Arkyn said. "The monsters here are not real, at least, they don't have bodies you can kill."

"If they were illusions, I would know," Erik said. "I am the Champion of Truth, and Marlin taught me how to do away with such magic."

"You are powerful, there is no disputing that fact," Lady Arkyn said. "But the world is vast and wide. I think the more you leave the Middle Kingdom, the more you will find that you are not all that powerful after all."

"You're saying I can't dispel these illusions?" Erik asked.

Arkyn nodded. "There is always something more powerful than you somewhere. Natchy Moors happens to be one place where I think you would find your skills and powers wanting."

"Then I can shift into dragon form and fly us all out of here. I could hold the vessel with…"

Lady Arkyn was already shaking her head. "The things out there will prey upon your mind, and play tricks upon you. Flying over it makes no difference. The evil will come for you whether in the water or above it."

"Manifestation of Hammenfein in the mortal realm," Erik repeated as he resigned himself to sit below deck helplessly. He then pointed to the door. "What makes Rafe so different?" Erik asked.

Lady Arkyn shrugged. "Some say that if you have no fears, then you can sail through the Natchy Moors, others say you need a special charm. Either way, Rafe is the only man I know of who has done it and returned to tell the tale. Many others have tried, but they have all perished. If we were to go above deck, you would see countless wrecked ships in the few moments before you went insane and the monsters took hold of your mind."

"If they are so powerful, then what prevents them from coming down here and getting at us anyway?" Erik pressed.

"Rafe said he lined this room with mithril. It keeps the monsters out."

"Wait, behind the wooden walls of this cabin is a sheet of mithril lining the entire hull?" Erik asked.

Lady Arkyn shook her head. "Not the entire hull, just this room. If we pass through the door leading up to the deck, or through the other door leading to the sleeping quarters, we would be vulnerable to the magic that taints these parts.

"I have seen mithril used like that before," Erik said. "In Valtuu Temple, they used a similar technique to protect Nagar's Secret, the book that held the spells Nagar and Tu'luh used to enslave the minds and hearts of living and dead creatures."

Lady Arkyn shivered as a talon or claw of some sort scraped along the outer hull. "Yes, mithril protects against various types of evil, but it has to be sealed to be most effective. That's why Rafe locked the door to the cabin from the outside."

Erik nodded. Something bumped into the bottom of the ship, knocking the vessel up and to the side. "For not having corporeal bodies, these things sure do pack a punch."

"It's best not to dwell on it," Lady Arkyn said. "Try to relax."

"Sure, I'll just relax inside a metal box that is hidden within a ship that happens to be under attack by sea monsters at the moment. That should be easy enough." It was meant to break the tension, but neither of them laughed.

Something hard scraped along the bottom of the ship. Erik tried breathing slowly to calm his nerves, but that did little, if anything at all to relieve the tension. He nearly jumped when something slammed into the side of the ship.

"Relax, Rafe knows what he's doing."

Erik nodded and tried to think of something to take his mind off of the situation. "Do you think Njar is all right?" he asked.

Lady Arkyn sighed. "I'm not sure. I know enough of Dremathor to understand that if he did somehow come back from the dead, and decided to go back into his old habits, he would be very destructive. Njar is no novice, and his warriors are among the best there are, but I am not sure if their magic would be enough."

"Can't be much more difficult than fighting Alkantar," Erik said quickly. "You and I got through that all right."

Tha-BUMP!

The ship tilted to the side and Erik hit his head on the wall behind him. He grunted and rubbed his head, then returned to the topic of conversation. "He could find us again, after he takes care of Dremathor."

Lady Arkyn cocked her head at him then. "Do you have no feelings for him?" she asked suddenly. "I mean, he is your father."

"He didn't raise me," Erik said quickly.

"You know as well as I do that he didn't abandon you either," Lady Arkyn put in. "Njar and Dimwater hatched the plan to get you away from Dremathor as a baby. With all his faults, he didn't abandon you and leave you at the orphanage."

Erik clapped his hands and leaned forward as the vessel was rocked to the side again. "True enough, but if he had kept me, he would have raised me to become a shadowfiend like him. Then where would we be? I would have been the first shadowfiend-sahale, and who knows what would have happened." As he said the words, he couldn't help but hear Alkantar and the demon from the monastery laughing at him. Perhaps he had been meant to be the Dark Sahale after all?

Something slammed into the side of the vessel, shaking it violently, but not cracking the hull.

Lady Arkyn smiled and nodded.

Erik caught the smile and realized what she was doing. "Ah, clever," he said. "That almost took my mind off of where we were."

"So, above you were talking about the Four Horsemen, do you have anything new to tell me?" Lady Arkyn asked, changing the subject.

Erik shook his head. "Not yet. I'm working on it, but no great discoveries."

"I had not expected Alkantar to talk of them," Lady Arkyn said. "I agree with you. It does seem to be a common theme that follows you in your life."

"Are you changing your philosophy?" Erik asked.

Lady Arkyn shook her head. "No, the present moment is what matters most, but it is an intriguing puzzle to work on. After all, before you were taken from Dremathor, your fate was to become something... well, something terrible."

Erik nodded. He had already learned this from Lady Dimwater. "And now?" he asked as something thumped across the deck above. He looked up. "Should I worry about that?" he asked.

Lady Arkyn shook her head. "It is no more real than the things hitting the side of the ship," she promised. "Now, as to your question about your current fate, I don't know. It's hard to see what might lie ahead of you. Does one escape destiny only to have something else written into the void, or are you free to make your own way in the world? Who is to say?"

"Do you believe in destiny?" Erik asked.

"No, but talking philosophy helps keep my mind off of the noises outside," she answered honestly.

"Well, at least I'm not the only one unnerved by it." Erik leaned back against the wall and sighed. "I don't know, about fate I mean. I used to think I was destined for something great. After the war against Tu'luh ended, I knew that I had done something wonderful, but I couldn't take all the credit for it. In reality I did no more than many others who fought with us."

"You know that isn't true," Lady Arkyn put in.

"Sure it is," Erik replied. "I have some talents and powers that others don't, perhaps, but everyone gave all they had. Marlin, Tillamon, Faengoril, Tatev, Salarion, Master Orres,

190

Gorin, Peren, they all fought with everything they had. Most of them could even say they gave more than I did, since all of them died except for Peren."

"Their sacrifices are great, but they don't diminish yours," Arkyn replied evenly. "We could not have won without you."

"Perhaps," Erik said. "I meant what I told Captain Deringer back in Gontin. Without Eldrik's help against Tu'luh, I don't know that I would have won that final battle."

"So because you didn't do it alone, you feel as though your accomplishments are less deserving of honor?"

Erik shook his head. "No, that isn't it. I just mean that while I used to think I was destined for greatness, I guess I imagined it differently. It didn't feel the way this feels. That may be hard to explain, but I guess I always thought I was something more."

"Something more than a sahale who can race among the clouds and save an entire kingdom?" Lady Arkyn scoffed. "That's a bit of a tall order, Erik."

Erik smirked and nodded. "Yeah, I suppose so." He sat and thought for a moment in silence.

"Lepkin is Dragon-born," Lady Arkyn said after a few seconds. "He has done many great things, but I bet if you were to ask him what he thought of you, he would say you are greater than he is."

That was hard to imagine. Master Lepkin was a living legend. Sure, Erik sometimes received similar treatment compared with how people reacted to Lepkin's presence, but it was hard to imagine Master Lepkin as something less than him. "No," he said as he continued to think on it. "I'm not greater. We just have different roles. He is every bit as vital to the success of the Middle Kingdom as I could ever have been, maybe more so."

Lady Arkyn smiled wide. "In any case, I am sure he would be proud to see that it isn't going to your head."

191

Something heavy slammed into the side of the ship and threw them both to the floor.

"Are you all right?" Erik asked.

"I think so," Lady Arkyn said as she put a hand up to her head. Erik saw a small cut on her forehead that was trickling blood.

"You're cut," he said as he reached out to steady her.

"I'm all right, but something is wrong," she said as she pushed him away. They both looked up and saw that the wood of the cabin wall was broken inward above where she had been sitting. Glistening mithril was visible, dented inward. Worse than that, a tear in the metal was leaking water.

"What in Icadion's name could do that?" Erik asked.

Lady Arkyn shook her head. "I don't know, but I think we are in trouble."

Chapter 14

Erik heard Rafe shouting from the deck. He ran to the door and pulled on it, but it was locked from the outside. The mithril lining in the door was going to be nearly impossible to penetrate, but on the other hand, if he changed into his dragon form, there would not be enough room in the cabin to hold him. The young warrior pulled his sword and ignited the magical white flames. With any luck, he could slip the blade into the gap and pry the door open. Telarian steel would be tested against the lock on the outside of the door.

He took three steps back and then charged the door. The burning blade crashed into the door, splintering the wooden casing and then clanged and jerked to the side as it struck the mithril lining in the center. Despite how thin the layer of mithril was, it turned Erik's sword aside, but Erik was undeterred. He used the momentum to drive his sword into the socket that secured the sliding door and then he pushed against the handle, using the weapon as a burning pry-bar. The flames ate away at the wood, making Erik's job somewhat easier and allowing him more area to maneuver his sword in. The resistance against his efforts was great, but he contracted every muscle in his body and pushed. His stomach tightened as he leaned into the sword and drove with his legs and chest, pushing with all of his strength. The sword stopped moving for a moment, and appeared to be stuck, but then it moved forward, slowly at first, a millimeter at a time as Erik strained against the sword. The door creaked and groaned, and then there was a metallic shattering and the door flew open.

Erik and Arkyn rushed onto the deck and found Rafe embattled with a winged monster that looked very much like an over-sized bat, but with three barbed tails. The black-haired sailor was cut along his left forearm, but otherwise unharmed. He expertly dodged the flailing tails and came up swinging, cutting at the monster's stomach.

Lady Arkyn pulled her bow and fired at a second beast diving down toward Rafe. The arrow struck it in the eye and the monster burst into flames, falling out of its dive and splashing down into the water.

"I thought you said the monsters here were not real," Erik shouted.

"Erik!" Rafe called from his position behind the wheel. "Take the wheel! Most of the monsters are illusions, but every once in a while the Natchy Moors like to throw the real thing at sailors as well, keeps us on our toes!"

Erik charged out into the open, ducking under one bat-creature's diving attack and slicing another's wing with his flaming sword. The bat flopped to the deck, but quickly jumped up to its hind legs. It hissed and bared its fangs as it stood every bit as tall as Erik on the ship's deck. Its left wing fanned out and the bat spun around, lashing out at Erik with its tails. Erik cut through two tails and jumped over the third. He then charged in and ran his sword through the creature's heart. It snarled and hissed as it convulsed and staggered backward to topple over the railing and into the water.

Something slammed into the ship and knocked Erik off his feet. His sword went skittering across the deck, flames vanishing as the weapon lost contact with him. A massive, purple tentacle with thousands of suckers rose from the misty depths on the opposite side of the ship. The tip wagged in the air high above them, and then came crashing down. The deck cracked and splintered in many places as the ship lurched to the side and then came to a halt.

"Behind you!" Lady Arkyn shouted at Erik.

He turned just in time to see a second tentacle careening toward him. He dove to the side, avoiding the slimy appendage by only a few inches as it *swished* over him and blasted the mast apart. The heavy sails above toppled over backward and in turn crashed into the wheel. Rafe was thrown aside, and slammed into the railing. Lady Arkyn moved in with her bow, firing arrow after arrow at the winged beasts hovering around the ship. Each time she struck one in the face, the creature would ignite and fall from the sky.

Erik rushed across the broken deck for his sword, but as the first tentacle ripped and pulled at the ship, one of its suckers snared the weapon and pulled it overboard. The young warrior didn't even stop to think. His instinct kicked in and he sprinted after the tentacle. He was not going to lose his sword to some overgrown octopus!

He dove over the devastated railing and into the water. The cool, salty liquid stung his eyes, but he paid it no mind. The massive tentacle swirled through the water, carrying the sword with it. Erik swam as quickly as he could. A burning hulk of flesh splashed into the water above him, he glanced up just long enough to see the charred remains of yet another bat-monster with an arrow sticking out from its face. He turned back to follow the tentacle and reached out to grab hold of it. The strong limb was softer than he had expected. Softer and much slicker. He lost his grip and came away with a copious amount of clear slime. He reached down and took a knife from his belt and then stabbed into the descending tentacle. A puff of black blood shot out from the knife wound, but otherwise the creature seemed to take no notice of the attack.

The limb dragged Erik down much quicker than he could swim, but it was also going far too deep. Erik looked up and realized the surface was slipping beyond his reach. He could hold his breath for a long time, but in his human form, he would likely not be able to swim back up. Luckily, there was no wizard here who could stop him from transforming.

He closed his eyes and brought his transforming power to the front of his mind. Rather than change immediately, he held the change at bay just long enough to allow the sea monster to bring him in close. He didn't want to scare the thing off before he could strike. Dragons made excellent swimmers, but against a natural being of the sea, he would easily be outpaced. The water darkened around him and the tentacle started to curl away. It was difficult to see through the gloomy water, but as Erik peered ahead he made out a massive form. It moved slowly, as if letting the currents carry its bulk toward him. A flap of skin raised upward, revealing a great, yellow eye that peered back at Erik.

He was close enough to strike.

Erik released his hold on his power and was enveloped in a flash of brilliant light. The sea monster shut its eye and recoiled against the sudden brightness, but Erik completed his transformation quickly enough to reach out and grab hold of four tentacles with his powerful claws. In his dragon form, Erik could pierce the murky waters with his vision clearly. The sea monster was as he had thought, a single creature not unlike a giant octopus, with eight thick, strong tentacles and one eye that stared back at him incredulously. The giant octopus pulled and struggled to free its four tentacles from Erik, and then started to reach forward with its other limbs. Erik knew that he had to win this fight quickly, ere the octopus caught him and drowned him in the sea.

He ignited the fires within his chest and unleashed a torrent of flame into the sea. For the first few seconds, the water directly in front of his mouth hissed and turned to steam as the flames died in the water, but as Erik persisted, spewing with his full force, the fire began to make headway, clearing and vaporizing the sea before him and creating a massive pocket of air. The octopus hissed and screeched, and then the flames bored into its eye. The tentacles went slack and the octopus emitted a cloud of ink as it tried to use its free limbs to swim away, but Erik wasn't about to let the thing go. He gripped tighter with his claws and ripped the four tentacles off, each making a sick, wet *schlo-POP!*

He then used his wings to propel him through the water and reached out through the dank, blueish black ink and seized the octopus by the wounded eye-socket. He clawed into the soft, gooey flesh and then punched his right claws through and out the other side. A copious amount of blood spilled into the water. The creature went limp. Erik turned upward and used his wings to ascend toward the surface while dragging the carcass along with him. He broke the surface with a desperate gasp for air, and then he flew upward into the mist. He heard Rafe utter a curse as the sailor noticed the dead, giant octopus, and then Erik tossed the thing out onto a nearby jetty of rocks. The wet corpse schlopped onto the sharp rocks and jiggled back and forth for a few moments as the last of its life blood oozed out over its purple flesh.

Erik then turned his attention to the winged bats. With a single blast of fire he destroyed seven of them, and the others that remained tucked their barbed tails and sped away.

"Huzzah!" Rafe shouted from below.

Erik turned his attention back to the depths below and then tucked his wings and dove back down. The water slapped his scales and then swallowed him as he shot into the sea like a massive, reptilian arrow. Using his superior sight, he located the sword, still stuck to one of the tentacles which was now resting on a sea vent that rose up from the bottom of the sea. Erik swam down and wrapped his talons around the sword and tentacle, and then he started to swim upward, but he noticed something shift in the depths below. He stopped and watched. There was not much that gave him cause to fear as a dragon, but for some reason he now felt very vulnerable. He glanced upward and saw that he was some two hundred feet below the surface. Whatever he thought he saw below him, was at least twice that far down, where not even his vision could pierce the darkness.

As he watched and waited, careful to remain very still in the depths, perched atop the sea vent, he heard the distinct sound of scales sliding across the ground. The slick, gritty scraping was unmistakable, yet he could see nothing. A rush of warm water came up to meet his body, and then a mixture of air bubbles and dust floated up into view from below. Erik remained still, moving only his eyes to try and discover what was lurking below. He looked out across the expansive sea and saw two additional sea vents some hundred yards away from him. One was spewing hot water and steam upward, the other was silent, pointed upward and unmoving. Preparing to escape quickly, he pulled the sword free from the sucker on the tentacle and decided he would leave the severed limb as bait if need be.

Erik looked below once more. His chest was starting to yearn for air, but he knew his dragon form could hold breath for several minutes at a time even while swimming. He looked down when he heard another slithering sound from below. He couldn't be sure, but it almost looked as if the entire sea floor was shifting in the darkness.

He then glanced up to the vents. To his surprise, a new one was now pointed upward, and standing between the first two. Erik focused on it, and realized that the third one was moving slightly, as if swaying with the under currents, or possibly...

The large, conical mound tilted to point at Erik and revealed its secret. What he had seen was not the birth of a third sea vent, but a great, unspeakably large serpent that had raised its head and pointed upward to match the silhouette of the other two vents. Now that it turned to face him, he could clearly see the narrow jaws, the two large, round nostrils, and the wicked green eyes that were now glowing and glaring directly at him.

The leviathan charged forward, striking out with unimaginable speed. Erik only barely managed to move out of the way and leave the tentacle he was holding in his place as the leviathan crashed through the vent he had been perched on and bit the severed tentacle in half, swallowing the large portion and then turning a grinning face toward Erik. Its evil eyes flicked up and caught sight of the other half of the octopus tentacle, sinking slowly and trailing a small stream of blood. Erik watched as the leviathan's nostrils flared. It attacked the remaining bit of tentacle. As it moved, it brought up several hundred feet worth of its body. Erik could see coils wrapped around the two vents from whence the leviathan had launched its attack.

He now realized why it had seemed as though the entire sea floor was shifting.

This was no ordinary leviathan.

Lady Arkyn had been correct. The Natchy Moors were an extension of Hammenfein, a portal to hell, if you will, and this was the great beast known as Vodklyk. Erik wasn't sure on all the particulars, but he knew that this monster spent most of its time guarding the second level of hell, under Hatmul's direction. He also knew that during the times it spent outside of Hammenfein, it loved to prey upon the hapless sea-farer.

Erik wasted no time. He shot upward through the water, aiming for the ship. Vodklyk hissed and shrieked in a shrill, ear-splitting tone as it flared its spined gill covers and bared its fangs. It was attracted to Erik's motion, but it also noticed the ship. Now they were both racing for the vessel rocking side to side upon the surface of the water.

Erik clawed at the water and beat it with his wings, driving himself upward as fast as he could. Vodklyk wasn't far behind, shooting upward and ripping the tops off of the distant sea vents as he violently slithered around them. Erik broke the surface just behind the ship and continued to ascend without slowing. He snatched out over the deck and seized Rafe and Lady Arkyn in his front claws and persisted to fly upward.

"What in the bloody—" Rafe shouted as he squirmed against Erik's grip.

Lady Arkyn wasn't too pleased either, but they both settled down when a thunderous explosion destroyed the ship and Vodklyk came crashing through with snarling fangs and flared, rattling spines on its gill covers.

"By the gods!" Rafe exclaimed. "It's Vodklyk! I thought he was a myth."

Lady Arkyn remained silent. Erik flew out and away from Vodklyk, but the giant serpent swam quickly upon the water's surface, giving chase.

"Can he traverse upon land?" Erik asked in his loud, deep dragon voice.

"Who cares?" Rafe shouted back. "Just fly west over Natchy Moors. The land will at least slow him down. Don't stop until we reach landfall in the northern territory, far away from this—"

"Erik, look out!" Lady Arkyn shouted, cutting Rafe off.

Erik turned his head to see Vodklyk hiss and jerk its head to the side. One of the spines from the flared set of gill covers on the left shot out like a missile. Erik dodged the first, but Vodklyk sent two more just as quickly. Erik dropped his altitude to avoid being struck by the ten-foot-long missiles.

"Don't go down!" Rafe shrieked. "Go up! Go up!"

"The barbs on the spikes are poisonous," Lady Arkyn warned.

Great! Erik thought to himself as he struggled to twist and turn to avoid several more strikes. Then, just as Erik flew upward, Vodklyk shot out across the surface of the water, passing by below them as quickly as a bolt of lightning crosses the sky.

"Oh- this is not good!" Rafe shouted. "He's in front of us!"

Vodklyk slithered atop a small, smooth outcropping of rock that jutted upward several hundred yards before the safety of the marshy moor beyond. The head and body rose up, equal in height to Erik, and then the fang-filled mouth opened and shot a stream of liquid at them.

Erik threw himself backward and gracefully turned into a dive.

The stream of liquid missed them, but Erik knew he had been out-maneuvered. He turned and beat his wings furiously, heading back the way they had come from. Some portion of the leviathan's massive body rippled upward, breaking the surface of the water. For a moment, Erik thought to attack, but when he saw the ridges of spikes along Vodklyk's back, he thought better of it. The monster was far too large, and just one strike from those spikes would mean death. The body below continued to pulse up and down, as a rope might when you shake one end and send waves down toward the other. Erik already guessed that Vodklyk was preparing to bring its tail up for an assault by the time Rafe made the same assumption and began screaming and slapping Erik's claws. Erik didn't respond to the sailor's frantic panic. Instead, he flew straight along the tail. When fighting with swords, one effective maneuver is the feint. Though Erik was in dragon form, he was outmatched and outpaced, which meant that his opponent might fall for a similar tactic.

He flew hard and straight, allowing Vodklyk to build momentum below by undulating his massive body in preparation for a tail whip. Erik was counting on it, for the longer he could keep the leviathan believing that the tail whip would win the fight, the more time the serpent's head and those cursed spikes would remain back at the rock outcropping.

He flew out beyond where the ship had gone down, and then saw the body start to narrow out. Knowing that he was reaching the end, he swerved off to the north at the last moment. The gargantuan tail came up out of the water just as he had expected, rising one hundred feet above the surface and slapping through the air where they would have been flying had they kept their previous trajectory.

The leviathan's angry snarl ripped through the air and the sea churned violently as the humongous serpent shifted around to chase them once more.

"Fly faster!" Rafe shouted as he slapped Erik's talons some more. Erik shifted his grip a bit so he could curl one of his talons over Rafe's mouth. While he couldn't hear Lady Arkyn's giggle over the sound of the splashing water below and his wings beating the air above, he could feel her body move in accordance with laughing. He grinned as well. A bit of mirth to cut the tension.

The relief was short-lived, however, for the leviathan gained on them even faster than it had the first time. Erik was doing everything he could to make it over a tall, green mountain that rose upward to meet the clouds just beyond the beach, but Vodklyk was coming in hard and fast. Erik's only hope was that the inlet leading up to the beach at the base of the mountain would slow Vodklyk down as the water became shallow. Vodklyk hissed angrily as it crashed through the shallow waters and churned up copious amounts of muck and seaweed. Fortunately, the beach did slow the creature down. Erik turned to ascend over the mountain, climbing hundreds of feet in a matter of seconds.

None of them saw the pair of spikes sailing through the air after them.

Vodklyk let out a final, vengeful snarl and then sank back down into the deeper waters. Erik looked back to ensure the creature was, in fact, retreating, and that was when he saw the two missiles, but it was too late. He twirled around and tried to tuck his wings, but one of the spines ripped through the fleshy part of his wing and severed the middle joint.

Erik cried out in agony as his wing fell limp at his side. They all began to tumble out of the sky, heading for the mountain peak. For several seconds, time seemed to slow and Erik could feel the full brunt of the burning pain in his wing. He couldn't hear Lady Arkyn's screams, or even orient himself. He spewed fire uncontrollably, and gasped for air at the same time. Then, just as his vision started to blur, he saw something on the top of the mountain that helped him calm himself.

Marlin, his very dear friend who had trained him in preparation for the Exalted Test of Arophim, was standing upon the grassy peak, waving and calling out to him. Though Marlin had died at Fort Drake, he looked as healthy and vibrant as ever now, there in the Natchy Moors.

"Erik, this way," Marlin said as he gestured for Erik to follow him.

I can't fly, Marlin. My wing is broken.

Marlin turned and walked down the opposite side of the peak, vanishing behind a veil of mist and fog.

"Marlin, wait," Erik said aloud. He focused all of his effort on stabilizing himself. He flapped both wings as much as he could, and then held them out as straight as possible. He had to fold his left wing into himself in order to prevent his crippled wing from dragging him off to the side, but with great effort, he was able to turn his rapid fall into a semi-steady glide. He passed the top of the mountain, clearing the grass only by a few feet.

"Let go of them," Marlin whispered on the wind.

Erik did as he was told and released Lady Arkyn and Rafe. The two of them tumbled in the soft grass, but both came to a safe stop before the slope on the northern face of the mountain. Erik then tucked his wings and tried to land, but his momentum carried him much farther down the slope. The dense fog made it nearly impossible for him to see clearly, and he struck a tree with his injured wing. The flash of burning pain yanked his mind out of focus and he once again lost control. He crashed down, shattering trees and splitting rocks until he skidded to a stop, digging a deep trench in the soft earth.

He craned his neck up to look at the peak looming high above him now. He could see Lady Arkyn and Rafe coming to his aid, but they were at least a quarter mile from him, and it would take time for them to reach his position.

"Erik," Marlin called as he emerged from the mists once more. "You must change back into your human form. If you remain as a dragon, Vodklyk's venom will kill you."

Erik was too weak to argue or ask any questions. He simply obeyed his trusted friend. His dragon form shrank away, taking the pain of the broken wing along with it, as well as the burning in his blood from Vodklyk's venom. As he lay there, naked and exhausted, his vision closed in around him, and he succumbed to absolute fatigue.

Chapter 15

Erik opened his eyes to find that the sky was dark. A roaring fire was popping and clacking nearby. He turned over and felt something tug at his legs. He looked down and saw some sort of strange patchwork pants covering his lower body, the legs stopping midway down his calves.

"Where did I get clothes?" Erik asked absently, remembering that he had been in his dragon form and the boat with their supplies had been destroyed.

"From my shirt," Rafe said as he walked around the fire, holding a plank of wood with roasted chunks of meat on it. "I figured you needed it more than I did."

Erik nodded. "Thank you," he said.

"How do you feel?" Lady Arkyn asked. "I have been monitoring you for fever, but you haven't had one, and I can't find any sign of the poison in your system. No swelling, no necrosis, nothing."

"Marlin said I would be fine once I changed back," Erik said, not realizing how it would sound to talk of a ghost.

"Who's that now?" Rafe asked as he set the plank of wood in front of Erik.

Erik glanced to Lady Arkyn. "I saw Marlin, in the mist," he explained.

Lady Arkyn sighed and looked to Rafe. "Marlin was the Prelate of Valtuu Temple. He died at Fort Drake several years ago."

Rafe nodded in understanding. "Many people see ghosts out here. Best not to trust them, the Natchy Moors are known for tricking even the strongest of minds."

"No, it was him, I know it," Erik said.

"Just, don't be so sure," Rafe suggested. "Maybe it was your friend, maybe it wasn't, but the next time you see him, it might not be *him*."

Erik reached out and took one of the pieces of meat. He plopped it into his mouth and chewed. It tasted like juicy, soft chicken. "What is this?"

"Found a moor croc while you were sleeping," Rafe said. "He and I had an argument about who was going to have dinner and who was going to *be* dinner." Rafe then patted a large, wide-bladed knife at his belt. "I won the argument."

Erik smiled. It was nice to see that Rafe had quickly rediscovered his courage after being chased by Vodklyk. Erik glanced around, seeing they were nestled in a grove of tall pines, and then looked to Lady Arkyn. "And Vodklyk? Any sign of the monster?"

Lady Arkyn shook her head and pointed toward the south. "After we crash landed, he did try to follow us, but we found a cave and hid inside. When he finally realized he couldn't get at us, he left and went back for the giant octopus carcass."

"Good thing you killed that other monster, gave Vodklyk something else to chew on," Rafe said as he took one of the pieces of meat off of Erik's plate. "That cave was the worst. We were all huddled inside for a day and a half, just hoping he wouldn't shoot one of his cursed spikes down into the hole at us—or spit that stinking acid stuff at us." Rafe's eyes went wide for a moment as he stopped everything and looked into the distance, obviously considering how close they had come to a horrible death. A moment later he shrugged it off and continued chewing his bite.

"A day and a half?" Erik asked. "Where was I?"

"We took you with us," Lady Arkyn said. "We couldn't very well leave you out in the open."

"Vodklyk came around the base of the mountain a few hours after we got to you. He was a lot slower on land, but still fairly deadly," Rafe said.

"Rafe carried you on his shoulders and I found the cave," Lady Arkyn explained.

"Thank you," Erik offered.

"You would have done the same for us," Lady Arkyn replied with a smile. "Now eat your food, you need your strength."

"Tomorrow we'll find our way out of this mess," Rafe added.

Erik ate another piece and then glanced at the trees around them. "Why are we out in the open now?" Erik asked. "What if Vodklyk returns?"

"Unlikely," Arkyn replied. "After eating the giant octopus, it is likely satisfied enough for now. Large snakes can live weeks on a single meal, I see no reason to believe Vodklyk is any different," she said.

"Except he is large enough to destroy ships in a single bite and guards the second level of hell," Erik replied evenly. "He isn't exactly a *normal* large snake."

Lady Arkyn shrugged, but didn't argue the point. "We were in the cave for a day and a half, but we have been traveling northward for another day. We have seen no sign of him, and we are within a couple days' travel of the northern beach."

"From there, we can try to make a raft and get across the channel to the northern territory," Rafe said. "Should be smooth sailing once we leave this place behind."

A shrill howl split the night air.

207

"Wolves?" Erik asked.

Rafe shook his head. "Banshees, but don't worry, they won't come near the fire."

Erik nodded and plopped another piece of meat in his mouth. He then dropped down onto his back once more and swallowed the food in his mouth. He closed his eyes, only intending to rest for a moment, but the next time he opened his eyes, it was morning.

The sun couldn't be seen through the thick fog, but the light did make it possible for them to see about twenty yards ahead of themselves. Lady Arkyn checked her bow and arrows while Rafe stomped out the last of the campfire embers.

"Morning sunshine!" Rafe said cheerily. "I should have warned you, moor croc can make you sleepy. Best not to eat too much at a time."

Erik pushed himself up and looked around for his sword. He was about to ask where it was when Lady Arkyn approached him and held it out.

"Looking for this?" she asked.

Erik nodded and took the weapon in hand. He strapped it around his waist and then checked it by pulling on the handle just enough to ensure it wouldn't stick in case he needed it. He took a couple of steps and realized that his naked toes were sinking into the spongy grass beneath his feet.

"I was going to make you some shoes," Rafe began, "but I don't have the right tools. The moor croc skin takes too long to cure, and I don't have equipment to work pine wood with."

"It's all right," Erik said. "I'm just happy to have some pants," he added as he lifted a knee and patted it for emphasis. "Which way?"

Rafe pointed to the north. "We make as straight a line as possible," he said. "If we're lucky, we can make the northern shore of this wretched place in two days, and then we can skip across the channel and happily find ourselves in the northern territory."

Without another word, the three began marching across the marshy ground, with Rafe in the lead, Erik in the middle, and Lady Arkyn bringing up the rear.

The fog made it so that Erik couldn't get much of a feel for the land. They occasionally came across sparse copses of trees, but there were not thick forests or expanses of undergrowth. Just wet, murky grass clumps separated by boggy mud and patches of murky water. Strange howls and cries cut the silence, but they sounded far off. Erik was about to ask if they needed a torch during the day to keep banshees at bay, but Rafe offered the explanation that such creatures slept during the day and would not bother them until nightfall without ever being asked.

After about three hours of walking, they crossed an odd section of ground that appeared to be made of sand and small bits of stone. The grains crunched under foot similarly to the way sea shells crack on stone when walked upon along a beach. Erik looked down at the sand and realized that the sand was, in fact, made of tiny bits of sea shells that had been crushed and ground down over time. The longer he studied the ground, the more shell fragments he started to see clearly. As they continued walking north, the fragments became larger and more frequent. Finally, they came to an incline made almost entirely of large shell fragments.

"Rafe," Erik said. "I think we should go around."

"Why?" Rafe asked.

Erik pointed to the ground. "Look, it's made of shells."

Rafe stopped and stared at the ground for a moment, and then his mouth went slack. "We're walking into a feeding ground." The three of them turned to go the other way, but they found a pair of large, blue-feathered birds as tall as Erik standing in the sand behind them.

"I didn't even hear them," Lady Arkyn said.

"Are they real?" Erik asked.

"Oh yeah," Rafe answered. "The monsters in the sea are fake, but the ones on this island are as real as they come."

"The ones we fought in the sea didn't seem so fake to me," Erik pointed out sourly as he slowly drew his sword.

"Well, the giant bats, octopus, and leviathan were all very real, but the ones that were attacking the ship before I called you up were fake, illusions brought about by our fears," Rafe clarified.

Each of the birds had an exceedingly long middle toe, tipped with a thick, curved claw that looked capable of slicing through a man as easily as a hot knife through butter. They were large, nearly as tall as Erik and Rafe from head to foot, with big, thick bodies covered in blue feathers. They had wings, but they were stunted, and appeared to have left these birds flightless. Large, red flaps of skin hung over the back of their heads, and a strong, yellow beak came to a fine point in the front. The birds eyed the group warily for a moment, then, seemingly disinterested, turned and walked away into the mist.

"That went about as well as we could have hoped for," Lady Arkyn said as she relaxed the tension in her bow string.

A chattering click came from behind. The group turned around to see an odd looking mammal creeping toward them on all fours. It was somewhat like an otter in shape and size, but longer in the body and with spikes along its spine. It clicked and clacked with its mouth, and then stood up on its back feet and let out a series of short, loud, clicks.

The mound of sea shells stirred beneath their feet as several more of the creatures burrowed up from under the surface all around them.

"This is not good," Rafe said calmly. He drew his sword and took a step backward, scanning the group of thirteen animals as they slowly advanced in on the trio. Lady Arkyn pulled back on her string again, but Erik had the distinct impression these animals were far too quick to go down easily.

He drew his sword and summoned the raging white flames as he let out a yell and charged the nearest spined creature. He swung his sword at the animal and it turned tail and sprinted away, loping up the slope and disappearing in the fog. The others clicked and chattered for a moment or two, and then did as the first had done.

"Nice call with the fire," Rafe said. "Looks like it scared them off."

"We should hurry before they return," Lady Arkyn said.

Erik and the others quickly made their way out to the west, not slowing their pace until they had found marshy grass once more. By then, the fog had thickened so much that it was difficult to see more than ten feet in any direction, and sometimes it was impossible to see even that far. The trio had to move slowly, using their ears to scan for danger more than their eyes. They persevered in a northerly direction until they came to a long, bubbling stream of black goo. Round bubbles forced their way to the surface, slowly pushing the viscous ooze out of the way and bursting above the stream with a release of green smoke.

"Don't use your flaming sword here," Rafe cautioned. "I have heard of this before. It's like a peat bog, but the gasses it emits are flammable."

"How do you know?" Erik asked.

"Family secret, if we live to reach the northern territory, I'll tell you."

Erik shrugged and looked to Lady Arkyn. She returned the gesture and scanned around. "We should look for a way to go around it," she said. "It's too wide to jump."

Rafe nodded. "We go east, then," he said.

"That's going to take us closer to those strange animals with spikes," Erik reminded him.

Rafe smiled. "Well, if they come after us, then you have my permission to light them, and the gas, on fire so we can all go out quickly and as painlessly as possible."

"Comforting," Erik replied.

Something caught the young warrior's eye a short ways off in the fog. He peered at the movement and reached for the hilt of his sword, but he relaxed when he saw Marlin standing in the mist. The departed prelate waved to Erik.

"Come this way," Marlin said.

Erik nodded and started to walk toward him, but then thought better of it. Rafe had warned him about this place playing tricks, and so far he had seen very little here to show him that anything was docile. Erik called upon his power as the Champion of Truth. He reached out with his innate gift and inspected Marlin. During training, Erik had been taught how to handle precisely this predicament. Marlin had once created doubles and illusions of himself and forced Erik to find the real Marlin. It had been difficult at first, but as Erik had grown comfortable with his powers, he had been able to tell the difference between illusions and the real Marlin with complete accuracy, regardless of whether there was only one illusion, or one hundred.

In this instance, Erik felt confident that this was the real Marlin he knew and loved. How it was possible, he didn't know, but if this place was accessible by demons from Hammenfein, then perhaps a good spirit could make their way to this place as well, and help the weary wanderer lost in the fog.

"Come," Marlin said. "Danger approaches. Come quickly."

Erik nodded, but thinking back on Rafe's warning he decided to use another test just to be sure before following Marlin. "What was the name of Valtuu Temple's librarian?" Erik asked.

Marlin cocked his head to the side and looked at Erik with his dull, gray eyes that he had had in life. Erik was a little confused to see that the man's natural color had not been restored after death, but then, he knew little of what happened to a person after their mortal life ended. "Tatev," Marlin said. "He had red, curly hair, and a love for books."

"And what were the special glasses he used?" Erik asked, referring to a magical instrument.

"The Eyes of Dowr," Marlin replied. "Now please, Erik, we must hurry."

Erik smiled and nodded. It had to be Marlin. No island could conjure up illusions that could both read minds and trick Erik's powers of discernment. This was Marlin, the same man who had helped him so many times in life. Erik reached out to stop Rafe as the sailor began walking toward the east. "We go the other way," Erik said confidently.

Rafe drew his brow into a knot. "No, we go this way. At least we know what awaits us if we find the sea shells again. If we go west, we could be walking into more dangerous territory."

Lady Arkyn stepped in close and agreed with Rafe. "If the spiked otters have built a home for themselves, then they are likely the most dangerous predators in that area, and possibly those strange birds we saw. If we go the other way, we might find whatever scares them enough to keep them in the east."

Erik shook his head. "But Marlin is here, he is telling us to go west. Look." Erik pointed toward Marlin. The others turned and looked, and then glanced at each other before Rafe shook his head and sighed.

"There is nothing there," Lady Arkyn said.

"Well," Erik began, "I can see him. Maybe he only appears to me. Come on, I used my power, I know it's him."

"Whatever powers you think you have, you should understand they won't work correctly here," Rafe said.

"Wizards have come to conquer this place only to find their spells impotent and their powers absolutely defunct. Come on, let's go."

Erik started toward the west. "No, we must follow Marlin." The ghost of the prelate was still waving him on, but it had turned and was now fading into the mist. "It's him, I know it is. He helped me when Vodklyk broke my wing and poisoned me, and he is helping us now."

"Rafe, perhaps we should listen to Erik," Lady Arkyn said. "If he says that he can see him…"

"Erik, don't go into the mist," Rafe warned.

"Come on," Erik said. The mist closed in around them. Rafe walked a bit to the east, and Erik tried to run a few steps to catch Marlin. Lady Arkyn stood in the middle, glancing between the two men. "Marlin, wait up!" Erik shouted. He had only gone three steps when the fog turned icy cold and thick as soup. He could still breathe, but with each inhalation came not only air, but a palpable amount of moisture. He spun around and rubbed his bare shoulders.

Lady Arkyn and Rafe were gone.

"Can you see me?" Erik shouted into the mists.

No answer.

"Rafe?" Erik shouted.

"We're here!" Lady Arkyn answered. She should have been only a few feet away, but her voice sounded distant, at least two hundred feet away. "Where are you? We can't see you."

Erik reached down to pull his sword free. He could light the flames and use it as a beacon for them, but he stopped short. He was still close to the odd stream of black goo with flammable gasses. If he lit his sword, he might inadvertently light the gas.

"Here," Marlin's voice said. "Come along this way, I will help you find them."

Erik turned and saw Marlin standing in the thick, cold mist. Not knowing what to think of the sudden change in the area around him, Erik called upon his powers of discernment once more. Still, they told him that Marlin stood before him, offering sincere help. "Is it really you?" Erik asked.

Marlin nodded. "Of course it is, but come, we don't have much time. The cassowacks are coming."

"The what?" Erik asked.

"The cassowacks," Marlin replied with a slight frown. "The giant blue-feathered birds you saw earlier. They prey upon animals, and they are highly territorial. The only reason they didn't attack you is because they recognized the area you were in as belonging to the spiked koshots. Had you still been in the marshes, the cassowacks would have attacked you for certain, and they are not only large, but extremely silent, as you have already discovered. Come, we must get you across the stream."

Erik nodded. He followed Marlin through the mist. The prelate's ghost could only go a few steps before waiting, otherwise Erik would lose sight of him, but Marlin was careful to remain close.

Lady Arkyn and Rafe continued to call out, and Erik would answer them, explaining that Marlin was helping him locate them. Their voices sounded closer with each call, but Rafe was still very disapproving of Erik's trust in Marlin.

"He isn't your friend!" Rafe kept yelling into the thick vapors.

Erik ignored him and continued to exchange progress updates with Lady Arkyn instead. At least her voice was pleasant and she was happy to have any help that brought them all back together. Within a few minutes of wandering in a snaking pattern through the mists, Lady Arkyn and Rafe broke through the fog and nearly stumbled into Erik.

"How did you get so far away from me?" Erik asked.

"I told you, this island plays tricks," Rafe replied. "Now, where is this Marlin fellow I keep hearing about?"

Erik pointed to Marlin, who was standing just a foot behind Rafe. Rafe turned and looked, Marlin waved, but Rafe apparently didn't see, for the sailor turned back around and glared angrily at Erik while shaking his head.

"You still can't see him?" Erik asked.

"You're blindly following an apparition that likely wants to eat you. I suggest you wise up, and fast," Rafe snarled.

"I say we follow Erik," Lady Arkyn said. "I trust his judgment."

The fog started to clear away to the west, so the trio continued that way, Rafe begrudgingly murmuring all the while.

"Don't mind him," Lady Arkyn said as she wrapped her arms around Erik's. "If you say that you can see Marlin, then I believe you."

"Thanks," Erik said.

Marlin walked beside them for some time, silently scanning the area around them and glancing back over his shoulder as the fog seemed to close behind them. Erik felt more than a little comforted to have him there. After a few moments, Erik realized that other than getting hopelessly lost in the mist, there were no pressing dangers, so he gave in to his curiosity, and started asking Marlin questions.

"Tell me what happens when you die," Erik said. "Is there not a way to reach Volganor?"

Marlin shook his head. "Volganor is sealed off from Terramyr. There is a Plane of the Dead, to which many souls find their way, but it is not the same as the Heaven City. It is a sort of limbo, where souls wander and socialize with each other. A few of the strong ones can remain here, and sometimes we are permitted to help those in need."

"How did you find me?" Erik asked. "I mean, how did you know I would be here?"

Marlin smiled with his milky eyes twinkling at Erik. "You find it surprising that I would watch over you, my young friend?"

Erik shook his head. "No." Still, as he thought about Volganor, he remembered that Hiasyntar'Kulai had taken his mother and father across whatever gulf there was between Terramyr and Volganor. Surely there had to be some way across, even if only the Ancients could traverse it. "The Father of the Ancients took my parents to Volganor," Erik told Marlin. "After the battle at Fort Drake was ended."

Marlin nodded. "Yes, I am aware of that."

Erik paused mid-step. "How did you know that?" he asked. "That occurred after you had been..." Erik couldn't bring himself to finish his sentence.

Marlin swept his arms out wide. "As a spirit, I am not bound by my previous limits of knowledge. I can see many things. I have been at your side since the day I was slain in battle at Fort Drake," Marlin replied.

Erik resumed walking. The answer seemed like it should satisfy him, but Erik had trouble fully accepting it. Marlin had been very wise during his lifetime. He had extensive knowledge of many subjects, but Erik had never once heard him speak about the afterlife in such terms as this. There were several occasions when comrades had died when Marlin could have comforted them with the knowledge that certain spirits were able to linger on as guardians... but he had never approached the subject like that before.

"I can see what troubles your mind," Marlin said suddenly. "In my spirit form, I can read your thoughts as easily as if you were speaking."

Erik stopped walking again. Lady Arkyn tugged on his arm.

"What's wrong?" she asked.

"Just a moment," he replied as he held up a finger. "Marlin, if you can read my thoughts, then how do I know it's

217

really you? You could have given me the answers I needed by taking them from my own head."

"Exactly!" Rafe shouted. "Now you're getting it."

Marlin stopped and sighed as he looked at Rafe. "He does not trust me, and I do not blame him. If you wish, I will allow you to scan me with your gift another time. Or, if you are untrusting, then I can leave. I will not force you to follow me. While alive, I never forced you to trust me. The choice was always yours. I am the same man still. Make your choice, and I shall abide by it."

Erik smiled. No, this was Marlin. He extended his hand outward toward Marlin. "No, it is you. It is good to see you once again!"

Marlin put his hand out to take Erik's, but his form went through Erik's hand with an icy chill. "Ah, sorry," Marlin said with a sheepish smile. "In my enthusiasm for seeing you once more, I forgot I cannot interact with you physically."

Erik shrugged it off and motioned for Marlin to lead the way.

"Is everything all right?" Lady Arkyn asked.

Erik nodded. "It's him, I am sure of it. Marlin will lead us to safety."

They walked for another hour before Marlin stopped and waved good-bye to Erik.

"I'll find you again, if necessary," Marlin promised. "You should be able to work your way around the head of the stream from here without me. The cassowacks have lost your trail. Best of luck, and tell Lepkin hello for me when you see him next."

Erik nodded. "I will for sure, but, do you have to leave us so soon?

Marlin nodded. "It is difficult to remain visible to you. Those of us in the spirit realm are meant to be hidden from those still alive. Continue on, and you should be all right."

"Before you go," Erik started. "Can you tell us why the giant octopus and Vodklyk came after us? I had been under the impression that the monsters in the waters were all illusions, meant to drive sailors mad and cause them to wreck upon the rocky outcroppings."

Marlin gestured toward Rafe. "As your friend has said, most of the time that is true, but sometimes the corporeal monsters do come out as well. Vodklyk is known to prowl the waters from time to time. Perhaps it was merely an unfortunate coincidence, or maybe the dark forces sensed your presence and wanted to come out and test your abilities, I am not certain. You have ever had a gift for finding danger. Now, I must go, I am growing weaker."

"Thank you, my dear friend," Erik said with a smile. Marlin then disappeared and the fog to the west lifted nearly entirely, allowing for the three of them to see their way around the end of the stream of black ooze.

"All right, I admit we should have come this way from the beginning," Rafe said. "Sorry I doubted you, Erik, it's just that I know a lot about the Natchy Moors, and I thought west would lead us into certain peril."

"No worries," Erik replied. "Let's just keep moving."

They walked around a large, pond-like spring of babbling and schlurping ooze making its way up out of the marshy ground and slowly pushing downstream as bubbles of green gas broke through the surface and erupted in the air above.

As they rounded the back of the spring, Erik heard something approaching from behind. He turned and saw two cassowacks running toward them. One of the birds squawked and redoubled its speed.

"Cassowacks!" Erik shouted.

Rafe and Lady Arkyn turned around and prepared to fight. Lady Arkyn pulled her bow and Rafe drew his sword, but before they could launch an attack, Rafe called out a warning.

"More!" Rafe shouted.

Erik spun around and saw seven of the creatures running toward them from the other side of the spring of ooze. Marlin was right, the birds were extremely sneaky. Erik pulled his sword.

"Careful, no fire," Lady Arkyn said.

Erik nodded. "I'll take these two back here, you both work on the larger group."

The two cassowacks slowed when they saw Erik's sword. They squawked and pawed at the ground with their long, deadly claws, but they didn't come closer than fifteen feet.

"Kill them!" Lady Arkyn shouted as she loosed her first arrow. A cassowack made a sound like a honking goose and then stumbled to the ground.

Erik advanced on the two cassowacks slowly. He didn't want to be out-maneuvered and flanked by the pair of large birds.

The cassowack to his right squawked loudly and pawed at the ground frantically. It then extended its right leg. Erik noticed a red X on the leg. That was odd. It almost looked like a brand of some sort. The cassowack on the left then squawked and stuck its right leg out. It also had an X.

"Don't hesitate, Erik, kill them before they strike!" Lady Arkyn shouted from behind. Erik heard the bowstring snap into place, followed by another honking cassowack.

"Go for the neck!" Rafe shouted.

Erik readied his sword, but as he brought up his arms into a high guard position, he noticed that he also had a red X on his right forearm. He stared at the mark and then back at the cassowacks. They anxiously waved their legs and squawked. Erik turned around and looked at Arkyn and Rafe. Rafe slashed through a charging cassowack's neck with his sword, lopping the head clean off and dropping the body. Rafe then turned to ready for the next strike, but as he did so, Erik noticed that there was no red X on the man.

What did it mean? It had to mean something.

Lady Arkyn turned around and glowered at Erik. "Kill them!"

The fury in her voice was something he had never experienced before. He was now equidistant to both Lady Arkyn and the two cassowacks behind him. He looked back and forth, trying to figure out the red X on his arm. Lady Arkyn looked and saw the mark too, and then her face became harder than Erik had ever seen before.

Lady Arkyn snarled and charged in at Erik. She was running at him, but her cadence seemed off somehow. As he watched, an arrow flew over his shoulder from behind and slammed into Lady Arkyn. For an instant, Erik's heart leapt into his throat and he was about to go into a rage, but then the image of Lady Arkyn melted away, revealing a cassowack with an arrow through its right eye and protruding out the back of its skull.

Erik wheeled around and saw Rafe and Lady Arkyn smiling at him. Rafe tapped the red X on his forearm and then touched his nose. Lady Arkyn prepared another arrow and fired. Erik spun around to see a second cassowack catch the arrow in the throat. The giant bird jerked to the side and stumbled into the bubbling black ooze. It made no sound as the goo pulled it down into its depths.

Beyond the spring, where the other cassowacks had been coming from, there was nothing but clear marsh. No bodies, no charging birds, nothing.

"I don't understand," Erik said.

Rafe came up quickly, his hands in the air as Erik nervously held his sword up.

"It's us," Rafe assured him. "I promise."

"But how?" Erik asked.

"As I said, this island plays tricks on the mind. The first time you saw Marlin, it likely was your friend. Or, it could have just as easily been a part of these creatures' attempt to lure you away from the group. Who knows? Either way, after we took you to the cave with us, we had already encountered something similar. So..." Rafe stuck his right arm out and displayed the red X.

"So you decided to—"

Lady Arkyn reached out and clamped a hand over Erik's mouth while making a sign with her other hand to be quiet. "Whatever we speak of on this island can be used against us."

Instantly Erik understood. The X was a visual cue, a sign to tell the real from the fake. He nodded his understanding and Lady Arkyn pulled her hand away. "Why not..." Erik displayed his arm and the mark, hoping they would understand that he was asking why they didn't tell him earlier.

"Watchers," Rafe said simply. "Anything we say can be used to assault our minds, but there are others who watch."

Erik nodded. "But Marlin said he could read my mind, could the watchers not read your minds and see what you were thinking?" Erik asked as he looked at the mark on Rafe's hand.

"The thing you think is Marlin might very well be able to read your thoughts, but I would imagine that is because you gave it your trust. I, on the other hand, suspect everything on this island is out to kill me, so I am not trusting any of it, not even the bloody grass."

Erik had more questions, but the fact that they had survived a terrible trap was enough for him at the moment. "In any case, we can go around the stream now," Erik said with a faint smirk.

Rafe laughed and nodded. "Around the spring and to the north," he said. "Hopefully with a bit more good fortune. By the way, you owe me big time, both for my ship, and for rescuing you from the cassowacks. They would have started eating you while you were still alive."

Chapter 16

The remainder of the journey to the northern shore of the Natchy Moors proved challenging, but uneventful. Erik did see Marlin a couple more times, but this time he knew better than to trust the apparition, and it knew better than to come too close. The fog stopped at the northern beach, opening onto a scene of tranquil beauty. White sands and peaceful waves lapping at the shore. The water was crystal clear, enabling Rafe to spear fish with great success. While Rafe cleaned and cooked the fish, Erik worked on finding wood for their raft.

There was a grove of pines some two hundred yards to the west of where Rafe had taken to spear fishing. Had Erik been able to change into his dragon form, he would have made short work of the trees. His wing would have given him pain, but that wasn't what stopped him. It was the idea that Vodklyk's poison might still be lingering on inside him, clinging to his dragon form somehow, and waiting to catch him. After they had arrived at the beach and appeared to have passed through all the horrors the Natchy Moors had to offer them, Lady Arkyn had confessed to Erik that she had never heard of anyone surviving Vodklyk's poison before. She promised to consult with Njar about an antivenom, but until then, she advised Erik to not use his dragon form.

Erik drew his sword and hoisted it up over his shoulders. He was grateful that his dragon form seemed to have absorbed all of the poison, though he wasn't sure how the transformation into his smaller, human body had managed to save him from death. Right now, as he prepared to chop down trees with his indelible Telarian steel blade, he was also thankful that he could not feel the pain of the broken wing. He cut down five trees, limbed them, and then began dragging the logs back to camp. By the time he finished moving all of the logs, Rafe had the fish ready to eat, and Lady Arkyn had found some edible fruit that grew along a thin outcropping that jutted out into the sea northward. She had also gathered a large amount of leaves and vines, from which she could make coverings for Rafe and Erik so they wouldn't get sunburned at sea the following day.

The three of them ate their fill, and then set about building large fires all around their camp.

They had heard the banshees cry every night while in Natchy Moors, and they had no intention of making it to the beach only to be harassed by the wicked creatures. When the morning came, Rafe made rope from long strips of bark from a copse of trees that Erik didn't recognize. The sailor worked the fibrous material for a long time, and then began making braided cords before finally lashing the logs together on the beach during low tide. When high tide came in, Lady Arkyn sat in the middle of the raft while Erik and Rafe each took a side of the raft and towed it out into the water. When they could no longer touch the bottom with their feet, they pulled themselves onto the raft and picked up the paddles Lady Arkyn had made that morning.

"Put these on," Lady Arkyn said as she set out the tunics and sunhats made from leaves and vines. "Don't need either of you blistering all up and down your backs. You'll be no good to me then."

Erik was pleasantly surprised to find that the leaves were fairly comfortable. They were supple and flexed with his movements. He had worried they would be scratchy and rigid.

"Leave it to the elf to weave cloth out of plants," Rafe said with a smile. "Thanks," he added quickly as he slipped his covering on.

They paddled for hours, Rafe calling out commands and letting Erik know when they needed to adjust their pacing or their bearing. The sun was just beginning to set in the west by the time they pulled their raft up onto the shore of the northern territory.

"Camp here for the night?" Rafe asked.

Lady Arkyn looked to Erik and then nodded. "Depends on how tired you both are after rowing all day," she said.

"I could use a rest, no lie," Rafe admitted freely as he stretched his arms. "We can prop the raft up on some rocks and make a bit of a roof over our heads. We can cut some of the weeds over there and make a loose thatch and bedding too."

Erik surveyed the land around them. A rocky beach spanned as far as he could see to the east and west. Twenty yards to the north, tall reeds and cat tails blew in the wind. The land sloped upward then, with some sandy dunes blocking a direct view of the tall trees that loomed in the distance.

"Let's get to the trees," Erik said. "We'd do better to find some cover. If we try to make a fire on the beach, we'll be visible for miles."

Lady Arkyn nodded. "There are orcs in these parts."

Rafe kicked at the rocks under foot. "It's almost dark as it is. We won't have much light to work with if we move into the trees."

226

"Leave that to me," Lady Arkyn insisted. "We just need to find the right spot, and I can take care of setting up the camp. Elves aren't just good for making clothes, we can see just fine in the dark too."

Rafe sighed and gestured for Lady Arkyn to lead the way. Erik adjusted his sword belt before falling in with the other two and heading inland. They didn't have to go far before Lady Arkyn found the husk of a once massive and vibrant redwood tree that was as big around as a small house. From the look of it, it had been mostly hollowed out by a lightning strike that had blown off the top of the tree and left a free standing natural wall. Animals had obviously been inside as well, as there were claw marks embedded into the charred wood, but the space was clear for the night. Lady Arkyn went to work cutting branches from nearby saplings for bedding, and to close the gap in the front of the hollowed husk where they entered. There was still an opening above them, but the night wasn't very cold, and it was still a relief just to be shielded from the wind.

Lady Arkyn took the first watch, and the two exhausted men fell asleep in short order, eager to rest their aching bodies.

Erik took the third watch, waking a couple hours before dawn and waiting until the sun rose. He was more than a little pleased when the only thing he noticed come nearby was an owl that was busy hunting field mice. When the sun finally popped up over the trees, Erik woke the others.

"We should move as quickly as possible," Erik announced.

"Uh-uh," Rafe said as he slowly stretched his arms out. "First, you break my ship, then you take my shirt and have me chasing you through fog to save you from cassowacks, and now you want me to skip breakfast? No. I'm going to eat."

"I think you left out the part about how I saved you from Vodklyk," Erik pointed out.

"A minor detail," Rafe replied. "Besides, I returned the favor by carrying you into a cave so the leviathan couldn't eat you, remember?"

"Not for nothing, but technically the leviathan is the one who destroyed your ship, not me," Erik said.

"I don't suppose you managed to grab a map with those big old dragon hands of yours?" Rafe asked.

Erik shook his head. "I didn't even have time to grab my pants, if you recall. That is the reason you gave me your shirt after all."

"Oh I remember," Rafe said. "I was there when we found you on the side of the mountain. I was just hoping you had it tucked away in some invisible, magical pouch."

Erik shook his head. Regretfully, when Rafe's ship was destroyed by Vodklyk, he lost everything he had taken from Alkantar, and he had lost the book given to him by the monks far to the south. He was going to have to hope that whatever knowledge the reclusive cult had about the Four Horsemen, they would be willing to share. While he was thinking about the book, his mind wandered back and plucked the memory of Tatev out from the recesses of his mind. He smiled as he recalled Tatev's curly red hair and child-like amusement and wonder when discovering new knowledge. It was a shame that he had not survived their trek across the Eastern Wilds. Had the barbaric Tarthuns not sacrificed him, he would have loved to visit the monastery in the south with its obscure texts and ancient tomes.

His memories turned sour as the image of Tatev being murdered by the Tarthuns took center stage in his mind. Tears threatened to well up in his eyes, so Erik cleared his throat and moved quickly to splash some water on his face.

"I'm going on ahead," Lady Arkyn called out. Erik looked up and wiped the water from his face to see that she was holding her bow in hand. "I think I found some tracks to follow. With any luck, I will be back with something to eat."

She then turned and vanished into the forest as quickly as a whisper on the wind.

Erik and Rafe moved toward the small stream a few meters away from where they had camped. Rafe bent down for a drink, and then splashed water over his face to help himself wake up. "You all right?" Rafe asked.

Erik turned a questioning look on the sailor and nodded. "I'm fine, why do you ask?"

Rafe shrugged. "Looked like you had something on your mind," he replied. "A lost friend, I am guessing by how distant your eyes became." Erik was about to speak, but Rafe held up his hand. "Before you ask how I know, let's just say that a sailor's life may not be as grand as that of the Champion of Truth, but it is not without its dangers and losses."

Erik nodded his understanding. "I lost a dear friend to a group of nomads in the Eastern Wilds," Erik explained. "Thinking about the map and the other book I had brought on this journey reminded me of him, that's all. It was a long time ago."

"But it still feels close, doesn't it?" Rafe asked. "I lost my grandfather when I was only seven. He had a growth on his neck the size of a small melon. Everyone said it was a goiter. It turned out to be a large tumor. He was in horrible pain for weeks on end, and then he died. I wasn't there when he finally passed, I was at sea with my father, but I can still remember how my grandmother told me what had happened. There had been no tenderness about it. I ran up to her house, she opened the door, looked down at me, and said he was dead and I didn't need to come around looking for him anymore. I broke down in tears. Cried right there in front of anyone passing by. It gets better with time, of course. It no longer feels like it was yesterday, but the old adage of time healing all wounds is a pile of gull droppings if you ask me. Time makes it a bit duller perhaps, teaches you how to live with the pain, but it doesn't heal anything. It may not feel as recent as yesterday to me anymore, but his death still feels close, like maybe it happened a few weeks ago, or last year. There's always a sadness."

Erik nodded and sat back against a cedar tree. "Yeah, it still feels close for Tatev and all the others too."

"And it probably will for the rest of your life," Rafe said. "I lost several friends to the sea, a few to disease, and one even hung himself. He just gave up and tied a rope around his neck and then jumped off his center mast. Never did understand why though, out of all of us, he had been the happiest."

Erik didn't understand that. Suicide was never something he could legitimize. "There's always another option," Erik commented.

"Oh, I agree," Rafe put in quickly. "Doing something like that only trades one kind of hurt for another. Better to persevere on this side of things, where your loved ones can help lift you up. I would have done anything to help him, if he had only told me there was something wrong." Rafe picked up a stick and chucked it at a bush. "Then again, maybe if I had been a better friend, I would have noticed something wasn't right."

"Can't do that," Erik cut in. "Blaming yourself is not the right way to go about it."

Rafe took in a breath and then moved to sit up against a tree trunk a few feet away so he could face Erik. "Sorry," he offered. "I had been planning on trying to cheer you up. Instead, seems like the conversation went down faster than a rowboat in a whirlpool."

Erik smiled and waved it off. "It's all right, but if you want to change subjects, then tell me why you weren't afraid to sail through the Natchy Moors."

Rafe wagged a finger at Erik. "Yeah, I did promise you some secrets if we made it this far, didn't I? Well, truth is, there are a few people who aren't affected by the illusions and mind games that the moors attack people with."

"Yes, I was told that it was either a charm or the absolute lack of fear," Erik said, referring to what Lady Arkyn had told him in the cabin of Rafe's ship.

"Well, given how I behaved when Vodklyk was after us, I think we can rule out infallible courage," Rafe said with a wink. Erik laughed and nodded his agreement. "Just promise not to spread that one around when we get back to Gontin, I would lose my livelihood as a ship's captain."

Erik held his right hand up in front of him and shook his head. "Secret's safe with me."

"There isn't any charm that would work either," Rafe said. "Charms rely on enchantments, which as you know is like taking something ordinary, and then putting magic on it to make it special, but the moors can cut through that. I wasn't joking when I said that wizards have died there either. There used to be scores of wizards that would go in there, hoping to rid the area of its curse and cleanse it for the use of all men, but none of them survived. I reckon there are some places on this world that are just evil, and there isn't anything to be done about it."

"It rendered my power useless as well," Erik said. "That has not happened since I learned how to use it, and I have traveled to many places and fought with many demons and monsters."

"Aye, I'm sure you have, but the Natchy Moors are a unique kind of evil."

"So what makes you different?" Erik pressed.

Rafe wrinkled his nose and dug his heel in the dirt in front of him. "You know how the cabin below was lined with mithril, and I said it would keep the illusions out?"

Erik nodded.

"Well, it's kind of like that, but I need to know that you won't tell anyone."

"Sure," Erik said quickly, eager to know the secret.

231

"No, I mean it, not even Lady Arkyn can know. I'll tell you because I owe you my life for getting me away from Vodklyk."

"All right," Erik said. "I shall not repeat what you say to anyone."

Rafe nodded. "I come from a line of people native to Gontin. We have a unique ingredient in our blood."

"You have mithril in your blood?" Erik asked incredulously.

Rafe shook his head. "Not exactly." He paused and sighed. "You know how when there is a lot of blood you can smell copper?"

Erik nodded.

"Well, we have that too of course, but our blood also has great amounts of a kind of silver metal in it."

"Silver?"

Rafe nodded. "It isn't exactly silver, but it isn't mithril either. It's something unique, and it only runs in the lines of a few families, all native to Gontin."

"How did you discover that?" Erik asked.

"Centuries ago, a vampire came to Gontin. He fed on one of my ancestors, and then immediately died. I am fuzzy on the details, because even now we aren't entirely sure of the progression of events, but after that there was some research done by that ancestor's brother. He tested a few other people in Gontin, and eventually discovered that there are people with this special metal in their blood. No idea how it got there or when it started, but it's there. As time went on and people started disappearing in the Natchy Moors, that same ancestor who did the research went out to the moors to see whether the illusions would have any effect on him."

"Brave man," Erik said.

Rafe nodded. "Or insane, but the two aren't mutually exclusive I suppose." Rafe smiled and gave another wink. "In

232

any case, he discovered that the illusions did not have any power over him."

"If that was so long ago, then why not take a ship full of people with this special blood and try to eradicate the monsters in the moors?"

Rafe touched his finger to his nose. "That is exactly what he set out to do. He gathered as many able-bodied men with the silver-blood as he could fit into a ship. For added measure, he hired on fourteen wizards as well."

"Wait, why not just use wizards who have the... silver-blood, as you called it?"

"Because that is the one down side," Rafe explained. "To date, not a single person born with silver-blood can perform magic."

Erik recalled Captain Deringer talking about failing time and time again trying to use the Nighthawk spell. "Captain Deringer is a silver-blood too, isn't he?"

Rafe's eyes widened a bit, but then he smiled and nodded. "You have a sharp mind and a keen sense of observation, my friend." Rafe then shifted his legs a bit and continued on. "In any case, the ship my ancestor took into the moors never returned. Everyone on it died in the moors. Since then, few have dared brave the waters, but I have done it on four separate occasions, not including our voyage. I had seen the bat creatures before, but had only ever been attacked once, and it was easily enough scared off by some shouting and a wave of my sword. I suppose we might have been fine as well, had Vodklyk not showed up."

"You suspect he stirred up the bat creatures and the giant octopus?" Erik asked.

"Seems as likely a reason as any, or I suppose it was just our lot and we were going to have a bad voyage no matter what. One can only play games of chance for so long before the winning streak turns dry."

Erik nodded. "Well, we made it through well enough, thanks to you and your quick thinking with those branding marks." Erik looked at his right forearm, but the mark had washed away when they had crossed the channel the day before.

"I try to keep a few tricks up my sleeve," Rafe replied.

"And what are you two chattering on about?" Lady Arkyn asked as she came bounding into view with a pair of slain hares slung over her shoulder.

"Just getting to know our fearless friend," Erik said.

"Fearless?" Lady Arkyn echoed with a scoff. "Then I must have seen someone else panicking when Vodklyk was chasing us."

"Ha, ha," Rafe said dryly with a slow clap of his hands. "If you don't make it as an adventurer, you can always try to become a court jester."

Lady Arkyn gracefully launched over the stream and plopped the two hares in Rafe's lap. "If I am to be the jester, then you shall be the cook. Get to work."

"Ouch," Erik said under his breath, but it was all in good fun. Rafe and Lady Arkyn were both laughing, and soon the catch was cleaned and roasting over a fire next to the brook. They tore at the food voraciously, having skipped breakfast, and then continued on their way north for another three hours before coming upon a large river flowing in a south-westerly direction. Erik took it as a good sign, because he had memorized the map taken from Alkantar, and the river marked the northern edge of the orcish lands, and signaled that it was time to alter their course to travel northwest, instead of simply north.

"With any luck, we'll find the cult at the base of the mountains about one hundred miles northwest of this point," Erik said happily.

"Assuming you can remember where to go," Rafe cut in.

"I know the map from Alkantar's notes well enough," Erik assured him. "I also had done some research of my own on their location before that. We move North West until we find their city or camp somewhere along the base of the Impassable Spine mountain range. In any case, we should be away from the orcs, so we can travel a bit more freely."

The three spent only a few minutes searching for a natural place to ford the river, and then continued along as the forest fell away and gave the land over to a vast valley filled with knee-high grasses and large, thorny bushes. Mice and rabbits ran across the ground in abundance, with a few eagles circling above or diving down to catch their quarry, but there were no signs of larger animals anywhere in the valley, except for the odd skull or bleached antler lying in the dirt.

After three days of walking and foraging for what they could find to eat, they came upon a stone fence in the valley, near the base of the mountain range. There were no signs or markings, but the fence appeared to be well maintained, with evidence of recent repairs plainly visible. However, there were no guards, or gates, and the fence was only four feet tall, so they could easily see beyond it, and they saw no structures of any kind in the near distance.

"A border marker?" Rafe suggested as they approached the stone barrier.

"Perhaps," Erik said. He wished he could take his dragon form and fly up to survey the area, but even if his wing hadn't been damaged, the Cult of Zammin was the supposed origination of the spell that could prevent him from using his gift as a sahale.

"Well, at least it looks like we are moving in the right direction," Rafe said as he placed his left hand on the fence and hopped over. "Shall we continue?"

Lady Arkyn nimbly jumped up onto the fence from a standing position, and then scanned the area from the slightly higher vantage point. "I see some animals," she said. "Look to be caribou perhaps."

"Well, then if we don't find the cult you are looking for, at least we can have some proper meat. I am tired of rabbits and mice," Rafe said as he rubbed his hands together eagerly.

Erik clambered over the wall and the three of them continued on. They approached what indeed was a large herd of caribou. The animals saw them, but they didn't spook or startle in any way.

"Seems they are used to seeing humans," Lady Arkyn said. "The fence may be a visual marker for the herd's grazing lands."

"A four foot fence wouldn't keep these animals in," Rafe said with a shake of his head.

"Unless they have been domesticated for a long enough time that they are trained to stay within their boundaries," Lady Arkyn replied. "Either way, we should be getting close."

They walked through the grazing herd and beyond them for two more miles until they came to a row of large, stone buildings. Smoke was gently rising out from the chimney of the first building. Rafe and Erik let their hands hover over their swords, but they needn't have worried.

The wooden door swung open and an elderly woman with wrinkled, tanned skin, dressed in thick layers of cloth and leather clothing came out with an empty basket. She looked up and smiled at the three of them.

"Hatcha mo, no'aka," she said as she bowed briefly before turning and continuing on around the house.

"Odd reaction to strangers," Rafe commented.

Erik nodded and watched as the old woman disappeared from sight. The door opened again, and an elderly man came out. He had a toothless smile and walked with a cane.

236

"Come," he said in Common Tongue. "I take you. Come." He motioned for Erik and the others to follow him. His upper body was slightly stooped over, with a noticeable hump in his back over the right side of his spine at the base of his neck, but he maintained a quick pace as he walked, leading them down a dirt path toward the mountain.

"Not at all what I expected," Rafe whispered to Erik.

"Me either," Erik replied. Where were the wizards and the strange relics? Where were the books and the weapons? What kind of cult cares for herds of caribou and keeps itself tucked away in the furthest reaches of the Impassable Spine mountain range?

They walked another mile or so until they approached a large dome made of gray stone. There were no windows, and only a single door in the structure. The old man turned and held out his cane to stop Erik and the others.

"You wait here. I go."

They watched as he went to the door and gave a series of taps with his cane.

The door opened and three individuals came out, all female. Nothing about this encounter turned out the way Erik had imagined. Instead of fancy clothes, the women all wore rough spun robes of brown. Their feet were protected with sandals, something which was never worn anywhere in the Middle Kingdom except inside of large homes when the weather was too hot to use slippers comfortably. Each of the women wore smiles, with their hair in braided buns atop their heads.

"Welcome, strangers," the black-haired woman in the middle said as they approached. The old man waved and smiled as he left Erik and the others alone with the women.

"How may we be of assistance?" a woman with gray hair asked.

"We… um…" Erik couldn't think of how to introduce himself. He had expected to find a peculiar group of people

237

dabbling in occult magic and rituals, not farmers and simple folk.

"I'm sorry, but we have come looking for the Cult of Zammin," Lady Arkyn said openly. "Have we come to the wrong place?"

The three women bowed at the waist. "That is the name outsiders call us by, though it is not the true name of our settlement," the red haired woman stated politely. "We are the Followers of Zammin."

Lady Arkyn bowed her head in slight deference. "No insult intended."

"None taken," the black haired woman said. "I am Zefra, the woman on my right is Oria, and this is our mother, Dora."

"I am Lady Arkyn, an agent to King Mathias," Lady Arkyn offered.

"My name is Rafe," Rafe said quickly, suspiciously leaving out his surname.

"I am Erik Lokton, the Champion of Truth," Erik added finally.

Zefra approached Erik and held her hand out toward him, palm out and level with his eyes. "You have a strange aura about you," she said. "Are you sahale?" Erik bristled while Rafe and Lady Arkyn tensed and prepared to reach for their weapons. "I have startled you," Zefra said apologetically as she pulled her hand back. "No harm was meant."

"She is the high priestess of Zammin," Dora put in proudly. "She has a gift for sensing gifts other people possess."

Zefra turned to Lady Arkyn and smiled. "May I?"

Lady Arkyn nodded.

Zefra raised her hand and closed her eyes. "Lady Arkyn is not only a skilled archer, but has powerful magic running through her."

"Destructive?" Dora asked.

Zefra shook her head. "No, mostly it is the ability to communicate with animals, though she does possess some healing abilities as well." Zefra then turned to face Rafe. She started to raise her hand, but he reached out and gently pressed it back down.

"I'd rather you didn't do that with me," he said.

"If the high priestess is to invite you inside, then she must inspect you," Oria explained. "It will not harm you."

"Well then, if it's all the same to you, I'd rather wait outside."

Erik nodded, figuring that Rafe was trying to protect the secret of his blood. "He can wait out here," Erik told Zefra. "He will not cause any trouble."

Zefra nodded her head and relaxed her arm. "Then, the two of you wish to come inside and join us, but he will remain out here and live with the caribou?"

"Live with the caribou?" Rafe echoed. "We didn't come to join your little commune, we—"

Erik held up a hand. "Actually, I just have some questions. We are here on official business."

"We do not recognize the authority of King Mathias here," Zefra pointed out. "These lands do not belong to him, nor do they belong to the dragons."

Erik called upon his power and did a bit of inspecting for himself. He checked all three of the women very carefully, and found only peaceful intentions within them. Knowing this, he felt he had a good idea of how to start the discussion. "I will be plain and straightforward," Erik said. "Recently, many sahale were murdered. I have taken up the investigation to find the party responsible. Now, I don't believe any of you three to be involved, but I have come because of a very special kind of magic."

"He speaks of the binding spell," Zefra told the other women.

"Zefra, are you certain we can trust him?" Dora asked.

239

"Yes, I am," she replied evenly. "We know of the magic you speak of. It was placed within our care many centuries ago, and has remained here in our stewardship until it was recently stolen."

Erik frowned. "You didn't create the spell that prevents a sahale from taking their dragon form?"

Zefra shook her head. "We have no need for such a spell. We live in peace, hundreds of miles away from anyone that would wish to do us any harm. We do not venture beyond our borders, and others do not trespass upon our territory."

"Then who gave you the spell?" Lady Arkyn asked.

Zefra nodded slowly. "It is best if we speak inside. The dome protects us from outsiders that would pry into our private lives with their unholy scrying magic."

Lady Arkyn and Erik shared a look. Now it made sense why Njar couldn't find the Cult of Zammin. The dome was deflecting the magic he used.

Rafe went and found a large rock to sit on while Erik and Lady Arkyn followed the women back toward the dome. Immediately upon walking through the portal, Erik noticed that the temperature was much warmer inside than outside. It wasn't unpleasant, but had he been wearing anything heavier than the covering of leaves and the patchwork pants, it very well might have been. The interior of the dome was not an open space, as he had suspected. There were hallways and doors in each direction he looked. In many respects, it resembled the interior of a large fortress. While the outer shell may have been rounded, everything on the inside was square.

Zefra led them into the hallway straight ahead and stopped at the third door on the right. She opened it and gestured for Erik and Lady Arkyn to go inside. "Will you be in need of refreshment? We have caribou milk, goat cheese, different types of fruits, and other items available at your request." Erik thought the idea of caribou milk sounded intriguing. He opted for some of that, while Lady Arkyn graciously declined the offer, insisting that she was not yet hungry. Zefra nodded and then looked to her mother. Dora bowed and then walked down the hall, presumably to fetch the drink. Zefra then looked at Erik's clothing. "The Followers of Zammin do not occupy their time in the pursuit of elegant clothing, but I think I can safely say that we might have something that would offer you better protection than what you are currently wearing.

Erik wiggled his dirty, bare toes and smiled. "I would be happy for anything you could provide." Zefra nodded and then looked to Oria. The red head smiled and started to walk, but Erik held up a hand and called out to her. "If I may impose, Rafe could also use a fresh change of clothes."

Oria bowed at the waist.

"Thank you," Erik said. "I'm afraid that I don't have money to pay you for your hospitality."

"The Followers of Zammin take pleasure in serving others. We have no use for money. Your thanks is more than enough to repay us for this small offering." Zefra pointed toward a simple bed. "If you wish to rest, please make yourself comfortable."

"I thought we were going to talk," Erik replied.

Zefra nodded. "Yes, once you have changed and refreshed yourselves, then we will speak. Please, take your time. I shall have a wash basin brought in for you." Zefra closed the door and walked down the hall.

Lady Arkyn moved to the door and quietly tested the knob. "Well, at least she didn't lock us in," she commented.

Erik smiled. "It's all right, they mean us no harm. I checked."

"And what if your powers are as useless here as they were in the Natchy Moors?"

Erik shrugged and took off the tunic of leaves and vines before dropping himself down onto the bed at the end of

241

the room. "This is much better than hollowed out trees or marshy grass," he said as he closed his eyes."

"You act as though you have never slept in a bed before," Lady Arkyn teased.

"Well, it feels like I have never been in a bed so comfortable before." He patted a spot next to him. "Come and see for yourself."

"This is hardly the time for a nap," Lady Arkyn commented.

Erik ignored her and flopped an arm over his eyes. He could hear her soft footsteps coming toward him. She settled into a cuddling position with him and placed her head and left hand on his chest. This was the most intimate they had been since reuniting, and though it excited Erik, it also made him slightly nervous. He put his arm around her and held her tight. Neither of them spoke. They laid there silently, enjoying each other's company and drifting on the edge of sleep and consciousness. Erik listened as Minrielle's breathing became deeper and more rhythmic. She didn't snore, but he could tell that she had slipped into slumber. Erik might have as well, except he was afraid of having a nightmare while so close to her, so he remained awake, thinking about the times they had shared before he had insisted they separate for a while. Lying here with her now, he felt foolish for sending her away. He realized now that her reassurances over the last couple of weeks had been far more powerful at calming his demons than any amount of meditating he performed at the monastery far to the south. She gave him a surge of strength that couldn't be imitated or replaced. Was that the difference between love and lust? The uplifting bond that made him more than he could be on his own, and demanded that he help her in the same way? Perhaps he had been a fool for sending her away. He had been unconscious back in the Natchy Moors, and neither she nor Rafe had complained about him thrashing about with nightmares.

A knock came at the door, pulling him from his thoughts. He slowly sat up as Minrielle woke and moved off of the bed before the door opened and a woman they hadn't met came in, struggling to carry a large, stone basin. She set it in the middle of the floor as another woman entered with two buckets of water and a large sea sponge. She set the items near the basin and then bowed as she left the room.

Erik went to the basin and poured a bit of water in so he could begin washing his feet. While he was doing that, Dora returned with a small wooden cup of caribou milk, and Oria came with a fresh change of clothes. Erik finished cleaning his feet and did a quick once over on his upper body with the sponge before dressing himself in the provided pants, tunic, and boots. Lady Arkyn used the remaining fresh water to wash her face, neck, and arms.

"Shall we go?" she asked as Erik downed the caribou milk.

Erik nodded. They went to the door and opened it to find Zefra standing just down the hall. She smiled at them and motioned for them to follow her.

"Do the clothes suit you?" she asked.

"They are excellent, thank you," Erik replied. He was surprised that they had managed to guess his size so accurately, but everything fit perfectly, even the boots. They walked down the hall and then turned right along a new corridor before finally coming to a large door. Zefra opened it and the three went into a library roughly twenty feet square.

Erik smiled. This was more like it. There were shelves of books lining the walls, more bookcases standing along the floor, and a large table in the center of the room for studying. Many of the tomes had languages written upon their spines that he could identify, but many more had foreign languages that he did not recognize.

"Do you know much of Zammin?" Zefra asked as she gestured for them to sit.

243

They both answered that they did not and sat down.

"No, I suppose most outsiders have little knowledge of our founder," Zefra said with a hesitant smile. "Well, in any case we do not often receive visitors. In your case, I could sense an urgency, however, and so I have allowed for a breach in our protocol and brought you directly into our inner library. I do not wish our society to be affiliated with the murders you spoke of. While we did care for the spell, it was neither of our design, nor could we use it ourselves. Our magical abilities align more with the pursuit of knowledge and peace. In a way, we seek to be like the Natural Races of Terramyr, trying to find harmony and balance within the world."

"I have to ask," Erik interrupted. "What do you know of the Four Horsemen?"

The color drained from Zefra's face. "I was not aware that was one of your interests," she replied.

Erik nodded. "We are here because of the murders, but, before we talk about those, I have to know something. Do you, any of you, know how to defeat the Four Horsemen?"

Zefra studied Erik curiously for a few moments while she chewed on her lower lip. "The Four Horsemen are not a topic we like to discuss. Before I answer, I must know why you ask."

Erik called upon his power once more and scanned Zefra to ensure that her intentions were indeed friendly. Afterward, he recounted to her his entire history with Tu'luh, starting with his training in Kuldiga Academy, and ending with the battle at Fort Drake. He was careful to emphasize how Tu'luh's vision had given him doubts concerning the fate of Terramyr, and that he wished to find a way to prevent the Four Horsemen from coming if he could, but that in the event they came, he wanted to know how to stop them from destroying the world. After he finished his recounting, Zefra sat quietly for a long time.

"I'm sorry to bore you with the details," Erik said. "But, I wanted to make sure you knew who I really am, and why I need to know everything I can about the Four Horsemen."

Zefra nodded. "I could tell you were special when I first met you, but I had no idea that you were so important."

Erik frowned. "I wasn't meaning to boast," he assured her.

"No, it isn't that," Zefra responded quickly. "What I mean is that there have been turning points in our history that many are unaware of. In the early days of our society, the Followers of Zammin were like you, battle-weary and looking for answers. Many of them had heard about the Four Horsemen as well, and so they began to study them intently. Unfortunately, most races and societies have either forgotten about the Four Horsemen, or they choose not to believe in them or their power. Those that do still believe in their existence are too afraid to discuss them openly, as you do. That is why your question took me by surprise. I have not heard mention of them by anyone outside of this dome for a very long time."

"You speak as though you have the life span of an elf," Lady Arkyn said.

Zefra nodded and gave a smile. "I may look young, but I am over three hundred years old."

"Do all of your people live that long?" Erik asked.

Zefra shook her head. "Only those who are descendants of the original founding members. There is a magic that runs through us which extends our life. Others who join us can live to the fullest of their normal lifespans, sometimes a few years longer, but we are the longest living people here, and as such the responsibilities of governing and protecting our society falls to us, as well as recording our history. When I am four hundred, I shall relinquish my station and give it to my younger sister, and the cycle shall continue."

"So, do you know something about the Four Horsemen then?" Erik pressed.

Zefra hesitated. "Not exactly," she said. "While it is true that many of our earlier members researched the topic greatly, in the last several centuries, we have become less interested in this area of study."

Erik turned his hands up on the table in a questioning gesture. "Why? What could be more interesting than this exact subject? What could have a more profound impact on Terramyr as a whole?"

Zefra nodded. "I understand your insistence, but you have to understand. We collected the best, most complete collection of materials on the Four Horsemen. None of the Followers of Zammin ever found a single clue to their weaknesses. In fact, we discovered only the opposite. The Four Horsemen have no weaknesses. Once they come to a world, and deem it worthy of destruction, there is nothing that can stop them. Our world is one of many in a vast universe that most mortals cannot comprehend. Many have lived and died before us, and one day, Terramyr will die as well."

"So you gave up," Erik concluded for her.

Zefra shook her head. "No, we just learned that sometimes there are problems for which no solutions exist. The only sure way to keep the Four Horsemen from coming to our world is to live in balance and harmony. That is what we have devoted ourselves to now. We have over three thousand people that live here, and not once during my lifetime has there ever been a theft, murder, or even a lie told."

"Truly?" Lady Arkyn asked incredulously.

Zefra nodded. "The Followers of Zammin are devout, and dedicated to keeping balance. While other humans give themselves to lust and greed, we temper ourselves and share all that we possess. We are not without disputes, of course, but by the time a child reaches the age of twelve, they are expected to behave in the proper manner."

"What if they don't?" Lady Arkyn asked.

"Then they are shunned and sent away. Sometimes those in exile return and ask for reinstatement, those who do so with sincere hearts are allowed to tend to the caribou herds you saw on your way in. In this way, they can atone for their reckless behavior with additional service and sacrifice, it is what maintains balance."

"Utopia will not stop the Four Horsemen," Erik said sourly. "At best, it will delay their arrival, but they are going to come, I have seen it in visions."

"That may be so, but there is nothing else we can do. We live for today, and allow tomorrow to come as it will."

"That sounds familiar," Lady Arkyn whispered.

Erik sighed and shook his head. "Is there nothing else you can tell me?" he asked. "Do you not have books that I can look at?"

"You would not understand them," Zefra replied. "They are written in Zammin's language."

"You mean the language the old lady spoke out at the stone hut by the caribou?" Erik asked. "Her husband could interpret for me."

"No," Zefra said emphatically. "Zammin was… special. He wrote in a language that is not to be found elsewhere on this world. There is no spoken language to go with the written system."

Erik sighed. Alkantar had told him the same thing back in Pracheloor Cave. "Actually, I had a book written in the same language. I was successful in translating part of it. I even memorized some of the symbols," he divulged.

Zefra shook her head. "Assuming you were correct in your translations, which is doubtful, it would still take years. And, as I have said, you would only come to the same conclusions that our predecessors did. It would be a futile exercise. I have summarized their conclusions, that shall suffice."

247

"What if we worked together? I could ask specific questions and you could translate for me then? It is very important."

Zefra shook her head. "When the Followers of Zammin realized there was no way to defeat the Four Horsemen, Zammin gave them instructions to live in harmony. He laid down a list of laws for us to follow that would help, and then he took the knowledge of his language with him. When I said it would take years for you to learn, I would have been more correct to say that it would take years for you to learn even if Zammin himself returned to teach you."

Erik grunted and thumped the table with his right thumb. "What is the point of a library if you do not utilize the information and knowledge kept within? Where did Zammin go?" Erik asked.

Zefra shrugged. "That was centuries ago. I am not aware of anyone who knows where Zammin went. He left behind some of his books, but we were given strict charge to keep them safe here. For the most part, we have obeyed well."

"For the most part?" Erik asked.

Zefra sighed and looked to a shelf on the opposite side of the room. "From time to time, there have been members of our society who have become fixated on the Four Horsemen, or on other points of interest, that have stolen from the library. The best book to offer you would be one known only as The Infinium, but it was taken from here many years before my birth, and has since been lost."

Erik straightened in his chair. He knew that book! Tatev had purchased it from a book store during their travels. "What was in that book?" Erik asked carefully, trying to see how much about it Zefra knew, and thereby determine the overall value of other knowledge kept by the Cult of Zammin.

"It is said to be the most complete book ever written about the Four Horsemen," Zefra said. "As I mentioned before, there have been other worlds before ours. The

248

Ancients, the mighty dragons that now reside across the waters to the south, came from a place called Kendualdern. The Infinium is an account of how their world fell into disfavor, and details the destruction of their world. The other information we have collected here is left by Zammin, who is gifted with special knowledge of the Four Horsemen, but even he said that The Infinium would be the key to understanding them. Unfortunately, those in our order who attempted to read the book would go mad. We could never pull all of its information from it, and now it is lost."

Erik nodded quietly and thought carefully about whether he should tell her that he knew where The Infinium was. Then again, seeing as how the Father of the Ancients, the first and oldest dragon to come to Terramyr, was now trying to decipher it with Al's help, there was little point in getting Zefra's hopes up, for she would not be allowed to take the book back.

"Now answer a question for me," Zefra said. "You said you had a book that contained our language. Where was it, and do you have it now?"

Erik described the book he had found in the monastery of the Monks of the Southern Light, far to the south of the orcish lands beyond Ten Forts. He talked about the monks who had it in their library, and explained where the monastery was. He then talked about the information he had parsed out of it, and described how he went about trying to decipher the language. Zefra listened intently, and then finally nodded and interrupted when Erik had told her enough for her to know which book it was.

"That was another great loss to our library. The book you describe has no title, as such, but is instead one volume in a series of chronicles that details the actions of a group known to us as the Grand Cosmic Council. The books were written in Zammin's language, but he told our forerunners that he had not written the books. Instead, he had acquired them and brought them to us for study."

"There are more of these books?" Erik asked hopefully.

Zefra nodded. "There are a few, but we no longer have them."

"It seems you have lost a lot of important books," Lady Arkyn said.

Zefra sighed. "In a society where everyone is so trusting, it is easy to take advantage. The thefts occurred before my time, as I said, there have been no crimes during my lifetime, but that is because we now have instated the inspection of all who wish to enter these halls. Had I suspected the slightest bit of guile from either of you, the doors would have remained closed and you would have been banished from our lands."

"I see," Lady Arkyn said.

"Where is the book you speak of?" Zefra asked Erik. "May I see it?"

Erik's cheeks went red. "I was, in fact, bringing it to you for help deciphering the parts that I could not understand, but it was lost in a battle at sea."

Zefra pursed her lips and folded her hands upon the table. "Pity." The three sat in silence for a few moments.

After a while, Erik's thoughts turned to different subjects. If the Cult of Zammin couldn't offer help with the Four Horsemen, then perhaps they would have information about Dremathor, or at least some insight into sahale. "Do you know of a person called Dremathor?" Erik asked.

Zefra frowned and shook her head. "No. I do not know that name."

"What about Alkantar?" Lady Arkyn asked, catching on to the new line of questions.

Zefra's face turned sour. "Yes, him I know, but not personally. He was one who ran away the day before he was to make the choice to follow our laws and customs. He was known by a different name while here, Kavin Colbreat. He was my nephew."

"How do you know of his alias, then?" Erik asked.

"Because, his father, who was my brother, went after him when it was discovered that Kavin had not only fled, but stolen several books from our library. It took several decades, but eventually my brother found his son. My brother had taken three others from our home here. As you know, traveling can be quite dangerous. In any case, by the time they found Kavin, he had made a pact with a demon. He had been granted dark magical powers, and he had turned from mischievous pranks to deadly passions. He slew all of the men who accompanied my brother."

"But your brother lived?" Lady Arkyn said.

Zefra nodded. "He was allowed to return to us so that he could deliver a warning not to follow Kavin. My brother told us that Kavin had changed his name to Alkantar, and was going to try to mount another attempt to find his son, but before we could find anyone willing to go with him, my brother died. Apparently, Kavin had cursed him, and cut his life short. That was over two hundred years ago."

"Alkantar is dead," Erik stated, trying to make his tone as soft as possible.

Zefra nodded slowly, but showed no hint of a smile. "If you are looking for thanks, you will not find it," she said. "I abhor the loss of life. While I cannot condone what Kavin did, I also cannot revel in his death."

"I offered mercy," Erik said. "But, he would not take it, and he attacked us twice. It was unavoidable."

Zefra turned and looked at Erik for a moment. "Then you are different from most men in this world," she said.

"That's what I keep telling him," Lady Arkyn put in.

Zefra said, "Many would call themselves heroes for slaying someone like Kavin, but you offered him mercy?"

Erik nodded. "I did."

Zefra smiled. "I am sorry I cannot help you with the other person you mentioned, but I have not heard the name Dremathor before today. Did he associate with Kavin?"

"That is what we are trying to figure out," Erik said. "Can you tell us anything about the sahale?"

Zefra nodded once and spoke. "I do not have extensive knowledge about them, but I can tell you what I do know. The spell that binds sahale to their human form was stolen from us as well. Another one of our families had a son who was always getting into trouble. I am not sure whether he knew Kavin, for he was only eight when Kavin had left and stolen from our library, but this boy followed in Kavin's footsteps. Upon his twelfth birthday, he was asked to either commit to obeying the law, or to choose exile. He swore to obey the laws, but that night he slipped into the library and took many spells, the binding spell among them. The others were mostly divination spells, mixed with a few healing charms, but the binding spell was never recovered. We tried to follow him, but were unsuccessful. I have no way of knowing how it got into the hands of the murderer you seek, but I do know someone who might be able to help. He will have answers about the sahale as well, and should be able to give you whatever information you need." Zefra stood and walked around a bookcase, only to come back a moment later with a rolled parchment. She gently untied the ribbon around it and unfurled it for Erik to see.

It was a map of the northern territories.

"We are here," Zefra said as she pointed to a blank spot on the map nestled at the base of a mountain. "The orcish lands lie to the east, with a great city some two hundred miles from here. On the eastern border of the orcish lands is a treacherous forest called the Dread Pines. If you can make it beyond that, then you will come upon the ruins of Galardene, which sits upon the Black River. To the south of Galardene are the Cliffs of Rontular, but you don't want to go that way. The cliffs are several hundred feet high and drop directly into the sea below. You want to travel up the Black River, through the ruins of Tarntin, and up into the mountains. The trek will be difficult, but if you can follow the Black River to its source, you will find Hermit's Hole." Zefra pointed to the origin of Black River, but there was no mention of Hermit's Hole on the map. "An ancient and powerful sahale lives there. He is the one who created the binding spell."

"A sahale created the binding spell?" Erik asked. "But why?"

Zefra sighed and shook her head. "The records of our people say nothing about it, but as I have searched through other tomes about the Four Horsemen, I did come upon something that may have an explanation. You see, the sahale who lives there was once a friend to our people. He never joined our numbers, but he admired our pursuits of knowledge and peaceful living. He had once helped a few of our scholars research something that they thought would spell disaster for our world."

"What was that?" Lady Arkyn asked eagerly.

Zefra frowned and took in a deep breath. Her hand started to tremble ever so slightly, but as soon as Erik noticed it, she rubbed her hands together and put on a smile for them. "It turned out to be a superstition, really," she said. "But, a little more than five hundred years ago, one of our scholars had a vision, something that is rare among our people, but taken very seriously. He saw the Four Horsemen come to Terramyr in answer to a reckless creature that was terrorizing all living things both in the Northern Territory, and in your realm, and beyond. There was much slaughter and devastation. It attracted the attention of the Four Horsemen, so they came to put an end to our world."

"This creature, did it have a name?" Lady Arkyn asked.

"In the vision, it came to our scholar that it had gone by many names, but the truest one was Daqn Saqr." Zefra reached up and rubbed her shoulders vigorously, as if a chill had overtaken the room.

"And so this sahale that was helping your people made this spell to stop the creature?" Lady Arkyn asked.

Zefra nodded. "But it never came to that. The creature was never born. Then, Nagar's Blight took over the land as you talked about earlier, Erik, and the scholar never had the vision again. The sahale that made the spell left it with us for safe keeping, just in case, but it has never been needed. I am sorry that it has been used to murder so many, it had been meant only as a defense."

"So if the spell was made to protect the world from this creature that would usher in the coming of the Four Horsemen, the creature known as Daqn Saqr must have also been a sahale, and the binding spell was created to make a fight against Daqn Saqr easier."

Zefra nodded. "I do not know much about Zammin's language, but I do know the language that this name comes from. It is an old form of High Terryn. In High Terryn, Daqn Saqr means Dark Sahale."

Chapter 17

Erik spent the next ten minutes throwing all sorts of questions at Zefra, but came away with nothing more of any value. If he wanted any additional answers about the Dark Sahale, he was going to have to find Hermit's Hole. When it was obvious that there was nothing more to be gained, the three of them rose from the table and exited the room. Erik had to fight against his urge to search the library for himself, but he was getting the sense that they were wearing out their welcome. Zefra was becoming increasingly tight-lipped, especially with questions regarding Zammin. He and Lady Arkyn exchanged a couple of glances that told him she was feeling the same as he was. Neither of them said it, but they could tell that Zefra knew more about Zammin than she was letting on.

They followed Zefra through the halls and back to the door leading out from the dome. They all exchanged polite bows as they said their good-byes, and Erik thanked Zefra for the map once more before they left.

Erik and Lady Arkyn exited the dome to find Rafe exactly where he had been, chewing on a long stem of thick grass. He motioned to three bags at his feet and smiled.

"The other ladies that came out to meet us dropped these off for us," Rafe said. "The backpacks are filled with bandages, food, and other necessities for our journey." Rafe tossed the chewed length of grass to the ground. "Good people here. Never met anyone so willing to just give me things. This would have cost quite a bit back home in Gontin."

"Yes, well, they seem eager enough to send us on our way," Erik put in.

Rafe arched a brow. "Oh, now what did you do? Did you break someone's house in there?"

Erik shirked off the jest and pointed eastward. "We should go." They set out immediately, not even waiting to spend the night and rest.

"So, did everything go all right?" Rafe asked as they left the dome far behind them. "Neither of you have said much since you came out of there. Was it strange on the inside? Sacrifices? Cannibals?"

"No, nothing like that," Lady Arkyn said flatly.

"Well what was it then?" Rafe pressed. "Something has you both spooked.

"We don't have time to explain," Erik said. "Let's just say that the murderer we are after might have something to do with the Four Horsemen."

"The Four…" Rafe stopped short and snorted. "You can't be serious, how can one person—"

Erik spun around and handed Rafe the rolled up map that Zefra had given to him. "You can stay if you like, but there are things that you should know." Erik filled Rafe in on all the details about Alkantar, the thirteen murdered sahale, and everything else they had learned along their journey so far. Rafe stood silently, listening to all of it with a straight face. After Erik finished, he said, "The shadowfiend I killed before coming to Gontin talked about a Dark Sahale, a being that would possibly end the world. Now, inside the dome, Zefra told us of a vision one of their scholars had that warned them about a Dark Sahale who would summon down the Four Horsemen by his actions. If you come with us, we don't stop to eat, and we only sleep as long as we have to until we find the sahale who made the binding spell that stops sahale from changing into their dragon form, and get all the answers we need from him so we know exactly what we are dealing with."

"Is it at all possible that we are chasing ghosts?" Rafe asked. "I mean, legends and myths are one thing, but we don't really know that a Dark Sahale is running around do we?"

Erik shook his head. "I don't know it for certain, but it feels right. The more we follow after the murderer who killed the thirteen sahale in Winter's Beak, the more it starts to make sense to me. There is something about this that has to be more than a coincidence. For the idea of a Dark Sahale to come up so often by groups who don't have any interaction with each other, there must be something more than simple myths and scary stories."

Rafe took the map from Erik and unrolled it. "And you are of the same opinion?" Rafe asked Lady Arkyn.

She nodded. "It could be that the shadowfiend who murdered the thirteen sahale in Winter's Beak is specifically targeting sahale to absorb their powers. If there was ever a creature that I would label as a Dark Sahale, it would be this one."

"Either way, the sahale in Hermit's Hole will have more answers for us than Zefra could give," Erik said.

"So we are going to this X marked at the head of the Black River then?" Rafe asked.

"As quickly as possible," Erik replied.

"Even if it takes us through orc territory and right by their stronghold in these parts?" Rafe asked.

Erik nodded decisively. "I can handle the orcs if we run across them."

"Wouldn't it be better to go around them rather than risk a fight?" Rafe insisted. "I mean, I'm as game as the next guy to swing a sword, but there are only three of us. An orc stronghold will be full of capable warriors."

"You are free to stay with the Cult of Zammin, if you wish." With that, Erik turned and continued on at a brisk pace. As the day wore on and the sun sank lower in the sky, turning the air cooler, they began to jog. Before darkness came, they had traveled thirty miles on foot. They ate some of their food from their packs while continuing to walk as night overtook the land. Lady Arkyn led the way now, using her superior vision to help them avoid obstacles. They traveled for five days like this, running for as long as they could and walking when they needed rest. On the morning of the sixth day, after sleeping for the last three hours before the sunrise, they found themselves surrounded by a group of orcs on horseback.

"I told you," Rafe said as he jumped to his feet and went for his sword.

A pair of orcs fired arrows into the ground next to his foot as a warning.

"I'll handle this," Erik said.

"Be careful," Lady Arkyn said. "If they know who you are, they aren't likely to be happy about how many of their kin you have sent to the underworld."

Erik smirked. He held his right hand up, and slowly loosened his sword belt with his left hand. After dropping the weapon to the ground, he walked up to a particularly large orc sitting atop a chestnut colored horse.

"Titalok a mi foldunkon," the large orc snarled.

Erik nodded. In pure, crisp orcish he replied, "I am sorry for the trespass, but it is necessary."

The large orc's eyes went wide and he looked to the warrior on his right. Then he turned his big, brown eyes back to Erik. "You speak our language? What kind of man are you?"

"I am a warrior, like you," Erik said. "I learned your language while staying with the Fire-oak tribe far to the south."

"The Fire-oak clan let you live?" the large orc asked incredulously.

"I performed a favor for the chief there, and was made blood kin to the orcs of the Fire-oak tribe."

The large orc swung down from his horse and pulled a massive knife from his belt. He put the blade up to Erik's throat. "You lie! No human scum can ever become blood kin to the orcs."

"Do I flinch, brother?" Erik asked as he remained perfectly still. He had expected the challenge, but knew from his time living with the Fire-oak tribe that the correct response was unflinching courage and a calm voice. "If you wish to make this a test of strength, then I will oblige, but that is not necessary."

From behind him, Erik could hear Rafe asking Lady Arkyn about his ability to speak orcish.

"Shut up!" Lady Arkyn said harshly.

Erik paid them no mind. He knew that Lady Arkyn would follow his lead. She may not understand the words he was using, but she knew him well enough to read his body language. So long as he did not make a move to attack, she would keep Rafe in check to avoid a struggle.

"Tell me, human, why would the Fire-oak clan accept you?"

Erik stared back into the orc's eyes without wavering or blinking. He knew that orcs would view breaking eye contact as weakness or guile, for only those who had no secrets to hide could look an orc in the eye. "I fought for the chief, and I slew many enemies."

"Why?" the orc pressed. "Why would he accept you to fight for him? Was he weak?"

Erik shook his head. "No, the chief fought bravely with me in every encounter. There are none in the Fire-oak tribe that are weak. The males and females all fought with me, and I was honored to fight alongside them, for we had a mutual enemy. There were seven demons that were coming up from the underdark. I was hunting the demons when the Fire-oak tribe caught me. When I explained my purpose, they let me live so long as I did not turn away from battle. We lost many good warriors as we assaulted the demons, but we killed all seven, and the Fire-oak tribe is now stronger for it, and has received Hatmul's favor through their valor."

The large orc grunted and came in closer with his face. He sniffed Erik with his large, greenish nose and then pulled back with a nod. "The human tells the truth."

"Then he is blood kin?" the other warrior asked.

The large orc nodded. "This is an orc in human skin, brothers. He is to be treated with respect."

"What proof does he have that he is telling the truth?" another warrior barked from somewhere behind Erik.

"What's going on?" Rafe asked nervously.

"Keep quiet," Lady Arkyn commanded.

"Do you have any proof?"

Erik slowly turned over his right hand and displayed a long, thin scar that ran across his palm. "This is where the chief cut me open to mingle our blood together," Erik said. "I have no other tokens or proof, but this, coupled with the fact that I can speak in your tongue, should be enough to show you that I speak the truth."

The large orc pulled his knife away from Erik's neck and sheathed it. "I am Lubbok, Prince of the Yellow-wing clan. I can lead you to our stronghold, and there we can feast your arrival, brother." Lubbok reached out and clasped Erik's right hand in his and gave it a hearty, single shake.

"I fear I cannot dally," Erik said. This refusal caused murmurs to ripple through the warriors on horseback, as he had expected. It was an insult to refuse an orc's invitation, but Erik knew the appropriate apology. "Though it pains me to refuse, I have a matter of honor that I must attend to, otherwise I would be unworthy to accept your offer."

Lubbok's angry eyes softened. "What troubles you, brother?"

"I am pursuing a murderer who killed many people dishonorably," Erik said. As violent and bloodthirsty as the orcs were, murder was not a crime their society tolerated. It was considered most foul and dishonorable to them to murder someone. The warriors on horseback all snarled and spat on the ground to display their disgust at hearing the word.

"Then I withdraw my invitation," Lubbok said. This was the sign that no offense was taken at being refused. It allowed both parties to save face in front of all witnesses, but Lubbok took it one step further. "As I have never before thought it possible that a human would fight alongside my people, I wish to offer my blade to you, now. Let me fight alongside you, and we will resolve this matter of honor together, and both thereby prove our valor."

Erik had not expected that at all. He nodded his agreement. "I am honored already by your willingness to assist me, brother," Erik replied.

"Then it is settled," Lubbok said. "Gonsar, Mordin, you will come with me. I will need three additional horses. The rest of you will return to my father and inform him that I am going with our brother to bring a murderer to justice."

Within seconds, three horses were brought to Erik and the orcs split into two groups.

"Allow me to tell my companions what is happening," Erik said. Lubbok nodded and waved toward Rafe and Lady Arkyn with a massive left arm that was covered in scars.

Erik returned to them with a large smile. "It seems that we will have some reinforcements," he said.

"Orcs?!" Rafe stammered. "But—"

Erik lightly backhanded Rafe in the stomach. "Keep your voice down. They have agreed to not only let us pass, but are also going to provide us with horses, and three warriors, including Lubbok, their prince. But, I must warn you, they will not tolerate insults, so keep your prejudices to yourself," Erik told Rafe.

"You believe we can trust them?" Lady Arkyn asked.

Erik nodded. "When I joked about Griselda... I left a few things out," Erik said. Lady Arkyn shot him a puzzled look. "We didn't get involved or anything, but she was the daughter of a chief whose tribe I lived with for a long time."

"You lived with orcs?" Lady Arkyn asked.

Erik smiled. "As I said, a story for another time, but to the orcs, I am considered a brother, an adopted member of their society if you will. So long as we avoid offending these orcs, then we will have no troubles."

"Well," Rafe began, "I thought we had gotten to know each other pretty good but it turns out you are just full of surprises." He smiled then and poked Erik in the ribs. "You don't happen to have a secret hoard of treasure somewhere I could dip into for a... business venture, do you?"

Erik answered the probing question with a wink and then turned back to speak to Lubbok. "The female is known as Lady Arkyn, and the male is called Rafe."

Lubbok nodded. "If they are with you, then we will count them as part of our group as well. Come, let us eat and discuss this murderer, then we can be on our way."

Erik knew better than to refuse this offer. He was in charge of the group, and Terramyr was indeed in great danger, but having three orcs along for the journey was like adding a compliment of ten human warriors to their group. Insulting them now and losing that, as well as the horses they offered, would hurt far more than the hour or two required for a proper orcish breakfast.

The six of them gathered around a large fire pit a few minutes later. Lubbok had his warriors go and fetch a deer, of which there were plenty a short distance away. They roasted the animal until the meat was done to perfection, and then they sat around the fire and ate until the meat was entirely devoured. The three orcs ate the larger portion of the animal, but Erik did well in keeping up with them. Lady Arkyn put away a surprising amount of food before she had to slow down as well, which impressed the three orcs. Rafe was the one who ate the least, which drew a bit of jeering from Lubbok.

"What is he saying?" Rafe asked after Lubbok had made his fourth comment about how little the sailor could eat.

Erik, not wanting to lie to either party and risk adding tension, turned and told Rafe the truth. "He says you must be weak, eating so little."

"I ate at least a couple pounds worth of venison," Rafe objected.

Lubbok wiped his mouth on his right forearm and gestured with his chin at Rafe. "What does he say, brother?" Erik sighed and interpreted what Rafe had said. Lubbok began to laugh. "My son can eat the same amount, and he is only three summers old."

Erik smiled and turned to inform Rafe what Lubbok had said.

The sailor grudgingly reached out and took a large portion of meat from the carcass and tore into it with a bite too large for his mouth, staring at Lubbok all the while. The amount of meat he had in his mouth was so much that he had to take gaping bites to try and chew it down, but rather than pull anything out and make it easier on himself, he continued chewing and chomping, with bits of meat hanging out over his mouth.

Lubbok smiled approvingly. "He has spirit," he told Erik.

Erik nodded. "He has done well on the journey so far."

"What dangers have you faced, brother?" one of the other orc warriors asked.

Erik stroked his chin and set his pile of ribs aside. "I slew a shadowfiend in Pracheloor Cave," he said.

Lubbok snarled and the three orcs spat on the ground. Magic users were only slightly more tolerable to orcs than murderers. "Magic is the way of cowards," Lubbok said in disgust. "You did well to slay the creature. An honorable feat."

Then there was a compliment of human archers and a wizard that followed us from the mainland when we began sailing northward."

"How many archers?" Chabba, the youngest of the orcs asked.

Erik shook his head. "Not sure, perhaps two score."

"And you defeated them all?" Chongor asked.

Erik nodded. "Lady Arkyn and I fought them together. We also killed a few dragon-slayers."

Lubbok pointed at Erik with a freshly cleaned thigh bone. "The archers are weak, save for the number of them, but dragon-slayers are great warriors. Another honorable victory, brother."

Erik bowed his head, accepting the compliment. "Later, we hired Rafe to sail us through the Natchy Moors."

"The what?" Chongor asked.

"The cursed waters," Lubbok explained. "The land was covered in a dense fog, and there were many monsters, yes?"

"Yes," Erik replied.

Lubbok nodded. "Then what you call the Natchy Moors, we call the cursed waters. Many orcs have tested their mettle in those parts, especially old males who have passed their prime and wish to die with honor."

"We slew many monsters there," Erik said.

"What kinds?" Chabba asked.

"Large things that were like bats, and a giant octopus that was trying to wreck our ship."

"How did you survive?" Chongor inquired. "No insult intended, but there are only three of you."

"Do you have magic, brother?" Chabba pressed. Their tones had gone from curious to distrusting and guarded.

264

Erik shook his head. "I am not a wizard," he replied. He decided it best not to mention the fact that he could transform into a dragon. "Lady Arkyn has some powers, but mainly she uses them to communicate with animals, nothing more."

"Speaking with animals is a skill," Lubbok insisted. "It is not magic, nor is it a tool used by cowards."

"And the sailor, does he use magic?" Chabba asked.

Erik shook his head. "He uses only a sword."

"And you slew the bats and the octopus?"

Erik nodded. "Yes."

"Then you are a great warrior indeed," Lubbok announced. Chabba and Chongor nodded their agreement. "No orc has ever returned from the cursed waters."

Erik thought about telling them of Vodklyk, but he knew that the orcs would not like hearing that Erik had retreated. Retreat was rarely a strategy used by orcs. They preferred to fight with their full force, never turning aside, as death in battle was preferable to running away. More than that, the orcs worshipped the gods that ruled Hammenfein. If he were to tell them that Vodklyk, a servant of those gods, had attacked them, the orcs may take that as a sign that Hatmul was displeased with Erik. They were impressed enough as it was, there was no reason to bring up any additional troubles.

"Tell me of this murderer," Lubbok said. "Is he strong?"

Erik shrugged. "To tell the truth, he is smart and cunning. He uses magic," all of the orcs spat in disgust, "and he has killed many men. I do not know his name, I am following his trail and looking for clues to his identity."

"But you are certain he is here, in our lands?" Lubbok asked.

Erik sighed and shook his head. "To be honest, I am not sure he is in the Northern Territory at all, but there is someone here who can help me. The clues I will find in the east will help me solve the riddle."

"I see," Lubbok stated as he tore off another piece of meat and chewed it quickly. "Then, we should hurry, and set out before the trail becomes lost."

Erik nodded.

Lubbok turned to Chabba and Chongor. "Scatter the bones and put out the fire. We ride to the east."

Erik turned and told Arkyn and Rafe that they were about to leave. Rafe rolled his eyes and looked down at a large amount of meat still in his hand while rubbing his burgeoning stomach. Erik then got to his feet. Lubbok stood and came in close, putting a massive hand on Erik's shoulder. He leaned down to Erik's ear.

"Brother, there is something you should know about the forest beyond our lands," he said. "There are elves there, but they are not like your friend. They are wild and savage, living in the trees and attacking anyone who enters the woods. It is not likely that we can get through without a confrontation." Lubbok pulled away and then glanced to Lady Arkyn. "You should warn her, so she understands that she will be fighting a people that look like her, but are not, in fact, her people. They are wild, savage creatures."

Erik nodded. "I will tell her."

"Is he talking about me now?" Lady Arkyn said as she approached them. "I ate more food than Rafe, so there shouldn't be anything to make fun of."

"I heard that," Rafe said as he struggled to get up, groaning like an old man after mid-summer's feast.

"No, he was warning me that there is a group of savage elves in the woods to the east. He says they will attack us, or anyone that enters the forest, upon sight. He wanted you to know that they are not your people."

"All elves are my people," Lady Arkyn replied indignantly. "I should be happy to see them."

"No, I don't think so," Erik said. "Remember, I can use my gift to scan the intentions of others, it works with orcs as well as humans or elves. He is sincere in his desire to warn you."

Lady Arkyn arched a brow over her bright, green eyes and put a hand on her hip. "What is the name of their city? I am sure we can arrange for safe passage."

"She does not believe me?" Lubbok cut in.

Erik held a hand up to ask both of them to wait. He was finding interpretation to be a little more work than he had expected. He turned to Lubbok. "You say the elves have no city?"

Lubbok shook his head.

Erik turned back to Lady Arkyn. "The elves have no city. He says they live in the trees. I suggest we trust him."

Lady Arkyn let her hand slip off her hip and then gave a single nod. "Very well, but if I get the chance, I will try to talk with them. No use shedding elven blood if we can use our words. We have enough people to fight."

Erik and Lubbok both bowed their heads as Lady Arkyn turned to gather her belongings.

"She also has spirit," Lubbok said. "I don't know her words, but it seemed to me that she wants to try reasoning with the savage elves, am I right?"

Erik smiled. This particular orc was smarter than he looked. "You are correct, brother."

"Then when she does, we will be nearby. When her words fail to convince the savage elves, we will be ready to shield her. You have my word, brother."

With that, Erik and Lubbok gathered their equipment and saddled their horses, which had been allowed to roam in the grasses nearby to graze. Once all six horses were ready, the group set out at a quick, but not grueling pace across the orcish lands. On the second day together, they came to a large, stone bridge that spanned the same river that Erik and the others had forded on their way to find the Cult of Zammin. Off in the distance to the north, Erik could see the stark towers and massive walls of the orcish stronghold.

"Behold, Ocht'nien, my home," Lubbok said as they crossed the bridge and continued onward. "My father, Chief Orgnin, has ruled there for five decades, longer than any chief before him. He is strong, and leads his people well."

"May his strength continue and his blade ever be sharp," Erik said, reciting the words of an oft given tribute among the Fire-oak tribe. Lubbok echoed the sentiment, and then they put the city to their backs and quickened their pace.

It took them three full days of riding to reach the edge of the orcish lands. Along the way, they saw four additional patrols of orc warriors, but none gave them any trouble once they saw that Lubbok was with them. At the edge of the orcish territory, there were several stakes driven into the ground with skulls lashed to the tops. It was a common border-marking between orcs and other civilizations. It served as a warning to all would-be intruders that orcs would not tolerate incursions into their homeland. The curious thing was that there had been no such markers on the western border.

"Lubbok, why did you not mark the border to the west?"

Lubbok turned around in his saddle and smiled. "You mean why do we not have hostilities with the caribou herders, yes?"

Erik nodded.

"They negotiated peace with us long ago. We trade with them."

"You... trade with them?" Erik asked incredulously. "I have ever heard of orcs trading with other races before."

"And until a few days ago, I had never heard of a human made blood kin to the orcs," Lubbok replied. "In any case, there is a legend among our people. Long ago, our ancestors sought to slaughter the people in the west and take their caribou. As our ancestors marched toward their dome, a tall man with green robes and a strange marking on his right cheek stood in the way. The people in the west called him by the name of Zammin, but to my ancestors he introduced himself as a guardian of Terramyr."

"A guardian?" Erik echoed. He recalled the descriptions of the guardian he had read about while studying in the monastery far to the south. This description matched perfectly with what he had read. Could it be that Zammin was that guardian? Was that why he had started the cult and tried to study the Four Horsemen early on? There were so many questions flooding Erik's mind that he almost forgot that he was in the middle of a discussion with Lubbok. He tempered his excitement and probed for more information. "He stood alone against an entire army?"

Lubbok nodded. "He said that the people who herded caribou and followed his teachings were not the kind who were allowed to take up weapons. He had forbad them from fighting and warring. Therefore, he said there was no honor to be gained in killing them. He suggested that we trade with them. We could give them leather goods and medicines, and they could give us caribou."

"And just like that, the army turned away?" Erik asked.

Lubbok laughed. "No. That is not the way of the orc. They tested the guardian by sending five orc warriors out to slay him. He killed them all. He then offered a challenge to the chief at that time. He said the chief could pick twenty of his best warriors, and they could all come against him in battle. If they won, then they could have the right to kill the people who herded caribou, but if they lost, then the guardian was to become our chief."

"Your father is chief," Erik said. "So I take it he died then?" *That would explain why the Cult of Zammin have not seen him since he left.* Erik thought.

269

"No, the guardian killed all twenty of the warriors and then held his weapon to the chief's neck. In front of the army, he killed the chief. The remaining warriors bowed down and were ready to make their pledge to him, but he told them that he did not want to be their chief, that he had other business which would take him far away. So, instead of taking what was his, he gave it back to us. It is said he spent the rest of the day examining the surviving warriors until he came to one known as Szabol. The guardian named Szabol chief of our tribe, and in return Szabol gave the guardian a blood oath coin. You know what that is, yes brother?"

Erik nodded. "It is an honor pledge to fulfill any favor the holder of such a coin may ask. To refuse the favor will bring dishonor, and a curse from Hatmul."

Lubbok nodded approvingly. "Correct. You know your culture well."

Erik smiled at that. Lubbok spoke as if Erik had been born an orc. He accepted him as fully as if Erik had tusks and green skin. It was good to be among such an open and honorable people. "So let me guess," Erik began. "The guardian used his blood oath coin to instruct your tribe to keep peace with the people in the west, and trade with them."

Lubbok nodded. "Also, because they cannot fight for themselves, should they ever ask us for military aid, we are to commit as fully as if our own kin were in danger."

Erik had to admit, he was liking how this guardian character behaved. To be sure, some had died during the conflict according to Lubbok's account, but he had saved many, many more and had established a unique peace that served both societies. This guardian, or Zammin, as the cultists called him, sounded like a person Erik would be happy to work alongside.

"Did he have a symbol on his collar?" Erik asked.

Lubbok shook his head. "I am not sure," he said. "It happened several centuries ago. I know only what I have told you."

Erik nodded. He was fairly certain that Zammin would carry the symbol upon his collar that Erik had memorized from the book. Unfortunately, unless he was also a person of extremely long life, it sounded as though Zammin might be dead by now.

As they approached what Zefra had termed the Dread Pines, Erik felt a chill creep up his spine. The trees were tall, thick and dark. Black and dark green beard-lichen hung down from the lower branches. The dirt below was well compacted, covered in dead pine needles and littered with pine cones and old limbs that had long since fallen from the trees on which they had grown. Some of the trees had thick, slowly moving streams of amber colored pitch oozing out from holes in the trunk and traveling downward.

A black and red woodpecker tapped at a nearby tree, furiously working his beak to get at the prizes behind the bark. Squirrels leapt from tree to tree in the branches above, chattering angrily and throwing small pine cones down at Erik and the others.

They pushed into the forest cautiously. Lubbok and the other orcs drew their weapons preemptively and continuously scanned the forest floor and the branches above for any sign of danger. Erik could sense a presence, but he wasn't sure where it was or whether it presented a threat to the group. Either way, they had to push through the Dread Pines in order to reach the ruins of Galardene.

Ever since Erik was a young teenager, he had wanted to visit Galardene, as it was Master Lepkin's birthplace. His former instructor had only mentioned it a few times, but never in great detail. Master Lepkin was usually quiet about details of his origin, as well as some of his greater feats such as the battle of Gelleirt Monastery where Lepkin defended the monks and their monastery against three hundred Tarthuns single-handedly. Erik had often tried to pry details out of Lepkin, but the man always deflected the questions, focusing solely on Erik's training. Now that Erik was on his way to Galardene, he was beginning to understand why the man had remained silent on this subject. Unlike Gelleirt Monastery, which Lepkin did his best not to talk about for fear of coming across as a braggart, Galardene was not a story with a happy ending. Erik was getting the distinct impression that whatever drove Lepkin and his people out of Galardene was still here, lying in wait for its next victim.

Whatever it was, it did not show itself that day. They made camp deep in the forest just an hour before sundown. Chabba and Chongor made themselves busy by creating pikes to set around the camp. Lubbok made short work of at least a dozen pine trees, cutting them down and thereby reducing how close any enemy could come by sneaking through the branches above. When he had finished, Lubbok enlisted Rafe's help to make a hasty lean-to shelter with the logs up against a rocky bluff to further shield them from unwanted attackers.

Lady Arkyn spent her time hunting, returning with two pheasants, a hare, and three quail. The group ate their fill, and then retired to the lean-to for the night. Lubbok took first watch, Lady Arkyn took the second, and Chongor took the third. Erik slept well that night, and woke refreshed as the first rays of sunlight broke through the forest.

They quickly cleared camp and resumed their journey. The second day in the forest was uneventful as well, as was the third. They made good progress, though they found that the weather had turned much colder and were even greeted by a layer of snow and frost on the morning of the fourth day. They gathered their cloaks about themselves and drew the hoods up to stave off the biting wind that assaulted them through the first part of the day, and welcomed the warmth of the sun when it finally broke through the clouds above the forest and thawed the area in mid-afternoon.

Their luck was not to last, though, for as the evening approached, the cold came back with a vengeance. Along with it, came a party of three elves. Lubbok was the first to spot them, hiding in the trees forty yards from their position. The large orc called a halt to the group and ordered Chongor and Chabba to prepare for battle. The elves were not like any others Erik had seen before. They did not wear elegant raiment, or even practical clothing. They were bare foot and wore only loin cloths. They were armed with savage looking bows that had barbs along the limbs. Their eyes were red, almost glowing in fact, and their ears were much more elongated than other elves. Their skin was different too. It was a pale grayish tan that gave them a rather feral, sickly look.

Lady Arkyn pulled her horse alongside Erik's. "Let me speak with them," she said.

Erik, not wanting her to be put into harm's way, called upon his power to scan the elves and discover their intentions. What he found was not comforting.

"Circle up!" Erik shouted to Rafe. "They are here to fight," Erik told Lady Arkyn. He then told Lubbok and the other orcs that they were about to be attacked.

Lady Arkyn didn't listen. She urged her horse forward and held out a hand in greeting. "I am Lady Arkyn," she said in Taish, the language of the elves.

The three elves in the branches looked at her, and then pulled their arrows and fired. Lady Arkyn was able to dodge the arrows, but her horse was struck in the side. It reared up and would have bucked her off if not for the fact that she was extremely nimble and quick. She managed to get to her feet and use the horse's momentum to launch herself up into a nearby tree. She then spun around and answered the attack with an arrow of her own.

One of the savage elves was struck in the heart. His body went rigid, and then he toppled out of the tree and slammed into the ground head-first. His neck broke with a resounding *snap!* Chongor and Chabba fired at the two remaining elves. Their aim proved as efficient as Lady Arkyn's, for they both hit their mark and the other two savage elves were slain.

Erik drew his sword and got down from his horse. He was always more comfortable fighting under his own power rather than relying upon an animal to carry him. He saw a flash of grayish skin dart behind a tree behind the group.

"I got him," Rafe said cavalierly as he ran off toward the assailant. Erik scanned the trees all around for more movement, but the other elves did not come from the trees above, or walk upon the ground. As Rafe ran to engage the one elf off in the trees, a hatch that had been covered with dirt and ferns flew open and three savage elves leapt out.

Rafe cried out as one of the elves managed to jab his left bicep with a spear, but the sailor did not give up the fight. He chopped down with his sword, severing both of the elf's arms at the elbow and dropping the detached limbs and the spear to the ground. He then whirled to the right and stabbed through the chest of a second elf. He would have likely taken the third as well, but Lady Arkyn fired from her vantage point above and struck the last elf down with an arrow through the right eye.

Rafe then ran on around a large pine tree. A moment later, the elf that Erik had seen running through the trees fell backward, his head missing from his neck.

Hatches opened up all around them then as savage elves poured out of the ground. Two were near Erik, but he dispatched them before they had a chance to escape their hiding spot. Chabba, Chongor, and Lady Arkyn let their arrows fly, killing nearly a dozen elves while Rafe hacked at a group of four that came after him, Lubbok trampled down several with his horse while yelling and shouting, and Erik engaged five more with his sword.

The fight only lasted for a few more moments before all of the savage elves lay dead upon the forest floor. Other than Rafe's wound, Erik's group came out of the battle unscathed, though they were a bit dirty for their efforts. They regrouped in the center of a nearby clearing and took stock of themselves before resuming the journey. Rafe tied his own bandage, refusing help from even Lady Arkyn. Erik assumed the sailor had a point to prove to the orcs. Apparently, it worked, for Lubbok gave Rafe a hearty slap on the back and brought the sailor his horse.

"You all right?" Erik asked Rafe.

"Fine, I've had scrapes bigger than this one," he replied evenly. "But it looks like Lady Arkyn's horse is a bit worse for wear."

Erik turned around and saw the large animal lying on its side, with Lady Arkyn gently stroking its neck as it grunted and twitched.

"He's hurt badly," Lady Arkyn said.

Erik approached and saw that two of the arrows were just behind the saddle, but they were embedded deep into the animal. The third was higher up, just behind the neck. Lady Arkyn was fortunate she had not been struck. The worst wound on the horse did not come from the arrows, however. After it had reared up and ran off, it had somehow managed to snap a branch and the sharp end had pierced the animal's chest just below the neck. Blood was flowing freely from the hole, and there was nothing any of them could do for the beast. Lady Arkyn spoke in her elvish language to soothe the horse. It closed its eyes and relaxed its neck, placing its head down upon the ground.

Lady Arkyn then drew her bow and positioned the arrow for a decisively quick mercy shot. She whispered one last phrase in Taish and then released the bowstring. The animal didn't so much as jerk or pull away. The shot was so expertly placed and executed that the horse felt no pain as it left its mortal shell behind.

"I see what you mean about talking with animals," Lubbok told Erik in orcish. "You are fortunate to have such companions."

Erik nodded. The group prepared to leave then, more than ready to put the Dread Pines behind them. Lady Arkyn shared Erik's horse, wrapping her arms tightly around his waist and leaning her head on the back of his shoulder as they continued along their way. Erik was not overly happy with the way Lady Arkyn had lost her horse, but he was more than a little excited to have her riding with him for the duration of the trip.

They finally left the Dread Pines behind for good in the middle of day five in the forest. After they were out of the woods, they could increase their speed a bit, but with Erik's horse now carrying two, they were not quite as fast as they had been before they entered the forest. Still, it was only one more day before they reached the Black River, on the other side of which, stood the darkened ruins of Galardene, Master Lepkin's original home.

Chapter 18

The Black River looked nothing like its name. The waters were a deep blueish green that flowed peacefully southward. A large bridge spanned the two hundred-foot wide river with stone columns holding up the bridge from below and wooden planks forming the walkway over the water. Erik supposed that back when the city was inhabited by Lepkin's people, the bridge would have looked beautiful, but at this time it was worn with age. Many of the wooden planks were cracked and broken, and there were several places where the wood had rotted away entirely. They had to cross the bridge in a single file line, moving slowly and walking their horses across using their reins to guide them along the sections that appeared strong enough to hold the weight. When they made the other side, they went straight for Galardene, which was another hundred yards away. Even from the distance they could see that many of the buildings had collapsed. As they entered the city, they could see that in addition to the collapsed buildings, other structures had been burned and hollowed out or covered with overgrowth and otherwise intact. They passed through what at one point may have been an outdoor market, with a few stalls still standing upright amidst waist-high weeds. From there they went into a district that seemed a mix of both houses and shops.

It was a strange feeling, seeing the remains of Lepkin's home. He had never been informed precisely what had driven them out. It couldn't have been the savage elves, for they were hardly fighters. They were more a barely organized rabble living wild in the woods. If Lepkin's people were anything like him, then it must have been something much more dangerous. Perhaps Lubbok knew. His people had apparently kept their history well, judging by the account of Zammin that Lubbok had shared with him.

"Brother, what happened to the humans here?"

"We do not know," Lubbok said. His eyes scanned the vacant buildings, looking for threats. His muscles were tense and the knuckles on his hands were turning white as he gripped the reins.

"Surely you must know something," Erik pressed. "Did they try to leave by heading down river?"

"The Black River leads to the cliffs in the south. If you were to take the river, then you would fall over the edge of the cliffs and die. The cliffs to the south are impassable," Lubbok commented. "When the humans fled this area, they used the river only until they reached the forest, and then had to cross the forest with the wild elves until they could get around the cliffs and down to the beaches. They crossed into our land, but it was obvious they were fleeing something, so we let them go and prepared to battle whatever had driven them out."

"So what was it?" Erik asked.

Lubbok shrugged. "We never found out. The humans escaped our grasp and nothing came to chase them. After more than a month of waiting, we entered the forest, but found only savage elves. We have been at war with those foul creatures ever since, but I do not think they are responsible for driving out the humans. The humans of Galardene were worthy

278

opponents, strong and large, like us. They were disciplined warriors and were an honorable people."

"How many humans escaped?" Erik asked.

Lubbok shrugged. "Not many. I don't know the exact count, but it was fewer than one hundred, that was why we assumed something great was pushing them out."

"And did your people ever cross the Dread Pines and come to these ruins?" Erik asked.

"Twice, but both parties found nothing extraordinary. So we ended our search."

"Strange," Erik said.

"What's he saying?" Rafe asked. "Does he know what happened here?"

Erik shook his head. "He said it's a mystery. They don't know what made the northmen of Galardene flee."

"There is a distinct evil here," Lady Arkyn said. "I can feel it."

As if on cue, several figures appeared on the rooftops around them. Some were armed with bows already drawn and trained on the party, others with swords or axes. Lubbok shouted orders to his warriors, but Erik told them to hold their fire. He knew these people.

They were tall, with lean, muscular bodies. The men wore loin cloths and the women wore coverings both over their groin and their chests, but otherwise the people were naked, save for black, swirling tattoos that covered their bodies.

"Blacktongues," Erik said.

"Impossible," Lady Arkyn said. "They were wiped out in the war against Tu'luh."

"Hold your fire, if they had wanted to attack, they would have already done so," Erik said. "I think they want to talk."

"Are you mad?" Lady Arkyn shouted. "They're assassins."

279

"Brother," Erik began, addressing Lubbok in orcish. "I will try to speak with them."

"Who are they?" Lubbok asked. "We have not seen their kind before."

"They are a race of assassins, a most wicked and vile people. I have fought many of them."

"Murderers who work with cowardly arts," Lubbok said. The three orcs spat in disgust.

"Are you flesh and blood?" one of the Blacktongue women asked. She walked toward the edge of the roof she stood upon and looked down at Erik. "I see that you are their leader, how is it a man walks alongside both elves and orcs?"

"How is it that Blacktongues live here in Galardene?" Erik said.

The woman tilted her head to the side and sneered. "You are alive then, and have your mind under your own control?"

"Last time I checked," Erik said. "Either come down and speak with me face to face, or I will come to you."

The woman dropped down from the roof as gracefully as a bird might land upon a branch. She stood and walked toward Erik, leaving her hatchets hanging from her belt as she came in close. Though her irises were a bright blue, the whites of her eyes had been tattooed black also, making for an intimidating visage. She showed no hint of fear, and as Erik scanned her with his power he found that she had not yet decided whether Erik and his party were a threat or not. Still, the idea of conversing with a Blacktongue was more temptation than he could resist. He had long ago set aside the hatred he had once felt for them, and was now discovering that he was almost happy to see that some of them had survived. While he did not mourn those he had fought against and killed, he found that as he focused on the idea of extending mercy to each of his foes in an attempt to keep the beast within himself caged, he did not much enjoy the thought of being a major contributor to the death of an entire race. The fact that he saw some here and now, and was about to talk with them, gave him a hope he had not experienced before.

He slid off his horse, pushing Lady Arkyn's hands back when she tried to hold him in place.

"I am Erik Lokton, from the Middle Kingdom," he said.

The woman nodded. "I know your name well," she said. "Among our people, you are called the scourge."

Erik smiled. "It has a nice ring to it," he said. "But, I must tell you, I am not here to bother your people. I am on an important mission."

"You are not the first person to come through here," the woman said. "Do you serve the first?"

Erik drew his brow into a knot above his eyes and folded his arms. "Who else came through here?" he asked.

"He was in the form of a man, but when he found us, he took the form of a demon. He slaughtered many of my people. He burned many of our homes."

"A shadowfiend," Erik stated. "No, I do not serve him. I believe he is responsible for the murders of many people back in my homeland, and I am following him."

"You are going to fight him?" the woman asked.

Erik nodded. "I am going to stop him."

The woman shook her head. "Then you will die, Erik Lokton of the Middle Kingdom, and all of your friends along with you."

"What is the ugly woman saying?" Lubbok shouted in orcish.

Erik held up a hand to silence him. It was a good thing that other humans did not take the time to learn orcish. If she had heard the insult, the conversation would have shifted to fighting in a heartbeat. "How long ago was he here?" Erik asked.

The woman was silent for a moment, and then she answered. "Two days ago. He came with a woman. She had dark hair, and fair skin. They appear to be working together. She had magic, and he fought with the soul of a demon." The woman gestured to the others on the rooftops. "We few are all that remain. Before the... shadowfiend came to us, we numbered four hundred strong. You cannot beat him. It is best to bury your dead and leave him be."

"I have to ask you something," Erik said. "When he fought with the power of a demon, how many shapes did he take?"

The woman narrowed her eyes and emitted a low grunt. "Two," she said after a few moments. "At first, he was like a monster, but then when more of us came out against him, he changed into a dragon."

"A dragon?" Rafe asked. "Just what in Icadion's name are we hunting?"

Erik nodded. "Then he is the one we are after," he said. Erik turned around to face Lady Arkyn. "This is the one who killed and absorbed the powers of the other sahale in Winter's Beak. He has to be the Dark Sahale."

"We will let you pass, but you cannot stay here," the woman said. "You are dead, all of you, unless you turn back now."

Erik smiled at her and shook his head. "If you know who I am, then you know that I am the only one who can stop the monster. Which way did he go?"

The woman pointed northward. "They went that way, toward the mountains."

"Erik," Lady Arkyn said. "He is going after the sahale we are trying to find."

Erik nodded. "Then we have no time to lose. We must track him down."

The woman gestured toward his horse. "If you survive, then you may pass through this way once more, but I do not expect to see you again. This is the end of the scourge."

"Tell me, how did you come here in such numbers?"

"We are of a different clan," the woman said. "We have lived here since the humans left this city. Before that, we lived in caves to the east."

"What drove the humans from this place?" Erik pressed.

"If you go northward, you will discover that as well," the woman replied. "If I were you, I would seek shelter before the sun goes down, otherwise, you may not live long enough to find your shadowfiend." With that, the woman snapped her fingers and the other Blacktongues on the rooftops disappeared as if made of vapor. The woman walked to an open door and vanished into the darkness of a vacant shop, leaving the six in the street by themselves.

Erik scanned the rooftops once more. He would be surprised if the Blacktongues actually let them pass through without a fight. If what the woman had said was true, then perhaps they might allow it in order to let Erik fight their mutual enemy, for no matter the outcome of such a fight, it would mean one less enemy for the Blacktongues. As his eyes searched the roofs, he saw another woman. This one was not like the Blacktongues. She wore a dark blue dress, and had long black hair that flowed out to the side with the wind. She looked at Erik and tilted her head to the side, staring at him. Erik reached out with his power and felt a strange mix of emotions coming from the woman. At once he felt contempt, curiosity, and respect emanating from her. The young warrior turned to alert Lady Arkyn to the woman's presence.

"Up on the roof to the south east, a woman, do you see her?" Erik whispered.

"There is no one there," Lady Arkyn said.

Erik turned back around and saw that the woman had vanished. "We need to hurry," Erik told Lubbok in orcish. "The murderer was here, and he killed many of their people."

"How many?" Lubbok asked. "They look like capable fighters."

Erik nodded. "She said they are all that remain of four hundred."

Lubbok's eyes shot wide, and then a great grin stretched the lips behind his lower tusks. "Then it shall be another good fight, brother, and we shall prove our valor."

They left Galardene as quickly as possible, riding northward alongside the Black River as Zefra had suggested. Despite the Blacktongue's warning, they were not able to find adequate shelter before nightfall. There was nothing with which to build a lean-to, so Lubbok and the other orc warriors pitched single man tents that they had with them. However, instead of sleeping in the tents, the group built a large campfire in the middle of the tents and then slept some fifty yards away. It was a simple ploy, but one that proved effective, for during the second watch, visitors came to call upon them.

Lady Arkyn woke the group quietly and they readied their weapons as a group of ten men snuck up on the camp from the north. They were crouched low, nearly crawling as they moved in close. They came within ten yards of the tents and then sprang up silently and began charging the tents with swords and spears. They ripped through the light canvas material and let out war cries as they stabbed down where they thought their victims would be.

With the aid of the camp fire's light, even Chabba and Chongor could effectively aim their bows on the assailants. Upon Lady Arkyn's signal, the three of them unleashed their arrows in a furious volley one after another until all of the attackers were slain but one. The last one they struck in the legs. He stumbled and fell into the camp fire, screaming and shouting in agony as he scrambled to roll out of the flames.

Before his clothes had stopped smoking, Erik was on him with his sword. The young warrior pressed the tip of the blade into the warrior's throat.

"Who sent you?"

The man looked up with savage, red eyes and lashed out with a free hand. Erik's sword pushed in, and the warrior fell to the ground. He turned and was about to speak to Lady Arkyn, but then an eerie green light rose from the Black River. It hovered just a few inches above the ground and started fanning out as it neared the camp.

"What evil is this?" Rafe asked.

"It's necromancy," Lady Arkyn said. "I have seen it before, outside of Winter's Beak." Lady Arkyn peered into the darkness, and then finally pointed beyond the river. "There, there she is!"

"Who?" Erik asked.

Chabba didn't need to understand Lady Arkyn's words to know what to do. He and Chongor lit their arrows in the campfire and shot in the direction Lady Arkyn was pointing. The flames illuminated the immediate area around them as they flew. When they reached the opposite side of the river, the group saw another dozen warriors with swords and spears. They were standing behind a woman with dark hair.

"That's her," Erik said. "That's the woman I saw after the Blacktongues left."

"It is the same woman I saw outside of Winter's Beak!" Lady Arkyn shouted as she fired her arrow at the woman. The arrow went wide and slammed into one of the nearby warriors. To their horror, the woman let out a blast of green light from her hand and the slain warrior rose back to his feet and pulled the arrow from his chest.

"Witch," Lubbok snarled. The three orcs spat. The green light stretching toward them began to fall upon the dead that had initially attacked the camp. The bodies started to stir. Lubbok reached down and removed a burning log from the

285

fire and used it like a club on the first reanimated warrior. Embers and sparks exploded as the log connected with the warrior's face. A sickening, wet crack rent the air and the warrior's head spun around on a shattered neck. "Come back from that," Lubbok growled. "Use fire!"

Erik smiled. He had fire, and whether it would bother his new brothers or not, now was the time to use it. He let his power and rage flow through him and ignite the blade. Chabba and Chongor lit their arrows in the fire, as did Lady Arkyn. Lubbok muttered some sort of curse at Erik for using magic, but he paid it no mind. He went to work taking the heads of the newly reanimated corpses before they could fully regain their senses.

The woman across the river screamed angrily as her spell failed to heal the burns on her warriors. There was little she could do, so she and the others across the river turned and fled after Erik and Lubbok finished off the rest of the original ten. Chabba and Chongor took down another two each as they fired arrows across the river. Lady Arkyn continued to fire at the woman, but none of her arrows hit their mark. Every time they came within a few feet, the missiles would unexpectedly turn and fly off to the side.

Erik watched the woman flee, but as he reached out with his power once more, he was surprised to discover that she had no fear of him or the others. She was retreating, but not because she thought she would lose. He could sense that she was holding back. Perhaps this attack had been meant to capture them instead of kill them outright. He wasn't sure, as the warriors had definitely fought hard, but he couldn't shake the impression that the woman didn't want to kill him. Perhaps they meant to kill the others, but not him.

"Magic," Lady Arkyn hissed as she finally gave up.

"It's all right, at least they've gone," Erik said, still trying to process his impressions of the woman.

Lubbok was not very pleased. After he was finished with the log, he tossed it aside and came at Erik, pointing an accusing finger. "You lied! You said you were not a wizard!"

"I am not," Erik said. "This sword is a special item, made from Telarian steel and endowed with a rare enchantment."

"A coward's weapon!" Lubbok spat.

If Lubbok didn't like the sword, then he would hate to find out Erik was actually sahale. "Brother, it was the only way to stop the witch's magic."

"I would rather die than use such a device!" Lubbok shouted.

Erik extinguished the flames and sheathed the sword. "Don't worry, Lubbok, you will never have to hold the sword. I, on the other hand, must use it as part of my station. It will aid us in the upcoming fight."

Lubbok stormed off, ranting about how he had half a mind to leave and return home and let Erik go on ahead without him. For a moment, it seemed as though he were going to do just that, for he walked far out into the darkness and disappeared. Even Chabba and Chongor stared off after him, though they did not look nearly as upset about the sword as Lubbok had been. Lubbok came back a minute later, having apparently calmed himself down a bit. He didn't offer an apology, or admit that he had come to terms with Erik's magic sword, but he did offer get the horses so they could continue onward.

Erik figured that was as close to a reconciliation as he could hope for.

They traveled through the night, keeping the river in sight, but not daring to get too close to it just in case the witch came back with her warriors. When they found a grouping of large boulders, they decided to camp for the remainder of the night.

The following day, they were up at first light. They continued along their way as quickly as their horses would allow, and maintained a grueling pace for two days, finally arriving at the ruins of Tarntin during the middle of the day.

"Do we expect any surprises here?" Lady Arkyn asked.

Erik shook his head. "If you mean more Blacktongues, they are all in Galardene. She did say that something in the north would show us why the other people left though."

"I bet she was talking about that witch and her crazy warriors," Rafe put in. "If you had an army that could never die, I bet you could run a whole slew of men out of just about anywhere." Rafe brought his horse up alongside Erik's. "By the by, how exactly did you see that kind of magic before?" Rafe asked Lady Arkyn.

"After I investigated the crime scene where the others were murdered, I was attacked during the night by a group of these same kind of warriors."

"Same as in similar, or same as in the exact same group?" Rafe pressed.

Lady Arkyn shrugged. "I used a natural gas explosion to kill the ones after me. I don't know if I killed them all, but I thought I had gotten the majority of them at least. I also thought I had killed the witch, because I didn't see her or the magic after the explosion."

"I see," Rafe said dryly. "You two sure do make your share of enemies, I'll give you that. I think I might need to raise my fee a bit."

"If we live through this, I can reimburse you enough to replace your ship," Erik said.

"Well," Rafe started as he tilted his head to the side and shined his nails on his shirt. "That will be a good start, but considering all the extra work that has gone into a voyage that was supposed to be a simple transport job..."

"If we live, then I am sure we can come to an arrangement," Erik replied flatly.

288

Rafe nodded and smiled, apparently satisfied. Lubbok, on the other hand, was still scowling at Erik any time the two happened to be looking at one another.

"He seems pretty upset," Lady Arkyn whispered as they neared the edge of the town.

"Doesn't like my magic sword," Erik replied. He was about to say something else, but he pulled up on the reins and stopped the horse. Everyone else saw him and copied his movement.

"What is it?" Rafe asked.

Erik didn't answer. He scanned the rooftops, and then checked the walls carefully. When his eyes couldn't find any sign of danger, he used his power to search the area. He was sure they had approached something very deadly, and very angry.

"Trouble, brother?" Chabba asked.

Erik nodded. "I can't see anything, it's just a feeling."

A black mist rose up from the ground behind them and started to close in. Rafe cursed under his breath and drew his sword. An arrow flew out from the darkness and caught Chabba in the right shoulder.

"Argh!" the orc wailed as he slumped forward and clutched at the wound. He shouted some very nasty curses in orcish and then snapped the protruding shaft off and pushed the head through. Once the missile was out of his body, he drew his sword in his left hand and turned the horse around.

A host of ten men came rushing out of the darkness.

Erik leapt down from his horse, allowing Lady Arkyn to use the steed. She expertly maneuvered the beast to run parallel to the growing wall of black mist and launched arrows at the oncoming warriors. Erik rushed the first one, noting that he was not like the men from last night. Instead, he wore a full set of chainmail over a leather hauberk. He ignited his blade and swung mightily. Chain links shattered and the sword cut deep into the attacker's chest, killing him instantly.

Rafe charged his horse at the attackers, as did Chabba. The first wave of attackers went down quickly, but they were replaced by a second wave, this time of twenty. Erik held his ground while Lady Arkyn and Chongor fired arrows at the attackers. Rafe and Chabba continued to assault the attackers directly, swinging their weapons and taking the heads from several warriors. Lubbok cried out angrily and then moved to flank the enemy. He came in from the far left and killed two warriors with his first swing. His horse trampled a third, and then a spear stabbed into his horse's neck, killing the beast and throwing Lubbok to the ground.

Erik rushed in, slicing through one enemy, and then another as he made his way to Lubbok. The mighty orc had lost his weapon, but was currently in the process of pummeling the spearman that had killed his horse with his meaty, green fists. Erik reached Lubbok just as a third wave of attackers came. Erik killed three and wounded another, giving Lubbok enough time to reclaim his weapon and stand beside him. They hacked at the enemy relentlessly, but no matter how many they slew, the enemy kept coming at them.

Bodies piled at their feet. To say that the attackers were not very good fighters would be a massive overstatement. Erik had only needed to deflect a few strikes the entire time, and he was up around fourteen kills. Lubbok was chopping them down as quickly as they ran toward him, and even Chabba was winning easily despite the uselessness of his dominant arm.

Still, no matter how many they killed, the black mist continued to inch forward, spewing out wave after wave of enemy, and driving the party back toward Tarntin. Soon, Lady Arkyn was out of arrows and was using her scimitar. Chongor was likewise down to his warhammer. Erik could hear that Rafe was starting to breathe heavily, and Chabba was leaning to the side from the pain and loss of blood.

"We have to move back!" Erik shouted to Rafe and Lady Arkyn. "There are too many."

"You retreat?" Lubbok guessed. He shot Erik an angry glare. "You have a burning sword!"

"If the mist reaches us, we will not be able to see," Erik explained.

"A true warrior can feel his enemies," Lubbok shouted. As if to prove his point, he continued glowering at Erik while a swordsman charged him from the side. At the last moment before the enemy struck, Lubbok lifted his sword and let the man impale himself, and then tossed the corpse aside. "Let the darkness come, for I will stand against it!"

"As will I!" Chabba shouted as his horse reared up and stove in an enemy's face.

"I will stand with you, brother!" Chongor pledged.

"Stonebubbles," Erik muttered, stealing a curse often used by dwarves. He knew that the orcs would rather stay and die than retreat. Lubbok had a point to prove, and he was indirectly challenging Erik's courage as well. Erik glanced up to Lady Arkyn, and she nodded knowingly.

"Rafe, come with me, we need to find cover," Lady Arkyn shouted. She and Rafe fled toward the city, and Erik took in a deep breath as the dark, cold mist rolled in around him. As he had feared, the mist was so thick he could only see a couple feet in front of him. The fire on the sword did nothing to pierce it. Whatever it was made of, it was cold and heavy, making it hard to breathe.

Footsteps came charging toward him. Erik closed his eyes. In that moment, he fell into his true self. He was not the dragon, he was not even the Champion of Truth. He was the warrior, taught by Master Lepkin and wielding the fabled flaming sword. Master Lepkin had once defeated three hundred Tarthuns single-handedly. Perhaps this was the battle where he would have the chance to do something similar. This time, there was no opportunity to extend mercy. The beast he fought so hard to cage within himself had to be unleashed in full.

Time seemed to slow as he calmly took in a breath and exhaled. He could hear the boots of an enemy plodding on the ground, coming his way. He could hear the man's heavy breathing. He pictured him in his mind, with a clenched jaw and wielding a sword up over his shoulders, ready to swing.

Then time sped back to its normal pace and Erik exploded into action. He twisted and swung his sword so quickly that the flames trailed behind it with a great *whoosh!* The attacker's head flew from his body and the rest of his corpse flopped to the ground.

A moment later a second came in from the left. Erik deflected the spear and stabbed through the attacker's chest. A third jumped in from behind. They were getting better now, faster and more adept in their movements. Erik stepped aside, flipped his sword into an upside-down grip and thrust the blade backward to skewer the third man through the abdomen.

Off in the distance, he could hear the battle cries of the orcs and the clattering of steel. Erik hadn't the time to try to find his allies. He was beset by another pair of attackers. He cut through them and then decided to take the offensive. He charged ahead into the darkness, cutting down every enemy he saw, but there was one enemy he had not seen, who would prove to be the creature the Blacktongue had warned him about.

*****

The sound of battle awakened Seroth's senses. His muscles tightened and ached for action. His nostrils flared as blood spilled upon the ground. The darkness hid him well enough that he could walk calmly for as long as he wanted, but his body yearned for the thrill, nay, the ecstasy of hunting live prey. He was a creature known by few in these parts of Terramyr, and that is what made him so successful. He stalked among the black mist, fully protected from the burning light of the sun.

He was not a vampire, for vampires were made from humans, and compared with him were about as dull and short sighted as most humans were when compared with the elegant elven races. Seroth, was a Verr'Tai, a twisted and evil undead elf with more power than most mortals could comprehend. More than that, he was a loyal servant of his lord and master, Hatmul, the ruler of Hammenfein. It had taken him centuries to make his journey to this place from his former home beyond the Nahktun Mountains, which stretched across a continent many thousands of miles away from the Heart of Terramyr, a shrouded island continent blocked off from the rest of the world by a ring of impassable mountains. Chasing out the pathetic humans from their cities had been his first victory, but this day would prove to be even more important. He could offer his master the souls of orcs today, and a sahale.

He sneered wickedly as he walked toward an injured orc. The creature was valiant, fighting vigorously and showing no signs of slowing despite his injuries. He would make a good addition to the ranks of those who served in Hammenfein. But first, Seroth was going to enjoy the orc's life force and strength. Though the mortals could not see him in the mist, he could easily see them. Their bodies appeared as deep red forms with humanoid shape as their blood called out to him through the darkness, glowing and beckoning for him to let it loose.

Three of his thralls attacked the injured orc and then fell by his blade. Seroth smiled and slipped in behind the orc. With his right hand he pierced the orc's neck with his sharp, elongated fingernails. The orc expectedly tried to lash out with his sword, but Seroth grabbed the orc by the left wrist and squeezed hard enough to break the bones in the joint. The sword fell. Seroth gripped harder with his right hand, letting the blood spill out over his fingers as he sniffed the

293

wonderfully metallic scent. He then lifted the orc up overhead and closed his eyes.

His favorite prey were those mortals who had magical powers, for their essence was always sweeter, but a strong orc was no meager morsel. It was a delectable treat in its own right. As the blood ebbed out from the orc, Seroth opened his mouth and devoured the very essence of the orc's being. A vampire feasted upon blood, but for Seroth the blood was like the whites of an egg. To be sure, it provided sustenance, but the real flavor was in the yolk, the unseen life force that was contained within a living body.

He consumed the orc's very aura, leaving a bare soul only to be sent down to Hammenfein. The body would remain with Seroth, though, for he would reanimate that as he had the hundreds and thousands of Northmen he had slain so long ago.

The orc was so delicious that Seroth couldn't help but roar in delight as he finished the last bit of the creature's energy. He felt his strength receive a boost, and his hands twitched as the new energy filled his body. He tossed the empty carcass aside and saw another orc, this one still atop a horse and chopping down Seroth's thralls.

Seroth leapt into the air and twisted about as he flew through the mist. With a tremendous force, he blasted into the large horse, splitting the animal in half and throwing the orc through the air to land in a heap. A host of thralls moved in for the kill, but Seroth issued a mental command to stay their hands. The victory was his, not theirs. The mist around him cleaned his body from the horse's blood, strengthening the spell of darkness as it absorbed the animal's life blood. Normally, Seroth would have jealously claimed the horse as well, but not on a day when he had such rare treats before him. He was going to save his appetite for them.

The orc rose to his feet and stood at the ready. He seemed confused when no one came to charge him. The darkness was so thick that Seroth knew the orc wouldn't be able to see anything. Still, the orc proved resourceful. He put his back to Seroth only to turn at the last moment and run his sword straight through Seroth's chest. Seroth felt his right lung collapse and his blood oozed out over the blade. The pain only angered him. He reached out and seized the orc's throat with his left hand. With a powerful squeeze he snapped the orc's neck. The orc twitched violently, but Seroth knew it was just the final impulses of a dead creature. He pulled the orc in close and devoured the creature's essence. He then dropped the hollowed body and turned for his final two victims.

The third orc was much stronger than the other two. He was going to provide a great amount of essence, and that was to say nothing of the foolish sahale fighting nearby. Why the sahale refused to change form was perplexing, but Seroth was not going to question his good fortune.

*****

Erik cut down another four enemies and then a wave of terror washed over him. He couldn't know what it was, exactly, but he could feel an intense presence, as if evil incarnate had descended upon the battle field. Without hesitation, he summoned Silverfang. The wolf would do no better in the darkness with his vision, but with his sense of smell he might be able to help Erik understand where the real threat was going to come from.

The wolf sprang into action, snarling and growling as it took down a pair of men in the darkness. Erik fought on, and then he heard a determined howl. Silverfang had indeed found something. Erik cut down the nearest enemy, and then turned to his right to follow after Silverfang's howls. He nearly stumbled over a pile of bodies, but managed to stay upright and continued running. Lubbok was nearby, grunting and shouting orcish curses as he continued to drop enemy after enemy.

Silverfang then snarled and there was a shriek that sounded more like the banshees in the Natchy Moors than it did anything around this area. For an instant, the mist dissipated, as if blown out from a central point by a great gust of air. In that moment, Erik saw Silverfang with his teeth sunk into a strange creature. It looked like an elf, except its skin was dead and rotting. It was taller than most elves, and more muscular too. There was also a bloody hole in the creature's chest. Whatever it was, it was not going down easily. It flung Silverfang aside and then the mist began to close back in. Just before the darkness blinded Erik once more, he saw the creature turn its attention to Lubbok.

Erik called upon his power and tried to pierce the gloomy veil, but nothing happened. The flames on his sword grew hotter as his rage boiled. He ran to intercept the creature. It must have seen him coming, for before Erik could react, it came at him from the side instead of straight ahead. Claws came in furiously fast, too fast for Erik to dodge or deflect the blow successfully.

A blur of gray fur launched through the air and took hold of the creature's reaching hand. As the wolf's teeth sank in, the mist dissipated just enough for Erik to see his foe.

Another shriek filled the air. Erik turned and ducked, lashing out with his flaming sword and catching the creature in the thigh. From the lack of resistance against the blade, it wasn't a deep cut, but it was enough to make the monster recoil back as green blood flowed out from the wound.

Silverfang tore and yanked on the arm, but the creature once again flung the wolf aside.

A sharp yelp followed by a series of short-breathed whimpers told Erik that Silverfang was hurt badly this time. He dismissed his companion back to his plane of existence where he could heal.

The creature came forward and Erik attacked. He pressed the fight, swinging and thrusting his sword. The creature held his hand out and a sword from one of the fallen attackers floated up to meet his palm. The grotesque elf-thing then sneered and counter-attacked. The swords clashed together in a shower of sparks and flames, but Erik had made a mistake. The real attack was a powerful kick that came in just a half second after the swords connected. Erik took the brunt of the assault fully in the chest and flew backward through the air. His sword fell to the ground, and the flames went out.

The mist closed in around him as Erik coughed and choked for breath. He struggled to get to his feet, but his body wouldn't respond. No air was coming into his lungs, and his legs were void of strength.

"Tell me, why do you not change form?" a voice called in the darkness. "I can smell your blood, I know what you are."

Erik pushed up to his feet, but his legs quivered and quaked to the point that they failed him, and he fell back to his knees. Never before had he ever been struck so hard by anyone. Had he not feared Vodklyk's poison, he would have changed form a long time ago, but as it was, he was stuck with his human body.

The mist directly before him parted just enough for the creature to emerge and be seen. The bite marks in his arm and the hole in his chest had closed, but the cut in his leg had not. The creature smiled wickedly and reached out. His claws were coming in quickly, but then there was a flash of green fire. The creature snarled and howled in pain as his forearm fell to the ground with a sickening *thump*. Erik looked up to see Lubbok, holding the flaming sword.

Green flames enveloped the black, Telarian steel, and for whatever reason, the weapon was hurting the creature beyond its ability to heal. Lubbok wasted no time in driving the sword through the creature's heart. The monster threw its head back and howled as the mist fell away.

Erik could see hundreds of warriors circled around them, but instead of charging in to help their master, they fell to the ground, as dead as stones.

Lubbok shouted angrily and jerked the blade upward, sawing through the creature's ribs and eventually ripping the blade out next to the creature's neck. The monster's head flopped to the side, providing an open target for the massive orc to finish the fight. He brought the flaming sword down and hacked the head off, thus ending the creature's miserable existence.

"Brother…" Erik started as he stood up weakly.

Lubbok nodded and looked at the flaming sword. He then promptly flipped it upside-down and stabbed it into the monster's corpse for good measure. "I suppose I cannot complain against you, now that I have also used magic."

Erik smiled and the two clasped hands once more.

The rift was now healed.

Chapter 19

Erik and Lubbok searched for Chabba and Chongor, and then took their bodies off to a grassy hill south of Tarntin. Rafe and Lady Arkyn were able to find three shovels in the ruins, and brought those out to help. Lubbok insisted on doing most of the digging himself, but eventually he let Erik help as well. Rafe and Lady Arkyn cleaned Chabba and Chongor's bodies as best they could and went back to Tarntin to find cloth with which to bury them in.

Lubbok performed their final rights in orcish, while the other three looked on.

"What is he saying?" Rafe asked quietly.

Erik hesitated, and then explained that Lubbok was calling upon Khefir to come and take the valiant warriors back to the halls of Hammenfein where they could serve at Hatmul's side in guarding the halls of hell.

"Sounds like a lame reward," Rafe commented quietly.

"In their culture, it is the highest honor to be worthy enough that Hatmul would choose them in death to guard Hammenfein. They keep mortals out, and prevent the spirits of the departed from escaping."

"They are cursed from the beginning of this world," Lady Arkyn put in. "As they were not created by Icadion, they are a cursed race, and can never attain a restful afterlife in the heaven city of Volganor. They are forever destined to return to the fires of hell. The best they can hope for is to prove strong enough to become captains in their afterlife."

Rafe nodded and the three continued to watch Lubbok in silence as he shouted the appropriate prayers and laid Chabba and Chongor's weapons in the grave with them. Then he motioned for the others to come and help pile the dirt on top.

After the graves were covered and the dead were buried properly, Rafe approached Lubbok and put a hand on the orc's shoulder. "I never thought I would say this about an orc, but they were good men, er, I mean good orcs."

Lubbok stared at Rafe for a moment and then nodded. Erik was about to come and interpret for them, but Lubbok waved him off. "Chongor, Chabba, good orcs," Lubbok said in Common Tongue. His words were forced and a bit clumsy, but clear enough to be understood. "Rafe, good man," Lubbok said as he poked Rafe in the chest with a thick finger.

Rafe nodded and patted Lubbok twice on the shoulder before turning back toward Tarntin. They found shelter in an old hut made of stone. For good measure, they sealed and barricaded the windows and the door. When the morning came, they made their way out across the plains again, heading northward toward the mountains and keeping the Black River at their left.

They made better time now that they had a horse for each person. They reached the base of the mountains before the first day ended. None of them said it, but they were all happy that this leg of the journey was without resistance.

They camped at the base of the mountains and feasted upon large steelhead which they fished from the Black River. When it came time for sleep, Erik volunteered for the first watch. He went out to the river and sat upon a large boulder near the water's edge. He watched as the sun dropped below the horizon and the glorious pinks and oranges in the sky faded to be replaced by a thick blanket of night. As the darkness grew and the campfire near the others started to die down a bit, Erik scanned the area around them and started to let his mind wander. He wondered how Njar was doing in his own quest. Had he managed to find and stop Dremathor? Was Dremathor the Dark Sahale? He shook his head. He knew that couldn't be it, or at least he hoped that was not the case. The Blacktongues had told Erik that they had recently seen the Dark Sahale come through and had tried to battle it. If that was in fact Dremathor, then that would mean that Njar had failed, and was dead. Erik could not bring himself to believe that Njar would have died. There had to be another shadowfiend that was the true murderer from Winter's Beak. Dremathor was certainly dangerous, but Njar had said he was certain that Dremathor did not have the power of the sahale in him.

He thought of the strange encounter with Alkantar and sighed. If only that shadowfiend had given him better information. Then he wouldn't be guessing at names in the dark while he sat at the edge of the Black River. He would at least know his enemy, and that would make the hunt more fair. As it stood now, he could only hope that the sahale living in Hermit's Hole could tell him who the Dark Sahale was. If not, then they would have come this way for nothing of any real value. The Cult of Zammin hadn't known any of the things Erik had hoped for. They didn't even know how to counter the binding spell that held a sahale trapped in their human form. Erik cursed himself for the wasted time.

"This guy better know what I need to know," Erik said as he rubbed his left shoulder to warm it up. It was not just a matter of thirteen murders in Winter's Beak now. The Dark Sahale was going to trigger the end of the world. All life everywhere. It was unthinkable, but it felt true. Somehow, this one creature held the power to attract the Four Horsemen, and that would be the end of Terramyr.

301

Erik snapped out of his thoughts when he heard the sound of shuffling footsteps approaching. He turned and scanned the darkness. He gripped his sword and was about to sound the alarm when a single man emerged from the shadows and approached him.

"I am not here to fight," the man said. His voice was familiar, but Erik couldn't quite place it. "Don't you recognize me, Erik Lokton?"

Erik stood up from the boulder, keeping his hand on his sword. "State your name," Erik said.

"My name, well, I go by several now," the voice said. "I have been called many things, but the two names I use the most are Aparen, and Eldrik Cedreau."

"Eldrik?!" Erik gasped. "But what are you doing here?"

Eldrik pulled back the hood covering his face and smiled softly. "I should have known you would follow me, Erik. You ever were a black or white kind of fellow, with little room for gray areas in life."

"Gray areas?" Erik said. "What are you...." In an instant, it clicked for him. Eldrik had committed the murders. He was the shadowfiend that had gone through the ruins of Galardene, first as a monster, and then in the form of a dragon. After all, Eldrik was sahale as well. "It was you in Winter's Beak?" Erik asked.

Eldrik nodded and stopped just out of arm's reach from Erik. "I tried to find you first, to explain why it had to be done."

"I am here now," Erik said. "I am not without mercy." Erik drew his sword, but he did not ignite the flames. "Explain to me now, and see if it can dissuade me from bringing you to justice."

"I needed their power," Eldrik explained as if it was all a simple matter. "Since leaving Fort Drake, I have studied everything I can about the Four Horsemen. The events with

Tu'luh affected me deeply, and I knew there had to be more I could do, and I was right."

"What do you mean?" Erik pressed. "You can't murder other people and expect that to stop the Four Horsemen."

"No, of course not," Eldrik agreed. "But, I did learn of a magic that can be used to stop them by force. You see, they are going to come anyway, so why not invite them here and set a trap in the meantime?"

"You're mad," Erik said. "You can't defeat them, no one can."

"Wrong!" Eldrik said angrily. "As a shadowfiend, I can absorb the energy and strength of others. If I can get to the World Seed, and absorb its powers, then I will have the ability to stop all four of them. You could help, be there at my side for the final battle!"

Erik stopped short of ranting at Eldrik. He had heard about the World Seed, but didn't see how it could be used against the Four Horsemen. Still, Eldrik was the first person to seem to have any inkling of something that might work. Perhaps it was worth it to at least hear what Eldrik intended to do. "How can you use the World Seed to stop them?" Erik asked.

Eldrik smiled. "There, finally, someone with enough sense to pursue the possibility!" Eldrik exclaimed. "The World Seed was used by Icadion to create the world," Eldrik began.

"Yes, I know of that," Erik interjected. Shermin and the other monks were more than happy to discuss their beliefs of how Terramyr was formed.

"The world Seed resides deep within our continent," Eldrik said. "Did you know that it is the very thing that the Four Horsemen will need to access in order to kill this world?"

Erik stared in disbelief. "No, the World Seed isn't connected to the world like that," he said.

Eldrik nodded. "Yes it is. From the seed grows a great tree, and from there sprang the life force that fills this world.

303

Kill the seed, and you kill the planet. That is why Terramyr created the Natural Races like the satyrs and the minotaurs; she was protecting herself after the Old Gods abandoned this world and let the forces of evil run amuck. But, we can use the seed, Erik. If you have enough power, you can absorb great strength and power from the World Seed. I am certain it is enough to withstand the Four Horsemen."

Erik shook his head. "This is madness. You are going to kill us all."

"No, no, no! Erik, don't you see? This is the only way. This is why I had to absorb the energy of the other sahale, that way I will be strong enough to absorb the power of the World Seed."

"You are talking about going into the heart of Terramyr and taking the relic used by Icadion to create the world," Erik said hotly. "No one can reach it, and even if they could, no mortal can absorb its power."

"Wrong again!" Eldrik snarled as he flared his arms out and whirled about. "You know of the demi-gods, yes?" Eldrik held up his fingers and listed a few of them off. "Basei, Lisei, Esei, and the others. They all started out as mortals, but how do you think they got *their* powers? They went and took them from the World Seed. There were at least fifty adventurers that attempted the quest, but only the strongest survived the transfer of power."

Erik turned and glanced toward the camp, considering whether to call for the others to join him, but Eldrik stepped in front of him, blocking off his line of sight. "Eldrik, while I agree that *if* it were possible to take powers from the World Seed, it would put us in a stronger position, there is nothing that I have read that indicates the powers of a Demi-god will be enough to stop the Four Horsemen. I have been researching this very topic as well, believe me!"

"None of the Demi-gods started as strong as I am now. I have the strength of nearly a score of our fellow sahale, and that is just the beginning. The best of the Demi-gods were only wizards and strong warriors when they went in. My research on the World Seed shows that it doesn't simply grant you powers, it grants you powers in an exponential sense, using your current strength as the base factor. As I am already much more powerful than any of the others, I should come out with powers much greater than the Demi-gods!'"

"Eldrik," Erik began with a shake of his head. "If the World Seed was the key to defeating the Four Horsemen, then why wouldn't the Old Gods use it themselves? Better than that, why didn't the gods of Kendualdern, or any of the other worlds destroyed by the Four Horsemen, try the very same thing?

"Because they were cowards!" Eldrik said. "Look at how easily the Old Gods fled from this world! Icadion was chased out by one of his own sons! Is it any wonder that he should cower to the Four Horsemen as well? But, if I am leading the fight, maybe some of the Demi-gods and Old Gods will join in the battle. Maybe we will be able to succeed where all other worlds heretofore attacked by the Four Horsemen have failed."

"Eldrik, listen to yourself, this isn't right." Erik said.

"Right?" Eldrik scoffed. "Since leaving Fort Drake, I have had visions. I have seen the Four Horsemen arrive and bombard this world with their massive fireballs. I have seen them kill thousands of innocent people with diseases and fires and floods, don't tell me that what I am doing isn't right. A few sacrifices made in order to save the whole. Those whose power I have absorbed shall be remembered as heroes. Their strength will make our final triumph possible. And then, once the Four Horsemen are gone, I will deal with the treacherous Old Gods as well, unless they vow to fight along my side against the Four Horsemen. I will bring peace to our world, and never shall there be strife again!"

There was a part of Erik that could understand Eldrik's words. It almost made sense. Even Zammin had been willing to slay more than a score of orcish warriors in order to save his own fledgling, but this plan felt wrong. It wasn't just the murders of the other sahale. Frankly, Erik could see the logic behind such a move even if he didn't agree with it, but something deep within him told him that this plan would not work. He had to make Eldrik see his point.

"Eldrik, you know I have a gift of discernment. I know that you believe in what you are saying, but this doesn't feel correct. Everything inside of me is telling me to stop you." Erik put a hand out on Eldrik's shoulder. "We fought together once, against Tu'luh. I would be honored to fight alongside you once more against the Four Horsemen, but not like this. There must be another way."

Eldrik threw Erik's hand off of him and stomped away. He folded his arms and threw his head up toward the sky as he took several deep breaths. After a few moments, he turned back around, marched up to Erik, and jabbed him in the chest with his right index finger as he glared at him. "You don't understand! This is the only way! I have searched for any answer I could find, and this is the only one I have found. Show me another way, and I will go with you." Eldrik poked him hard enough to shove Erik back two steps. "Well?!" Eldrik demanded. "Tell me *your* plan to stop them! Tell me how to end the nightmares that have plagued me. Tell me how to save our home world!"

Erik couldn't understand what had driven Eldrik to this point. The last time he had seen the man, they had fought alongside each other to bring Tu'luh down. Now, Eldrik was speaking of murdering sahale, overthrowing demi-gods, and even storming Volganor. He was clearly not himself. Erik scanned Eldrik with his power to see the extent of Eldrik's madness, but it did little to comfort him. Eldrik fully believed in what he was doing. It would be nearly impossible to convince him to stop the insanity.

"I don't have a plan yet," Erik answered truthfully.

"Ah," Eldrik snarled. "Well, then my plan is the only viable option." Eldrik stepped back and folded his arms once more.

"What of the sahale in Hermit's Hole?" Erik asked, trying to change the subject and see if he could calm Eldrik down enough to have a rational conversation.

Eldrik shook his head. "That old buffoon had to be stopped. He was going to launch a counter movement against me. I could not let him live."

"So you have killed him as well?" Erik clarified.

Eldrik nodded. "I thought he would understand," Eldrik said. "He was supposed to be among the wisest of the sahale, but he was as stubborn as you are. He kept telling me that I would not be able to absorb the power of the World Seed, and that even if I did, the Four Horsemen would be able to conquer this world. He did not understand."

"So you killed him and took his power as well?" Erik asked.

Eldrik nodded and then looked off toward the river. "His power was great, a fine addition to my strength. Oh, don't you see, with each one I absorb I get not only their physical powers and their magical abilities, but I get their memories. I absorb their experience. It makes me better in every area. The Four Horsemen cannot hope to stand against me once I have achieved my plans."

"Their memories?" Erik echoed. "So you know everything that the sahale from Hermit's Hole knew?"

"More than that," Eldrik said. "I know everything Dremathor knew," he said.

Erik balked. He had not expected that.

"Your father loved you," Eldrik said.

"He isn't my father," Erik replied. "I am the son of Lord Lokton."

"No, Trenton Lokton wasn't your father. He was my father. Or at least, he was supposed to be my father, before a group of witches got involved and messed things up. Them and Njar, meddlers the lot of them."

Erik didn't need to use his powers to see what had really happened between Dremathor and Njar now. It was as plain as the contemptuous expression on Eldrik's face when he spoke Njar's name. "You attacked Njar, didn't you? Somehow, you used your powers to resurrect Dremathor and use him as a pawn."

Eldrik spat on the ground and kicked a bit of dirt over the spittle. "The old goat was always meddling, but never fully aware of what he was doing. Don't you realize, if you and I had lived out the destinies that we were supposed to, I would have been the Champion of Truth, and you would have become a shadowfiend like your father? I can see the darkness in you, even now. Who is to say that if the roles were the way they were supposed to be, that you and I would not be having this very conversation right now, only you would be in my shoes, and I would be in yours?"

The words of Alkantar and the demon from the south came back to Erik's mind again, but this time, so did Lady Arkyn's words of comfort and support. "No," Erik said. "Whatever the fates may have had in store for us, I choose my own destiny now, just as you do. I choose to develop the good, and suppress the evil that is within me. Whether it comes from my father, or I was supposed to be some sort of shadowfiend, it doesn't matter. I am I. I am Erik Lokton, and I am the Champion of Truth."

Eldrik began a slow clap and gave Erik a mocking smile. "And that makes you better than me, does it? Bah! You are still the naïve idiot you were when you attended Kuldiga Academy. Quick to judge and fight, but slow to learn."

The feeling of dread in Erik's gut grew and caused his blood to stir. Eldrik was on a path that would not lead to victory against the Four Horsemen. Instead, he was going to call them forth early, and take away any hope Erik had of finding a real solution to the problem. Erik couldn't allow that. "Eldrik," Erik said sternly. "I strive to offer mercy to everyone I meet who has done wrong, or is planning to do so. I would extend the same to you now. Your quest will only end in destruction for all of us. I can feel it with my power. I can sympathize with your reasoning, but it is flawed."

"And yet you can offer no alternative," Eldrik spat.

"Eldrik, this must end." Erik's sword roared alive with white flames that illuminated the area in a thirty foot radius. More than that, it would signal the others to the danger, for he knew that none of them were likely asleep as of yet. They would come to his aid, and the murderer would be stopped. "I am sorry, my friend, but you must choose. Either you can renounce the wicked deeds you have done, and work with me to find a tenable solution to the nightmares that plague us both, or we must fight here and now."

"Then, I am also sorry," Eldrik hissed. "I had hoped you would see reason. After all, you did question whether fighting against Tu'luh was the right thing to do. Why not at least consider my proposal now. I will not make slaves out of the people of this world, but I will ensure peace, and I will rescue us all from the Four Horsemen that would destroy us out of hand."

"No," Erik said decisively. "I have considered what you said, and I cannot let you go through with your plans. But, you can join with me. As our fates are so intertwined, why not come with me? We could be a great force for good. I promise, I will not rest until we find a way to stop the Four Horsemen."

Eldrik shook his head. "I have already found the correct way, but you are too blind to see it." He snapped his fingers and the area around them lit up as if the sun was high in the sky. Lubbok, Rafe, and Lady Arkyn were lifted into the air and held by an invisible force. "Move to attack, and they will all die."

"If I let you leave, then the Four Horsemen will come and kill us all anyway," Erik replied evenly. "You are the Dark Sahale, and you must be stopped."

A scream filled the air, stopping Erik in his tracks. He turned and saw Lady Arkyn's face turning red as she struggled to claw at something around her neck.

"You see, I know you," Eldrik said. "Your weakness will ever be your heart."

"Eldrik, this is between you and me," Erik said.

Eldrik smiled and without a word or a move of his hands, sent a spell at Erik that knocked the warrior to his knees. Erik struggled to push against the ground with his hands as something heavy forced him downward. "Erik, I have given my word to someone that I will not harm you. If I were to break my word, then I would lose a portion of my power." Eldrik moved in close and the weight shifted off of Erik's back as something else snaked around his body and raised him up to eye level with Eldrik. "You see, I knew your father, you *real* father. Before he gave me his powers, he made me swear that I would never harm you. Had I broken that oath say, a year or two ago, then likely the power of the wizard's oath would have killed me, but I have found a way around it. Now, the worst that will happen to me is I will lose the portion of power that Dremathor gave me. But I will not die. So, believe me when I say the only thing keeping you and your pathetic friends alive is the simple fact that I respect you."

Eldrik grinned. "Since you know of Dremathor, then I should warn you, he is not the only one I brought back."

Erik narrowed his eyes on Eldrik and tried to fight the spell. "What have you done?"

"Do you recall a warlock by the name of Gondok'hr? Or did you know him better as Senator Bracken?"

310

Erik's heart skipped a beat and jumped into his throat. Gondok'hr was the warlock responsible for his adopted father's death. True, it had been Eldrik that had stabbed Trenton Lokton in an alleyway, but it was Gondok'hr, masquerading as Senator Bracken, that had arrested Trenton Lokton and had him tried before the senate tribunal. He had also led an assault against Kuldiga Academy, and Lokton Manor, and had personally killed Master Orres, the former head of Kuldiga Academy. Erik may have been able to come to terms with most of his enemies, but Gondok'hr was one that he had never stopped hating.

"I can see the anger in your eyes," Eldrik said. "But it is true. Gondok'hr walks among the living once more, and he does my bidding."

"Eldrik, this has gone too far already, you must stop."

"No, it is *you* who must stop. Get in my way again, and I shall not let you escape. This is your only warning, Erik Lokton. Should we cross paths again, then I will destroy you, and everyone you love." Eldrik glanced over to the three he held suspended in the air and a wicked, sly look came over his face. "This is so you will understand how serious I am."

Erik tried to move and lash out at Eldrik, but the spell holding him was too strong. He was helpless as Eldrik turned toward the others. Erik tried to shout, but as he opened his mouth, a coil of energy filled it and gagged him. He tried to summon Silverfang, but he found that even that spell was blocked from his abilities.

Eldrik was in complete control.

He went to Lubbok first, and then to Rafe, and finally to Lady Arkyn. He raised his right hand slowly. Eldrik then snapped his fingers, and Lady Arkyn's left leg was twisted around, breaking the bones in several places. She writhed in agony as Erik fought futilely against the spell holding him. Eldrik then turned to Rafe and pointed at the man's wound in his arm where the spear had struck him. Rafe's arm ripped open and the bandages failed to contain the amount of blood that rushed out. Then Eldrik moved to Lubbok. The orc had only anger and determination in his eyes as he watched the Dark Sahale approach. Eldrik turned and smiled at Erik.

"So that you will know the extent of my powers," he said. He slapped Lubbok in the stomach and the mighty orc fell to the ground. At first, Erik feared the orc was dead, but then he realized that Eldrik had given Lubbok a much worse curse. The green skin darkened to a deep tannish brown. Lubbok's tusks disappeared and his head shape changed from its strong, square appearance to take on a smaller, rounder shape. Dark hair grew from the top of Lubbok's head and his muscles shrank to roughly match Rafe's size. The orcish clothes began to hang loose as Lubbok was fully transformed into a human, never able to return to his father again.

"Erik, do not follow me. Stay out of my way, and we can part as old friends. Follow me again, and I shall destroy you entirely." Eldrik leapt into the air and turned into a dark cloud of smoke. Then, he was gone. The spells released all of them and Erik rushed over to Lady Arkyn.

"I'm coming," he shouted.

She pointed to Rafe with a quivering hand. "Help him first," she said through her tears.

Erik didn't like the idea, but he knew she was right. He sprinted to Rafe and quickly went to work to stop the hemorrhaging. Before he had finished, Lubbok regained his consciousness and sat up to examine himself. He began to curse, but he no longer spoke orcish. Eldrik had even changed Lubbok's language.

Lubbok looked to Erik with his once proud eyes filled with tears. "I am shamed," he said.

Erik finished working with Rafe and then moved to help Lady Arkyn. He gently examined her leg, finding the femur broken in the middle, the tibia and fibia broken several inches below the knee, and the ankle entirely separated from its appropriate position. For the first time in a long while, Erik was overwhelmed. He wasn't sure what to do. He sat back and held Lady Arkyn's hand for a few moments, staring at her twisted leg and shaking his head while she cried.

"Here, let me help."

A hand fell on Erik's shoulder. He turned, expecting Lubbok, but saw instead a man in a white robe with a long, gray beard that fell to his waist. A pair of sparkling blue eyes sat behind a thin-rimmed pair of glasses. His hair was as long as his beard, but neatly groomed. He narrowed his eyes on Erik and the thick, white brows pinched in close together.

"Don't tell me you don't remember your own grandfather?!" Allun Rha said in a sour voice.

Allun Rha bent down and placed a hand on Lady Arkyn's leg and a flash of white light wrapped her in a gentle embrace. Her leg was twisted back into place and the bones mended themselves, but without causing additional pain. Lady Arkyn looked up and smiled with teary eyes, but Allun Rha didn't tarry with her. He moved to Rafe and healed the man's arm wound.

Lastly, he walked to Lubbok and knelt before the transformed orc.

"I can change you back," Allun Rha said. "But it will take a lot of my energy. Afterward, I will need to rest before I can help you further."

Lubbok nodded eagerly. Allun Rha placed a hand on each of Lubbok's shoulders. He spoke in a language Erik didn't understand, and the two were caught up in a great cloud of gold and red smoke. Lightning streaked across the outside of the cloud and miniature thunder claps erupted from within. When the cloud cleared, Lubbok was smiling his big, proud grin and touching his green fingers to his tusks.

"I am whole again!" Lubbok exclaimed.

Erik approached Allun Rha and looked at him questioningly. "How did you know where to find me?"

313

"It took some doing," Allun Rha said. "But I felt a disturbance in the energies back at my tower. I would have consulted with Hiasyntar'Kulai, but he was unavailable. They are working to decipher the Infinium, and cannot be reached. You know better than I how extensive their caves are under the ground."

Erik nodded. He had been in the deepest depths of the Ancient's palace far in the east. If the dragons did not want to be disturbed, then no one would be able to bother them in the inner most chambers. "But, I thought you were supposed to stay in the tower and guard the way so that no one else could find the Palace of the Immortal Mystics?"

Allun Rha nodded and put a hand out on Erik's shoulder to steady himself. "This seemed a bit more pressing, to be frank," he said. "If you recall, I once asked you about Aparen, but you seemed not to know the name."

Erik nodded, vaguely remembering what was said in their first and only encounter.

"Well, I have been trying to find out who became Aparen since that day. You see, it was supposed to be you, but something changed that."

"And so you found Eldrik," Erik finished dryly. "He was here."

"Oh, I know. That is how I found you. I used my scrying table for years, but only found you when the two of you came into contact with each other. Only then was the disturbance in the magical essence great enough to show up at my tower. I came as quickly as I could." Allun Rha looked around disappointedly. "But it appears I came too late to catch Aparen."

"He wants to use the World Seed to gain enough power to fight the Four Horsemen," Erik said.

"Yes, I know. That is what you were going to do, if your fate hadn't been switched and Dremathor had been allowed to raise you."

314

"So the things that I feel inside of me…"

"If you are asking if I can see a blight on your soul, you are wasting your breath. It is not what you are supposed to do that matters, boy. Only what you *actually* do is what decides who you are. As long as you are willing to stand on the right side of things, that is enough for me." Allun Rha looked back toward the camp. "Have any food? I'm hungry."

"Did we lose?" Rafe asked as he suddenly regained consciousness and pushed himself up. "All I remember is this wizard guy ripping my arm open after attacking Lady Arkyn."

"I'm all right," Lady Arkyn said.

Rafe shook his head and stood up. His eyes shot open wide as he saw Allun Rha. "Nope. We're dead. I knew it! We lost and now we're all dead. Hopefully Nagé will take us before Khefir comes for Lubbok." Rafe put his hands in the air and glanced to Lubbok. "No offense."

"You aren't dead, though your head might have sustained some amount of injury that my magic failed to repair," Allun Rha said.

"I don't know who this ghost is, but tell him to bugger off!" Rafe shouted as he turned and walked back toward the camp. "I'm tired of ghosts, I'm tired of demons and magic, and all I want to do is take a hot bath and drink a bottle of ale. Anyone gets in my way, and I'll…well I'll slap them with my ghost-hands!"

Lubbok snorted and began to laugh. "I don't understand them anymore!" he said in orcish.

Erik smiled and patted Lubbok on the shoulder. "Ready to continue on our journey?" Erik asked him. "We have ourselves a chase, and our quarry has a head start."

"So we haven't lost?" Lubbok said as he rose to his feet.

Erik shook his head. "We didn't lose, brother. Not yet."

315

"Well, then in Khullan's name, let us go forward and strike our enemies down!"

EPILOGUE

Zefra sat alone in her chamber, idly running her brush through her hair and staring at a spot on the stone floor. Her thoughts drifted here and there for the most part, but no matter what she tried, they always seemed to return to Erik Lokton. The young man was impressive to say the least, but there was more to it than that. There was a fire in his heart. She rose up from her chair and moved to an oblong box of black stone near the foot of her bed. She set her brush down on the floor and opened the box. Inside was a book with golden leather binding. Zammin's symbol was embossed in red on the front of the book. She gently ran her fingers along the symbol, wondering if she should have told Erik all that she knew.

No. That would have gone against the commandment they had received from Zammin. He was more than the founder of their society, she knew. He was a guardian of the world. To go against his wishes and instructions would put the world in great danger. There were not only dark forces upon the face of Terramyr, there were also the Watchers, those that would punish Zammin if he was caught interfering with Terramyr.

She sighed and closed the lid on the stone box.

"You did well," a voice called from inside the room.

317

Zefra jumped to her feet and glanced toward her door. It was closed, with all the bolts securely in place. She turned on the stranger and was about to cast a spell, but then she saw who it was.

A man sat in her chair, with green robes over a red jerkin made from dragon skin. The black collar of the tunic underneath stood up around the stranger's neck. On the collar was a red symbol that matched the symbol on the book. Across the table lay a great, silver spear, and at once she realized who was in her room.

Zefra dropped to her knees and placed a hand over her heart. "Forgive me, I didn't expect you to come," she said.

"I cannot stay long," he said. "The Watchers are very active of late. If they see me here, then my actions will be found out."

Zefra nodded, but kept her gaze on the floor in an attempt to remain reverent.

"I am not a god, Zefra, stand up," he said. "I came to speak with you about the man that was here."

"Erik," Zefra said with a nod as she rose to her feet once more. "What about him?"

"I think I would like you to talk with him again," he said. "I want you to wait for him down on the shores where the Cliffs of Rontular end and the beaches begin. I have already visited the orc chief in the east. He will have three of his best warriors waiting for you."

"I am unmarried," Zefra said. "I am not permitted to be alone with others of the opposite sex without private sleeping quarters."

"It's all right," he said. "The warriors are all female. They shall remain close to you and protect you."

"What shall I tell Erik?" Zefra asked.

"Tell him everything," he said. "Take the book with you, and work with him to understand it."

"As you command," Zefra said with a bow of her head.

318

"I must go now, but I will try to come to you again if I can." He rose to his feet and took his spear in hand. "Zefra, the days ahead are going to be very dark. Your mission is of the utmost importance. This Erik may be the one I have been waiting for, do you understand?"

"I do," she replied.

"Good. Then work with him, and tell him my true name, so he knows who I am."

"I will, Reshem," Zefra promised.

There was a flash of silver light, and the man was gone.

About the Author

Sam Ferguson is a fairly average guy.

That's it.

No, really, that's it.

Oh- you are actually reading this?

Well… the truth is that Sam is a very *lucky* guy. He juggles work in such a way that he makes sure to spend enough time with his loving wife and five sons. He is blessed to be writing full time now. In his spare time he is an avid powerlifter, and competes from time to time.

He spent nearly five years serving as a U.S. Diplomat and absolutely loved the experience, but decided to move back home. Outside of the U.S. he has lived in Latvia, Hungary, and Armenia. He speaks Russian, Hungarian, and Armenian. (He used to speak some Latvian too, but he has no one to practice with anymore…)

He has a large, happy dog.

He plays the Elder Scrolls series.

His favorite superhero is Wolverine, but Batman is a close second.

If the kids go to bed at a reasonable hour, he will cuddle up with his wife to watch Scrubs reruns, the Big Bang Theory, Castle, and Burn Notice.

See, really just an average guy after all.

If you enjoyed this book, then join Sam Ferguson's Facebook page, sign up for alerts on his Amazon page where we would encourage you to leave reviews on the books you have read, or you can follow Sam on his author blog:

www.talesfromterramyr.com/ and on his weight lifting blog: www.steeldads.blogspot.com

You can also find new books and special deals each month by following Dragon Scale Publishing on twitter @dragonscalebook, or by liking our Facebook Page or subscribing to our newsletter.

See the full collection of Dragon Scale Books by visiting:

WWW.DRAGONSCALEBOOKS.COM

Other Books by Sam Ferguson

The Sorceress of Aspenwood Series
The Dragon's Champion Series
The Wealth of Kings
The Netherworld Gate Series
The Dragons of Kendualdern series
The Fur Trader
The Haymaker Adventures
Flight of the Krilo
The Lost City of Alfarin
Winter's Ghost (Novella)
The Moon Dragon
The Beast of Blue Mountain
The Dwarves of Roegudok Hall comic Episode 1

Other Books by Dragon Scale Publishing
The Protector of Esparia by Lisa M. Wilson
Kingdom of Denall Series by Eric Buffington:
The Troven
Secrets at the Keep
The Changing
Tales of the NoWhere and NeverWhen by Jason Hauser
Codex of Light by E.P. Stein

Also available exclusively on the
Dragon Scale website:
Tharzule's Tome of Wishes by Malinda Smiley
Orcs and Elves by Bethan Owen

About Terramyr

This book is a story from the world of Terramyr, a world which is part of a grand fantasy universe.* The world of Terramyr is rich in stories of adventure and magic, where struggles of the small and mighty alike are worthy of being told. Each story reflects a different point in time where the course of Terramyr's history is affected; all paths leading to a moment when the life of Terramyr will be weighed in the cosmic balance.

Terramyr is a palimpsest of fantastic history and magic, where different ages of gods and mortals have given rise to heroes and villains of all sorts, from each corner of the world.

The life of Terramyr is measured in five major eras of time, each a testament to the strength of will of mortals and those who would seek to become gods. Covering over 12,000 years of Terramyr's history the struggles of each race, from orcs to demigods, from elves to gnomes, are recorded by author Sam Ferguson.

We invite you to take a walk in the wild jungles of Prirodha, explore the verdant seacoast of the Elven Isles, climb the snowy peaks of the Dryden Range, delve the mighty caverns of the Dwarves of Roegudok Hall, discover the hidden treasures of the merpeople of the Ilion Ocean, and to share the adventures which take place in many more beautiful, exciting locations across the world of Terramyr.

You can learn more about the World of Terramyr at Terramyr.wikia.com
And
www.TalesFromTerramyr.blogspot.com
And
www.DragonScaleBooks.com
*Related worlds include Kendualdern, a world where dragons rule.

While each series or stand-alone book which is part of the World of Terramyr can be enjoyed on its own, the more you explore, the more you will find easter eggs, learn about the mythology and history of the world, and the more you may come to discover the extent of the powers interested in guiding Terramyr to its final end.

You can enjoy the stories in any order you choose, but for readers who are interested in knowing where in the chronology of Terramyr a given story falls, here is a chronological list of the stories (those currently available, and those yet to come) that take place on the World of Terramyr.

Pre–history and Creation Era	The Dragons of Kendualdern series The Dragons of Kendualdern: Dominion (Coming Soon) The Dragons of Kendualdern: Hunted (Coming Soon) The Dragons of Kendualdern: Rebellion (Coming Soon) The Dragons of Kendualdern: Annihilation (Coming Soon) The World Seed (Coming Soon)
Ancient Era (1,000 years)	
Dark Ages aka The Era of Kings (3,500 years)	Flight of the Krilo (Year 365)
Age of Demigods (5,000 years)	The Haymaker Adventures (Year 3,500) The Sorceress of Aspenwood Series (Years 3,676 – 3,677) The Dragon's Champion Series (Years 3,709 – 3,711) The Netherworld Gate Series (Year 3,710) Winter's Ghost (Year 3,710) The Wealth of Kings (Year

	3,711) Dark Sahale (Year 3,718) The Fur Trader (Year 3,720)
Common Era (1,700 years)	
Enlightened Era aka Age of Wonders (1,000 years…?)